PRAISE FOR
THE ANDROMEDA EVOLUTION

"*The Andromeda Evolution* is both a kick-ass sequel and a loving tribute to one of the greatest science fiction novels ever written. Daniel H. Wilson has taken up Crichton's mantle and reinvented the techno-thriller by continuing the tale that invented that genre. This is a meticulously crafted adventure story, packed with action, mystery, wonder, and just enough hard science to scare the hell out of you. So good!"

—Ernest Cline, author of *Ready Player One*

"The stellar cast of characters makes the story more than just a series of events but a tale that carries weight. The structure of the novel reads as if the reader has been granted access to a top secret file that provides an overview of the incident, which follows the exact layout of Crichton's classic novel. Wilson invokes the best of that story and updates everything with terrific flair."

—Associated Press

"Ingenious. . . . Wilson is a good choice for carrying the master's work forward. . . . The episodes set in outer space are particularly thrilling. . . . Would make Crichton proud."

—*Washington Post*

"Wilson has perfectly captured the suspense of the original."

—*Newsday*

THE ANDROMEDA EVOLUTION

MICHAEL CRICHTON

THE ANDROMEDA EVOLUTION

A NOVEL BY DANIEL H. WILSON

HARPER

NEW YORK • LONDON • TORONTO • SYDNEY

HARPER

A hardcover edition of this book was published in 2019 by HarperCollins Publishers.

FIRST HARPER PAPERBACKS EDITION PUBLISHED 2O2O.

Designed by Lucy Albanese
Illustrations on pages 279, 291, and 303 by Alexis Seabrook
Photograph details on page 271 © Shutterstock

The Library of Congress has catalogued the hardcover edition of this book as follows:

Names: Wilson, Daniel H. (Daniel Howard), 1978– author. | Crichton, Michael, 1942–2008.
Title: The andromeda evolution / a novel by Daniel H. Wilson.
Description: First edition. | New York, NY : Harper, [2019]
Identifiers: LCCN 2019023408 (print) | LCCN 2019023409 (ebook) | ISBN 9780062473271 (hardcover) | ISBN 9780062473288 (ebook) | ISBN 9780062956668 (international edition)
Subjects: GSAFD: Science fiction.
Classification: LCC PS3623.I57796 A85 2019 (print) | LCC PS3623.I57796 (ebook) | DDC 813/.6—dc23
LC record available at https://lccn.loc.gov/2019023408
LC ebook record available at https://lccn.loc.gov/2019023409

ISBN 978-0-06-247329-5 (pbk.)

21 22 23 24 LSC 10 9 8 7 6 5 4 3 2

For M.C.

ANDROMEDA EVOLUTION

MACHINE SCORE REVIEW BELOW

ACKNOWLEDGMENTS

I N THESE PAGES YOU WILL FIND THE METICULOUS RE-construction of a five-day scientific crisis that culminated in the near extinction of our species.

It is important to recognize up front that the advanced technology that is the hallmark of our modern world was not itself the cause of this crisis—though it exacerbated it. The response to the Andromeda Evolution was unprecedented in its coordination and scientific sophistication. Yet it was this same scientific mastery that enabled tragic errors resulting in terrible destruction and loss of life.

Nevertheless, it is vital this story be told—now more than ever.

A greater number of human beings walk the earth today than at any other point in the history of our species. We are able to survive in our billions thanks only to the technological infrastructure we have built to sustain ourselves. And every last one of us could be gone tomorrow, confronted with the failure of that same infrastructure.

My hope is that this rigorous account of events will demonstrate both the capabilities and the limits of scientific progress—the good and the bad.

An accurate and detailed reconstruction was only possible thanks to the generous contributions of those who were involved in the disaster, directly or indirectly, as well as a small army of domain experts and fact-checkers. I wish to thank them all, though I must take responsibility for any errors or omissions that have crept into this manuscript.

For their chapter-by-chapter technical corrections, my sincere gratitude goes to Captain Jake B. Wilcox, US Air Force (Ret.); Liu Wang, PhD, China National Space Administration (CSNA); Deepayan Khan, PhD, Carnegie Mellon Robotics Institute; David Baumann, Chicago Dynamics Incorporated; Ricardo Boas, Department for Isolated Indians, FUNAI; and Jane Hurst, PhD, NASA Johnson Space Center.

The bulk of this work depended on the efforts of Dr. Pamela Sanders, a US Army colonel, professor, and head of the Department of Electrical Engineering and Computer Science at the US Military Academy at West Point. With the help of her indefatigable students, Dr. Sanders was instrumental in securing, transcribing, and categorizing thousands of hours of video footage, audio recordings, and raw sensor data recovered from body-mounted cameras, the logs of the International Space Station, salvaged aerial drones, and satellite-based surveillance systems (in cooperation with the National Reconnaissance Office).

I especially wish to thank the surviving members of the second-generation Project Wildfire, who were able to sit with me after their debriefings to verify even the most minute details. And for those members who did not survive, I offer my heartfelt thanks to the friends, coworkers, and family members who set aside their grief to share the intimate stories necessary to convey their loved ones' unique constellations of personality, expertise, and motivation. It is thanks to their gracious efforts if these pages are able to breathe life and humanity into what could otherwise be a dry and technical treatment of events.

By compiling a multitude of personal viewpoints along with hard facts, I have attempted to capture the fear and wonder that fueled the deadly events of these five days. In some cases, the reader must bear with practical reports based on little more than hard data, but when possible, this reportage has been bolstered with subjective opinions, thoughts, and emotions reported after the fact. By using both avenues of information, I have taken the liberty of reconstructing events to provide a more traditional narrative experience.

Lastly and most importantly, this account would never have been possible without the groundbreaking work of the late Michael Crichton, MD—a visionary who shattered a code of silence and introduced a stunned world to the precursor events to this crisis. The original account of the Andromeda Strain, published fifty years ago, opened the eyes of millions of readers to the great potential and dire limitations of scientific progress. Along with countless others, I am forever in awe of and deeply indebted to Crichton's contributions.

It may seem disheartening that this new crisis unfolded along the same fault lines of human hubris, miscommunication, and plain bad luck as the first Andromeda incident. However, it is not my intent to vilify or blame any institution or individual. In the moment, each of us necessarily believes we are the hero of our own story—even those of us later judged to be villains.

I will leave such judgments to you, the reader.

The scientists, astronauts, and soldiers who lived through the events described in these chapters were human beings, with strengths and flaws. Some showed surprising heroism in the face of annihilation, while others failed at crucial moments. But none acted in vain—for at the very least, we all of us are *still here*, still alive to read and learn from this unlikely chronicle of human survival, a saga known now by its code name: the Andromeda Evolution.

D.H.W.
Portland, Oregon
January 2019

DAY 0

CONTACT

> The future is coming faster
> than most people realize.
>
> —MICHAEL CRICHTON

Event Classification

WHEN IT ALL BEGAN AGAIN, PAULO ARANHA WOULD have been bored. Bored and sleepy. He was only a year from retirement from the National Indian Foundation of Brazil, known under its Portuguese acronym FUNAI. Stationed on the outskirts of government-protected land stretching across the Amazon basin, the *sertanista* was in his mid-fifties and had spent his career protecting the undeveloped interior of Brazil. He was sitting under a flickering, generator-run light-bulb, lulled to drowsiness by the rising morning heat and the familiar sounds of the untamed jungle outside the open windows of his monitoring station.

Paulo was at least thirty pounds overweight, sweating in his official olive FUNAI uniform, and seated before an old metal desk loaded with an eclectic array of electronic equipment. As was his habit, he was squinting down at his lap, his concentration focused intently on hand-rolling a tobacco cigarette with his blunt yet surprisingly agile fingers.

His movements were sure and quick, with no hesitation or trembling, despite the gray whiskers jutting from his cheeks and his steadily failing eyesight.

As he lit and puffed contentedly on his cigarro, Paulo did not notice the red warning light flashing on his computer monitor.

It was a small oversight, normally harmless, and yet on this morning it carried consequences that had already begun to snowball exponentially. The unseen light was hidden behind the curl of a yellow sticky note (directions to a local fishing hole). It had been blinking unheeded since late afternoon the day before.

The flashing pixels were signaling the beginning of a global emergency.

A THOUSAND FEET overhead, an Israeli-made unmanned aerial vehicle (UAV) the size of a school bus was thrumming steadily over the vast Amazonian jungle. Dubbed the Abutre-rei—"King Vulture" in Portuguese—its wheels were caked in reddish jungle mud from a rough landing strip and its white hull streaked with the corpses of insects. Nevertheless, the drone was sleek and predatory—like an artifact from the distant future that had slipped backward in time to hover over this prehistoric land.

The Abutre-rei was on an endless mission, sweeping back and forth over a green sea of jungle canopy that stretched to all horizons. The unblinking black eye of its gyro-stabilized, self-cleaning camera lens was trained on the ground below, and a Seeker ultra-wideband synthetic-aperture radar unit invisibly illuminated the complex terrain with timed pulses of radio waves that could penetrate rain, dust, and mist. Back and forth, back and forth. The drone was specialized for environmental monitoring and photogrammetry—relentlessly constructing and reconstructing an ultra-high-resolution map of the Amazon basin.

Inside his monitoring station, Paulo only half watched as the constantly updating image knitted itself together on his monitor. An occasional haze of stale bluish smoke rose from the spit-soaked cigarro parked in its usual spot at the corner of his mouth.

Everything changed at precisely 14:08:24 UTC.

At that moment, a new vertical strip of mapped terrain was added to the composite image. The unseen warning light was displaced fifty pixels to the left, just peeking out from under the sticky note.

Stunned, Paulo Aranha stared at the pulsing red spot.

In recovered webcam footage, he could be seen blinking frantically, trying to clear his eyes. Then he snatched away the sticky note and crumpled it in his fingers. The dot was located beside a small thumbnail image of something the Abutre-rei had found in the jungle. Something Paulo could not even begin to explain.

Paulo Aranha's job at FUNAI was to monitor and protect an exclusion zone established around the easternmost region of the Upper Amazon—over thirty-two thousand square miles of unbroken jungle. It was a priceless treasure, site of both the largest concentration of biodiversity on earth and a *terra indigena* that was home to approximately forty uncontacted Amazonian tribes—pockets of indigenous human civilization with little or no exposure to the technology and disease of the outside world.

With such natural riches, the land was under constant attack. Like an army of termites, destitute locals were motivated to sneak into protected territory to fish virgin rivers or poach valuable endangered species; loggers were tempted to bring down the huge kurana, cedar trees that could fetch thousands of dollars on the black market; and of course, the hordes of *narcotraficantes* stopping over on their way from southern Brazil to Central America were a constant and brutal menace.

Preserving the wilderness required unwavering attention.

With a nicotine-stained finger, Paulo pecked a key to activate Marvin, a computer program housed in a beige plastic box wedged under his desk. Acquired years ago from a joint research effort with an American graduate program, the battered box was unremarkable save for a faded printout of an old *Simpsons* cartoon character taped to the outside.

On the inside, however, Marvin housed a sophisticated neural network—an expert system that had been trained on thousands of square miles of real jungle imagery, and over a hundred million more simulated.

Marvin could reliably identify a quarter-mile airstrip hacked out of the remote jungle by drug couriers; or the logging roads that threaded like slug trails into the deep woods, with larger trees intentionally left unmolested as cover; or even the occasional maloca huts built by the uncontacted tribes—rare and intimate glimpses of another world.

Most importantly, the program could scan ten square miles of super-high-resolution terrain in seconds—a feat impossible for even the most dedicated human being.

Paulo knew that Marvin was *muito inteligente*, but it had outright rejected this new data as not classifiable. This was something the algorithm had never seen, not in all its petabytes of training data.

In fact, it was something nobody had ever seen.

The output simply read: CLASSIFICATION RESULTS: UNKNOWN.

Marvin hadn't even offered a probability distribution.

Paulo didn't like it. He made a kind of surprised grunt, the cigarette trembling on his lower lip. Tapping keys rapidly, he enlarged the thumbnail image and examined it from every available angle, trying to dismiss it as a glitch. But it was no use—the strange sight defied explanation.

Something black was rising from the deepest jungle. Something very big.

Paulo waved smoke away with one hand, his gut pressing against the cool metal desk. He squinted at the dim screen, pushing his face closer. His balding head was coated in a cold sweat, gleaming under the stark light of the bulb overhead.

"No," Paulo was recorded as saying to himself. "Isto é impossível."

Thumbing a switch on a battered 3-D printer, Paulo waited impatiently as the raw image data was transferred to the boxy machine. The shack soon filled with the warm wax smell of melting plastic as an array of pulsing lasers set to work. Inch by inch, a hardened layer of plastic rose from the flat bed of the printer. As the seconds ticked by, the formless sludge resolved into a three-dimensional topographic map.

The pale white plastic was rising up in the detailed shape of the jungle canopy, looking for all the world like a bed of cauliflower.

Rolling and lighting yet another cigarette by instinct, Paulo tried not to watch as a new world slowly emerged from the unformed ooze. Each layer hardened in seconds, quickly firming into a scale model of the jungle. Wheezing slightly, Paulo cracked his knuckles one by one, staring blankly and smoking in silence.

In the rare instance that Marvin returned less than an 80 percent classification probability, it was up to Paulo to make the final determination. He did so by employing a carefully honed method that was strictly unavailable to the machine: his sense of touch.

Touch is the most ancient sensory faculty of any living organism. The human body is almost entirely covered with tactile sensors. The neural circuits related to the somatosensory system overlap with multiple other areas of sensing, in ways both unknown and unstudied. Of particular sensitivity are the countless mechanoreceptors in our lips, tongue, feet, and, most especially, our fingertips.

This was Paulo's talent—one area where man rose above machine.

Eyes half closed, he began with static contact, lightly placing all eight of his finger pads on the model surface. Gently, Paulo added steady pressure to establish a touch baseline. And finally he scanned his fingers laterally over the meticulously rendered folds of jungle canopy.

Properly honed, the discriminatory power of skin receptors can exceed visual acuity. Every inch of the model's texture corresponded to roughly one hundred yards of real-world terrain, resulting in contours only detectable through a cutaneous spatial resolution far superior to any computer's image analysis, no matter how clever the machine.

Paulo could run his fingertips over the roof of the jungle and *feel* whether an unclassified data sample was the ragged, chainsawed destruction of an airstrip or the smooth banks of an innocent new river tributary.

Eyes closed, limp cigarette in the corner of his mouth, Paulo slouched, his face to the ceiling. His outstretched hands traced the surface of the jungle as if he were a blind god touching the face of the planet.

When his questing fingers found the hard, unnatural lines

of the . . . thing, Paulo Aranha swallowed a low moan in the back of his throat. Whatever it was, it really did exist. But there were no roads nearby. No sign of construction. It could not be possible—out there alone and colossal among the primordial trees—and yet it was as real as touching the stubble on his own face.

The thing in the jungle rose at least a hundred feet above a skirt of raw wilderness, long and slightly curved, like a barricade. It spoiled the sanctity of a rain forest otherwise unbroken for thousands of square miles. And it seemed to have appeared from nowhere.

Around the perimeter of the structure, Paulo could feel a crumbling sensation. It was the texture of death—thousands of virgin trees collapsed and sick. This thing was a kind of pestilence, polluting everything nearby.

For a long moment, Paulo sat and contemplated raising an alert on the antiquated FUNAI-issued shortwave radio sitting on his desk. His eyes lingered on its silver dials as the generator puttered outside, providing the trickle of electricity necessary to connect this isolated shack to the rest of the world.

Pushing away from the desk, Paulo felt blindly under the drawers until his fingers brushed against a business card taped beneath. It contained the phone number of a young American who had recently contacted Paulo.

Claiming to be a businessman, the man had explained that a Chinese aircraft had recently been lost over this territory. His company was willing to pay a hefty price for information about it. Paulo had assumed (and continued to assume) that the American was looking for pieces of airplane wreckage, although he hadn't said that. Not exactly. Instead, the man had said specifically to report "anything strange."

And this was definitely that.

Using his palms to wipe away the sheen of sweat that soaked his face like tears, Paulo stared at the business card and punched a number on his desk phone.

A man with an American accent answered on the first ring.

"I'm glad you called, Mr. Aranha," said the voice. "I was right to trust you."

"You already know?" Paulo asked, glancing at the computer screen.

"Marvin rang me just now, when you registered the anomalous classification," said the voice. "He's smarter than he looks."

The Americans and their trickery. It never ceased to amaze Paulo. A people who seemed so trusting and forthright—all smiles . . . and yet.

"What now?" asked Paulo.

"You can relax, Mr. Aranha. We've got people taking care of it. You'll be well compensated for your assistance. But I am curious," asked the voice. "What do you think it is?"

"I know it is not an error, senhor. It's really out there. I have touched it."

"Well, then?"

Paulo thought for a moment before answering. "It is a plague. Killing everything it touches. But I can never know what it is."

"And why is that?"

"Because that thing out there . . . it was not built by any human hands."

Fairchild AFB

NEARLY FIVE THOUSAND MILES AWAY, NEAR SPOKANE, Washington, Colonel Stacy Hopper was arriving to a quiet morning shift at Fairchild Air Force Base. A skeleton crew of intelligence analysts who had worked overnight were just clocking out, leaving behind dimmed monitors on neat desks and a meager work log indicating that, as usual, nothing much had happened.

Crisply uniformed in her air force blues, complete with a service cap, tie tab fastened neatly around her neck, and sensible black hosiery, Hopper eyed the windowless control room. A thermos of coffee rested in the crook of her arm. Her morning crew of eight uniformed intelligence analysts were settling into their consoles, saying their good mornings, and slipping on headsets. Many of them had damp shoulders, having just arrived to work on another rainy morning in the Pacific Northwest.

Hopper sat down at her own console at the back of the room, enjoying the soft murmuring of her analysts' voices. Glancing up at the telemetry monitors lining the front wall, she saw nothing out of the ordinary—just the way she liked it.

It was said by her colleagues (in private) that Hopper, a calm, gray-eyed woman, had the patience of a land mine. In fact, she was perfectly satisfied with the slow pace of this job. She was the third acting commander of the project. Both of her predecessors had devoted the entirety of their careers to this post. As far as Hopper was concerned, it would be perfectly fine if Project Eternal Vigilance lived up to its name.

By the account of her longest-serving analysts, Hopper was fond of the rather pedantic saying "Absence of evidence is not evidence of absence."

It was a sentiment that had begun to go stale among her staff.

This low morale was ironic, considering that at its inception, Project Eternal Vigilance had been considered the prime posting within all armed forces, and every roster spot vigorously competed for (by those with the security clearance to even know of it).

The project had been spawned in the aftermath of the Andromeda incident—a weapons research program gone horribly wrong, detailed in the publication popularly known as *The Andromeda Strain*.

In the late 1960s, the US Air Force deployed a series of high-altitude unmanned craft to search for weaponizable microparticles in the upper atmosphere. In February 1967, the Scoop VII platform proceeded to find exactly what the military men were looking for, except that the original Andromeda Strain was far more virulent than anyone could have guessed.

Before it could be retrieved by military personnel, the recovery capsule was compromised by overly curious civilians. The microparticle proceeded to infect and gruesomely wipe out the entire forty-eight-person population of the town of Piedmont, Arizona—save for an old man and a newborn baby. These surviving subjects were discovered and rescued by the acclaimed bacteriologist Dr. Jeremy Stone and the pathologist Dr. Charles Burton. The two survivors were isolated for study in an underground cleanroom laboratory, code-named Wildfire. Their fates were eventually classified to protect their privacy.

It was in Wildfire that a team of eminent scientists, hand selected for this situation, raced to study the exotic microparticle later dubbed AS-1; they found that it was one micron in size, transmitted by inhalation in the air, and caused death by near-instantaneous coagulation of the blood. And although its microscopic six-sided structure and lack of amino acids indicated it was nonbiological, AS-1 proved capable of self-replicating—and mutating.

Before the Wildfire team could finish their tests, the Andromeda Strain evolved into a novel plastiphage configuration called AS-2. Though harmless to human beings, AS-2 was able to depolymerize the plastic sealing gaskets that isolated the laboratory bulkheads. A nuclear fail-safe was triggered and heroically disarmed moments before detonation.

However, remnants of the AS-2 variety escaped, the particles outgassing into the atmosphere and dispersing globally. Although this new particle was not harmful to humans, it wreaked havoc on nascent international space programs that depended on advanced polymers to reach orbit.

Thus began Project Eternal Vigilance.

Hours after the Andromeda incident, the founding members of Project Wildfire lobbied the president of the United States for emergency resources. The goal was to begin worldwide monitoring for new outbreaks of the Andromeda Strain or its subsequent evolutions. Their proposal was given immediate and generous funding from the Department of Defense black budget, staffed with top analysts, and officially activated three days later.

But that was over fifty years before, and every scientist involved in the first Andromeda incident had since passed away.

Today, Colonel Hopper watched as the rows of computer monitors came on, bathing her analysts' faces in bluish light. The colonel sighed at the view, ruminating on the huge expense necessary to secure every bit of satellite time, every analyst hour, and the immense amounts of data transfer and storage.

Colonel Hopper was well aware of her unit's dwindling influence. At every morning shift, she noted the increasing mileage on her equipment, the attrition of her best analysts, and the encroaching needs of the other units at work in Fairchild AFB.

In particular, Air Mobility Command (AMC) had been pushing for more satellite time to ease their daily task of coordinating KC-135 Stratotanker aerial refueling craft in the thin air high above Tibet and the Middle East. The acting commander of AMC had even gone on record with the opinion that Eternal Vigilance was a pointless waste of resources.

And it seemed he was correct.

Eternal Vigilance had been on high alert for over fifty years—with Hopper at the helm for the last fifteen. And before today, it had never found a single thing.

IT IS A WELL-ESTABLISHED Achilles' heel of human civilization that individuals are more motivated by immediate private reward than by long-term, collective future benefits. This effect is particularly evident when considering payoffs that will take longer than a generation to arrive—a phenomenon called inter-generational discounting.

The concept was formally introduced by the young French economist Florian Pavard during a poorly attended speech at the International Conference on Social Economics on October 23, 1982:

> The average span of a human generation is twenty-five years. Any reward occurring beyond this generational horizon creates an imbalance that undermines long-term cooperation. In short, we as a species are motivated to betray our own descendants. In my view, the only possible solution is the institution of harsh and immediate punishments for those who would be unfaithful to the future.

It has been subsequently theorized that our species' seeming inability to focus on long-term existential threats will inexorably lead to the destruction of our environment, overpopulation, and resource exhaustion. It is therefore not an uncommon belief among economists that this inborn deficit represents a sort of built-in timer for the self-destruction of human civilization.

Sadly, all the evidence of world history supports this theory.

And thus, despite well-known deadly high stakes, Project Eternal Vigilance suffered from endemic human shortsightedness. Over the years, the operational capacity of the program had been deferred, discounted, and diminished. And on this particular rainy morning, the project was on its last legs, barely functioning . . . but still viable.

At 16:24:32 UTC Colonel Hopper was seen on internal video, sitting at her desk with perfect posture. Her half-empty thermos of coffee rested atop a pile of equipment requisition forms that she must have known would be denied, and yet had forced herself to complete anyway.

A call came through.

Sliding on her headset, Hopper punched a button on her comm line, her monitors erupting into life.

"Vigilance One. Go ahead," she said, speaking in the clipped tones of a lifelong data analyst.

The voice she heard had a distinct American accent, and she recognized it from her dwindling team of field operatives.

"This is Brasileiro. I've got something you'll want to see."

"Private channel is open, pending certificates."

"Pushing through now."

Tapping keys, Hopper granted the request.

All at once, the bank of four flat-panel monitors lining the front wall flared with data. Each monitor showed a discrete overhead view of the Amazon jungle: a basic unenhanced digital camera image; a light detection and ranging (LIDAR) map; an enhanced-color hyperspectral view of the canopy; and the minutely detailed gray-scale topography of synthetic aperture radar.

The drone footage was live, being generated in real time.

One by one, the eight analysts looked up at the front screens, pushing their chairs away from desks and murmuring to one another. Personalized workstations began to blink with ancillary data, information flowing to specialists according to their domain of control. Colonel Hopper stood.

In the dead center of every image stood something unexplainable.

It appeared to be a featureless block, curved slightly. It rose above the steaming expanse of jungle, laid directly across a river tributary. At its base, sluggish water flowed from underneath. Behind it, the blocked river had pooled into what looked like a giant mud puddle, flooding the surrounding jungle. The nearby trees and vegetation that hadn't been swamped seemed frail and bent, dying.

"The anomaly is located on the descent trajectory of Heavenly Palace," said Brasileiro, over the room speakers. "The Tiangong-1 space station was directly above—"

"Roger that, Brasileiro. That will be all for now," replied Hopper, putting the connection on hold.

With a glance, Hopper checked the latitude and longitude. The anomaly was perfectly equatorial, with a line of zero degrees latitude to seven decimal points—a precision of approximately one yard. She added this observation to the incident notes. It was an odd detail, seemingly important, and yet catastrophically misleading.

Dale Sugarman, the senior signals intelligence analyst, stood up and turned to face Colonel Hopper, his headphones dangling around his neck. In five years, she had never seen the huge man demonstrate excitement about anything other than video games. Now, the senior airman's shaky voice echoed sharply through the all-room speaker loop: "This data is impossible, ma'am. There are no roads, no airstrip, no way to build anything out there. Sensor error. I advise overhauling the drone. Send in—"

"'Impossible' is the wrong word, Airman," said Hopper crisply, crossing her arms. A conviction crept into her voice as she continued, "What we are seeing is not impossible. It is simply an ultra-low-probability event."

The room fell silent as the analysts considered her words.

There exists a certain class of event that can technically occur, yet is so incredibly unlikely that most laymen would consider it impossible. This false assumption is based on a rule of thumb called Borel's fallacy: "Phenomena with extremely low probabilities effectively never happen in real life."

Of course, the mathematician Émile Borel never said such a thing. Instead, he proposed a law of large numbers, demonstrating that given a universe of infinite size, *every event with nonzero probability will eventually occur.* Or put another way—with enough chances, anything that *can* happen *will* happen.

For the rare patient ones among us, the data-driven, those who are not afraid to delay gratification and save their dessert for last—these low-probability events aren't inconceivable; they are inevitable.

Colonel Hopper was supremely patient, and as the world accelerated faster, she seemed to move more slowly. Indeed, she had been carefully selected by her predecessors for this particular ability.*

Fifteen years of toiling without reward or the promise of one, without encouragement, and often without even the respect of her colleagues—and Hopper had never once wavered in her commitment to the job.

And in this crucial moment, her persistence paid off in spectacular fashion.

COLONEL HOPPER FISHED out a thick binder from her top drawer and thumped it onto the desk. She was determined to make sure the rest of this encounter unfolded according to protocol. Using an old-fashioned letter opener, she tore through several seals to access the classified, laminated pages within. Although most emergency procedures were now automated, these

---

* Arthur Manchek, who first held this post, was also said to slow down as the world moved faster, appearing to grow more disinterested as those around him became overexcited. It was an ability he had honed over the years to maintain a clear head in an emergency, and one he prized in his recruits.

instructions had been set down decades ago, and they called for a trained and capable human being to be in the loop every step of the way.

Pulling the headset mike closer to her lips, Hopper began issuing orders rapid-fire, with the certainty of an air-traffic controller.

"Brasileiro. Establish a thirty-mile circular quarantine zone with an epicenter at the anomaly. Pull that drone out of range immediately and land it at the perimeter. Once it's down, don't let anyone go near it."

"Roger that, Vigilance One."

Advanced computer models of the original Piedmont incident had indicated thirty miles as a minimum safe distance for airborne exposure. On screen, the real-time video shuddered and jerked as the Abutre-rei drone wheeled around and sped away in the other direction. After several seconds, the low-hanging nose camera had turned itself back one hundred and eighty degrees, and the anomaly reappeared on-screen, shrinking into the distance.

"Colonel, what does this thing have to do with us?" asked Sugarman in a quiet voice, his eyeglasses winking blue light from his workstation.

Hopper paused, then decided not to answer directly. Brasileiro's earlier mention of the code name Heavenly Palace already represented a possible breach of classified information. Instead of responding, she moved to confirm the piece of information of most interest to Eternal Vigilance.

"Can you reconfirm that equatorial location?"

"It's confirmed," said Sugarman, hunching over his desk. "The anomaly is located on the exact equator, ma'am. Down to the centimeter, it looks like."

Hopper took a deep, controlled breath. Aside from muted

static, the room was utterly quiet. When Sugarman spoke, his voice was surprisingly loud.

"Why would an equatorial location matter?"

Hopper's silence was jarring. The question could not be answered without compromising the security of the mission. It was information that could only travel up the chain of command, not down.

"Airman. Requisition the Transat Four satellite cluster, please. We need situational awareness on this, exquisite level."

"Ma'am, that's a collateral system. It's being used by someone else. Currently logged for . . . CIA overseas usage—"

"You have my authorization to transmit Clear Eyes priority."

Sugarman swallowed. "Yes, ma'am. We are seizing the satellite feed now."

After a flurry of keypunches, an active satellite image blinked onto the front screens. It showed an infrared view of a jeep convoy speeding across dark desert terrain, leaving twin white tire tracks visible in the sand. Crisp black targeting crosshairs were overlaid on the image, above horizontal range lines.

From the in-room speakers, an unfamiliar and angry voice began to sputter, "Attention unidentified Clear Eyes permission. Get off this channel. You are currently interrupting a sensitive—"

"Rezone that eye to our coordinates," said Hopper. "And mute that man."

"Yes, ma'am."

The room fell back into silence, except for the frantic typing of the analysts, each focusing their laser-like attention on a few drops of the rolling tide of data pouring into their monitors from the trunk feed.

Somewhere above, on a classified orbital trajectory, the lens of a spy satellite adjusted silently in the vacuum of space.

The image of the jeep convoy blurred and disappeared from the monitors. Seconds later, the eye settled onto a patch of the Amazon jungle, and the camera iris spiraled into crystal clarity.

Across the monitors hanging high at the front of the room, the anomaly appeared in complex detail—its metallic-looking surface beaded with droplets of jungle mist, faint hexagonal imprints etched into its skin, and the whole of it gleaming like a beetle's waxy shell in the rising midday sun.

"Infrared," said Hopper.

On the second monitor, the image appeared in gray scale, with lighter pixels indicating hotter surface temperatures. The image of the surrounding jungle canopy dissolved into a grayish mass of what looked like storm clouds. The anomaly itself was pure white now, so bright it briefly washed out the rest of the image.

"It's hot, ma'am. Really hot," said an analyst. "See how the nearby vegetation is curling back?"

Hopper nodded, pointing at the monitor. "What are those faint speckles? All of them seem to be the same temperature, but cooling fast."

At his desk, Sugarman put his face close to his dedicated feed. He spoke briefly into his headset to another analyst. Finally, he responded.

"We believe those are dead bodies, ma'am. About fourteen of them. Human."

"You can't possibly confirm that, Airman. Plenty of large primates live in that area of the world."

"Some of them are carrying spears, ma'am."

Hopper was silent for a moment.

"I see," she said.

On screen, the thermal image flashed to white, saturating the sensor and washing out the screen. As the exposure slowly returned to normal, the anomaly seemed different. The fading specks were now closer to it.

"What was that?" asked Hopper.

"I . . . it appears to be growing," responded Sugarman. "And there's something new emerging from the middle of the lake. A smaller, six-sided structure."

The third monitor lit up with splotches of color. A hazy cloud of blue and orange appeared in the atmosphere above the anomaly. It seemed to be drifting east on a slight wind current.

"We've got an ash cloud," said another analyst. "The atmosphere down there is soaked with it. It must have been ejected from the anomaly somehow. More readings incoming . . ."

The colonel drew a finger down a column of figures on the top-secret laminated binder page. The vital information had been laid down as simply as a child's book report, created with the age-old maxim of K.I.S.S.—"Keep it simple, stupid"—in mind.

Her finger stopped at a mass spectrum graph. There was a tremor in her voice as she issued her next command:

"Get the mass spec readings from the drone."

"Already on it, ma'am."

Seconds later, a junior analyst slid a mass spectrograph onto the colonel's desk.

Once again, Hopper ran a finger across the laminated sheet. When she stopped and looked up, the tremor in her voice was gone.

"We have positive ID," she said.

"Of what?" asked Sugarman, pivoting to face his boss. His lips were pale, voice dry and on the verge of cracking. Behind him, the entire room of analysts had turned to watch Hopper, solemn in their fear.

"The signature peaks are an almost exact match," she replied, "to the Andromeda Strain recovered in Piedmont, Arizona, over fifty years ago. Somehow, something made of a similar substance is down in that jungle right now. And based on the visuals, it's getting bigger. Those bodies are almost underneath it."

"But that's not—" Sugarman stopped himself. "You mean to say . . ."

Every person in the room knew the purpose of this mission. Yet none of them had ever actually believed the strain would reappear. Not even now, in the face of overwhelming evidence. Except for one.

Hopper stood and addressed her incredulous staff, tucking the binder under her arm.

"Project Eternal Vigilance has just fulfilled her purpose. Our work here is done. I wish you well on your future assignments, whatever they may be."

Colonel Hopper then turned and walked directly toward the high-priority communications room—a soundproofed closet, really. The analysts watched her go with their mouths open, speechless.

Over her shoulder, Hopper issued her final orders.

"Alert your colleagues at Peterson AFB and transfer those feeds. Based on an exponential rate of growth, tell them I estimate we've got less than four days."

"Four days? Until what?" asked Sugarman.

"Until that anomaly spreads all the way to the ocean."

And with that, Project Eternal Vigilance was complete.

Alert

RAND L. STERN WAS ALREADY DEAD TIRED, AND THE day had hardly begun. A four-star general with a sprawling family and a rocket-powered career, Stern faced a constant and overwhelming demand for his attention. For his own part, he was simply looking forward to eating lunch for fifteen uninterrupted minutes.

Stern was a compact African American man in his fifties and only now going gray at the temples. A top graduate of the US Air Force Academy, he had spent thousands of hours as a command pilot in an F-16 Fighting Falcon, hundreds of those in combat. Afterward, he had done a stint as a professor at West Point. And for the last three years, he had been in charge of the United States Northern Command (USNORTHCOM) and the North American Aerospace Defense Command (NORAD), after his nomination was confirmed unanimously by the US Senate in 2016.

Stationed at Peterson Air Force Base in central Colorado, General Stern oversaw the activities of thirty-eight thousand individuals concerned with monitoring and protecting American interests in the area from two hundred to twenty-two thousand miles up, a volume of space dwarfing that of the entire planet. His annual budget was in the tens of billions, comparable to the world's largest multinational companies.

If asked, he would respond that his most complex command assignment was the parenting of four preteen girls alongside his wife, a research scientist in the Department of Psychology at the University of Denver.

At home, Stern's voice was only one among many. At work, however, he spoke for over three hundred million American citizens.

In his first-day briefing packet, Stern had been informed of twelve high-priority ongoing top-secret projects of extreme significance to national defense. Among them was something called Project Wildfire, created in the aftermath of the Andromeda incident of some fifty years before. Wildfire had seemed like an innocuous footnote compared to the ambitions of the Chinese and the astonishing amount of unaccounted-for nuclear material that had been lost in orbit. Yet during his tenure, no other project had been a bigger thorn in his side.

Dealing with the Andromeda microparticle had gone from a purely scientific undertaking to a secret arms race with the sort of global repercussions not encountered since the height of the Cold War. As a result, Project Wildfire had grown to consume a disproportionate amount of resources. It had become a gargantuan feat just to hide its dozens of subprojects from the public view, costing billions of dollars and millions of man-hours.

All of it weighed heavily on the general.

In a later interview, he described the job as "feeling like Atlas,

crouched there alone, holding the planet in my arms—and nobody knows what I'm protecting them from or why. Not even
my girls."

Among the classified downstream projects, the existence of
Eternal Vigilance was peripheral at best. Serious fear of another
spontaneous mutation from the Andromeda microparticle had
evaporated over time. Instead, what was most important were
the possibilities of intentional weaponization by enemies of the
state.

In typical human fashion, attention had turned away from
the wondrous contemplation of extraterrestrials and settled
squarely and mundanely on the countries (allies and not) who
had inevitably learned about the deadly version of the microparticle called AS-1, and its plastic-eating cousin, AS-2.

Both varieties had proven to be dangerous in their own ways.

Upon inhalation, AS-1 was almost always immediately fatal.
The relatively benign AS-2 variety, which had evolved sponta-
neously in the heart of the Wildfire laboratory, had shown itself capable of lingering in the upper atmosphere, turning most
plastics into dust—a development that had set back the US space
program by decades. It also made AS-2 samples freely available
to any nation with the scientific acumen to go up and collect
them.

No other varieties of Andromeda, natural or manufactured,
had been detected—though not for lack of trying.

And now, the call Stern had been dreading for years had
come from an utterly unexpected direction—not from his
agents scrutinizing the China National Space Administration,
or the spies sent to investigate disease outbreaks around the
world, or even from a certain secret clean room still buried under a cornfield in Nevada.

The call had come from Eternal Vigilance.

Ensconced in his private office at Peterson Air Force Base, Stern had at first reacted to the emergency notification from Colonel Hopper with mild annoyance. Although false positives would normally be eliminated before reaching him, his assumption was that one had slipped through.

Dismissing an incongruous screensaver of kittens shooting rainbows from their mouths (a gift from his youngest daughter), the general accepted Hopper's information push. As his screen flooded with images of the anomaly, he leaned back in his chair with fingers knotted over his stomach and closed his eyes in frustration.

"Colonel Hopper. What is this?" he asked.

"I have a theory."

"You have a theory. I'm late for my lunch. Since the promotion, they've got my days regimented into ten-minute increments. There are only so many of these increments in one day. You are occupying one now. I would rather it be occupied by a bacon, lettuce, and tomato sandwich."

"Yes, sir. Did you see the trajectory?"

"I see a static object in the jungle, Colonel. There is no trajectory."

"On April tenth of this year, the Tiangong-1 Chinese space station fell into destructive reentry and disintegrated. That anomaly is perfectly equatorial, and directly in the debris trajectory of the fallen station. You may recall the incident was code-named Heavenly Palace."

General Stern sat up abruptly.

"We can't confirm what the Chinese were experimenting with on that space station," Hopper added.

"But we have a pretty good guess, don't we?" responded Stern, the data on his screen.

This problem had just moved into a sphere of his thinking

that outranked meals. It was an area that concerned not only national defense but the defense of the species.

The general's mouth moved as if to speak, and then it closed.

"Good work, Colonel. We'll take on your feeds and any information you've collected. I'm . . . why, I can't believe I'm saying this . . .

"I am now issuing a Wildfire Alert."

IT IS A little-known fact that human logistics experts have not independently planned or executed a major military endeavor for the United States of America since early in the Vietnam War. Every operation, from single-element transports to coordination of an entire operating theater, is at least partially computer generated under the umbrella of a sprawling and complex collection of algorithms known as automated logistics and decision analysis (ALDA).

In this aspect, the Andromeda response was no different than any other complex military response—it was machine generated.

Given General Stern's initial data, ALDA activated the Percheron supercomputing cluster located in the chilled depths of the Air Force Research Laboratories beneath Wright-Patterson AFB in western Ohio. Kicking or delaying thousands of other lower-priority computing threads, ALDA connected to a massive, constantly refreshed data set of personnel and resources, coming back with a full mission loadout within fifteen minutes.

Yet even with its unprecedented level of processing power and data, ALDA had always been wisely deployed with an 80/20 rule—which holds that an algorithm should be depended upon to reach only 80 percent of the solution, with human common sense and intuition applied to the final 20 percent.

In this case, General Stern saw no technical i
default loadout, which read as follows (still in part
code):

PROJECT WILDFIRE V2—CREW DOSSIER

NIDHI VEDALA, MD-PHD (AGE: 42)

Wildfire Clearance (FULL)

Designated: Command, 001 ***

Location: Massachusetts, Amherst >>> Travel Duration: ~12H
***

Specialization: Nanotechnology; materials science;
Andromeda Strain: AS-1, AS-2 ***

Misc: Leadership quality; domain expert ***

HAROLD ODHIAMBO, PHD (AGE: 68) ***

Wildfire Clearance (ACADEMIC) ***

Designated: Lead Field Scientist, 002 ***

Location: Nairobi, Kenya >>> Travel Duration: ~15H ***

Specialization: Xenogeology; geology; anthropology; biology;
physical sciences; . . . <CONTINUES>

Misc: Broad knowledge base ***

PENG WU, PLA Air Force, Major (AGE: 37) ***

Wildfire Clearance (PEOPLE'S REPUBLIC JOINT ALLIANCE) ***

Designated: Field Scientist, 003 ***

Location: Shanghai, China >>> Travel Duration: ~18H ***

Specialization: Taikonaut; soldier; medical doctor:
pathologist ***

Misc: Combat training; survival training; possible domain
knowledge [REDACTED] ***

ZACHARY GORDON, US Army, Sergeant First Class (AGE: 28)

Wildfire Clearance (PRELIMINARY) ***

Designated: Field Medic, 004 ***

Location: Fort Benning, Georgia *** Travel Duration: ~14H ***

Specialization: Ranger elite light infantry; battalion senior medic ***

Misc: Trauma surgeon ***

SOPHIE KLINE, PHD (AGE: 32)

Wildfire Clearance (NASA) ***

Designated: Remote Scientist, 005 ***

Location: International Space Station *** Travel Duration: N/A ***

Specialization: Nanorobotics, nanobiology, microgravity research ***

Misc: AS-1, AS-2 EXPERT ***

*** END DOSSIER ***

Stern paused at the inclusion of Major Peng Wu, a Chinese national who normally would have been excluded as a security concern. Then he shook his head, cracking a wry smile. The ALDA algorithm was relentlessly logical yet had often proven itself capable of nonintuitive decision-making. Given the situation with Heavenly Palace, it was a stroke of genius to bring in a Chinese military candidate who had been waiting, preapproved, in the Wildfire candidate pool.

Peng Wu was not just any taikonaut—she had actually participated in the first manned voyage to the Tiangong-1 space station. Stern knew she wouldn't divulge any Chinese military secrets—they'd already tried discerning that—but her knowledge of what had happened up there could still save lives.

At this point, General Stern's only duty was to give a verbal confirmation. However, a final exchange took place in the seconds before the go order was passed on—both upward to the president of the United States and down to the enlisted men and women immediately dispatched to execute first steps.

The following is a partial transcript of the last-minute exchange between General Stern and one of his most trusted officers:

< . . . >

0–10 GEN
_____
Strike the last field candidate. I have a replacement.

S-OP-001
_____
Zack Gordon? Are you sure, General?

0–10 GEN
_____
Send Stone.

S-OP-001
_____
I'm sorry, sir?

0–10 GEN
_____
James Stone. Out of Palo Alto. You'll find him on the standby list.

S-OP-001
_____
[short pause] Sir, do you mean the son of Dr. Jeremy Stone?
From the first Andromeda incident? This guy hasn't got the clearance.
His prep work is also out of date. I believe he was always a tangential candidate, too special-purpose.

0–10 GEN

I know. Send him anyway.

S-OP-001

There will be a delay while we wait for his security clearance.

0–10 GEN

Understood. Scramble my personal C-40 transport and go get him. That'll help mitigate the delay.

S-OP-001

[long pause] You were close friends with Dr. Jeremy Stone, weren't you?

0–10 GEN

Your point?

S-OP-001

I'm just afraid . . . you should consider the optics on this.

0–10 GEN

Listen, son. It's not your career on the line. I'm invoking directive 7–12, citing top-secret situational knowledge that must remain opaque. My voice is my clearance, and I am General Rand L. Stern.

S-OP-001

Acknowledged, sir. Dossier approved and . . . the mission is live.

[typing sounds]

S-OP-001

Enlisted liaisons are being dispatched now to retrieve our field team. You are advised to report to local command and control to assume overwatch duties. Good luck, sir.

0–10 GEN
_____
Roger that. And thank you.

S-OP-001
_____
Sir?

[brief pause]

S-OP-001
_____
Sir. If you don't mind my asking. Off the record . . .

0–10 GEN
_____
Nothing is off the record. You know that.

S-OP-001
_____
Well then, on the record, but between us.

0–10 GEN
_____
All right. Shoot.

S-OP-001
_____
Why James Stone?

[long pause]

0–10 GEN
_____
It's just a hunch. Nothing more.

[end transmission]

Conservative estimates from the DC-based Nova America think tank conclude that Stern's hunch likely saved three to four billion lives.

DAY 1

TERRA INDIGENA

There is a category of event that, once it occurs, cannot be satisfactorily resolved.

—MICHAEL CRICHTON

Emergency Debris Avoidance Maneuver

TWO HUNDRED AND FORTY-EIGHT MILES ABOVE EARTH, Dr. Sophie Kline floated quietly in a nimbus of her own long blond hair. It was just after 6:00 a.m. Greenwich Mean Time—the official time zone of the International Space Station, as a compromise to accommodate Mission Control in both Houston and Moscow—but her blue-gray eyes were wide open and alert. This early, both of her fellow astronauts were still in sleep cycle, and the observation cupola was shuttered, empty, and dark—the only sound a faint whirring from the Tranquility module ventilation systems.

It was Kline's favorite time of day.

She punched a glowing button, and the hull began to whine as the exterior cupola shutters rose. The gentle glow of Earth's surface lit the interior of the module, and Kline enjoyed the usual thrill in her stomach. She loved the feeling of being alone and suspended, looking down on the planet from on high. It gave her a sense of utter superiority, as if everything below were a part of her own creation.

This small daily ritual (confessed in a personal flight journal salvaged after the incident) might seem arrogant, but it was simply a dream of freedom.

As it was, Kline was floating in the windowed cupola with her paralyzed legs bound tightly together with Velcro straps to keep them out of the way. It was only in these quiet moments of weightlessness that she could almost forget the searing cramps and spasms that writhed through her devastated muscles.

Sophie Kline had not been able to walk since she was six years old, so she had chosen to fly. She was tall, despite her disability, and as she focused on the cupola window, her striking eyebrows and gaunt cheeks lent her a predatory appearance, softened only by a smattering of freckles across her nose and forehead.

Her path to the stars was so unlikely as to almost satisfy Borel's fallacy. When Kline fell and broke her right arm at the age of four, her parents assumed she was simply clumsy or unlucky. Only one was true. At the hospital, an attentive pediatrician noticed that the little girl had a concerning tremor.

The incredibly unlikely juvenile amyotrophic lateral sclerosis (JALS) diagnosis came at the age of five, with the degenerative disease attacking her relatively newfound ability to walk. Sophie began her life in a wheelchair, though she had no intention of ending it there. With an almost inhuman resolve, particularly for a child, she had set her ingenious mind and iron will to escaping the bounds of gravity.

She had succeeded.

Every reputable doctor had predicted she would be dead by the age of twelve. Instead, she had persevered, taking advantage of each new medical advance, and eventually become a world-renowned scientist and an American astronaut.

Kline found that the chronic pain in her muscles nearly disappeared in microgravity, and her wasted body wasn't a disadvantage the way it was on earth. In constant free fall, she was as physically capable as any astronaut. More capable, in fact, since she did not have to worry about the muscle-wasting effects of weightlessness.

Thus, using only her arms, Kline turned her body to face the circular porthole in the center of the viewing cupola. Six trapezoidal panes of glass splayed radially out from it—the largest window ever put to use in outer space. Beyond, the face of the planet slid past, surprisingly close. Today, she saw an endless jungle vista—a dense landscape of treetops twined with gleaming rivers that looked to Sophie like the wriggling trace of neurons.

It was a view that absolutely should not have been there, and the sight of it indicated that a serious emergency had occurred during sleep cycle.

Internal ISS video footage showed Sophie Kline muttering in disbelief, frantically scanning the computer monitors ringing the neck of the cupola. Physiological monitoring logs reported her heart rate elevating as she took hold of two slender blue handrails and pulled her face to within inches of the central porthole. The terrain scrolling past below would have been utterly unfamiliar to the seasoned astronaut.

Like the other two crew members on board the ISS, Kline's body was instrumented with wireless physiological sensors. Unlike her crewmates', however, Kline's monitoring extended further—at one-second intervals, her mind was being read. As a teenager, Kline had been implanted with a Kinetics-V brain-computer interface (BCI) at her own insistence, so she could continue her college courses via computer as the disease progressed through her nervous system.

The BCI device was a golden mesh of thousands of wires, soaked in a biocompatible coating to prevent foreign body rejection, and sunk into the jelly-like surface of Kline's motor cortex. Upgradable via radio, the current software iteration employed a deep-learning algorithm to map the electrical activity of neurons in Sophie's brain to actions in the real world. The unique interface linked Kline mentally to the ISS computer systems—an almost telepathic connection.

Kline realized that the ISS had undergone a severe trajectory change. Such an event could only signal imminent disaster, and it should have been a cause for panic. Indeed, her outward reaction to the unexpected terrain had been consistent with surprise and shock. However, routine monitoring of her brain implant's data stream showed that Kline's predominant state of mind was an alpha brain wave varying between 7 and 13 Hz—a state of nonarousal, relaxed alertness in the face of mortal danger.

It was a small discrepancy that would go unnoticed until much later.

Kline opened a comm channel to Houston flight control and requested information from CAPCOM.

The initial response was static.

A lot had happened during the astronauts' sleep period, beginning at precisely 23:35:10 UTC when, under the auspices of General Rand L. Stern, the USSTRATCOM Command Center issued an emergency notification to ISS Mission Control in Houston.

USSTRATCOM advised of a likely close approach of the ISS to multiple red threshold objects. Such notifications were fairly common, as the command center is tasked with monitoring any object in low orbit with a diameter larger than one and a half inches.

Officially, the debris source was attributed to a failed NSA satellite deployment, but console operators at Houston were backchannel notified that the orbital debris was in actuality the aftermath of a classified antisatellite weapons (ASAT) attack performed against China by Russia.

In public, these space warfare operations were universally condemned for scattering dangerous space junk in low Earth orbit. Yet it was an open secret that since the 1960s every spacefaring nation had been enthusiastically experimenting with ASAT platforms—from simple kinetic kill warheads to more sophisticated reusable approaches deploying shaped-charge explosives.

The attitude determination and control (ADCO) officer, at Mission Control, Vandi Chawla ran a simulation on the USSTRATCOM-supplied data and confirmed the high likelihood of a conjunction in the orbital pathway. Because they were red threshold objects, not yellow, there was no debate about the primary response. She immediately authorized an emergency debris avoidance maneuver (EDAM), even though the orbital modification would result in several missed launch opportunities over the next months, none of them critical resupplies.

While the astronauts slept, commands for a prolonged thirty-nine-minute avoidance maneuver were issued from the trajectory operations manager (TOPO) console. The ISS's four 220-pound control moment gyroscopes shifted rhythm immediately. Made of stainless steel, the circular flywheels generated the torque that leaned the ISS forward at a constant four degrees—keeping the station's floor pointed at Earth's surface and maintaining an Earth-centered, Earth-fixed (ECEF) diving orbit. The electrically powered gyros began to modify the station attitude in preparation for the maneuver.

Once situated, the next step would normally have called for an extended thruster burn from the robotic Progress cargo module attached to the Pirs docking compartment. However, due to the substantial translation needed, TOPO decided to authorize use of an experimental solar electric propulsion (SEP) device.

Electrical power gathered by onboard solar arrays was routed to a cluster of highly efficient electrostatic Hall thrusters, conserving precious supplies of traditional chemical propellant. On activation, the thrusters pulsed in perfect rhythm, ejecting a flickering plume of plasma exhaust. The resulting force pushed the ISS upward directly through its center of gravity, while also translating the bulky structure to a southward trajectory.

A typical reboost maneuver would change only the altitude of the ISS, but in this case the azimuth was also modified from fifty-four degrees to zero, resulting in a highly unusual equatorial orbit. The maneuver was completed within the allotted time, and a summary press release was issued, citing a routine debris avoidance maneuver and praising the success of the SEP device.

General Stern had managed to coordinate the entire effort without ever informing NASA, RNCA, or JAXA of the true underlying emergency.

And yet Sophie Kline knew right away the trajectory change had something to do with Andromeda. This was not surprising, since Kline was one of the very few people intimately aware of the true purpose of the International Space Station.

The full, unclassified transcript of her initial exchange is below:

ISS-KLINE

Houston this is Station, come in. Requesting status update. What . . . [unintelligible] Why am I seeing Brazil moving east west?

HOU-CAPCOM

Just, uh, had an EDAM, Station. Orbital debris. Good news, though. The SEP thrusters worked perfectly.

ISS-KLINE

That is good news. But, this is so far . . . listen, I'm initiating a special query request. Have you been contacted by Peterson Air Force Base?

[static—four seconds]

HOU-CAPCOM

I'm sorry, Station, we've got no record—

[transmission lost]
[static—eleven seconds]

PAFB-STERN

Kline. This is Stern. We are on a private channel. I've got an update for your to-do list.

ISS-KLINE

Go ahead.

PAFB-STERN

Your scientific mission is suspended as of now. Until further notice, knowledge of your reassignment is to be restricted from all space agencies, including NASA. Do you understand?

[short pause]

ISS-KLINE

Yes sir, General Stern.

PAFB-STERN

You've been placed in an equatorial orbit that passes over the debris field of the fallen Tiangong-1 space station. We . . . It, it's been hypothesized the station may have triggered a ground contamination upon reentry.

ISS-KLINE

In the *jungle*?

PAFB-STERN

Something is down there. Some kind of anomaly. It's already killed people, and it's spreading.

ISS-KLINE

I see.

PAFB-STERN

Project Wildfire has been reactivated, Dr. Kline. Your role is orbital lab support. The other ISS crew members will monitor for any remnants of the Tiangong-1 that are still atmospheric, under the guise of an emergency scientific mission.

ISS-KLINE

Understood.

PAFB-STERN

You will also monitor our field team from above. Eyes and ears. Got it?

ISS-KLINE

A field team? You're not sending people into that jungle? General, please, at least wait until I can—

PAFB-STERN

No time, Doctor. Report to the Wildfire Mark IV laboratory module. It's already begun.

• • •

THE EXISTENCE OF the executive order can seem contradictory to democratic government. In times of emergency or in peace, the president of the United States may simply dictate national policy and have it executed in an instant—without review.

This act has been previously described as: "Stroke of the pen, law of the land."

The first executive order was used by George Washington on June 8, 1789, to instruct the heads of all federal departments to create a State of the Union for the newborn country. In 1863, Abraham Lincoln issued one that became known as the Emancipation Proclamation—ultimately freeing three million slaves. And nearly a century later, Franklin Delano Roosevelt issued a 550-word executive order that called for the United States government to incarcerate over a hundred and twenty thousand of its own citizens and residents of Japanese descent in concentration camps constructed across the Western United States.

It is a great and terrible power to wield, and one that can lead to historic repercussions—if it is ever made public, that is.

The classified executive order NSAM 362-S (known as a "National Security Action Memorandum" at the time) was issued three weeks after the first Andromeda incident and the subsequent back-to-back losses of the American *Andros V* manned spacecraft and the Russian Zond 19 mission. Within government circles, the order was widely regarded as symbolic. Off the record, many politicians considered the task to be on par with the Pharaohs' orders to erect the great pyramids of Giza.

A portion of the order read:

TOP SECRET/FORMERLY RESTRICTED DATA ATTACHMENT
NATIONAL SECURITY ACTION MEMORANDUM NO. 362-S

                      April 10, 1967

THE PRESIDENT   Ordering the Creation of
                      a Microgravity Laboratory
                      Module to be Placed in a Space
                      Station in Permanent Orbit.

By the authority vested in me as President by the
Constitution and the laws of the United States
of America, I hereby determine that it is vital
for national security and the safety of our
species itself to study the extra-terrestrial
microparticle known as the Andromeda Strain in its
natural microgravity environment, i.e., a state-
of-the-art laboratory placed in low Earth orbit.

The estimated cost of the endeavor in 1967 was $50 billion, twice the cost of the Apollo program and (adjusting for inflation) approximately the same as the entire national military budget of 2018. In the upper echelons of government executives who were authorized to read the order, the president's demand was met with derision and disbelief.

But the practical need to study the particle remained.

By the fall of 1967, the tiny town of Piedmont, Arizona, had been sterilized from top to bottom and the forty-eight bodies (including two US Army personnel) cremated. Every structure and vehicle was deconstructed and placed in hangar-like storage facilities built in the desert by the Army Corp of Engineers for this purpose. The task was accomplished carefully and with no casualties, thanks to the findings of the Wildfire team. The effect was so sudden, and the town so small, that within two decades the very existence of Piedmont was erroneously thought by many to have been fictional.

Once every splinter had been accounted for, the next step was to determine exactly what had happened. It was a multibillion-dollar question, and the world couldn't know it was being asked without risking a civilization-ending panic.

As the Indian-born British historian Romila Chandra states in her classic tome, *Fallen Empires of Man*, "The instinct of the human being upon contact with a foreign civilization is to flee. If that is not possible, it is invariably to attack. Only after surviving first contact is there an overwhelming urge to learn more. But do not mistake this response for altruistic curiosity, rather it is simply a need to understand the *other* in order to protect oneself from it . . . or, more likely, to attempt to destroy it." It is an apt description of how humanity behaved in the aftermath of Andromeda—especially after Russia and China learned of and responded to the events in Piedmont, Arizona, through their own spycraft.

The Russians were first, managing to push the Salyut 1 space station into orbit by 1971—only four years after the Andromeda incident. The United States attempted to catch up two years after that, but the Skylab launch was compromised by the "benign" plastic-eating strain of Andromeda still lingering in the upper atmosphere. During Skylab's initial ascent, exposure to the AS-2 plastiphage resulted in a partially disintegrated heat shield, spewing debris that severely damaged the station.*

---

* Officially, the damage was attributed to an accidental deployment of the micro-meteoroid shield during launch.

Skylab lasted six years. The Mir space station lasted longer, at ten years. Both failed to achieve their secret goal of studying Andromeda in microgravity. As it turned out, the problem was too big for one nation to solve alone—even a superpower.

In 1987, President Reagan called for the creation of an International Space Station, a joint venture between the Soviet Union and the United States, with more partner countries to come. Eyebrows went up around the world, as the Russians and Americans made for strange bedfellows. Privately, both nations were motivated by a mutual fear of allowing the Andromeda particle to go unstudied.*

Even then, a permanent space station was only the first step.

It was not until 2013 that the Wildfire Mark IV laboratory module arrived (disguised as a Cygnus automated cargo spacecraft), and docked to the nadir port of the Harmony node at the front of the station. Its activation coincided with the beginning of Dr. Sophie Kline's scientific missions to the ISS.

The top-secret module was born in the depths of the original Project Wildfire facility beneath Nevada, constructed entirely by sterilized robotic arms. Those robots were teleoperated by on-site workers who were themselves in an ISO Class 1 clean room. The final laboratory enclosure was completely self-contained and launched aboard an Antares-5 rocket from Cape Canaveral Air Force Station on January 17, 2013.

Once docked, the laboratory module constituted the only biosafety level (BSL) 5 containment facility ever created, much

---

* Though never fully substantiated, several declassified CIA reports from the early 1970s independently reference a small Siberian town called Verlaik. Reports indicate that residents there came into accidental contact with a microparticle captured from the upper atmosphere by the Russian Sovok space program. Despite these mentions, further evidence of the town's existence has been impossible to verify.

less placed in orbit. The Wildfire microgravity laboratory was self-irradiated every four hours with high-intensity ultraviolet light, and it contained no breathable atmosphere. It was instead pressurized with a combination of noble gases—odorless, colorless, and with virtually zero chemical reactivity. The cylindrical space inside the laboratory module was phenomenally clean and sterile, precisely because it was unoccupied.

There were only two potential organisms on board, and they were what the module had been built to study: material samples of the extraterrestrial microparticles known as AS-1 and AS-2.

The interior of the module had never been touched by a human being, and never would be. Every aspect of the laboratory's functioning was remote-controlled via radio contact from outside. And this was exactly why Dr. Sophie Kline had been the first astronaut with ALS deployed to the International Space Station.

The wasting effects of Kline's disease had made her the perfect recipient of a brain-computer interface at a young age. Years of training with the interface had given her the ability to control most computers as naturally as breathing—a crucial ability while handling highly dangerous samples through a remote connection.

Though there had been other operators, only Sophie Kline could control the Wildfire Mark IV laboratory module with her mind.

WITH GENERAL STERN'S orders to report to the laboratory module still ringing in her ears, Kline hesitated for one moment. Her left eye twitched almost imperceptibly as she activated the muscle groups necessary to communicate with her personal computer, which activated a monitor along the lower wall of the cupola.

A real-time camera feed of the Kibo science module appeared. There astronaut Jin Hamanaka, apparently also alarmed by the change in trajectory, was busily checking propellant levels on her laptop. On a feed of the Zvezda service module, the cosmonaut Yury Komarov was outside his sleep station, calmly stowing his gear and preparing for an exercise routine during the hour window before morning conference.

Kline watched both feeds carefully. As far as she could tell, the other astronauts were not panicking or behaving erratically.

Pushing herself backward, Kline floated away from the cupola and "up" toward the exit in the ceiling. As she floated away, she watched the sprawling rain forest hundreds of miles below. The vista was already rotating away, replaced by the Atlantic Ocean as the station continued its eastward orbit.

In another time, the young Sophie Kline would have been abandoned to a sanitarium, immobile and forgotten—assuming she survived her childhood. The sole reason she had transcended gravity was humankind's ever-growing mastery over nature. Looking down on the planet from the perspective of a god, trapped in a body that refused to obey her orders, she was acutely aware of this fact.

But—as history has proven time and again—in the hands of human beings, increasing power is increasingly dangerous.

Heavenly Palace

THE COALITION OF COUNTRIES THAT FUNDED THE
International Space Station (and hoped to share in its discoveries) had neglected to include one of the largest and
most ancient civilizations in the world—a proud and capable
nation with the strength to develop its own competing effort to
study Andromeda.

Alone and forced to act unilaterally, the People's Republic of
China inevitably set out to do just that.

Suspicion, distrust, and competitiveness had fractured the
international effort to understand the Andromeda Strain. Although the AS-1 microparticle had proven that it would kill any
human with equal savagery, no matter their ethnicity, the vaga-
ries of politics blunted what could have been a united response.
And that enmity came to a head with the creation of a new space
station.

The Tiangong-1, whose name meant "heavenly palace" in Chinese, was launched on September 29, 2011. It was an auspicious date for both travel and grand openings, according to the astrological predictions of the Chinese zodiac calendar, the Sheng Xiao. After a successful launch, the station was placed into orbit at a slightly inclined attitude of nineteen degrees—a trajectory that coincided perfectly with regular resupply launches from the Chinese Xichang Satellite Launch Center in Hainan Province.

Although the launch had not been advertised, American spy agencies watched intently and continued to monitor the station until its premature demise.

The end occurred in 2013, only two years into the multibillion-yuan effort, when China suddenly announced that the project was over. Authorities there officially hailed Tiangong-1 as an "unmitigated success for the China National Space Administration and the Chinese people."

However, around-the-clock observation from a series of earth-based imaging assets revealed a narrative very different than that of the official reports. It seemed Chinese Mission Control had lost radio contact, including telemetry, with their station.

Without any means of control, the Tiangong-1 fell into a decaying orbit.

Thermal readings from multiple spy agencies determined that life support had been shut off, with the surface of the station as cold as the space around it. Abandoned, the station continued to orbit the earth for several years, engines offline and radios silent.

On April 10, 2018, the scant air particles percolating in the upper atmosphere finally managed to drag the station into destructive reentry. The metal cylinder was ripped to superheated shreds by atmospheric friction, reduced to a flaming confetti that rained down on the planet below—directly above the primordial jungles of the eastern Amazon.

Thus, the entire effort ended in a brief streak of light and heat.

The failure would likely have been deemed harmless were it not for a single, final bit of information. During the continuous monitoring of the space station—from launch, to resupply missions, to its last fiery reentry—operatives had noticed something the Chinese space agency never mentioned publicly.

The last crew of three taikonauts had never emerged from the Tiangong-1.

Code Name Andromeda

BARELY FIVE HUNDRED FEET ABOVE A JUNGLE CANOPY that itself soared a hundred and fifty feet high in places, a Sikorsky H-92 Superhawk helicopter thundered over shivering trees. The gray metal chopper was streaked with jungle mist, nose jutting out like the beak of a predatory bird. In its wake, bands of monkeys hooted in the treetops and colorful birds took startled flight.

James Stone didn't remember falling asleep.

Even with the thudding of the rotors in his ears and the vibration of the window glass on the rolled-up jacket he was using for a pillow, he'd had no trouble nodding off.

Later, when every detail of his life was declassified and dissected, splashed across the front pages of newspapers and magazines, it became well documented that Stone had the ability to fall asleep anywhere, at almost any time—to "turn off," to use the parlance of soldiers.

James had been able to do this since he was a little boy.

Part of it must have been out of sheer necessity. Young James spent his childhood accompanying his famous father—the Nobel Prize–winning polymath Dr. Jeremy Stone—on his scholarly travels around the world. Well dressed and soft-spoken, little James seemed nothing like his loud, impatient father. Together they were an odd couple, circumnavigating the globe every few months as Dr. Stone delivered lectures, attended scientific talks, and toured various international scientific projects.

James very rarely saw his mother, Allison, after his parents were divorced near his ninth birthday. And although the two were so obviously different from one another, Stone's father was clearly dedicated to ensuring that the boy learn something new every day of their never-ending travels. Today, this type of roving education is called world schooling.

Yet according to private interviews that were not splashed across the tabloids, there was another reason that Stone had become very good at falling asleep—it was because he so frequently woke up in terror, his skin crawling with the cobweb remnants of a singular nightmare. This time, aboard the Sikorsky, would have been no different.

In recovered cabin security footage, Stone woke with a start and stared dazedly at the stripped-down interior of the former military helicopter. The sun was low on the horizon outside, flooding the interior with ruddy morning light. His jaw tightening, Stone blinked a few times before apparently forcing himself to relax.

By his own account, the dream was always the same, its familiar images having solidified over the years into a kind of half memory. Stone described it as a gruesome stream of blood, wine-dark, flowing over white desert sand. The spreading stream stopped, suddenly still, *wrong* somehow, as the surface of the blood seemed to congeal all at once, the gleaming slick shrinking in on itself and solidifying into tiny grains of ocher dust—fine particles of dried blood that swirled up and away on the oven-hot breath of desert wind.

Stone shook his head to clear it.

Putting the dream out of his mind, he focused on the brightening jungle outside. He must have felt a sense of raw anticipation. As a child raised by a daredevil scientist, he had finally, at the start of his fifth decade, found himself joining an adventure to rival his father's.

Briefing documents lay spread out on the empty seats beside him, covered in dire warnings and classifications. Among them was a stiff, waxy photograph accompanied by a few pages of technical readouts.

It was truly a stunning image.

The ultra-high-resolution picture had been created by the army's adaptive super-resolution image reconstruction algorithm, which combined multiple video frames, still images, and radar-generated topographical information to construct a three-dimensional image and paint it with light in spectacular detail.

Even so, it still looked like a hoax.

The structure reminded Stone of his trips to the ancient Mayan temples of Guatemala and the Yucatan Peninsula. How the surprisingly intact rock edifices peeked their heads out of misty jungles, like giants frozen midstride over a primal landscape that had grown up around them.

Similar, except that the appearance of this particular structure had triggered the scrambling of an international coalition of esteemed scientists to the most remote jungle on the planetary surface. It was apparently worth hiring a black-market chopper for a surely outrageous price, and sending a trio of polite but firm active-duty soldiers to retrieve Stone from a guest lecture before a college class, midsentence, confiscating his phone and firmly escorting him away.

And yet Stone had only glanced at the glossy image. The structure was obviously interesting, but it wasn't what had piqued his curiosity. That would have been the other readout:

MASS SPECTROMETRY RESULTS

/// These data were collected by [redacted] High-Resolution Spectral Analysis suite and are intended for AFSPC USE ONLY. ///

*** UNAUTHORIZED USE PROHIBITED. CLASSIFIED TOP SECRET—DISSEMINATION IS SUBJECT TO CRIMINAL PENALTIES INCLUDING SUMMARY EXECUTION WITHOUT TRIAL ***

Unknown reading /// Unknown reading. N2. Saturation. /// Composition analysis . . .

. . . Incident in PIEDMONT, ARIZONA. MATCH *** MATCH *** MATCH ***

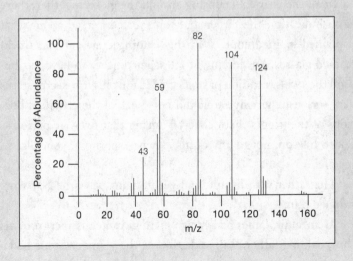

The atmospheric readings were startling in that they very nearly replicated the exact composition of air rising off the sunbaked plains of Piedmont, Arizona, in the aftermath of the Andromeda incident.

And with that, a haunting name was invoked:

PROJECT WILDFIRE * PROJECT WILDFIRE * PROJECT WILDFIRE *

The words would have undoubtedly caused deep, conflicting feelings in Stone. Over fifty years before, his father had played a significant role in stopping the spread of the Andromeda Strain. While under preliminary consideration for inclusion on the Wildfire roster, James Stone had been given access to a slew of classified documents. He had used the opportunity to pore over every detail of the incident—and especially his father's part in it.

Yet to try and discuss it with the old man would have been impossible—literally illegal.

In all the years of traipsing around the globe together, there is no indication the father and son ever conversed about what happened in Piedmont. With his balding crew cut and thick-framed glasses, Dr. Jeremy Stone seemed never to have left behind the 1950s tradition of stoicism. He took his top-secret status very seriously. Jeremy Stone did not speak of the classified portions of the events that occurred during that five-day period—not to his son, not to any of his ex-wives, not to anyone else in his life.

The father was distant, and yet in many ways the boy worshipped him.

As an adult, James had grown up to be quite distinct from his thin, balding father. Tall and athletic, the younger Stone had a head of thick dark hair (graying now) and a quiet, driven personality. He had reached the highest level of professional success as a roboticist and artificial intelligence expert. Where his father had operated within the hallowed traditions of academia, James had become an industry darling, a perpetually single workaholic who consulted across a variety of high-tech corporations—both start-ups and venerable institutions—wielding a razor-sharp intellect to collect massive paydays.

The elder Stone passed away still a bachelor, having married (twice to the wives of his colleagues) and divorced four times. James Stone apparently decided to forgo the entire process, never marrying or having children of his own. Despite their differences, James was his father's son in so many ways.

According to Stone, after receiving contingent approval to join the modern-day Project Wildfire early in his career, not telling his father about it was one of the hardest things he had ever done in his life.

But it's exactly what his father would have done in his place.

THOUGH RECORDS OF the Sikorsky H-92 pilot and copilot do not exist, word of mouth indicated that they were Brazilian *narcotraficantes*—subjectively a pair of criminals, but objectively the best in the world at navigating the largely unpoliced cross-basin routes favored by the Colombian cartels.

The pilot did not understand why he was flying an *americano*, much less during the daytime; he also did not know of the huge, unmarked cash payment made to his superiors; and he was not completely sure he would make it out of this job alive.

This last concern was actually quite valid.

At Peterson AFB, the Sikorsky was under constant surveillance. An F-35B Lightning II stealth fighter had been hastily launched from just off the Pacific coast, where it was stationed aboard the Nimitz-class aircraft carrier USS *Carl Vinson* (CVN-70). The carrier strike group had been dispatched under the guise of a joint American and Peruvian emergency response exercise. If the Sikorsky helicopter were to show any sign of contamination, the high-altitude fighter was one trigger word away from launching a bevy of AIM-120 AMRAAM long-range air-to-air missiles.

The helicopter pilot was unaware of this information, but certainly suspected something was wrong. Wisely, he chose not to deviate from the prescribed course in the slightest—despite what was about to unfold.

"Agora, nos descemos," the pilot said to the American. "Brace. Brace yourself."

In the cabin, James heard the static-filled voice of the pilot over his headphones.

"Why here?" he replied, scanning the unbroken jungle below. "We need to be closer."

"*Quarantena.* Thirty miles."

Quarantine zone. So the government *had* learned something since Piedmont. If the AS-2 plastiphage microparticle were airborne near the site, it could infect low-flying aircraft. In recovered cabin video, James can be seen hastily checking the rubber of the window gasket—running a finger along the soft plastic seal and examining it.

Still intact.

The second evolution of the Andromeda Strain, called AS-2, was known to dechain the polymers that made up synthetic rubber, especially the early blends synthesized before the microparticle had been studied. And although the information was classified, James Stone knew that Andromeda still permeated the nitrogen-rich mesosphere high above them.

Stone exhaled a deep breath.

If an AS-2 strain had infected the helicopter, he'd know it already. With vital engine parts disintegrating, they would have careened into the jungle and died in a crunch of metal and dirt—as had the unfortunate pilot of the F-40 Scavenger jet that had streaked over the Piedmont site after first contact. Or like the *Andros V* spacecraft, which had come crashing down in a fiery blaze on February 17, 1967, its tungsten-and-plastic-laminate heat shield turned to sterile dust.

Confident that his fiery demise wasn't coming in the next few seconds, Stone turned to what lay beyond the window. Everything outside was Terra Indigena—mile after mile of government-protected land. He wondered whether the Brazilian government had even been informed of this mission.

He doubted it.

Stone caught sight of a plume of red smoke outside, rising from a clear-cut patch of jungle near a riverbank. A smallish, recently constructed maloca hut sprouted from the center of the clearing, surrounded by hacked vegetation and fallen trees.

It looked like a scar to Stone, a cigarette burn on the face of the pristine jungle.

To the pilot, however, the clearing looked like the only landing pad within five hundred miles. Flying past and gaining altitude, he wheeled the bird into a wide circle to surveil the area and alert the people below that he would be coming in for a landing.

In the audio logs, a burst of confused and frightened dialogue can be heard ricocheting between the pilot and copilot. Three seconds later, the pilot yanked the control stick and dropped the Sikorsky into a stomach-churning descent. The anomaly was barely discernible on the horizon. But for an instant, something else had been briefly visible in the treetops—still several miles away.

Stone clearly saw it, too.

"Wait!" he called over the radio. "What was that? In the trees?"

The chopper only sank faster, spiraling, rapidly losing altitude.

"Go. Now!" the pilot shouted at Stone, tapping his copilot.

The copilot climbed back into the cabin, reaching across Stone's lap and unceremoniously yanking open the rolling side door. Shrinking back, Stone saw they were still a hundred feet up. Outside, a roaring mass of jungle canopy shuddered under the pounding rotors, and the cabin was filled with a wash of humid air.

Craning his neck, Stone was able to snatch a final, puzzling glance of the bizarre scene in the distance.

Then the Sikorsky sank below the tree line, jolting onto the ground, tires bouncing on the red mud of the clearing. As the helicopter settled, the pilot left the controls and joined his copilot in the cabin, rushing to detach Stone's luggage where it was secured in webbed fabric. They ignored the American, shouting to one another in Portuguese, leaving the engines running and the rotors spinning.

Stone still could not quite understand what it was he had seen.

It appeared at first to be a wave of darkness washing over the tree canopy. A swarm of black shapes, thrashing like a school of salmon going upstream—a ripple of movement under the electric green foliage.

"Senhor!" shouted Stone, over the noise of the rotors. "What was that? Were they—"

Stone's voice cut out as the pilots turned to him.

It was the naked fear on the faces of what he would later describe as "hard men" that took Stone's breath away. And at that moment, some symmetry in the twisting shapes he had seen coalesced in his mind.

The pilot and copilot tossed out Stone's black hard-case luggage. Stone hastily gathered his papers, snatched up his duffel bag, and got to his feet. He stood in the open doorway for a moment, a lean silhouette against the crimson sunlight outside.

Stone turned to the pilot, his voice hollow as he spoke. "Those were monkeys, weren't they? Swinging through the upper branches in a panic. Hundreds of them. A thousand."

The pilot said nothing, emotionless behind mirrored sunglasses. Without warning, his copilot took hold of Stone's shoulders and roughly shoved him through the helicopter door. He tumbled out and fell to his knees on the muddy ground.

The Sikorsky had already lifted off before Stone could get to his feet.

Boots on the Ground

D R. NIDHI VEDALA WAS ANGRY. AND IMPATIENT. SWATTING at a mosquito with one hand, she heard the thundering approach of the Sikorsky H-92 and her dark eyebrows knit together in a frown. The makeshift clearing around her was scattered with muddy black hard-case luggage, each containing precious equipment that needed to be checked for damage. The noise and commotion of incoming rotors sent squawking birds streaking past her and startled a young caiman on the riverbank into the water.

She ignored it all, consciously forcing herself to unclench her fists and continue inspecting the hard-cases. The jungle didn't frighten her. Not much did.

Vedala had grown up an orphan in the Morarji Nagar slums of Mumbai, a member of the Dalit social caste—called the "untouchables," often beaten and discriminated against. Though impoverished, she saw the world with the clear focus of a naturally keen intellect. Even as a bone-thin child under a mop of reddish-black hair, she never had a doubt that she would some-day escape the narrow alleyways, fetid community toilets, and sickening miasma of the toxically polluted Mithi River.

During her first round of mandatory statewide merit test-ing, Nidhi had come away with the top score out of approxi-mately fifteen million school-age Indian children. Starting from nothing, she had painstakingly earned her place among these distinguished scientists on this high-stakes mission.

The leader of the expedition and a founding member of the next generation Project Wildfire, Vedala had been dragged away from her laboratory at the Massachusetts Institute of Tech-nology by armed goons, driven an hour to Hanscom Air Force Base, and placed on board a wildly inappropriate C-130 Hercules military turboprop. Her mobile phone and laptop were confiscated, along with her identification. The cargo plane had been fueled up and waiting on the tarmac, but still set in an armored vehicle transport configuration, with only a few jump seats available for passengers.

None of this had startled her in the least.

Vedala was a small woman with an impish face and an effi-cient pixie haircut. She often scowled while concentrating, un-consciously intimidating others. She wasn't tall, but nonetheless projected a large presence, and her military escort quickly de-cided to retire to the cockpit up front with the two pilots and loadmaster. For the next twelve hours Vedala sat alone in the cavernous belly of the great beast, sleeping occasionally, but mostly rereading a fat red packet of files by the stark glow of the interior floodlights.

From the first moment, she understood that only one type of threat could possibly justify this level of expenditure—it had to be a global crisis with existence-level repercussions. A true world-ending scenario.

And Vedala welcomed it.

This was, after all, exactly the situation to which she had devoted her career. A materials scientist with a nanostructure specialty, she had spent her public life rising meteorically through the ranks of academics.

Her relentless exploration of new metamaterials had exploited the quirks of quantum mechanics to miraculous effect. Among the many discoveries made in her laboratory were novel materials that could absorb electromagnetic energy to render a perfect retina-draining blackness, or allow light in the visible spectrum to slide away entirely in a blurry sort of invisibility cloak, or imbue a surface with perfect smoothness, a near-zero friction to which no viscous liquid could stick.*

But Vedala's true career had not taken place in the public eye.

Early on she had been approached by a major general in the US Air Force, an ambitious former fighter pilot named Rand L. Stern who had transitioned to a faculty position at the US Military Academy at West Point with a specialization in theoretical mathematics.

At that time in her life, Vedala hadn't known that academics and the military could mix. But the determined general wouldn't be ignored. He told Nidhi that her expertise was needed for a historically momentous project, and all she had to do was sign on the dotted line. He mentioned she had already passed every background check and intelligence test that his analysts could administer.

Vedala had only blinked at this information.

She had not been aware that she was under any scrutiny.

---

* This patent would eventually prove very effective at coating the inside of ketchup bottles, potentially solving a small but widespread problem forever.

Now, she wondered at just how specific the *New York Times* crosswords had been getting the last few weeks, and she began to question the increasingly complex problems her graduate students had been bringing to their office visits.

In any case, Vedala had never failed a test in her life.

Choosing to accept Stern's offer of military clearance, she had listened intently to every detail of the incident in Piedmont, Arizona. When it was over, she understood her role perfectly.

At first assumed to be an organism, the Andromeda Strain actually seemed to have more in common with a new area of science—nanotechnology, the study of machines less than one hundred nanometers in size.

Vedala had devoted her career to understanding the topography of nanoscopic structures, and the construction of artifacts small enough to fit on a pinhead (along with however many angels wished to dance there). She knew there was vast potential waiting for humankind in the realm of nanoscale. After a single conversation with Stern, it became her life's work to understand this mysterious extraterrestrial microparticle.

So far, her studies had been a resounding success.

Vedala's most brilliant insight had been to expose the two varieties of Andromeda to each other. Studying the results at a nanoscale, she discovered that each strain ignored the presence of the other. As close cousins, the substances seemed to have entered into a kind of noncompete agreement.

Essentially, AS-1 and AS-2 were invisible to each other.

Realizing this, Vedala had been able to mass-produce a spray coating with a nanostructure mimicking the contours of both Andromeda strains, creating a surface that was nonreactive to both. Vedala's brilliance did not extend to naming her creation, however; the antibonding mechanism was dubbed simply "aerosolized nanocrystalline cellulose-based Andromeda inhibitor."

The inhibitor had been utilized so far to protect low-orbit spy satellites and government rocket launches from atmospheric AS-2. This represented humankind's first mastery over the strange, plastic-eating microparticle after decades of highly classified study in the laboratory. Now the time had come for Vedala to test her creation face-to-face against the first documented "wild" appearance of Andromeda. And she did not intend to fail.

It was nearly noon. Every other member of her team had already arrived, whisked away from their respective lives to the middle of the Amazon jungle.

All of them had been on time, except for one: James Stone, PhD.

As a roboticist, Stone's skills were not mission appropriate. In Vedala's estimation, he should have been replaced with a microbiologist or a bacteriologist. Any number of more multidimensional researchers would be better suited. And yet General Stern had been intransigent on Stone's inclusion.

Standing beside a muddy river with no name, Vedala knew the stakes of this mission. She also knew its legacy. And thus she had her own idea of why James Stone had been forced onto her roster.

As Stone gathered his luggage, Vedala spit on the ground, turned, and walked away to inspect the hard-cases.

Vedala was an orphan and a self-made success. Her assumption was that James Stone, son of the famous scientist Jeremy Stone, had been included on her field team for a reason she could fundamentally never respect—his family pedigree.

Meanwhile, the civilian scientists were still adjusting to life without their smartphones or the Internet.

Methodically breaking down her traveling backpack to separate out the extra scientific goods that could be hauled by one of the native porters, Peng resolved to stay close to the guides—doing so would maximize her survival probability and therefore the success probability of the mission as a whole.

"FINALLY, WE'RE ALL here," said Vedala.

The Indian woman barely glanced in the direction of James Stone as he stomped across the muddy clearing, huffing and puffing, dragging a black plastic hard-case full of equipment. Wearing a brand-new khaki outfit, the roboticist was in his early fifties but looked younger. His face was already sweaty in the oppressive heat of high noon.

"Let's begin," she added.

Vedala stood under the low ceiling of a maloca—a simple thatch-roofed hut the guides had hastily constructed beside the gurgling brown river. A paper topographic map was spread across a folding table and weighted at the corners with muddy stones. Across from her stood the immaculately outfitted Peng Wu. The PLA Air Force major stood perfectly straight, with martial precision, trim and athletic in a long-sleeved jacket and khaki pants neatly tucked into her boots.

With her military bearing, Peng stood out in stark contrast to the much older Harold Odhiambo, a robust Kenyan man with close-cropped salt-and-pepper hair, a gently amused attitude, and a disheveled outfit complete with cargo shorts and an Australian bush hat with one side pinned up.

Odhiambo turned his kind eyes to Stone as the bedraggled man joined the group under the thatch roof.

"Welcome, Dr. Stone," said Odhiambo, with an English accent. "I enjoyed your work on collision avoidance using low-resolution imaging. Very efficient."

Stone was speechless for a moment, surprised that the famous xenogeologist would have bothered to read his work. Then he recalled that Odhiambo supposedly read *everything*, and with that, his manners returned.

"Thank you, Dr. Odhiambo. That's very flattering. I apologize that I haven't caught up with your latest—"

Vedala cut in.

"You can take that offline. Harold has dabbled in just about everything over his career," she said. "Which is why he's perfect for our mission. He's not just a specialist."

The words hung in the air long enough to be awkward before a modulated ringing interrupted.

"Back to the agenda," she added.

Vedala picked up an Iridium satellite phone from the table. The chunk of black plastic was a restricted military model commissioned by the Defense Information Systems Agency (DISA). It had been ruggedized, weatherproofed, waterproofed, signal-encrypted, and fitted with a hot-swappable antenna adapter. Currently it was attached to a thin black antenna wire strung around the wooden poles supporting the hut. The ice-blue LED screen glowed coolly in the heat of the jungle, four out of four connection bars illuminated.

"Dr. Sophie Kline is joining us from the International Space Station," Vedala said, depressing a button to answer the call. "Good afternoon, Doctor, how's the view from up there?"

"Beautiful, Nidhi, and not a single mosquito."

The voice on the speakerphone was confident and feminine, but a few lightly slurred syllables and a slight tremor betrayed its owner's neurodegenerative disease. "I'm over top of you now, but in a few minutes my orbit will carry me beyond the horizon again and our comms may not be so clear."

Looking at her crew, Vedala continued. "I assume you've all read my personal briefing letter, as well as the red folder docs sent by the Department of Defense—"

James Stone raised his hand, and Vedala stopped, lips pursed in annoyance.

"Yes?"

"Sorry to interrupt, Dr. Vedala, but I didn't get a briefing document."

Vedala blew a curl of hair away from her eyes in irritation. "No, of course you didn't. You were a . . . late addition."

"Oh, I didn't know—"

"It's not your fault," she snapped, more abruptly than she meant to. "Our fearless leader, General Stern, approved the final details of this expedition, and I'm not privy to all the information he had. You can pick up the details as we go—it's almost time to start the day's march. This is Project Wildfire, so you all understand the stakes."

"The fate of the world . . ." Odhiambo smiled.

"You may not be far from the truth," said Vedala. "Agenda item number one, let's talk situational background. Twenty-six hours ago a terrain-mapping drone detected a . . . structure in the deep jungle, thirty miles from here. This anomaly is two hundred feet tall, and it appeared within the last two weeks in the middle of impassable jungle, without any known roads or a landing strip. And now for the reason we're here. Subsequent mass spectrometry readings detected a chemical fingerprint closely matching the original Andromeda incident. Any questions?"

"Another outbreak," said Odhiambo, in a thoughtful voice. "But why would it be located here, so far from anything else?"

Kline's voice came in over the satellite phone: "The Chinese Tiangong-1 space station broke up in the atmosphere over Brazil six months ago. It spread bits of wreckage between here and the Atlantic Ocean. We think . . . ah, the Americans think, the Chinese may have been experimenting with Andromeda."

Peng seemed to have been waiting for this. The former soldier kept her face blank as the others looked to her. Kline's accusatory tone had not gone unnoticed, and Peng's response seemed prepared as she spoke.

"Of course I have no official knowledge of this," said Peng. "However, it would not be an unprecedented scenario, considering the *many* international efforts under way to study Andromeda in a microgravity environment."

Vedala nodded, half smiling. Peng was making a pointed remark about the existence of the Wildfire laboratory module on board the ISS, but she was at least willing to acknowledge the reality—an infected sample from the fallen Chinese space station could have contaminated the jungle.

"Regardless of how the anomaly got here, we are facing the reality of a large structure growing in the middle of the jungle with a chemical composition that matches Andromeda. Our plan is to hike into the quarantine zone and find out what this thing is before it gets any bigger. Thanks to the last Project Wildfire, we know a lot more than the people who tried this in Piedmont. Our respirators and inhibitor spray will protect us, and we have toxin detectors operating constantly."

"I'm surprised the feds didn't already nuke it on reflex," said Stone, venturing a joke.

Vedala only scowled. "And start a world war? We're not in

the United States, Dr. Stone. The contamination didn't appear in our own backyard this time around. We weren't that lucky—"

At these words, Vedala noticed a change in Stone's demeanor. He looked away at once, cheeks flushing with anger. She immediately realized how callous her words must have sounded.

"Obviously, what happened in Piedmont wasn't *lucky*. But this incident is happening in one of the most ecologically delicate places on the planet, severely limiting our options. We're in protected indigenous territory, a place where by Brazilian law uncontacted tribes are meant to be left alone. Harold can elaborate."

"She's right," said Harold Odhiambo, addressing the group. "This is Terra Indigena. The indigenous people who live here are isolated, surviving quite comfortably at a mostly pre–Stone Age level of technology."

Harold spread his long arms, gesturing at the trees.

"We are standing in Earth's lungs. These tree species spread their roots wide and shallow, cutting off almost all access to bedrock. The people who have lived here for millennia never had the opportunity to develop stone tools. Even their arrowheads are carved from bamboo, completely biodegradable. They have been spared the never-ending progression of technology."

"You say that as if progress is a bad thing," said Peng, quietly.

"It is not a bad thing . . . until we show up. Exposed to superior technology, these tribes are vulnerable to being exploited, killed, or enslaved. In the best-case scenario, they will covet our technology—especially our steel and guns. When they do get hold of it, they forget the traditional ways of living and become dependent on tools they can't reproduce. Any contact, with good or evil intentions, will destroy them. Outsiders either take their lives, or their way of life."

Odhiambo's manner had turned grave.

"Our presence in the jungle is highly dangerous. History has played out the same way across every continent, from the indigenous people of Africa to those of Australia and the Americas. It always ends in death."

"And that's why we're not contacting anybody," said Vedala, pointing to the tree line where the quasi-military men were waiting. "Those are our guides, and they're going to keep us far away from the locals."

The dozen uniformed men had collected in shady spots around the edge of the clearing, standing or squatting and talking quietly to each other. From a distance they looked like soldiers, wearing camouflage, with machetes hanging from their hips and shotguns casually strapped over their shoulders.

But looking closer, Stone could see they were indigenous, their crisp military uniforms complemented by traditional clamshell earrings that stretched their earlobes and stiff bamboo shoots poking from their nostrils like jaguar whiskers. Most of the men had waves of bluish lines tattooed across their upper cheeks and thick black hair chopped in bowl cuts.

"Are they not Indians?" asked Peng.

"Those are Matis frontiersmen," responded Vedala, "and they know this territory well. Until forty years ago, they were one of the uncontacted tribes."

Vedala nodded to a large man with a sweat-stained green shirt neatly tucked into military fatigues. Unlike the others, this soldier was Anglo, and he carried a high-tech battle rifle strapped over his chest. The weapon appeared well-used, bristling with after-market attachments.

"And the final item on our agenda," said Vedala. "Meeting our guides."

As if on cue, the soldier stood and began to stride toward them, heavily muscled arms swinging. The bearded Brazilian American spit out a toothpick as he approached the group, snapping words at them with a Portuguese accent.

"Listen up, people. My name is Sergeant Eduardo Brink, United States Army Special Forces. I have been instructed by General Stern to handle you with kid gloves. But this is the Amazon wild. This jungle does not care for your credentials. It does not care for your intelligence. Or for your technology. It was here before you and it will be here after you are gone."

"If we're lucky," muttered Stone.

Brink flashed a cold stare down at the roboticist before continuing. "You are already deep into the territory of indios bravos, wild Indians of Brazil. Make no mistake. You are not welcome. It is sheer luck that I was stationed here with FUNAI and available to accompany you. Our rendezvous with command is in forty-eight hours, at the prescribed destination. If we are not there, command will assume we were killed in action and proceed with alternate plans. My job is to get you where you're going, on time . . . alive."

Brink's voice lowered, and he stepped closer to Stone.

"And let me be very clear, amigo . . . without me, you *will* die here."

The group of scientists exchanged worried glances, and the sergeant seemed satisfied. Turning, he spoke rapid-fire to the native soldiers, who tossed away cigarettes and rose to their feet. Some pulled tumplines over their foreheads, using the woven straps to carry luggage while leaving their arms free. A few others set off into the jungle without a word. The whistling snaps of machetes were audible as they set about hacking a new path through the dense wall of undergrowth. Brink turned back to the scientists, pulling a toothpick from his shirt pocket and clenching it between his teeth in a wide, menacing smile.

"You don't have to like me, boys and girls. You just have to obey me. Because the very last thing you want is to end up out here all alone."

Manifest

DISPATCHED TO THE AMAZON JUNGLE ON AN HOUR'S notice, the Wildfire field team had been as well equipped as possible given the abbreviated logistical timeline. The following partial manifest is technical in nature, but nonetheless illuminating in its content. Previously classified, the full inventory is now stored in the National Archives.

*** APPROVED STANDARD ISSUE MANIFEST—ALL TEAM ITEMS ***

Tropical loadout as determined by Marine Corps Jungle Warfare Training Center (est. Okinawa, Japan). All items stowed in Umlindi all-weather backpack, Tarahumara attachment, chest-mounted heavy recon kit bag. ATTIRE to incl. standard-issue civilian jungle dress, USMC-approved boots, Merino blend socks x4, tactical wind

shirt, rain gear. TOOL and TOOL ROLL to incl. machete,
whistle, compass, flashlight, fire starter, multi-tool,
all-purpose utensil, leather gloves, trowel. SLEEP SYSTEM
to incl. hammock w/ bug screen and rain fly, mountain
serape, cordage.

Local guides to carry SURVIVAL KIT / COOKING KIT /
TRAUMA KIT / WEAPONS KIT.

*** APPROVED SPECIAL MANIFEST ***

NIDHI VEDALA, MD-PHD
Aerosolized cellulose-based Andromeda inhibitor, 200 oz.
Based on subject's Wildfire research and developed in
cooperation with Indian Institutes of Technology (IIT),
Delhi campus. (Protected by US top-secret classification
and IIT Act in the Republic of India.) Contains no latex
elements. Mimics the Andromeda nanostructure to remain
invisible to known microparticle varieties (AS-1 & AS-2).
Multiple interleaved layers are self-cleaning, providing
a low-viscosity surface that repels liquid, dust, etc.
Totally inert, indigestible, and requiring infrequent
reapplication.

HAROLD ODHIAMBO, PHD
Projectile-tipped seismic sensor package, 16 count.
Single-use deployment, locally networked and AI-enabled.
Developed under Kenyan government research grant KIR-
2300B and designed for detection of wildlife migration,
geological activity, and criminal poaching. Fine-
tunable for surface or subsurface events, with innate

machine-learning capability for pattern recognition
and noise cancellation. Additional specialty loadout,
incl.: compact infrasound detector; soil moisture meter;
portable core saw.

PLA MAJOR PENG WU

Chinese-made Dyclone-Wa portable field science and
engineering kit—including packable light microscopy;
portable autoclave; mass spectrum analyzer; gas
and liquid chromatograph; pH meter; refractometer;
microcentrifuge; wireless data logging and backup;
satellite upload capability; twenty-seven built-in
sensors and autosampler; and automatic sensor testing
and calibration. Appropriate for field experimentation
across multiple disciplines.

JAMES STONE, PHD

Palm-size "canary" self-charging mini-drones, 12 count.
Charging base station integrated into portable backpack.
Mounted with five-axis radial blade, four propellers
with redundant, interchangeable parts. Sensor package:
miniaturized laser rangefinder (submillimeter precision);
low- and high-res camera imaging; gyroscopic inertial
measurement unit; toxin-detecting environmental
sensors (including AS-1 and AS-2 detection). Capable
of concerted real-time map-building; collision avoidance;
three-dimensional path-finding. No extra payload
capacity.

SERGEANT EDUARDO BRINK, US ARMY

<REDACTED by order of US Government Approved
Presidential Secret Order #3028.>

DAY 2

WILDFIRE

In a disaster . . . individual personality does not matter. Almost everything you do is going to make it worse.

—MICHAEL CRICHTON

Dawn Discovery

ON WHAT WOULD BE THEIR FIRST AND ONLY NIGHT OF decent rest, the group of four scientists and twelve guides successfully camped beside the nameless river, sleeping in hammocks covered by mosquito netting. They were exhausted, despite having hiked for a mere six hours and covering fewer than ten miles. No problems were reported by Sergeant Brink in his official logbook or by Nidhi Vedala in her morning status notes.

But something happened during the night.

Upon reviewing the personal field diary of James Stone (a decidedly low-tech waterproof notebook and pen recovered after the incident), a paragraph stands out: "Slept fitfully. Woke from the dream, as usual. Thought I saw someone in dark but can't be sure. Guides seem spooked. Caught Matis searching the tree line for something. Said nothing when asked about it."

In the aftermath of the incident, every surviving Matis scout blended untraceably back into the FUNAI-protected tribal villages and river shanties deep in Terra Indigena. Only one scout, Ixema, was eventually located, having spent his wages in a single day in the nearby gambling city of Leticia. He returned to where he had been contracted, looking for another payout. A sum was agreed upon, in exchange for information about the journey.

Of the first night in the jungle, Ixema would say only one thing: "In the morning, something was wrong." When pressed as to what exactly had happened, he admitted someone had left footprints around the camp. Several items were moved, but nothing had been taken.

Finally, after much prodding, Ixema added one detail.

Whoever had come in the night had also left something behind. Something Brink ordered the Matis to quickly remove from view, before the scientists could see it. Ixema described the head of a skinned monkey, brown eyes large and round in a skull covered in pink flesh, fangs bared in an agonized grimace.

And its mouth, open as if screaming, was filled with gray ash.

Twenty-Mile Perimeter

THE FOUR SCIENTISTS AWOKE TO FIND THE MATIS already breaking camp. The smoking remnants of last night's campfire had been doused, and the scouts were quietly divvying up the scientists' heavy equipment. Without a word, two heavily tattooed Matis frontiersmen set off in single file into the trees, shotguns slung over their shoulders. Their pale, flashing machetes were quickly swallowed within the dim jungle.

Watching them go, Vedala approached Sergeant Brink where he stood among the remaining scouts and porters.

"Where are they going?" she asked.

"Directly toward the anomaly. We follow in twenty minutes. Get your people packed and ready."

In response, Vedala walked to a waterproof hard-case lying on the slick mud of the jungle floor. She felt a sense of growing unease. The team was drawing nearer to the anomaly, and yet she had no idea what level of lethality to expect. Her only hope was that the inhibitor spray worked as well in practice as it did theoretically.

Shaking off her unease, she cracked open the hard-case and retrieved several aerosol canisters. Passing a canister to Brink, she began spraying her arms, torso, and legs in short bursts, explaining: "This inhibitor solution protects any surface from contact with the Andromeda nanostructure. Apply it over your clothes and on your exposed skin. Give it to your men, too. Tell them to think of it as sunscreen. It should last a few days."

She closed her eyes and held her breath, spraying her face. Without a word, Brink headed over to his guides. Once he had moved away, Vedala opened her eyes and pulled out the government-issued Iridium satellite phone.

Quietly, she tried to raise General Stern at Peterson AFB.

Under the omnipresent tree canopy, the finicky phone didn't register a single connection bar. Wary of wasting the batteries, Vedala gave up quickly. Further communication would be impossible until they found a break in the canopy. That likely wouldn't happen until they reached the clearing beside the anomaly.

Rendezvous with command was still set for noon on the following day, and until then, it appeared the team would be on its own.

The two lead scouts had left behind an easy-to-follow trail of hacked plants—saplings and branches cut off at sharp angles, which looked oddly like spear points waiting to impale anyone who strayed from the path. Sergeant Brink and several of his Matis companions soon set off in single file, followed by the scientists, safely sandwiched between scouts in front and porters behind.

The day's march progressed largely without incident.

Armed with detailed topographic map information collected by the Abutre-rei, Brink and his guides were able to lead the group around steep hills, avoiding sudden drop-offs and choosing to cross the many river tributaries at shallow points or where huge trees had fallen to create impromptu bridges.

Though the path was twisting, the team made excellent time.

The complex jungle environment proved to be disorienting for the scientists. Peng Wu and Nidhi Vedala marched without speaking, frowns creasing their foreheads. James Stone walked behind them, sweating profusely, eyes wide and constantly scanning.

Only Harold Odhiambo seemed to be perfectly at home, laughing and joking quietly with the Matis guides as he tromped through underbrush in his khaki shorts with his white tube socks rising out of muddy, well-used boots.

Nothing gave the Kenyan scholar more satisfaction than sinking the teeth of his intellect into a new and exotic problem— and this one was unparalleled, given his interests. After years of wide-ranging studies, Odhiambo had devoted the twilight of his career to the geology of other worlds. Though seeing the utterly foreign architecture of the anomaly had frightened him deeply, it had also aroused his curiosity. Now he felt like a child again, riding in the back of his father's ramshackle fishing boat—a thrilling experience, if not particularly safe.

Stone was moving more cautiously. He wore a bulky metal-framed backpack swarmed by a dozen gently whirring canary drones. For now each small drone stayed within thirty yards or so, periodically returning to self-dock and rapidly recharge its batteries. The effect was that of a man carrying a thriving bee-hive on his back.

The Matis guides were much amused by the birdlike devices, pointing and calling to them with uncannily realistic birdcalls of their own.

Each of the nimble, hand-size quad-rotor drones carried an

array of onboard sensors, as well as a chemical sensor package tailored to detect the signature of the AS-1 and AS-2 varieties. The toxin-detecting sensors continually scanned the air, and as the drones occasionally alighted on stable surfaces, a passive end effector could rasp surfaces to scratch off physical samples for testing.

Cruising through dappled shadows cast by the tree canopy high above, the drones moved like phantom hummingbirds, slightly above eye level, exploring in a cone-shaped pattern out ahead of the group.

A small flat-screen tablet computer hung over Stone's chest by a lanyard. It displayed a crude drone-generated map, topographic, with the position of each flying robot identified and large objects marked as dots of varying diameters. In one corner, a grainy live video showed one drone's camera feed. Despite the constant flow of information, Stone rarely stopped to check the screen. He was too afraid of losing the rest of his team in the thick foliage of the jungle.

It was a claustrophobic experience for the scientists, who were unaccustomed to the sheer density of life concentrated in such a small area. On average hundreds of species of plant grow in every acre of the Amazon—a bewildering confusion to eyes used to seeing only a dozen or so species in North American forests.

Soaring trees rose up around them, with roots stretched out like the tendons of extinct dinosaurs, and all of it crawling with vines, flowers, and creepers. Every inch of the jungle was alive with insects and birds and animals—biting ants making their tiny highways, rooting anteaters snuffling through the underbrush, and the flickering neon streaks of macaws winging through the air.

This fecund crush of plant life all around and the spongelike soil beneath seemed to swallow up every sound. Staying close together became a priority for the field team. Even a conversation a few feet away was muted into muffled whispers, and none of the scientists relished the idea of getting lost and needing to blow on an emergency whistle until found.

Marching along with one eye on the unreadable Matis guides, James Stone had begun to harbor suspicions. Entries in his recovered field diary indicated that, for one, he did not believe the team had permission to be on this land. He suspected that nobody, including the Brazilian government, had been notified of the existence of this expedition, much less its purpose.

Thus Stone assumed that if they were to fail, it would likely be a case of disappearing into the jungle forever.

More importantly, he had become increasingly worried about the behavior of their field guide, Eduardo Brink. Stone possessed an uncanny eye for details, a trait shared by his father. Briefly and quietly, Brink and the Matis had huddled together at various times for several worried discussions in an unintelligible pidgin of Portuguese and the native Panoan language.

Brink never shared the content of these discussions.

In one instance, Stone watched as a Matis pointed out an indentation on the path. Brink promptly stamped on it with a jungle boot. When Stone inspected the soil a few minutes later, he saw what could have been a naked human heel print. In another instance, Stone noticed several branches bent at about waist height along the path, as though a person had marked his or her trail through the jungle. Either the lead scouts had begun marking the path after hours of not doing so, or someone else had already been here.

Finally, after hours of marching, Stone spotted a branch that had been laid across the path—insubstantial, but with a clear message: go no further.

Stone was beginning to suspect that the team was under surveillance by an outside group. In any case, he was certain that Brink and his scouts were keeping secrets. Without proof, however, he wasn't ready to make accusations.

Not yet.

And though his suspicions would turn out to be true, during the course of the day's hike Stone would find them to be among the least of his worries.

"DR. VEDALA! EVERYONE! I've got something!" shouted Stone, his voice thin and indistinct in the hanging curtains of vegetation. "Stop where you are, please. Make your way to me. Don't stray from the path."

Moving single file, calling out to each other, the scientists slowed and stopped. Tired and muddy, the field team converged on Stone. The roboticist was breathing hard, holding up the small screen that hung around his neck. Sergeant Brink emerged from behind a tree and stood watching them. He was clearly irritated by the slowdown but said nothing.

On the glowing display, a series of near-identical dots stretched out in a staggered line through the jungle a hundred yards ahead. None of the dots were directly on the path before them, but the scattered line crossed their position. With a finger swipe, Stone sent the canary drones on a wider reconnaissance pattern. More dots began to appear, an irregular line crossing deep into the jungle.

"Look here," said Stone. "These objects are all nearly the same size. Laid out in two rough lines."

Odhiambo examined the screen, tracing his rough fingers along the line of dots. In the corner, a thumbnail-size video feed showed a clump of something dark lying on the jungle floor. "Plants do not grow like that. In straight lines."

Stone stared down at the screen as more dots emerged. "Actually, they aren't in lines. Not exactly. Look at how they curve. Whatever is out there is lying in two concentric arcs."

A shotgun blast rang out from farther ahead.

The dull thump of noise faded quickly, but the jungle fell into an immediate, unnatural silence.

"Stay here!" shouted Brink, jogging up the path alone. The team shared a worried glance, and then followed behind him. Stone brought up the rear, keeping an eye on his screen. In particular, he was watching for toxin alerts.

Emerging at last from behind the exposed roots of a sprawling kapok tree, Stone stopped with the rest of the group and stared in disbelief.

Ahead, he could see the dots were actually black, furry lumps—dead howler monkeys, a staggered line of them, unseeing eyes clouded, fangs bared. Beyond the howlers, Stone could make out a few woolly monkeys, covered in fine reddish fur.

With a lot of cursing and gesturing, Brink was calling back the two Matis forward scouts, one of whom still had his shotgun out. The armed woodsman shrugged and replied in low tones as Brink angrily berated him.

"What happened?" called Vedala.

"He says he put one out of its misery," said Brink.

"Right. Keep your men back. We're holding here until we can get a full sitrep," ordered Vedala, just as Brink began to walk out toward the nearest primate corpse.

"Stay with me, Sergeant," added Vedala, firmly.

The large man kept walking a few steps, then thought better of it. Gesturing to the Matis to join him, Brink returned to lean against a tree. Unlatching the stubby battle rifle from his chest, he began to clean the barrel with a worn piece of rag.

Vedala turned to the group of scientists, speaking with urgency. "Something killed these animals. We need to know what it was, right now."

James Stone had crouched on a tree root, his eyes fixed on the monitor hanging from his neck. With quick gestures, he directed the canaries to survey the field of corpses, the soft whir of their rotors the only sound in the still jungle.

"Not picking up any airborne toxins," he reported.

Squinting into the shadowed jungle, Vedala studied the minefield of simian corpses stretched out before them. The Matis had gathered together, speaking urgently among themselves and not making any move to proceed. Peng had already retrieved her portable field laboratory. The device was half unpacked from a dirt-streaked hard-case. She was methodically ripping open the vacuum-sealed equipment from its Chinese-marked packaging.

Staring into the wilderness with naked concern, Odhiambo began to ruminate out loud.

"These primates are not the same. They are separated by species," he said. His eyes rose to survey the canopy.

"They fell. Moving through the trees. In two lines."

After conferring quickly with a Matis in both sign language and broken Spanish, Odhiambo turned back to the group.

"He says the black ones move faster than the red ones. That must be why they made it farther. It also tells us the direction they were going."

"They were running from something," concluded Vedala.

"If the lines are concentric arcs," added Peng, "it means they were all running from the *same* thing—a single point in the jungle."

"Our anomaly?" suggested Odhiambo.

"We'll see," said Stone, tapping his screen. "I can use the radius of the arcs to estimate an origin point."

On Stone's command, the swarm of canaries rose higher, their flickering shapes milling about in the lower canopy. From around sixty feet up, the dotted remains of the monkeys took on a clear pattern of two arcs.

Stone reverse-pinched the screen to zoom out to a larger map, largely blank. Each corpse was marked as a black dot. Drawing with his fingertip, he connected the dots until he had traced an entire rough circle.

And in the dead center, their destination waited.

"Dr. Odhiambo is right," said Stone. "They were fleeing the anomaly."

Looking up, Stone was startled to see Vedala leaning beside him, her cheek nearly pressed against his as she peered into the monitor. A low-resolution live video feed in the corner showed the sneering face of a dead monkey. Its lolling tongue was streaked with what looked like gray ash.

"What the hell is this?" she asked, pointing and looking into Stone's face.

Suddenly aware of how close she was to Stone, Vedala backed up, stumbling over a root. Under a layer of dirt and sweat, she was surprised to feel heat rising on her cheeks.

"There was something in its mouth," she said, covering her embarrassment. "You should have pointed it out immediately. It's a disease marker."

On her knees in the dirt a few yards away, Peng had finished assembling her portable field science kit.

"I'll tell you what it is. But we need a sample," she said.

The scientists looked at each other, and even the Matis guides perked up, watching to see who would volunteer.

"I'll do it," said Vedala.

Reaching into the kit slung on her hip, Vedala retrieved a half-face respirator. She pulled the contoured device down over her mouth and nose. It was dark blue and smooth, with two cylindrical black filters on either side. Slipping on a pair of purple nonlatex exam gloves, she took Peng's sample kit and tromped away toward the nearest corpse.

"Wait for me," said Stone, pulling on his own respirator. "I'm going, too."

ENVELOPED IN A cloud of a dozen canary drones, the two figures moved through shadowy layers of undergrowth. The rest of the field team watched silently from afar as the two were engulfed by the jungle.

The day was already nearly half over.

Fortunately, the sample retrieval process was brief and proceeded without event. Of more importance is the unknown exchange that occurred between Nidhi Vedala and James Stone while they were momentarily alone.

Returning from the jungle, Nidhi handed the sample bag to Peng and then turned to the sergeant. Getting directly to the point, she asked Eduardo Brink whether he was aware of any immediate danger to her team. Fixing a steely glare on James Stone, the sergeant crossed his bulky arms and responded that the team was not in any more or less danger than they had been upon their arrival.

Stone-faced, Brink issued a final bit of advice: "There's nothing out here I can't handle. Trust me, I've got instructions for every eventuality."

These words would turn out to be fateful.

Meanwhile, Peng Wu had begun to fit the test tubes into a

vacuum-sealed portal of her portable laboratory. The contents of each vial were sucked into the compact machine, where they were pulped by a diamond impact hammer, and various specimens were routed to different compartments.

In this way, Peng was able to run dozens of experiments with her miniaturized and specialized hardware. She also had the benefit of already knowing the findings of the scientists who survived the first Andromeda incident.

First, she used the mass spectrum analyzer to determine that the gray ash exhibited a chemical signature matching Andromeda (confirming the onboard sensors of the Abutre-rei drone). Even with the added granularity of chromatography, however, she could not determine whether the sample was an exact match to AS-1 or AS-2. Such results would require either comparison to live samples, or more advanced (and nonportable) lab methods such as X-ray crystallography.

Isolating the positive samples, she nonetheless continued to experiment.

Next, Peng tried to stimulate growth. Routing samples to environments with varying levels of vacuum, carbon dioxide, and ultraviolet light, she exposed each to a variety of potentially reactive substances, including fabric, epithelial tissue (i.e., skin), and Vedala's inhibitor substance.

The samples refused to react in any way, save for two exposures: blood and latex. And in both of those cases, environment did not seem to matter in the least to the voracious microparticle.

Focusing her final (and rather limited) light microscopy analysis on these two reactions, Peng was perplexed to observe a mix of outcomes. On direct contact with blood, the infected samples caused coagulation at an alarming speed. Similarly, exposure to latex created a dustlike substance. Both patterns had been seen before in AS-1 and AS-2.

It was what happened afterward that put a dismayed frown on Peng's face.

The microparticle seemed to grow visibly larger, self-replicating on exposure. With limited scientific resources in the field, Peng could not observe in any finer detail. Based on the outcome, she assumed her samples had been cross-contaminated and deemed the results largely untrustworthy.

Only now did Peng have enough information to turn to the group.

"The gray substance from the tongue has tested positive for Andromeda," reported Peng. "I can't confirm exactly which variety. The results are confused and most likely corrupted."

"Even so, what did you find?" asked Vedala.

Peng spoke carefully. "The specimen appeared to coagulate blood on contact, like AS-1. But it also partially dechained polymer-made material, in the manner of AS-2. And . . . it seemed to self-replicate, using the substrate materials as fuel."

Nidhi Vedala exhaled. "So at the very least, we know the primates were infected. The question is, by which strain?"

"Impossible to guess, without a full laboratory analysis," said Peng.

Odhiambo spoke up in a steady, rumbling voice. "The trees are unbroken between here and the anomaly. There are no babies among these monkeys. The infants must have been left behind. And primates are capable of brachiating at over thirty miles an hour through dense canopy such as this."

"We're less than twenty miles from the anomaly," added Vedala, grasping Odhiambo's point. "At maximum speed, these animals survived a little more than half an hour, postinfection."

"That's consistent with the Piedmont incident," said Stone. "Some victims there died immediately of blood coagulation, but others . . . they lasted longer. Long enough to record final mes-

sages, to wander the streets, and to commit suicide. None survived more than an hour."

"Except the baby and the old man," corrected Nidhi. "They
each had an abnormal blood pH that prevented infection."

"Right," said Stone, his voice hollow.

"We should get these results up to Kline in the Wildfire
module," said Peng. "With living Andromeda samples for comparison, she can tell us which strain we're dealing with. We
need to find a clearing."

"Wrong," replied Brink, looming over the four scientists.
He scanned the jungle as he spoke. "We need to keep the team
moving. There is a rendezvous to make. Besides, you'll find
no line of sight to the communications satellite out here. And
therefore no way to make radio contact."

"That's not exactly true."

Brink turned to glare at James Stone, who stood holding a
dinner-plate-size drone in his hands.

"What's that supposed to be?" asked Brink.

Stone shrugged, wearing a sheepish grin.

"She's my baby, highly customized. I brought her in my personal effects, instead of a change of clothes."

Brink snorted in disgust, turning away.

Moments later, the carbon fiber drone was rising slowly
through the canopy, picking its way through a maze of branches
and vines. A string of wire filament trailed below it like a fishing
line. The buzzing drone soon emerged through a small gap in
the upper tree canopy, an alien visitor to the sun-soaked roof of
the tropical rain forest.

Vedala dialed a direct line to the International Space Station.

An instant after the satellite uplink was established, a frantic
flurry of invisible data leaped up from the green expanse of trees
and into the blackness of the void above.

A Higher Analysis

A T THE HEART OF THE INTERNATIONAL SPACE STATION, several hundred miles above the Amazon jungle, a humanoid form stood shrouded in shadows, still and silent. As it drifted slightly in the microgravity, the reddish pulse of a status light shone from the sinuous curves of its outer casing. The anodized aluminum was smooth, honed to a perfect golden sheen, but most of all it was clean—indeed, it had never been touched by human hands.

The experimental Robonaut R3A4 humanoid robot had been constructed inside this room by its predecessor, had never left its sealed environment, and was the sole permanent occupant of the Wildfire Mark IV laboratory module.

Although untouched by human hands, the Robonaut was often touched by human *thoughts*.

One by one, a ring of white lights blinked on inside the cylindrical laboratory module. LEDs on the upper chest of the R3A4 blinked from red to green. And in a subtle, complex symphony of movement and attention, the Robonaut appeared to come alive. The machine glanced down at its own hands, flexing each finger with startling dexterity. It then turned to face a wall of containment cabinets, each housing a separate experiment, stacked together like brightly lit fish tanks.

Invented and perfected through multiple grant iterations by NASA's Dexterous Robotics Laboratory at Johnson Space Center, the R3A4 occupied the same form factor as a human astronaut. A one-to-one match with the human body made for easy teleoperation—although the R3A4 was stronger, faster, and had better sensory capabilities than its human operators.

And this R3A4 was especially unique.

The Wildfire Robonaut had been tailor-made for Dr. Sophie Kline. The brain-computer interface Kline had used since childhood had been modified to wirelessly transmit her most subtle gestures to the R3A4. Locked inside its permanent home, the machine could carry out her experiments without risk of bacteria, dirt, or any foreign bodies that might compromise the platonically perfect cleanliness of the Wildfire laboratory.

The R3A4 went to work.

Twenty yards away in the Destiny laboratory module, Sophie Kline floated beside a remote workstation, wearing a slim pair of virtual reality goggles and instrumented gloves. She could see through the machine's eyes, feel with its hands, and mentally inhabit the Robonaut with little effort. Over the years, the machine had become an extension of her own body—a hard metal incarnation of herself that Kline secretly relished inhabiting.

In the Amazon rain forest far below, the Wildfire field team had sent up a barrage of data collected from dead primates. Now, Kline had the eyes of her second skin set to maximum magnification, comparing the incoming data to a live sample of the Andromeda Strain AS-1—a specimen that had been retrieved directly from Piedmont, Arizona.

The transcript of her communication with the field scientists, monitored by NORTHCOM and confirmed against the audio logs of a salvaged canary drone, was as follows:

GRND-VEDALA

Kline. Data transfer is complete. We have limited time. Our drone can only loiter in communication range for a couple minutes.

ISS-KLINE

Roger that, Vedala. Preliminary results do confirm a match to Andromeda.

GRND-VEDALA

Our results concur. But which strain are we dealing with? Can you compare to the Piedmont samples?

ISS-KLINE

Hold on. [fifteen seconds elapse]

ISS-KLINE

It . . . this isn't AS-1 or AS-2. You've hit on something new.

GRND-VEDALA

[static] Another evolution?

ISS-KLINE

Call it AS-3.

GRND-VEDALA

Is it dangerous?

ISS-KLINE

Affirmative. I advise you abort mission and retreat to the quarantine perimeter. The anomaly is growing out of control. And another unidentified structure is rising from the lake. There is nothing more your team can do, you understand?

GRND-VEDALA

We've got a lot of dead primates down here, and not a lot of time. What exactly did you find? Will it react to inhibitor?

ISS-KLINE

It's nonreactive to the inhibitor, but the sample exhibits deadly properties of both previous strains.

GRND-VEDALA

I assumed as much. We're continuing.

ISS-KLINE

Nidhi, listen. The first Andromeda strain triggered on contact with life. It killed those people in Piedmont and then evolved into AS-2, which eats the plastic necessary for spaceflight. It's *not* a coincidence.

GRND-VEDALA

So you're hypothesizing that Andromeda mutated in order to trap our species on Earth's surface? It's an interesting theory, but irrelevant.

ISS-KLINE

Not irrelevant if you consider this new evolution. AS-3 has appeared for a reason. There is an alien intelligence behind this. We are facing an unknown enemy who is staging an attack over the gulf of a hundred thousand years and across our solar system and likely the cosmos. This is a war, Nidhi, and you are on the front lines of it. I repeat. Do not approach that anomaly.

GRND-VEDALA

[static] We'll take your theory under advisement. Over and out.

ISS-KLINE

Run. Disobey orders if you have to. Get out of—

[connection lost]

Incomplete Information

A STUNNED SILENCE SETTLED OVER THE SCIENTISTS. They stood shoulder to shoulder around the satellite phone as Kline's final words were cut off. A hot wash of air came from above as the PhantomEye lowered itself through the sun-soaked jungle canopy to rejoin the team.

Vedala was the first to move back into action, and she did so in her typical brusque manner. "Respirators on. Everyone recoat your uniforms and skin with the aerosolized inhibitor solution. Use light bursts to conserve it. Tuck your pants into your boots and wear gloves. We're not taking any chances we don't have to."

Then, after a deep breath, she added, "We're moving on in five."

"Listen, lady," said Brink. "Didn't you hear what your friend just said—"

"Brink," interrupted Vedala. "Tell your guides to reapply the inhibitor. Watch them. Make sure they do it properly. I don't want anybody on our team to end up like these primates. Because we are moving on in five."

"Who says?" asked Brink, standing to his full height, the snub-nosed battle rifle hanging from his chest like an exclamation point.

"*I do*," said Vedala, standing toe to toe with the sergeant, a full head shorter and no less intimidating for it. "I am not about to explain my qualifications, but if you have read and comprehended your mission briefing, then you will intimately understand the . . . the *goddamn* consequences of disobeying me."

Brink stared down at her, jaw clenched, slowly turning red with anger. Before he could respond, a hand appeared on Vedala's forearm, gently pulling her back.

"Wait," said Peng. The rare sound of her calm voice was enough to cause everyone to step out of the moment, turning away from Brink to listen.

"The soldier is right. We need to discuss this. As a group," said Peng.

"What is there to discuss?" asked Vedala, glaring at Peng with suspicion. "That *thing* out there represents an existence-level threat to humanity. Out of everyone on the planet, we four are the best prepared to learn more about it, and possibly to stop it from spreading. We knew this was dangerous from the start."

"This is true," said Peng. "But if Kline is right, then it could be a suicide mission. The anomaly is the focal point of a virulent new infection. Ground zero. Perhaps we could do more good by studying it from afar. Establish a perimeter, like Kline suggested."

Vedala snorted, tugging the straps of her backpack tighter and stepping toward Peng. "Kline has put forth a *theory*. Without evidence, that's all it is. We are scientists. What we need is understanding. And we aren't going to get that by staying on the perimeter."

Peng stared coolly back at Vedala, while Brink watched them both with a wry smile.

"Major Wu is right," came a deep voice. "Let us stop arguing, stop rushing off, and start *thinking*."

Odhiambo cracked his knuckles, taking a deep breath and letting the green-filtered sunlight dance over the gray stubble on his cheeks and chin. The rest of the group waited, their heart rates slowing as they watched the calm man simply breathe.

In his rigorous, methodical way, Odhiambo began to work through the problem. "If what Dr. Kline says is true, and this anomaly is an attack, then the original Andromeda Strain must have been lingering in our atmosphere for thousands of years. And probably for millions. It is an old and patient thing—a trap designed to wait for intelligent life to evolve before springing. Once triggered, the strain evolves to isolate life on the planet's surface by eating the plastics necessary for spaceflight. Am I correct so far?"

Looking at each other, the group nodded affirmation.

"Well, if this hypothesis is true, then how would the strain know to wait *here*? Out of all the places where intelligent life could evolve?"

"It wouldn't," said Stone. "A weapon like that only works if the microparticle spreads everywhere life could possibly evolve—all over the galaxy—lingering in the upper atmosphere of any planet or moon *with* an atmosphere. It's John Samuel's Messenger Theory—one of the first ideas put forth by my father to explain the Andromeda Strain."

"Clarify," said Vedala.

"The Messenger Theory was proposed as the best, and possibly only, way to communicate with intelligent life across galaxies. Send a self-replicating craft to a neighboring plane-tary system, have it find raw materials to build copies of itself, and then launch those copies to other systems. The fleet would spread exponentially, covering every planet in the galaxy in only a few thousands of years . . ."

Odhiambo smiled at James Stone and finished his thought. "Indicating an alien intelligence. And thus we have come to our conclusion. We have no evidence that Andromeda has prolifer-ated throughout our solar system. No sample-return mission has ever tested positive for the microparticle, correct?"

In the reconstructed video, acquired from the canary drones as they milled around the small clearing, Nidhi Vedala can be seen watching Peng Wu closely at this moment. Peng's face is carefully blank, and as Odhiambo finishes his thoughts, she turns to face the jungle.

"Not that I've seen," said Stone.

Peng Wu is seen taking a breath as if to speak . . . but the former taikonaut lets it out without saying anything. Her silence in this moment was surely spurred by conflicting desires—her duty to her team on one hand, versus her duty to maintain the secrets of her homeland on the other. With every word tanta-mount to a chess move, her decision to take no action here would prove a costly blunder.

And an unnecessary one.

In the grand scheme of things, all human beings are part of the same family, regardless of origin.* The divisions we have built between ourselves along the lines of race and geography are illusions. If our species is ultimately able to see past these

---

* Based on modern genetic variance, it is estimated that an ancient and catastrophic near-extinction event reduced the human population to a mere six hundred individuals. This tiny group of shared ancestors went on to give rise to all of us in our billions.

biases, it will be our shared genetic stamp of humanness that will outlive the cultural contrivances that distract us in our day-to-day lives.

And yet even in the face of a species-wide threat, loyalty to nationality won out in this moment. Peng Wu said nothing.

"Then I do not see how Kline's hypothesis could be true," continued Odhiambo. "If the microparticle exists only in our atmosphere, it must have evolved naturally from a terrestrial source or arrived randomly from the cosmos. If so, the Messenger Theory does not apply, and there can be no malevolent intent. Based on the information we have, we are dealing with a very dangerous specimen, but one that does not have a will of its own."

There was no disagreement from the scientists, though Sergeant Brink grumbled unhappily and pushed off his tree.

"We have a rendezvous to keep," confirmed Vedala. "Let's get on with it. Everyone?"

Standing in the silent jungle, the members of the group regarded one another without speaking—an assured conviction settling over them. It was Brink who broke the silence, the whine of his machete slicing off a branch as he wordlessly turned and forged ahead. The oil-slick gleam of the inhibitor spray lent a surreal shimmer to his brawny arms as he marched away among soaring tree trunks.

"Come on," called Brink, the dense jungle muffling his words. "We've wasted too much daylight already."

Second Camp

OVER THE REST OF THE SECOND DAY'S MARCH, THE Wildfire field team followed their expert Matis guides past the corpse perimeter and deeper into the thirty-mile circular quarantine zone around the anomaly. They were glad to leave behind the smell of death, and the unsettling remains of the fallen monkeys. Under the canopy of pristine rain forest, the team must have felt vulnerable, effectively invisible to satellite imagery or surveillance aircraft, and cut off from radio contact.

Rendezvous was at noon the next day—in eighteen hours—and the team was on schedule.

Their progress had been aided by the canary drones employed by Dr. Stone, which were primarily engaged in topographical exploration and environmental toxin screening in an area a few hundred yards ahead of the group. However, because the canaries were so employed, very little video footage exists of the interpersonal interactions that occurred during this portion of the journey.

Instead, the events of the afternoon have been reconstructed through postevent interviews with survivors, the logbook of Dr. Stone, and a cache of information inadvertently collected by the sensor array of the PhantomEye drone.

Approximately twelve miles from destination, the group continued following Sergeant Brink as he cut a brisk, winding path across river tributaries and around rugged hillsides—moving as fast as possible, given the harsh terrain and constant obstacles. As the team marched single file in the footsteps of their advance scouts, the jungle floor was stamped by many feet, deteriorating from a barely cleared trail littered with foliage to a red mud slick that had the scientists occasionally scrambling along on all fours.

The brutal pace was intentional; Brink could sense that the group (including his team of Matis frontiersmen) had been spooked by the strange events of the day. The sergeant felt that physical exertion would help abate the growing fear and distract the group from ruminating on negative possible outcomes. It was a good instinct, and an approach commonly and successfully employed among soldiers.

Moving quickly had the added bonus of reducing the number of questions voiced by the breathless scientists. In particular, Brink seemed irritated by the persistent comments of James Stone.

In a partial video segment captured by a far-off canary, Stone could be seen pulling Brink aside at the top of a small ridge. From a distance, the two had an emphatic exchange, bordering on an argument. It appeared the men nearly came to blows on the ridge, before Stone stomped away angrily.

As shadows began to grow in the high canopy, the air seemed to shimmer with waves of dusky sunlight, filtering through endless leaves and vines. Reaching an area of high ground, Brink turned to the Matis and declared the day's march over.

"Ten-mile perimeter," he said. "We stay here tonight. Be at the destination by noon tomorrow."

The nervous guides immediately set about hacking at the jungle, establishing the night's camp with quiet urgency. Within minutes, however, they discovered that the clearing was infested with *tracuá*—a local breed of small, voracious carpenter ants who are known to vigorously defend their territory. A familiar nuisance to the Matis, the ants were pervasive in many parts of the forest. Their bites felt like wasp stings, and they were quite capable of traversing cordage to invade hanging hammocks. The insects began to emerge in the gloom, slowly at first, but in rapidly growing numbers.

Dr. Vedala exhibited immediate skepticism regarding the camp selection, noting that there was still at least an hour of fading daylight remaining in which to choose another site. Her concerns were summarily ignored by Sergeant Brink, who considered the ants a trifling annoyance. The dismissive interaction further added to the tension and fear enveloping the team.

As the canary drones returned from scouting and converged on the campsite, their video feeds revealed lines of worry and tension on the faces of every field team member, save one.

James Stone was working intently.

The roboticist had unpacked his PhantomEye drone again, extended the four rotors, and switched in a fresh battery. Within minutes he had sent the humming black drone up into the jungle, letting it pick its way forward through stripes of shadow and light. Accelerating through tangled vines and tree limbs, the

AI-enabled drone employed a high-fidelity laser rangefinder to avoid obstacles and accelerate to fully autonomous speeds of up to fifty miles per hour.

At that rate, it should have been able to scout their destination within twelve minutes.

Swatting at biting ants, trying to ignore the wild hacking of the Matis's machetes and the grumbling complaints of his fellow scientists, Stone studied the monitor hanging from his neck. The image showed a real-time, gyro-stabilized video feed of the drone's progress. In the last glow of daylight, Stone was hoping to catch an actual glimpse of the mysterious anomaly.

Nine minutes into its journey (still two miles from its destination) the PhantomEye reported a gyroscopic exception and dropped out of radio contact. Stone's frantic efforts to reconnect with his precious robot were unsuccessful, and the entire hundred-thousand-dollar unit was lost.

It would never be recovered.

Cursing and typing, Stone found he had been left with only a data log of the drone's final moments. A quick forensic analysis determined that the PhantomEye had lost stability as it was crossing a stream. It had flipped violently and likely splashed into the water.

Noticing Stone's distress, Harold Odhiambo made his way over.

The Kenyan was worried, having noted that although the Matis guides were finished clearing the camp, they had now moved on to cutting large branches, sharpening them, and placing the jagged stakes along the camp perimeter. Indeed, it appeared to Odhiambo that the Matis were preparing for war.

"A collision?" asked Odhiambo, squatting beside Stone.

"Possible, but not likely," said Stone, his face illuminated by the glow of the monitor. "It was over a river—the only real clear place around. And it was navigating the jungle fine up until then. Look."

Stone moved through each frame of the saved video feed. In the final second, the image shuddered violently. After that, the screen devolved into a blur as rotor stabilization failed and the drone began to spin.

"The failure comes out of nowhere. Like it was hit by something," mused Stone.

"A bird strike?" asked Odhiambo.

"Could be," said Stone, continuing to advance frame by frame through the swirl of river and jungle. The image on the monitor was nonsensical at this point, just a meaningless smear of color.

Stone shook his head in disgust.

"Wait," urged Odhiambo. "Stop there."

Puzzled, Stone stopped the frame.

"Go backward, please," asked the Kenyan. "Again."

As Stone moved back a single frame, he saw it, too—a reddish oval hidden among the trees. Peng and Vedala had silently joined them. Now the entire field team watched as Stone zoomed in on the red blur.

"It looks like a face," he said, confused. "But something is wrong with it. Could it be an optical illusion?"

Though pixelated in its enlarged form, the face—if that's truly what it was—seemed distorted. The features were almost demonic, eyes burning black and bright. The skin was reddish, as if coated in blood.

"This is most certainly what destroyed your drone," said Odhiambo.

"What's out there?" asked Stone, eyes lifting beyond the

bright, fresh-cut tips of wooden stakes ringing the perimeter. Peng and Vedala stood a bit closer, the four of them small in the darkening woods.

"It is not a question of what," added Odhiambo, lines of worry creasing his forehead as his watery eyes searched the depths of the jungle. "But *who*."

IN CERTAIN DREAMS, we have all experienced an uncanny distortion of the passage of time; experiences in which precious seconds telescope toward infinity, usually in the face of impending catastrophe. Having suffered from such a recurring vision since childhood, James Stone described the next hour as a living version of his worst nightmares. A sense of foreboding had fallen over the jungle and pervaded everything the scientists did with a sense of déjà vu.

Recovered canary video footage effectively conveys the languid atmosphere that fell over the "golden hour"—a period closer to forty-five minutes and occurring just before dusk—of the second day's march. As the simmering crest of the sun descended ten degrees past the horizon, a suffusion of indirect light imbued every leaf, vine, and flying insect with a radiance that seemed to come from within.

In this golden aura of shifting shadows and faint glimmerings, a feeling of helplessness had settled over the field team. As the light began to fade, their eyes grew wider, trained on the shadowed folds of jungle.

The stillness was shattered by a shrill whistle.

In the newly created clearing, a Matis stood before a thick round tree trunk, holding an unstrung hammock in his hands. His hat cocked back on his head, the man was thoughtfully chewing a bundle of coca leaves, the small lump bulging from his cheek like a tumor. He stared up into the last light with hollow black eyes. Following his gaze, the scientists saw their first Amazonian rubber tree.

A long, wet-looking film of white sap, like candle wax, rolled down the rough, spotted bark.

Colloquially known as "the trees that bleed," this species had instigated one of the darkest periods of Brazilian history. The Amazon rubber boom, beginning in the late 1800s, brought voracious swarms of prospectors and rubber barons deep into the virgin jungle. Tens of thousands of indigenous people were enslaved, threatened with death, and forced to tap the trees to collect the leaking sap. It was the first, but not the last, systemized plundering of the Amazon by outside colonizers.

The Matis spit the wad of coca leaves to the ground. He spoke quickly to Brink without looking away from the tree. In the fading light, the bamboo shoots embedded in his nostrils gave him an unearthly presence.

"What do you mean, the tree is not supposed to look like that?" said Brink quietly, brushing an ant off his forearm as he turned to the group. "It's just a rubber tree. It's supposed to bleed."

The frontiersman reached out to point and stopped. Vedala had clamped a hand over his wrist. She slowly pulled his arm down, her eyes locked on the surface of the tree.

"No," cautioned Vedala. "Don't touch."

Halfway up the trunk, the weeping sap darkened to a metallic gray. The surface was flecked with luminous green spots. Around the edges, the chitinous coating traced its expansion in six-sided ridges.

As Vedala watched, the scabby layer flattened out, spreading an inch in all directions. A creaking groan came from inside the tree, followed by an ominous splintering sound.

Vedala immediately moved back. Sergeant Brink stood watching with his mouth partly open, a forgotten toothpick dangling from his lip.

The lead scientist spoke to the group, her eyes hard and bright. "Everyone," said Vedala. "This is a live infection site. We can't stay here tonight. Get ready to move on."

"You've got to be kidding."

The group turned to Brink, who stood breathing hard, his sudden anger masking a rising fear. Dusk would soon give way to night. The evening birds had begun their lonely evening calls.

"I am dead serious," replied Vedala, scowling at the Matis as they ignored her and watched Brink for orders. Several were looking warily out into the jungle, murmuring to each other in low tones. Brink paused, put a hand to his forehead, and then lowered it.

"I can't believe this," he muttered. Then he nodded to Vedala. "All right. Quickly."

The Matis porters began to move, collecting baggage and preparing to leave.

Stone hastily checked the toxin detectors on his canary drones, finding nothing. Nonetheless, he pulled the respirator from his pocket and slid it over his mouth and nose, feeling the familiar heat of his breath washing over his cheeks.

"It is a rubber tree," said Odhiambo. "Latex. It makes perfect sense that Andromeda would settle here. My guess is we are looking at AS-2, or some variant. A cousin of the microparticle that consumed the seals of the original Wildfire laboratory."

"If it only eats rubber, then it's not a threat," insisted Brink weakly.

"Ah, but it evolves," said Odhiambo, his voice almost melancholy. "We are indeed witnessing an Andromeda evolution. And it is impossible to properly gauge the amount of danger we are in."

"Harold is right," said Vedala.

Brink slid a headlamp across his forehead and illuminated it. Unsheathing his machete, he motioned the lead scouts forward before stomping off after them. He could be heard muttering as he left, "This is without a doubt the stupidest, most foolhardy expedition I have ever been involved with."

The hulking soldier disappeared into the foliage, swatting angrily with his machete.

Peng marched past the others, following close behind Brink. Her black eyes shone over the dark blue mask of a respirator. She barely spared a glance at the infection spreading across the deformed tree trunk. Since the conversation with Kline, she had been even quieter than usual—searching for the right moves in what was becoming an unwinnable game.

Stone watched her go.

It struck him that nobody had taken so much as a sample. They were too far in, it was too late in the day, and they had already seen too much. This jungle had been sickened, infected by something, and the disease was clearly coming from the inexplicable anomaly approximately ten miles away.

Up ahead, Stone could hear Brink speaking quietly to a guide.

"Dark soon," said the Matis.

"I know," replied Brink. "We cover as much ground as we can. Make camp on the very next ridge. Damn these eggheads."

And with that, the team marched onward into the night. They left behind a short-lived camp hacked out of the raw jungle, along with its swarms of biting ants and the long, sharpened poles that surrounded it. This last-minute decision to move on, and the subsequent necessity of setting up camp in the dark, with fewer defenses, would prove to be pivotal.

It was a choice that meant not all of the team would survive the night.

DAY 3

ANOMALY

I believe in the future.

—MICHAEL CRICHTON

Night Ambush

A PORTABLE INFRASOUND DETECTOR CARRIED BY HAROLD Odhiambo registered gunfire forty-nine minutes before the dawn of the team's third day in the Amazon, coinciding with the darkest point of the night. With the already faint light of the stars and moon hidden behind a ceiling of thick jungle canopy, the floor of the Amazon jungle would have been ink black.

Eduardo Brink and his men had established the new camp hastily and in the dark the night before. They were in an unfamiliar location, exhausted, and they could see next to nothing. In short, the field team was utterly unprepared to defend themselves from a coordinated onslaught.

The strike came without warning.

The handful of attackers were experts at navigating the jungle. Forensic evidence later collected from the scene indicated that their eyesight had been enhanced by exposure to the juice of the sananga root.* In this way, the assailants were able to maneuver confidently by the first, almost unnoticeable glimmer of dawn.

The following events unfolded in just under eleven minutes.

Dr. Nidhi Vedala was awoken in her hammock by a blood-curdling shriek. Later, it was determined that the scream came from a Matis porter who had been impaled through the upper chest with a sharpened bamboo spear. Perhaps having heard a noise, the man had apparently gone to the camp perimeter and illuminated his headlamp.

Inhuman roars, jaguar-like, resounded in the jungle for the next thirty seconds as the frightened team of scientists flipped out of their hammocks and into the dirt, blinking sleep from their eyes. Confusion ensued as the scientists and porters attempted to scramble to safety under a hail of bamboo-tipped arrows that fluttered into the campsite from all directions.

Sergeant Brink had wisely placed his rugged frontiersmen in a perimeter around the less experienced scientists—both to keep the newcomers protected from prowling animals and to prevent them from simply wandering into the woods and getting lost. The nearly defenseless scientists strategically occupied the center of the camp, their hammocks radiating from the shared base of a walking palm tree.

The Matis were first to face the danger while the scientists fumbled into partial shelter among the walking palms' thick, stiltlike roots. Dozens of arrows were raining down around

---

* When rubbed in the eyes, the sananga root enhances color perception and visual acuity—useful for hunting and warfare. Although modern science does not yet understand the underlying mechanism of its action, spoken-word records indicate that the root has been in use by indigenous Amazonians for over two thousand years.

them, their needle-sharp tips coated with a poisonous curare plant extract normally used for hunting monkeys.

After the first few volleys, Brink's voice could be heard barking out hoarse commands. In moments, the small clearing around the great walking palm tree erupted into a cacophony of gunfire. The sharp smell of gunpowder and the pungent aroma of shredded bark and leaves filled the camp. The piercing crack of rifle shots and booming shotgun blasts reverberated almost nonstop for several deafening minutes.

All of this noise was punctuated by the stuttering discharge of Brink's snub-nosed M4A1 battle rifle. The lethal black weapon was lighter than standard-issue and outfitted with a Mark 18 close quarters battle receiver (CQBR)—a 10.3-inch barrel appropriate for the close-up nature of jungle warfare, a favorite among special forces units.

As he crawled on hands and knees through the flickering light of muzzle blasts, Stone caught glimpses of the demonic, twisted red faces of devils. The monsters were scampering through the brush along the perimeter of the camp with long black axes held high. Remembering the smudge of red in his drone footage, Stone could now confirm it had not been a visual artifact.

This was first contact.

Faces smeared in red urucum paint, the devilish-looking warriors were in reality only men, small and agile, chests tattooed in solid black bars and hair coated with tufts of bird down. They were emissaries from an uncontacted tribe, and almost certainly the group who had been following and watching the scientists' journey. They had warned the field team in myriad ways to go no farther into forbidden territory.

Now it was too late.

On examination of documented sightings registered by

FUNAI in the preceding year, this group matched closely with a tribe known colloquially as the Machado—named for their use of rare stone axes. Having retreated to the Amazonian interior only a generation ago, this group would certainly have retained extensive knowledge of guns and their capabilities. This explains how they knew to use the trees as cover to avoid weapons that barked and spat bullets into the night.

The Matis, who had until recently been in the same situation as their attackers, seemed to immediately recognize the indigenous tactics. They well understood the lethal stakes of this fight. Each of the Matis fired his weapon wildly into the jungle, emptying magazines and ejecting spent shells, filling the air with the rolling thunder of explosions.

It was an impressive show of force, and that was the point.

Sergeant Brink had been surprised to his core by the brazen attack. But his disbelief and fear intensified as the fighting continued beyond the initial barrage of gunfire. The noise and destruction were expressly meant to shock the enemy into retreat. Even having seen only glimpses of these ferocious warriors, Brink suspected that something was seriously wrong with them. Intertribal warfare in the deep Amazon was not unheard of, but attacks on Westerners were rare and almost never continued past an initial demonstration of overwhelming firepower.

Worse, Brink understood that his command over the Matis scouts was tenuous at best. And as he watched in dismay—shouting desperate orders over the whip-crack reports of his own battle rifle—Brink's worst fears came true.

One by one, the guns went silent.

After his initial scream, the wounded Matis had quickly collapsed. His nervous system had been invaded by sticky black curare, a naturally occurring neurotoxin primarily employed to paralyze large primates during hunting expeditions. His body lay inert, the LED headlamp on his forehead still illuminating a bright slice of jungle floor. Meanwhile, in an act of silent cooperation, the rest of the Matis guides had quietly retreated together.

Brink's harshly shouted orders and threats had no effect except to further frighten the scientists still huddled among the roots of the walking palm.

Continuing to risk life and limb on an inscrutable mission for outsiders would have made no sense to the indigenous mercenaries. Having been exploited for decades by various visitors to the Amazon, the Matis had much more in common with the Machado than with Sergeant Brink or the Wildfire field team.

The guides, many of whom were related, would have been secure in the knowledge that in only a few days' hike they could reach the ancestral maloca huts of their families in the deep jungle. In addition, a deep-seated (and well-earned) distrust of whites had left them suspecting that this mess had been caused by foreigners of one sort or another. Better to withdraw and let the situation take care of itself.

Within six minutes of the attack, every non-native member of the Wildfire team had been left to fend for himself.

Only Eduardo Brink was armed and capable of defending the camp. As the confident soldier stalked through the pitch-black jungle, he would have known that if he were to even be nicked by a poisonous spear point, the entire science team would likely be slaughtered.

"Lights out!" Brink shouted.

James Stone had turned on a flashlight in the center of the camp. The light only made him a target. Plus, it would interfere with Brink's last-ditch plan of attack. The camp was quickly enclosed in darkness again.

Brink crouched and wedged the butt of his battle rifle into

the hollow of his shoulder, pressing his cheek against the cold metal. With a dirt-covered thumb, he flipped on the green-glowing AN/PVS-17 night sight. Normally, his night vision would be helmet-mounted, but this was supposedly a civilian operation, and his orders had been to keep the military hardware to a minimum.

Scanning the walking palm tree in the amplified light of the rifle scope, Brink was glad to see the scientists staying together in the folds of bark. In addition, some enterprising individual had dragged over a few pieces of hard-case luggage to provide cover from stray arrows.

Brink swept his night sight across the face of the open jungle, the glow tracing a green circle over his right eye.

He began to discern the silhouettes of his attackers as they loped between the black stripes of trees. The sight of them was grotesque—the features he could make out were caked in gritty layers of red paint that appeared black in his sight. Beneath the mud, he could see cheeks, lips, and eyes that were twisted and deformed. The surface of their skin seemed to be erupting in gruesome dark splotches.

Something was indeed very wrong with these men.

The job of the *sertanistas* is to never harm the indigenous people they protect, even at the cost of harm to themselves. One of the most famous sayings among the FUNAI is actually a dire warning: "Die if you must." But on this night, Brink was revealed to be a veteran soldier, not a conservator. Like most visitors to this place, he was not willing to risk his own life to protect this tribe who lived deep in the Amazon jungle.

Brink was not, in fact, affiliated with FUNAI, as he had indicated. Instead, he was a seasoned veteran with a tenacity borne of countless clandestine operations for obscure agencies in remote places throughout the world. Moving like a machine, he crept forward, scanning the jungle and occasionally squeezing the trigger of his battle rifle.

Each shot was a death sentence—his aim was impeccable.

Brink had been abandoned by his own indigenous mercenaries. He was outnumbered and facing annihilation in the form of primitive but deadly axes and arrows. Operating on a lifetime of soldier's instinct, he employed superior training and a fifty-thousand-year gap in weapons and sensor technology to ruthlessly eradicate the threat before him.

Stepping carefully through the jungle, rifle on the high ready and one eye on his scope, Brink fired at anything that moved. He was not worried about whether the target was a friendly Matis guide or a hostile Machado—he considered them all enemies now.

In three minutes, Brink had nearly accomplished his objective.

When the bite of a stone ax glanced off his shoulder blade, Brink spun and fired on instinct. His bullet punched a fist-size hole in the Machado before him and sprayed a blood mist over the waxy leaves of a nearby kapok tree.

At first, Brink assumed he was fine. The blow had only grazed the meat of his shoulder. While painful, it had not shattered any bones, and he still had free range of motion. He could feel a warm wetness spreading down his back and into the seam of his trousers. After a few seconds the feeling went away.

Though Brink could not see it, the rivulet of blood trickling down his back had quickly clotted into a fine red dust.

For thirty seconds, Brink continued walking, sweeping his rifle back and forth and finding no remaining targets. He kept one eye on the brightly lit scope, occasionally closing it and opening his other eye (still adjusted to the dark) to scan the area around him.

Eleven minutes had elapsed, and every attacker lay dead.

Seven corpses were sprawled among the trees. Five of them were the bodies of the devil-like Machado. The other two Brink would have recognized as his own Matis workers. Nevertheless, Brink's mission parameters were satisfied.

The scientists appeared safe, if terrified. The operation could now continue, with the field team easily reaching the destination in time to make the noon rendezvous the next day. At this thought, Brink leaned against a tree in relief. Lowering his rifle, he allowed himself a grim smile.

He had cheated death yet again.

The rueful smile was still on Eduardo Brink's face as dawn broke over the jungle twenty minutes later. His body was found leaning peacefully against the blood-spattered tree trunk, fingers still wrapped around the grip of his battle rifle.

Alpha and Omega

I N THE PREDAWN DARKNESS, PENG WU HAD LISTENED from her hiding spot as the other three scientists scrambled to safety in the myriad roots of the walking palm. As the attack unfolded, Peng slipped out of her hammock and crawled to a large nut tree at the edge of the clearing. Drawing her PLA-issued combat knife, she crouched to make herself a smaller target, keeping a solid wall of wood behind her. From this strategic position, she resolved to stab anything that might come at her from the front.

Peng had assumed that if the Matis failed to defend the camp and a final attack came, it would wipe out the helpless scientists who were clustered together. She did not intend to be among the victims. So she sat alone, blindly scanning the darkness and catching details through the lightning-strike flashes of gunfire.

The close-packed jungle foliage deadened the barking reports of weapons. Occasional screams and shrill war cries seemed to come from nowhere and everywhere. These sounds soon became more sporadic, eventually dying out altogether after ten long minutes. Peng listened carefully, tensed for a last attack. She heard only a final gasp of surprise, and guessed correctly that the noise had come from Sergeant Brink.

Whatever had gone wrong, Peng was determined to figure it out first.

As the other scientists began to compose themselves in the first gray light of morning, Peng carefully unfolded from her hidden perch. She noted a pale scrape of bark near her face, where an arrow had narrowly missed. Moving quickly and quietly, she crouch-walked to the camp perimeter, knife out and extended before her.

Along the way, Peng spied several corpses lying sprawled among the underbrush and gnarled tree roots. The tree trunks and foliage had been blasted and shredded by bullets, leaves stained red with horror-movie spatters of blood and soft tissue. These bodies would bear more inspection. Even at a glance, the skin seemed covered in a reddish pigment that was clouded with blotches.

Peng kept moving, giving the mangled bodies a wide berth. In the distance behind her, she could hear the hushed voices of the field team.

Seconds later, she spotted Brink's burly silhouette. He was leaning casually against the fat base of a rubber tree, holding his battle rifle on the low ready. The night scope projected a green circle of light onto his bicep.

"Brink," whispered Peng, stepping closer.

Approaching from behind, Peng put out a finger to tap his shoulder but stopped before touching him. Something felt wrong. Unnatural.

This was not Eduardo Brink, not exactly.

Peng worked to contain a thrill of panic. She was reminded of being a little girl with her parents gone away on PLA business, left behind to face unknown rules and consequences. She had learned to distance herself from overwhelming feelings by treating the world like a game. Over the years, Peng had become a cool and methodical person precisely because she struggled with anxiety.

Struggled, but never lost to it.

Backing away carefully, controlling her breathing, Peng glanced behind her. She was still alone.

Slowly, she circled around Brink.

The corpse was still smiling, eyes clouded over with gray flecks of a metallic-looking substance. It seemed he had leaned against the tree to catch his breath and then somehow been frozen there in death. Across his broad shoulders, Brink's tan jungle shirt was ripped open. A small skin laceration was visible, partially hidden from view where it was pressed against the mottled bark of the rubber tree.

His body sagged, but something was holding him upright.

In this brief moment, Peng Wu was not foolish enough to touch the corpse. Instead, she hastily unzipped the interior pockets of Brink's personal kit bag. As a former soldier, she would have known this compartment was where special forces troops often kept mementos, maps, and ongoing mission notes.

Among Brink's effects, Peng discovered a small waterproof packet labeled:

FAIL-SAFE—FAIL-SAFE—FAIL-SAFE

Unraveling the packet, she extracted a black plastic container about the size of a Zippo lighter. Inside this protective case was a vial containing a sickly-looking amber liquid. It would have been obvious to the former soldier that the thick fluid was some kind of nerve agent—a deadly and discreet poison.

The glass vial was etched with the code word OMEGA. It was the final letter of the Greek alphabet, signifying the end of all things.

The growing distrust between Peng Wu and the rest of the team had just blossomed into full-blown paranoia. Peng had hard decisions to make in these few remaining seconds alone. It was not clear who among her colleagues had retained her trust, if anyone.

When Brink's smiling corpse was discovered and searched by the rest of the field team later that morning, the Omega vial was no longer among his effects.

In the Morning Light

THESE WERE JUST MEN. NATIVE MEN," SAID HAROLD Odhiambo, his voice somber. "More victims, among many."

Pulling on a pair of purple exam gloves, the Kenyan scientist stood over the muddy corpse of a Machado. The small man was sprawled facedown in the dewy undergrowth. With careful movements, Odhiambo turned the body over.

The Machado's cheeks were smudged with dried red urucum, his nostrils and lower lip pierced by bamboo shoots that splayed in a fearsome imitation of jaguar whiskers. These traditional adornments, subtly different than those of the Matis, confirmed the tribal identity of the body.

But that was not what most concerned Odhiambo.

The man's mouth, open in a pained snarl, was coated in a grayish, ashy substance. His upper lip was caked with it. Most disturbing, the skin of his face was scabbed in hexagonal patches of what looked like metal.

"It appears to be the same material we found on the howler monkeys," said Peng, watching from a distance. "Something farther in, probably the anomaly, has infected them. Infected this whole jungle."

At the top of the Machado's bare chest, Odhiambo made another grisly discovery—the puckered, bloody hole of an entry wound.

"He was shot down like a dog," said Odhiambo, his voice cracking with emotion. "All of them were. Brink did this."

"Would you rather he hadn't?" asked Vedala.

Turning to Vedala, Odhiambo's voice rumbled with deep anger. "If he were truly from FUNAI, Brink would never have shot them dead. Certainly not every single one. The indigenists are trained never to harm the indios bravos, only to scare them away."

Odhiambo looked away with tired eyes.

"Die if you must," he said, almost to himself. "But do no harm."

"I'm sorry, you're right," said Vedala. "We still need to discuss our unfortunate Sergeant Brink. And I'll need both of you to help with the examination, at the very least as a sanity check."

Nidhi Vedala could feel that her team was balanced on the knife's edge of panic. They had all silently realized that they'd been abandoned by their native guides. All were mulling the constant threat of another attack. The situation was bleak, even without factoring in the existence of a deadly contamination event somewhere ahead of them.

Quietly, Vedala was also considering the repercussions of missing today's noon communications rendezvous with General Stern. She guessed that twelve hours of missed contact would likely result in a change of plans, giving the team until midnight to reach the anomaly and make contact. If the group was considered killed in action, Stern's response would likely be drastic.

Looking at each of her team members, Vedala found herself thankful. The strict, mechanical precision of Peng Wu and the calm competence of Harold Odhiambo were comforting. It was James Stone, the robotics expert and last-minute addition to the team, who worried her. Moments ago she had brusquely ordered him to repack his crucial equipment. Now he was kneeling in the mud near the walking palm tree, muttering to himself as he worked.

Without porters, each scientist would have to carry a full load. Whatever couldn't be repacked would have to be left behind. Even so, Vedala had given Stone the repacking order primarily to keep him occupied while the rest of the team examined the corpses. The sight of him had disturbed Vedala. His eyes were vacant over protruding cheekbones and a growth of reddish beard stubble. He had been rubbing his face and speaking in low tones about nightmares of "blood like dust on the wind."

Leaving the struggling roboticist behind, Vedala pulled on a pair of latex-free examination gloves. She led the two other team members back to the remains of Sergeant Brink. His body was still leaning against the trunk of a rubber tree, that horrible smile stuck on his face.

As part of standard training, every member of the Wildfire roster had of course studied the incident in Piedmont. One of the first observations of the original field team was that the corpses did not bleed. And here, in the deep jungle more than fifty years later, Vedala found herself re-creating a field experiment she had only read about in historical case files.

With a scalpel, she drew a line across Brink's muscled scapula, exposing the bone of the shoulder blade just below the pre-existing wound. Peering into the clean, razor-sharp lip of the incision, Vedala could see each layer of the dermis in perfect relief—from the tan surface of the epidermis to the pale white dermis and the fatty yellow hypodermis. Below that was a layer of pink muscle and then whitish-pink bone with a clean notch in it.

Speaking into a voice recorder, Vedala noted what she was observing: "Deep laceration to subject's scapula. The wound is clean of blood. A preliminary examination indicates the red blood cells are desiccated in the area near the wound, and possibly throughout the body. The corpse demonstrates no lividity."

"In other words, his blood has been turned to red dust," said a hollow voice.

The three scientists turned to see James Stone, standing gaunt and trembling a few yards away. His backpack was strapped on tightly, crowded with canary drones. For once the entire swarm was quiet, all of them perched on their docks to recharge. Stone's eyes burned with a haggard intensity Vedala hadn't seen before.

"It's just like the first time. It's Piedmont all over again. We should all be dead by now. I should be dead—"

"No, James," said Vedala in a steady voice.

She didn't like the way Stone was breathing in shallow gasps, or how his eyes were darting back and forth across the oddly upright body of Sergeant Brink. "It's not quite the same as before. Look here. Focus."

Vedala carefully tugged on Brink's shirt, ripping the fabric open where it had been split. Peng Wu gasped audibly as the skin of Brink's shoulder was revealed. Where it came into contact with the weeping sap of the rubber tree, the bloodless flesh had begun to meld with the bark.

Brink's corpse was fusing into the tree.

Vedala held up her recorder, steadfastly maintaining a clinical tone in the face of this new horror. "The naturally forming latex from the rubber tree is disintegrating, consistent with infection by the AS-2 plastiphage variety—as witnessed when the seals failed on level five of the original Wildfire facility."

Vedala stopped to take several steadying breaths.

"In addition, coagulation of the subject's blood is consistent with an infection of the lethal AS-1 variety, which killed the victims in Piedmont, Arizona."

She paused.

The cry of insects was loud against the silence. The group of scientists must have been feeling very alone in the jungle, aware of the thousands of miles between them and any hope of rescue or safety.

"This evidence confirms the existence of a novel mutation, with elements of AS-1 and AS-2," continued Vedala. "There is a noticeable alteration of the subject's flesh where it comes into contact with the latex sap. The two materials seem to be . . . combining. A hexagonal growth pattern of hardened gray particulate matter, possibly metallic, can be observed on both flesh and bark."

Unfolding a geologist's hand lens, similar to a jeweler's loupe, Odhiambo studied the bark under magnification.

"These hexagons are smaller versions of the same patterns we have seen in images of the anomaly," he said. "And on a microscopic level, we know these same patterns form the fundamental cellular structure of the Andromeda Strain."

Odhiambo snapped the lens shut and returned it to his pocket.

"So, what is our diagnosis?" asked Peng.

"I have to agree with Dr. Kline," replied Vedala. "We're not dealing with AS-1 or AS-2, exactly, though properties of both are present. My best hypothesis is that we are witnessing a new evolution of the Andromeda Strain. We can call it AS-3 for simplicity, but there is very little to understand so far, except that it retains the deadly properties of both its predecessors. AS-3 seems to coagulate blood on contact, acts as a plastiphage, and converts those raw materials into some kind of metallic substance."

Standing in tree shadows, James Stone had managed to calm himself down. Now, he spoke quickly and quietly. "That's all well and good, Nidhi, but if we want to stay alive out here, the real question is, How was he infected?"

Nidhi Vedala was silent for a moment. She could feel the heat of the jungle growing as the sun rose somewhere beyond the canopy. Finally she spoke, calming herself with a logical, scientific thought process.

"That's a good question, James," she said. "The inhibitor barrier is intact on his skin. So it appears that this Andromeda variety is nonreactive with its predecessors. His nostrils and mouth are clear of any residue. It's unlikely he inhaled it or absorbed it through a mucous membrane. He also appears free from facial deformities, unlike our attackers. In fact, all the damage seems to emanate from this single wound to his shoulder. My suggestion is that we begin looking for a fomite."

"A nonorganic vector for disease," clarified Odhiambo. "And I believe the solution is right before us."

Odhiambo turned his eyes to the curved head of a stone ax, where it rested on the muddy ground. The handmade ax head glimmered grayish-green. Odhiambo grasped it lightly by the wood handle.

"Dr. Odhiambo," said Peng, her voice rising. "I thought you said the Amazon had no stone?"

"Barely any," replied Odhiambo, lifting the ax. "Whatever there is has to make a long journey down from the Andes."

Turning the weapon gingerly in his gloved hands, Odhiambo's gaze ran along faint hexagonal etches embedded in the surface of the ax head. "But I don't believe this ax head is made of stone. It is much too light. And much, much too sharp."

"Well, then, what do you think . . ." Vedala said, trailing off as she realized the obvious.

"Human beings are enterprising, Dr. Vedala. Adaptable. This tool has been crafted from a material that must have appeared only recently."

"They've mined the anomaly," breathed Peng.

Putting a hand to her forehead in dismay, Peng stepped away. She spoke almost to herself, a flood of words coming out as the realization swept over her. "Of course. Of course they did. They're human beings, just like us. They would have noticed the anomaly immediately. Recognized it as a potential source of new technology. They would have studied it, mined it, built ax-heads or arrowheads from it. Used it however they could, trying to improve their lives."

Peng glanced up at the other scientists, an embarrassed look on her face in the wake of the uncharacteristic outburst.

"And yet, one wrong move and AS-3 can kill," added Stone. "I don't get it. Why would anyone risk working with such a dangerous material?"

"They probably didn't know. Or if they did, maybe they saw it as a positive attribute," responded Peng more quietly. "Not useful for hunting, as the infection would make meat inconsumable. But good for defense . . . killing your enemy with one blow would be a significant advantage, whether it was a man or a jaguar."

"This could also explain why they were so brave to attack us, despite our arms," mused Odhiambo. "It was simply a question of superior firepower. And the tables had finally turned."

"That, or anger," said Stone. "They may have assumed we

were responsible for this . . . thing that's invaded their world. And there is truth to that assumption."

The group of scientists stood mulling this for a moment.

Historically, indigenous peoples have often been judged for not having "evolved" the same weapons, religious beliefs, and societal infrastructure as those in the West. Even the word *civilization* is a loaded term, as its definition is traditionally dictated by self-appointed gatekeepers of progress. These isolated people had found a new material in their midst, and their instinct was not a primitive urge to flee from it, destroy it, or simply ignore it.

Their human instinct was to *use* it.

The anomaly had already impacted the local population along familiar vectors of curiosity and self-interest—the same qualities that caused the citizens of Piedmont, Arizona, to watch a government satellite fall from the sky and decide to open it to see what was inside. The mistake that led to these deaths in the jungle was human; it had been made before and it would be made again in the near future by others who considered themselves more "civilized."

In the heart of this still jungle, four of the brightest minds on earth stood ready to take on the greatest threat in human history. The Wildfire field team was armed with two thousand years of iterative scientific progress, backpacks bristling with advanced scientific tools, minds comforted by a total faith in their superior knowledge. Up until this moment, the team had imagined they were infinitely more advanced and prepared than the "wild Indians" of the forest.

Now they were realizing that this was a false assumption.

Cut off from the rest of the world, without guides or the knowledge of how to survive for long in the jungle, the Wildfire team was staring into annihilation.

James Stone was the first to speak.

"We have to communicate with command," he said. "My drone is lost, and there are no clearings around here. I see no other choice . . ."

"Yes. Back to the mission. We'll head to the clearing beside the anomaly to get a line to the satellite," continued Vedala, with growing authority in her voice. "It's our only hope. Stern can authorize reinforcements, or extract us."

From her expression, Peng Wu was not so convinced.

In recovered drone footage, she was seen with hands hidden in her pockets, appearing to secretly clasp an unknown object. It was most likely the plastic case containing a lethal nerve agent. She had just opened her mouth to speak—perhaps even to confess to her discovery and warn the others—when she was interrupted by something incredible.

"Everyone," said Odhiambo. "Please be very still and don't create a panic."

"What's the matter, Harold?" asked Vedala, concern on her face.

The older Kenyan nodded in the direction of the forest before him.

"We have a visitor."

Turning as one, the group spotted a small red face. Halfway up a leaning tree trunk, a pair of eyes were watching them from behind a splay of leaves. It was the face of a child—a boy. His cheeks were caked in red urucum paint, with clear evidence of tears having streaked ravines through the dried dust.

Counting the Wildfire team, he was now the fifth survivor.

Outcomes

A THOUSAND MILES TO THE WEST, A CARRIER STRIKE group was still stationed off the coast of Peru. On the flight deck of the USS *Carl Vinson*, a squadron of four specially selected F/A-18E Super Hornet combat jets were prepped and waiting. In the dead of night, a cargo of mysterious snub-nosed underwing packages had arrived on two unmarked V-22 Osprey transports. The vertical replenishment effort was carried out by an uncommunicative delivery team, none bearing a visible military affiliation.

These newcomers had been solely approved to handle weapons loading.

This was much to the consternation of the regular-duty group of navy ordnancemen. The veteran "ordies" were full members of this elite fighter squadron and felt a sense of ownership over not only their airplanes but also their pilots. Orders were orders, however. So the disgruntled men and women had stood at the base of the flight control tower in their red shirts,

grumbling to each other and sneaking cigarettes while mysterious outsiders did their jobs for them.*

Each bullet-shaped payload was designed to fit seamlessly
into an underwing weapon station. The jets were quickly outfitted with a full complement of four payloads on each of their
inboard hardpoints. Complete with boosters, the total weight
was nearly six thousand pounds of pure cellulose-based Andromeda inhibitor, in liquid form. Existence of this prototype
substance was officially classified, and its weaponization into a
standard combat loadout a closely guarded secret.

The delivery team stood guard on the flight deck for the rest
of that day, working in shifts. Wearing mirrored aviator sunglasses and with arms crossed, none of the newcomers seemed
capable of speech. Meanwhile, word of a new launch had gone
out in the combat direction center.

Felix squadron had been put on alert posture from midnight
until six a.m.

While on alert, the squadron of Super Hornets was primed
and ready to roar off the carrier's steam catapult at a moment's
notice—specifically the bow-cat, due to wind conditions. Given
the word, they would be launched one by one onto a covert journey east over the depths of the Amazon. Their presence would
break a dozen treaties in force, including the founding Treaty of
Peace and Friendship between nations signed in 1828. Despite
any altruistic intentions, an armed sortie onto a foreign nation's
soil without permission would be viewed as nothing less than
an act of war—the clandestine mission being in clear violation

---

* Surprisingly, US Navy surface ships still allow smoking and will likely
continue to do so for the foreseeable future due to a federal law that requires all navy ships to sell cigarettes and tobacco—a result of the tobacco
industry's intense lobbying in the 1990s. Banning smoking on board US
Navy ships will at some point literally require an act of Congress.

of the definition of aggression as set out in the Charter of the United Nations.

The hope was that it wouldn't come to that.

Maximum clean wing speed for a Super Hornet is Mach 1.6, but with weapons on, the squadron faced increased drag. Estimated flight duration to target at a maximum velocity of Mach 1 was three hours forty minutes. At dawn of the next morning, Felix squadron would be in position to unleash hell.

This last-ditch attempt to contain the anomaly via aerial bombardment with the Andromeda inhibitor was deemed necessary by Wildfire protocol, despite the high likelihood of triggering an international conflict. The hope was that coating the structure surface with inhibitor would stop its expansion. The associated risks were deemed acceptable in the face of the most likely alternative scenarios of Andromeda infection if the threat was not contained.

The following eschatological taxonomy was introduced in classified reports commonly associated with the Andromeda incident, describing non-nation-centric outcomes of the potential spread and dissemination of the Andromeda microparticle.

Scenario A (65%): Regional Disaster

Similar in scale to severe weather incident or minor asteroid impact. Contagious particles spread but are contained to quarantine zone. Death rate: 100 to 1,000s.

Scenario B (21%): Global Human Dieback

Similar in scale to global thermonuclear war. Microparticles spread globally, but either through preparation or luck, survival rates hover well above zero and governmental institutions continue to exist. Death rate: 1M to 100M.

Scenario C (9%): Civilization Extinction

Similar in scale to severe asteroid impact or volcanic eruptions contributing to sudden global warming events. Traumatic die-off worldwide on a scale that destroys government infrastructure and plunges humanity into pretechnological phase. Death rate: Billions.

Scenario D (4%): Targeted Human Extinction

Similar in scale to biowarfare plagues. Likely a human-engineered outcome resulting from the weaponization of the Andromeda microparticle and the failure of an aggressor nation's prophylactic vaccines. Resulting in total or near-total human extinction, while possibly not harming other biological organisms. Survival rate: 10,000 to 100,000s.

Scenario E (<1%): Biosphere Extinction

Similar in scale to an astronomically adjacent gamma-ray burst. A rampant Andromeda microparticle, engineered or in its "natural" state, absorbs enough energy to disseminate globally, feeding impartially on biological organisms of all forms, effectively sterilizing the planetary biosphere and reducing Earth to a lifeless rock. Only nonplanetary humans (ISS, other orbital vehicles/structures) with samples of life could survive, though likely not for long. Human survival rate: 10s to 100s.

Scenario F (<.01%): Total Planetary Extinction

Unprecedented in scale, other than the eventual envelopment of Earth by the dying sun as it expands in approximately 7.6 billion years. Theoretically possible as the "gray goo" scenario of expanding nanoparticles. Experimentally, the Andromeda Strain has been seen to adapt to consume different materials in a pure energy conversion. If this process were to repeat unchecked, the entire mass of the planet Earth could be consumed. Survival rate: Zero.

Indios Bravos

REALIZING HE HAD BEEN SEEN BY THE SHOCKED WILDFIRE team, the boy decided to come down from his tree. He carefully descended from his hiding place, poised to run away. Hesitantly, he stepped into a gap between tree roots and faced the scientists from a distance.

The boy was perhaps ten years old, barefoot and brown-skinned, black hair chopped close to his skull. He carried a hand-made length of rope twined over both his shoulders like bandoliers. Standing proudly, red dust still clinging to his cheeks, he thrust out his small chest. He held a blowgun in one hand like a staff, nearly twice as tall as himself, with one end planted firmly into the muddy ground.

Shouting in his fiercest voice, the boy moved his free hand in a clear gesture of "Go away."

The four scientists, alone in a foreign jungle, clearly had no idea how to respond. Still standing over the body they had been examining, they did not take their eyes off the child. On instinct, they moved slowly and spoke calmly, keeping their hands visible.

"He's not infected, as far as I can see," said Stone.

"Probably too young to have handled the contaminated weapons," said Peng.

Harold Odhiambo began to step backward, his palms flashing as he raised them. A sad smile had surfaced on his face. "We should move away from here for the moment," he told the group.

"Why?" asked Vedala. "He's only a little boy. He's not a threat."

"I believe it is likely we are standing over the body of someone he knows, perhaps a father or uncle," replied the Kenyan, gently.

As a group, the team backed away.

The boy crept toward the fallen man. Kneeling beside the corpse, he placed his forehead against the ground. Tears had sprung to the child's eyes, and his chest shuddered. His lips curled down in a pure expression of grief.

The scientists watched from a short distance.

"We shouldn't let him touch the body," said Stone.

"How do you propose we stop him?" asked Vedala.

"I have an idea," said Stone.

"You always seem to," retorted Vedala.

Stone called out in a gentle voice, but only evoked a cringe and another shout. Crouching over the body protectively, the boy was tugging on a limp hand, trying to drag the corpse without success.

Palms up, Stone advanced a few slow steps. Alert and afraid, the boy stood suddenly. Stone ever so slowly reached around to his backpack and plucked a canary drone from its recharging perch.

Stone held out the small black device on his flat palm.

The boy's eyes narrowed in suspicion as the four rotors spun into a blur. A whoosh of air spread below the drone. With a small smile that he hoped was reassuring, Stone lowered his hand and retreated.

The canary drone remained hovering in the air before him.

The boy's eyes widened in wonder and curiosity. Looking quizzically at the other scientists, he tried to gauge the level of danger from this mystical bird.

Inch by inch, the drone flew nearer to the amazed child.

Confident of the temporary distraction, Stone detached the monitor hanging around his neck and handed it to Vedala. Speaking quietly, he told the group, "All the canary's sensors are piped into here, including the camera. Use this to examine him for infection. I'll be busy for the next few minutes."

With skeptical approval, Vedala took the monitor and flipped the image to infrared. Examining the boy's skin temperature, she launched into a hushed discussion with Peng Wu regarding what might be the most obvious visual signs of infection.

Meanwhile, Stone had slid a ruggedized laptop that looked like a brick of black plastic out from his backpack. Sitting on the ground, he unfolded a portable keyboard from the back casing and balanced it on his knees.

He began to type frantically.

Vedala examined an up-close image of the boy's face through the monitor, zooming in on the nose and mouth. She relayed her findings to the other scientists in a hushed voice, without looking up.

"Unlike the others," she said, "he hasn't got any of the dark ash around his mouth or nose. And I see no sign of metallic growths on the epidermis."

Vedala glanced over the monitor at the boy. He was standing on a log, watching the canary drone with bright, alert eyes. It hovered around him in slow circles. He looked like a kitten, ready to pounce.

"Motor and coordination seem to be functioning fine," she added.

Stone continued typing, elbows sticking out awkwardly from his laptop. Peng was rifling through a leftover hard-case for sample bags. And a few yards away, Odhiambo was stooped over a compact utility shovel, struggling to scoop dirt as rivulets of sweat coursed over his temples.

"Harold, what are you doing?" asked Vedala. "I could use your help."

Odhiambo turned to face her, still hunched over a shovelful of silty jungle soil. He nodded toward the body, then let his eyes move to the distracted boy.

"Oh," said Vedala.

Although she was focused on a grand scientific adventure, Vedala had to remind herself that these were human lives that had been lost. Odhiambo had a way of maintaining perspective that she appreciated. It wasn't a strength she possessed.

"Stone. What about you?" asked Vedala. "The kid won't be distracted forever by your silly drone."

Stone responded without looking up from his computer. "That silly drone, as you call it, is a sophisticated robot with all kinds of capabilities. Specifically, it has a camera, a microphone, a small speaker, and copious amounts of AI."

"So what?"

"Did you notice how the boy moves his hands when he

speaks? I think he's using a subdialect of the Panoan language. What the Matis guides spoke."

"Great, but none of us can understand it," said Vedala. "Nobody outside the Amazon has ever even heard this language. They're uncontacted, remember?"

"No such thing. We're all connected in history at some point. Every human being. And his language is sure to have plenty in common with the other local dialects. Anyway, we'll find out soon."

Stone looked up to Vedala, smiling with pure, almost child-like delight. He tapped a button on his laptop. "I admit I'm a specialist, but my robots aren't. I brought along a universal speech recognizer and extensive gesture-recognition libraries. What's more, the diagnostic speaker on the drone is now connected to a text-to-speech synthesizer—"

"Wait," interrupted Peng, looking over from a disemboweled backpack splayed out in the dirt. "The drone has speech recognition? And a voice?"

Stone smiled at the group. "Our little bird is a translator now."

"Yes. This is a good idea, Dr. Stone," added Odhiambo, nodding and smiling. "The boy will talk to the bird. In almost every indigenous mythology, birds serve as messengers. This is a very good idea."

"I'll believe it when I see it," muttered Vedala.

"First," said Peng, her brow furrowing as she thought through this new potential advantage, "ask him how he survived, while the rest of his group was infected. He could be the key to saving all of us."

Thirty yards away, the boy was reaching for the hovering drone. It deftly moved out of the way when his hand approached, performing reflexive object avoidance. The graceful movements seemed to delight the child. Within thirty seconds he had made a small game out of trying to catch the "bird."

The group of scientists watched the child intently. His knowledge could be invaluable to them.

Stone unleashed a final flurry of typing, his dark blue eyes focused on the screen as his fingers moved rapid-fire across rows of waterproof keys. Nidhi Vedala watched him as he worked. She was beginning to wonder if Stone's technological adaptability hadn't made him a useful addition to this mission after all. The knowledge she traditionally respected was stored in other peoples' heads. But the roboticist seemed to have spread his skill sets outward, into the technology he carried with him.

"Okay, here we go," Stone said.

Moving gently, the canary lowered itself back within reach. It began blinking its diagnostic lights in a pattern. Fascinated, the child stopped swatting at it and watched with anticipation. Nearing eye level, the drone chirped once, testing the speaker. The boy flashed a startled frown at the device, sitting back against a log.

After a deep breath, Stone held the monitor in both hands and spoke quietly into its microphone.

"Hello. What is your name?"

On the laptop, a universal translator library converted the English into broken Panoan and fed the words to a text-to-speech synthesizer on the drone. Half a second later, the canary emitted a series of vocalizations reminiscent of the language of the Matis guides. Stone had chosen a voice synthesizer with the voice of a young man, hoping the boy would relate to it, but even so the syllables sounded computer generated and strange.

Nevertheless, startled recognition flashed over the boy's face.

Taken aback, he hopped away from the canary. He stared at

the hovering device with concern. Then he looked beyond it, directly at the scientists. With one hand he slowly reached up and touched his bare chest.

He tapped it twice.

"Tupa," he said.

First Contact

I MUST WARN YOU ALL BEFORE WE BEGIN," SAID ODHIAMBO in a grave voice. "This is first contact, and Tupa is only a boy. We have no other choice in the matter, and I understand that. But we are nobody's savior. We are in all likelihood his worst enemy, no matter our good intentions."

James Stone nodded solemnly, hunched over the monitor as he made final tweaks to the canary's speech recognition interface. As the boy conversed more in his distinctive language, the speech library had automatically strung a web of probability between unrecognized words and likely corollaries from the half dozen or so related dialects included in the universal translator library.

After only ten minutes of conversation, a bedrock of common words had begun to emerge, some of them nearly identical to existing dialects and others idiosyncratically distinct.

For his part, the boy was quickly picking up on the unique accent of the drone. He seemed adept at discerning its meanings, even when the language used was wrong or the pronunciation incorrect. This uncanny problem-solving ability led Odhiambo to hypothesize that despite their isolation, the Machado must have interacted at least occasionally with outsiders.

It didn't hurt that the boy Tupa was an exceptionally quick learner.

With her arms crossed, Vedala watched Stone and Odhiambo conversing over the monitor. She forced herself not to fidget. The backpacks were prepared, and the morning mist had evaporated. She had even set aside extra supplies for the young newcomer. Making first contact was clearly a delicate operation, and the boy surely had valuable information, but she could feel the urgency to set out rising along with the morning sun.

The field team desperately needed to reach the anomaly and reestablish contact with NORTHCOM. Throughout the entire march, not a single break had appeared in the canopy large enough to establish radio contact. The clearing beside the anomaly would be their last best hope.

Vedala assumed that missing the midday rendezvous with General Stern would be construed as a mission failure, with probable nonsurvival of the team. Though it was ludicrous, she couldn't shake a horrifying vision of a nuclear strike engulfing the quarantine zone, imagining the blood-boiling heat of a supersonic blast wave front ripping through the jungle.

As Vedala half listened to the conversation and puzzled over their next steps, Peng Wu finished breaking camp. She had packed her samples and portable laboratory, and was now laying out a midmorning meal in the form of military rations that were too heavy to bring along. Three backpacks were loaded and ready to go. The fourth was sitting beside James Stone and Harold Odhiambo, its batteries powering the laptop that was processing their exploratory conversation with Tupa.

As Peng worked, she watched the others and tried to determine who among them could be trusted.

"We need to move soon," Peng said to Vedala in a quiet voice. "And we need to figure out what to do with the child."

Vedala nodded.

Tupa sat on a winding tree root with his blowgun across his knees. He spoke softly to the hovering drone, scarcely paying attention to the collection of human beings only a few yards away—a group of people of many colors, but clearly none of them his kin.

The boy was reeling from the violence of the morning, yet he was able to accommodate the questions of this magical speaking bird, whom he immediately took to calling "Sashi."*

Whether the bird was magic or science, it made no difference.

"Boom!" called the boy, gesturing with both hands before continuing in the stuttering syllables of his own language.

The canary watched and listened via camera and microphone, occasionally speaking to the boy through its speaker, and Stone's portable computer translated out loud into English: "It began with a loud noise."

––––––––

* The canary drone fit into a mythology prevalent across many tribes of Brazil. Saci Pererê of Tupi-Guarani folktales is a mischievous child spirit in a red cap with a glowing pipe. He is famous for transforming into an elusive bird—the *matitaperê*, whose calls are notoriously hard to track down. Tupa seemed to associate the steady red glow of the drone's battery LED with that of a pipe, and its hovering flight matched well enough with the bird form.

The following paraphrased transcription was completed by the team at Translingua Expressar do Brasil. Advanced technical support (including audio and video data reconstruction) was provided by students of the US Military Academy at West Point under the direction of Dr. Pamela Sanders.

The account is based on translated gestures as well as language, employing civilian builds of the CIA-funded Universal Translation Library (UTL) and the Gesture Recognition Engine Analysis (GREAn) Machine. Words are chosen by probability, and perfection is not guaranteed. For access to a full word-for-word transcription, or raw audio and video files, please contact the United States National Historic Register.

How did you get here, Tupa?

Three [days | suns] ago, all was good. We were moving between [family | communal] maloca huts along the river. My [uncles | older men] were digging up [turtle] eggs on the riverbanks. One day's hike. I was helping.

Then a roar shook the jungle. Like thunder without the smell of rain.

What did you do?

We waited. Uncle said it was the shout of an angry god. The other men thought it was a great jaguar, hunting. I felt very [scared | worried]. The noise was from the direction of our family [camp | home].

The jungle became quiet.

The men were quiet, too. We heard, very [faint | distant] . . . screaming. Fierce screams. I began to pray. There were more shrieks, closer. I put my head between my knees. Everywhere was wild noise.

The light in the [high canopy] grew dark. Tree branches shook and jumped. Leaves were falling and we covered our heads. Then a [large group | horde] of monkeys passed by in the trees overhead. Hooting and screeching. They were running away from something.

I was [happy | relieved] it was only monkeys. The men were angry [we had] only one blowgun. There was [good meat] moving through the trees.

But something was wrong.

Monkeys [forage] slow. Take their time. These were crazy. Some fell, hitting the ground like [large seed pods]. The fallen ones who lived kept trying to run with [broken bodies]. It was a panic. And not just the monkeys.

All of the jungle was running away.

All of the jungle? Who is that?

Monkey. Sloth. Birds and [pigs | peccaries]. Even the snakes. They all ran away.

Where did you go then?

We moved along the river, toward the thunder. But the river had also run away. The banks were muddy. Pale [catfish] were flopping. We followed the [river's corpse] until we found an [evil | bad thing] in the jungle.

It was a black mountain, with a mouth that breathed smoke and fire.

[side conversation]

WU
_____

It sounds like (. . .) an explosion. Do we have intel on an explosion near the anomaly?

VEDALA
_____

Sure. Something had to eject an ash cloud over the site. That's what Eternal Vigilance detected. It matched Andromeda and triggered Project Wildfire.

WU
_____

Then there could still be particulate in the atmosphere. It could be as highly infectious as the Piedmont site—

ODHIAMBO

The boy is upset. Let us get this back on track.

[end side conversation]

What did the men decide to do next, Tupa?

Uncle told me to stay back, to hide among the trees. Near the black mountain, dark ash was falling like [slow raindrops] or [cotton wood fluff]. Smoke came from the empty mouth (. . .)

The [smoke | ash] got in their eyes. The men coughed. I heard them complain their lungs were burned. It was not a sacred smoke.

On the ground were pieces of black rock. Some were very jagged. The men picked them up. The rock was even sharper and lighter than the thing called steel.

The stone flakes were good. My uncle replaced two ax heads right away. He argued the flakes were a gift from the gods. Others said the place was cursed. They would not touch the stone of the black mountain. After a little while, they decided to follow the monkeys and recover their meat.

I was glad to leave behind the bad place.

Were all the men sick? Or only the ones who touched the stones?

I don't know. I was sent [home] with the turtle eggs. Uncle told me to warn our family. I ran home (. . .) but the maloca was empty. The others were gone. Maybe the roar frightened them. And they (. . .) they left behind (. . .)

Is there something else?

More stones. At our maloca. I did not touch them. Someone else [had also] visited the black mouth. I stayed there for two nights, waiting. Nobody came back.

[crying]

It's okay, Tupa. Take your time.

I decided to go and find the men.

But when I saw them (. . .) they were different. Their faces were [injured | wrong]. And they were angry, painting for [battle]. I was scared. I watched from the trees. They were shouting about [intruders] in the jungle. They had [found | tracked] enemies. I painted my face, too. But I was too scared to join them.

And then (. . .) and then they [attacked | fought].

Uncle died. All of them died. They were peaceful men. The black mountain made them crazy. It killed them.

I am sorry, Tupa. Do you know where the black mountain came from? How long it has been there?

No. I think that (. . .) it came from [hell | underworld]. It breathed fire and a black smoke that is poison. It hurt my family. And now it is eating the jungle.

These men and women want to stop the black mountain. To make sure it doesn't hurt anyone else. Do you remember where it is?

Yes.

Do you remember how to get back there?

(. . .) Yes.

[side conversation]

STONE
_____

If there were stone flakes at his camp, they're probably all infected. He could be the only survivor.

VEDALA
_____

Ethically, we can't further expose him to Andromeda. And he obviously doesn't have Wildfire clearance. We can't bring him.

STONE

[snorts] That anomaly is sitting in the equivalent of his living room. This isn't even a choice, it's our responsibility. He's only a boy. We have to protect him.

VEDALA

It *is* a choice. His. We'll let him decide whether to join us, or to stay out here on his own and look for his people.

(. . .)

STONE

Fine, Nidhi.

VEDALA

Don't forget, James—this jungle is his home. This is where he belongs. To assume we can save him from his own home is pure arrogance.

STONE

No. This *was* his home (. . .) until Andromeda took it from him. It's taken his family, too. Now, this little boy doesn't belong anywhere.

[end side conversation]

Tupa, you aren't safe here. These men and women are your friends. They need your help. But it is your choice, if you want to go with them or not. Do you want to stay here, away from the danger? Or will you lead them to the black mountain that spits smoke? Will you help them fight this evil?

(. . .)

[end transcript]

As he listened to the last of the canary drone's questions, Tupa sat and watched the jungle for a long moment. He ran his fingers across the blowgun, thinking. Overhead, insects flickered through rare shafts of sunlight that streamed through the chattering canopy high above.

Finally, Tupa looked past the hovering canary drone and at the Wildfire team. Focusing directly on James Stone, the boy touched his chest. Eyes never wavering, he spoke quickly to the canary.

A half second later, the laptop quietly articulated a translation.

"What is your name?"

A look of relief spread over Stone's face. Standing up on legs numb from sitting, he took an awkward step forward. He touched his own chest, voice breaking with emotion as he said his first words to the boy.

"James," he said. "I am James. Good to meet you, Tupa."

Watching the two of them approach each other, man and boy, Vedala frowned. She had registered a note of true feeling in Stone's voice. The roboticist seemed deeply sensitive to the fate of this young survivor. It was unexpected, coming from a childless bachelor. The raw emotion she saw on Stone's face in this moment would continue to haunt her for the remainder of the mission.

Plan B

FLIPPING AN INDUSTRIAL-GRADE LIGHT SWITCH, GENERAL Rand Stern watched as bank after bank of fluorescent lights kicked on, illuminating the massive sweep of the Ambrose High Bay laboratory, a stadium-size area buried under a half mile of solid granite known as Cheyenne Mountain.

The Cheyenne Mountain Complex had housed the command center for NORAD before operations moved to Peterson AFB. For the last decade it had been placed on warm standby, staffed only when necessary. The entire five-acre underground complex was now manned by a skeleton crew.

But this afternoon, Stern wasn't interested in its human occupants.

Stern proceeded alone, walking in the shadow of a towering equipment rack on his left. He fought the urge to shiver under the loud and constant breeze of the air conditioning. His boots clanged on a strip of metal grating laid into concrete. Beneath the latticework, he could see thick braids of cable snaking off toward self-contained laboratory pods lining the right side of the corridor. Each pod housed some form of robot.

The buzzing fluorescents had been illuminated specifically for Stern.

Few of these machines required light to run their repetitive trials. It gave the general a slightly nauseous feeling to think of them down here in the cavernous darkness, complex tools thrashing about endlessly without human supervision.

Stepping onto solid concrete painted with yellow safety lines, Stern stopped before a glass and metal cage. It had always reminded him of a zoo exhibit—the type designed to contain dangerous predators. Indeed, the modified BSL-4 enclosure was designed to contain incredibly dangerous organisms—although usually microscopic in size.

Beyond triple-paned glass, a twin iteration of the ISS-based Robonaut R3A4 was awkwardly conducting an experiment. It was oblivious to the general, moving in slow, jerky motions. Stern tapped the touch monitor hanging outside the cage, and it flickered on. The display indicated that the current telepresence occupant in control of the robot was a student. Data was being piped in from Australia on a feed owned by the Royal Melbourne Institute of Technology.

Swiping a key card, Stern tapped in a code and peered into a camera to offer biometric confirmation of his identity. The feed to Australia immediately cut off. Without any commands, the Robonaut returned to a default posture. Turning to face Stern, it squared its shoulders and stared blankly ahead.

After tapping a contact number into the monitor, Stern clasped his hands behind his back and rocked onto his heels.

Waiting, he watched as a satellite uplink was established with the International Space Station. Stern was growing anxious about the mission, particularly the fact that Kline hadn't been more helpful, and he was hoping to use this opportunity to see what she would say off the record.

The robot remained as still as a statue.

With telepresence-enabled applications, Stern had always found the moment of animation to be fascinating. Watching a remote human being take control of a robot was like seeing a soul inhabit a body. Yet after a few moments of waiting, he began to feel uneasy. The connection was already made, but nothing was happening. Something must have gone wrong.

And then Stern realized that the Robonaut was *watching* him.

Dr. Kline was so adept at inhabiting these machines, her control of them so smooth and natural, that she had given no outward indication that she was occupying the Robonaut's body. Only something in its expressionless camera eyes, some hint of awareness, had triggered a surge of animal adrenaline in Stern.

"Kline," he said roughly, ignoring the spooky gaze of the subterranean robot.

"General Stern," replied the low, husky voice of Sophie Kline.

Her words had been transmitted securely from the International Space Station and out of a speaker embedded in the exterior of the enclosure. Each syllable seemed to slither into the metallic depths of the empty high bay laboratory. Stern had to remind himself that he wasn't talking to an actual robot, just a robotically determined woman currently residing in a free-falling capsule some three hundred miles over his head.

On the ISS, Kline was wearing her head-mounted display and gloves, able to control this Robonaut as easily as any other.

"Why are you contacting me this way?" she asked.

"Security," responded Stern. "Unlike everything else up there, your telepresence data is encrypted and transmitted as machine instruction. The other voice and data lines are encrypted, but well, you know the Russians."

The robot nodded, an uncannily human movement that Stern found disconcerting.

"Go on," said Kline.

Clasping his hands tighter, Stern continued.

"The Wildfire team has missed its noon rendezvous. Since you spoke to them, we've had no contact."

"They're only overdue by a few hours."

"Nevertheless, we are putting alternate plans in motion."

"We?"

Stern ignored the question.

"Containment, Kline. A spire has grown half a mile out of the lake, straight up, and the main structure has more than doubled in size. We are moving to suppress the anomaly before it grows any larger. There are several routes along which we could choose to proceed. Some are more . . . egregious than others."

"You do recall the first Andromeda incident? If you go nuclear, the strain will only feed on the energy. You'll turn a bad situation into hell on earth."

"We're the military. We remember everything. For instance, we remember how the Russians defeated Napoleon and his Grande Armée after he invaded Moscow in 1812 with overwhelming force."

The robot was silent. It stared into Stern's eyes without expression. Stern blinked first, necessarily.

"They burned everything, Dr. Kline," he continued, voice dropping. "They destroyed their own homes to starve out the enemy. Without shelter, the French troops froze. Without anything to eat, they starved."

"And so did the Russian peasants," replied Kline. "General, can I assume you are proposing a scorched-earth policy? You mean to burn everything near the anomaly, salt the earth with some form of that Andromeda inhibitor solution, and then push the circle inward and repeat."

"You catch on quickly," replied Stern. "Believe it or not, the US Air Force still makes napalm. It works just as well as it ever did."

"There are people living there, tribes, each of them a civilization unto itself," replied Kline. "Not to mention that our own team is probably still alive. And you want to decimate the entire area?"

"I don't want to do this. I *have* to. Unless there is another way."

"Is this an international decision? Are all nations in agreement?"

"This is a unilateral decision that was made more than fifty years ago, when the fail-safe protocols were written in the aftermath of the first Andromeda incident. It transcends nationhood. It's a hard rule, made in hard times, to secure the future of humankind at any cost."

"Which part of humankind? This will mean the extinction of an unknown number of indigenous cultures with whom we've intentionally never made contact. What are their lives worth to you?"

"I wish I were here to argue ethics, Dr. Kline. But I'm not. I am here for your expertise. This is our last chance. Do you see another way to contain the Andromeda Strain?"

Drawing itself up to its full height, the R3A4 trained its two camera lenses on General Stern and regarded him silently. The military man found the gaze of the machine unnerving, but he did not turn away.

"The best way to contain it," said Kline, "is to *leave it alone*. Give the Wildfire team another twenty-four hours. Have faith that they're still alive."

General Stern let the air out of his lungs slowly.

"I will take that under advisement," he replied.

The Anomaly

THE WORLD HAD GONE DIM AND CLAUSTROPHOBIC under a seemingly endless ceiling of foliage. Loaded with the extra baggage formerly carried by Matis porters, the Wildfire field team struggled to follow the fleet-footed Tupa. The boy was tracing a path alongside the muddy tangles of a rapidly drying riverbed—or the "river's corpse," as the canary translated.

Tupa's route could not be found on any map, though he led them with the certainty of someone walking across his own town. For nearly eight hours, he had been marching confidently ahead through muted sunlight, accompanied by a whirring swarm of canary drones. The rest of the team stumbled along, machetes flashing as they tried to keep their footing on the spongy edges of the riverbed. Around them, the monolithic columns of tree trunks soared, blocking out the sky. Over the hours, red mud had coated their boots and khaki pants, spatters and smears that soon took on the gruesome appearance of dried blood.

The team did not speak much during the journey, moving too fast for conversation. Their moist, sucking footsteps and the brush of leaves over their legs were punctuated by the occasional splintering crash of a far-off tree falling or the gurgle of water flowing around some half-submerged obstacle.

Odhiambo observed the yellowish water with concern. In the recent past, the river had clearly been much higher. The exposed roots of trees lining the banks were still drying out. Odhiambo was at a loss to understand what had happened. The river seemed to have just disappeared.

It was yet another mystery, among many.

All seemed still and calm in the failing light of day when, unheralded, the jungle broke. There was nothing obvious or momentous to signify the end of their journey. In fact, it was just the opposite.

Peng Wu saw it first.

Maneuvering around the roots of a vine-encrusted wimba tree the size of a fifteen-story building, Peng stepped into what looked like a sudden nightfall. Her machete, which had been in constant motion, wavered in the air with nothing left to slice. Looking to her left and right, she saw a crush of plants, trees, and vines that curled away from a monstrous shadow.

The team had reached the anomaly.

Peng blinked at the emptiness before her, mouth open in wonder. For a moment, she felt as if she were back in orbit within the Tiangong-1, staring into the reeling infinity of space. She turned and saw Tupa watching her with a mixture of fear and curiosity. Snapping her mouth shut, Peng dropped the expression of wonder from her face.

Seconds later, the three other scientists stumbled to a stop at

Peng's side. All were silent as they gazed at the featureless skin of the anomaly.

The structure was darkly menacing. Its color was the black, green, and purple of solar panels, almost oily, reflecting the sporadic sunlight in greasy rainbows. At its base, the structure seemed to have cratered into the ground, leaving waves in the dirt like a rumpled skirt, and a not unpleasant raw-earth smell.

And rising beyond it, barely visible through the upper foliage, was the stark silhouette of a narrow six-sided column. It had risen higher than anyone could believe was possible, like a seam in the sky. Its purpose was utterly inscrutable, and Odhiambo later mused that it reminded him of the spiky crystalline growths found in deep cave systems.

"My god," someone murmured, but otherwise the scientists were silent as they finally observed the reason for this mission in person.

James Stone rested his hands on his knees, steadying himself. He could feel his pulse throbbing in his temples, his vision quivering with each beat of his heart. The sight ahead had sparked an instinctive fear that coursed through his body with the fire of pure adrenaline—a fear of something impossible, yet haunting and too familiar. Stone couldn't help thinking of his recurring dream.

In the diseased vicinity of the structure, he thought he could glimpse the ruby sparkle of congealed blood. The dirt at his feet resembled granules of dried plasma. Stone could feel a fetidly hot breeze coming off the anomaly, sending grains of dust airborne—like a stream of blood evaporating on desert sand.

Stone sensed Vedala standing at his elbow. She was holding out the satellite phone in one hand. He scrambled to check his environmental monitoring.

"I'm not detecting any toxins. The ash must have settled. What now?" Stone asked, swallowing with difficulty.

"Our clearing is gone," Vedala said matter-of-factly. "The anomaly must have grown since we set out. We've got no line of sight to the communications satellites."

She craned her neck, spying only a narrow slit of blue sky between the towering face of the anomaly and a wild confusion of jungle that crept to the very edge of it. She stood with the satellite radio in both hands, holding it like a baby. The phone had been fitted with a black antenna shaped like a tongue depressor. The connection bars sat flat and dark.

Tupa watched from beyond the tree line, highly entertained by Vedala's gesticulations. The rest of the field team was not so amused, as her worried expression clearly telegraphed the danger they were in.

"Is this really our only approach? It isn't going to work," said Stone.

Vedala replied, not looking away, "It's an Iridium phone. Coverage is provided by over sixty satellites on polar orbits a couple hundred miles up. It's always shifting, so there's still a chance we'll hit a connection."

"And if we don't?" asked Stone.

Stopping, Vedala turned to the group.

"If we don't rendezvous, they'll assume we're dead. And if they believe we're dead . . . they'll move on to contingency plans."

"And that's bad?"

"It is not good," said Peng Wu. "The military instinct will be to wipe out the entire area. Purge it completely, and us with it."

The team was now past rendezvous by over five hours.

Peng Wu threw her pack on the ground beside the anomaly. She hastily extracted hard-copy topographic maps of the surrounding area. Head down, eyes trained on the data, she said,

"Nidhi is right. Everything has changed. Mainly, this thing is a lot bigger than it was when we first set out."

"Haiya," exclaimed Odhiambo in his native tongue. "How can that be? I see no evidence of construction. It's not as if this thing is *alive*."

"Okay, we can start with a canary survey—" began Stone, before Odhiambo shushed him with a wave of his hand.

"No, wait," said Odhiambo. "Listen to that."

The twisted, curled branches and dried leaves around them had begun to rattle. A mass of warm air was cascading up the face of the anomaly and brushing against the tree line.

"Strange. There is rarely wind beneath the canopy," said Odhiambo.

"The anomaly is tall. It must be channeling a breeze," offered Vedala.

"Not likely," said Odhiambo. "This air is moving upward."

Tupa whimpered and backed away, his dark hair fluttering in the rising rush of wind. A deep, subterranean groan was emanating from the dirt beneath their feet. The scientists put their arms out for balance in the quaking jungle, shooting terrified glances at each other.

Stone glanced at the feed from a canary drone on the monitor hanging around his neck, switching from visible light to infrared. The face of the anomaly erupted into blazing white light.

"Move away!" shouted Stone, stepping back. "It's heating up fast!"

"What is this?" cried Peng. She stood near the wall, machete clenched in her fist. Her long black hair flew in the whirlwind of air rushing upward. "What's happening to it?"

The unearthly groan rose in pitch as tons of dirt and rock and roots were violently shifted somewhere underground. Meanwhile, the surface of the anomaly was pulsing—as if it were vibrating at a rate too fast to see.

"I think we are about to find out," said Harold, pulling on Peng's shoulder. She did not move, continuing to stare up at the anomaly with calculating eyes. Her machete trembled in her outstretched hand. Shrugging away from Odhiambo's grasp, Peng stepped forward and pressed the tip of the machete blade against the trembling surface.

"Peng!" called Odhiambo, backpedaling away from the heat. "Stop this!"

For a moment nothing happened.

Then the steel machete blade began to change color in a slow wave, from the tip moving back, darkening to a dull red and then brightening toward orange. The tip finally erupted into an incandescent yellow-white color. With a cry of pain, Peng dropped the blade to the jungle floor. It lay there steaming, bits of carbon in the superheated steel twinkling like stars against an apocalyptic sky.

"Oxidation," she said, backing away with a forearm across her face. "Over a thousand degrees Celsius, based on the color of that steel."

The ragged border of jungle canopy had begun to writhe, leaves chattering and branches creaking. Seed pods plummeted down from hundreds of feet above, thudding into the ground, followed by a dry snowfall of crisp leaves and lichen and bark.

Shielding themselves from falling debris, the group stared in awe at the face of the anomaly from the safety of the forest. What they saw next was impossible to reconstruct in video, despite extensive attempts to utilize super-resolution techniques on recovered footage.

The skin of the anomaly erupted in rotating hexagonal lines,

a hypnotic chaos of overlapping patterns. Nidhi Vedala postu-
lated directly afterward that the artifacts could have been a
macro-level effect sprouting from the cellular structure of
trillions of smaller Andromeda microparticles. These etched
shapes revolved in a repeating pattern that optically froze in the
way fan blades seem to stop spinning against a white ceiling.

It was by all accounts a mesmerizing sight.

Satellite footage showed that the surface of the anomaly
throbbed once and then lurched, a trembling shudder that seemed
to ripple through the structure. The seismic activity and pattern
of rotating lines were disorienting, so much so that Peng Wu fell
to the ground unconscious.

A final, intense blast of heat swept off the wall and flowed
through the wet rain forest. Among the trees, the team cowered
together.

"I know what this is," said Vedala, shouting just to hear herself. "I know exactly what this is!"

Finally, the entire anomaly flashed purple before *expanding*—
erupting outward and upward, and growing by nearly a foot in
all its dimensions. The illusory hexagonal shapes grew more
defined before fading, rotating back into nothingness like the
aperture of a camera lens collapsing to a pinprick.

The jungle was still.

"Impossible, impossible," muttered Odhiambo, hoarse with
fright.

"It grew," called Stone. "It's even bigger now."

Stone helped Peng up from where she was sitting tangled
among roots. During the event, none of the other scientists had
realized she had fainted. Though muddied and nursing a lump
on the back of her head, Peng did nothing to indicate she had
been in distress.

Vedala looked around at the field team as if noticing them

for the first time. Her face was flushed. All of them had suffered minor sunburns. The group had witnessed something unexplainable, but as a materials specialist Vedala understood at least one thing—the anomaly represented an unimaginable leap forward in technology.

Vedala spoke in a steady, quiet voice to the group.

"What we have just witnessed is beyond any known human scientific capability. Once I get a sample of it under a microscope, I'll confirm, but my bet is that we will find that this entire anomaly is made of an Andromeda-based nanomaterial. The structure just underwent a form of . . . mitosis is the best description. Like cell division. Each microparticle split and produced a copy of itself."

"That sounds familiar," said Stone. "My father documented this behavior during the first Andromeda incident. Except that he and Dr. Leavitt only observed it happening on a microscopic scale. It flashed purple, and then it underwent something akin to cellular division."

"How?" asked Peng. "What could it use as fuel out here?"

"Nitrogen. Carbon dioxide. Phosphorus. A rich variety of elements, all readily available in massive quantities," replied Odhiambo. "A pure conversion system."

"You mean the dirt itself . . . the air," said Stone.

"Yes," replied Vedala. "Our friend Tupa had it right from the start. The anomaly is eating the jungle itself."

Fail-Safe

T WAS NOW CLOSE TO THE END OF AN EXCEEDINGLY long day. Nidhi Vedala called for camp to be set up deep among the trees, but still in view of the anomaly. Among the remaining team members, only Peng Wu had any real training in jungle survival. She had completed her final basic training in the Xishuangbanna tropical rain forest in the Yunnan Province of southern China. Despite her academic qualifications, Peng's skill set made her the best choice for establishing a safe campsite.

This suited Vedala fine, as she felt that at the moment the former soldier needed something to focus on. Peng had seemed especially shaken by the disturbing growth event.

Reclaiming her singed machete, Peng set about clearing a spot beyond the shriveled trees—a dozen yards or so from where the muddy river streamed out from under the anomaly. Beside the water, the team had discovered the hexagonal tunnel mouth described by Tupa. It was no longer breathing black smoke, but the dark passage remained foreboding nonetheless.

The dull thumps of Peng's machete echoed flatly. The early evening light felt murky and thick as it wafted down through burned leaves.

The bizarre anomaly loomed in the dusk—both the bulk of the main structure and the dark column rising beyond—their metallic-looking surfaces absorbing the last of the daylight, glittering like the pebbled skin of a leviathan surfacing from impossible depths.

Since the team had been dispatched three days ago, Vedala estimated the anomaly had grown nearly twice as large. The group instinctively felt safer among the trees, well beyond the barren strip of churned red earth that separated the structure's face from the jungle.

Alien and implacable, the anomaly seemed to exert an ill will.

As Peng worked alone, the others set about their familiar routines of science. Abandoned by their guides and unable to contact NORTHCOM, the field team was now demonstrating why it had been selected. A sense of curiosity and wonder had settled over them, despite the recent traumatic events.

The greatest mystery on earth was within arm's reach.

Vedala obsessively ran and reran the routines to establish a satellite uplink with command and control, walking the perimeter and looking for a tree break. She was a small, determined figure beside such an imposing mass, but the expanding structure had created a maze of wreckage that was nearly impenetrable. No matter where she wandered, the connection bars on her satellite phone stubbornly refused to budge.

Meanwhile, James Stone and Tupa had become inseparable. At the tree line, Stone was shaking a canister of inhibitor spray. He aimed it at his own forearm as Tupa watched with curiosity.

He pulled the tab, and a fine mist of protective sealant hissed from the canister mouth. Tupa dived back, feet scrabbling in the dirt, his fingers forming an unmistakable fanged sign.

"Jahmays!" he said, in dismay.

Laughing, Stone shook his head.

"No, not a snake," he said. "Armor. Strong."

A nearby canary whispered its translation. Tupa hesitantly put out his arms and allowed Stone to apply a coating. Squeezing his eyes closed and holding his breath at Stone's direction, he looked like any child being daubed with sunscreen at the beach. When it was over, his eyes popped open and his front teeth flashed in a grin as he repeated the words back to James.

"Armor," he said. "Strong."

For his part, Harold Odhiambo was sitting on a shattered tree trunk, taking meticulous count of a number of complicated seismic sensors. It was tedious work, but he seemed to enjoy the slow, practiced motions, checking each sensor before slipping it into a mesh pocket on the exterior of his rucksack.

Though the others naturally shied away from the incomprehensible structure, Harold Odhiambo found its bulk oddly comforting.

The esteemed scientist had spent the last decade studying extraterrestrial geology—the inner workings of other worlds—and in this anomaly he did not see a deformity of something natural, but the beauty of truly nonhuman architecture.

As a boy growing up in Kenya, Odhiambo had always been enamored of the gigantic termite mounds that dotted the landscape of the wild plains. Fully insulated against the elements, predators, and the occasional wildfires that raced over the dry grass, each self-contained mound was built from naturally occurring materials and housed over a billion small creatures capable of operating complex societies that could and did last for millennia.

In a recurring game of make-believe, the young Odhiambo had imagined himself exploring the tiny hallways of such a megatropolis—the winding passages reflecting the utter non-humanness of the design. As he grew into an adult and traveled the world to complete his studies, Odhiambo had watched human beings everywhere he visited continue to encroach on nature, destroying and remaking everything they touched, a wave of annihilation that impacted every possible habitat.

The more Odhiambo had seen of humankind's scientific triumphs, the more he appreciated those termites and the enduring megacities they built. Constructed from the mud of the plains, the alien-seeming mounds thrived in balance with the ecosystem. It was a feat he had not yet seen a human civilization accomplish, except for perhaps the humans who lived in and cultivated this rain forest.

His rucksack fully loaded with sensors, Odhiambo seemed satisfied. He hopped down from the log and set out on a path along the anomaly. Surveying the ground, he stopped and crouched on surprisingly limber knees for a man of his age. He withdrew a fist-size seismic sensor from the mesh pocket and firmly pressed the barbed tip of the device into the ragged dirt. With a well-practiced motion, he twisted the top half sharply. A blue LED began to glow, and a charging sound ramped up.

As Odhiambo stood, hunched under the weight of his rucksack, the corkscrew seismic device released a burst of pent-up energy, twisting its proboscis into the ground. By the time it had disappeared under the raw dirt, Odhiambo was already moving on.

In this manner, he implanted sixteen sensors along the

perimeter, focusing an extra few sensors on the "mouth" that led into darkness, near the yellowish river.

Eyes on her satellite phone, Vedala continued to pace the anomaly. She walked right past James Stone, who was busy cleaning mud from the recharging docks on his specialized backpack. As Stone worked, he demonstrated the inner workings of the instrument to Tupa, who had proven to be an astute student. Surrounded by several loitering canaries, the closest of which would occasionally offer a translation, the two of them looked perfectly content.

As Vedala passed by yet again, Stone stopped and cocked his head to listen.

"That's the sound of interference," he said.

"What?" asked Vedala.

"Those satphones are digital. They don't hiss like a radio. What you're hearing is electromagnetic interference, like from a microwave oven."

"I'd agree with you, except what electrical source could be putting off that much interference?"

Vedala knew the answer before she finished the question, of course. She craned her neck, looking up at the greenish-black structure. Walking slowly toward it, she held the satellite phone out like a dowsing rod. She listened as the hissing grew louder. The short antenna nearly grazed the surface, and the static hissed ferociously.

"We weren't advised of this," said Vedala, her shoulders slumping.

Stone stood up, putting his hands to the small of his back and stretching as he observed the anomaly. He squinted as the last rays of sunlight flitted across it in a wavering streak. "Well, it's gotten bigger since we left. The interference may have only started recently."

"But why would it be transmitting electricity?" asked Vedala.

A large rucksack hit the dirt nearby.

"Of course it does," said a voice.

Stone and Vedala turned to see a sweat-soaked Odhiambo. The older man stood with his eyes closed for a moment. Deeper in the jungle, birds screeched from the lower canopy as Odhiambo took great long breaths in through his nose.

"Electrical power," he said. "Yes."

"What have you got, Harold?" asked Stone.

Odhiambo opened his eyes, grinning.

"I do not know how this thing came to be here. I do not know why. But I believe I can tell you what it is."

Peng Wu joined them, listening with curiosity.

"My seismic sensors have been pulling data from the area," said Odhiambo. "Mostly concentrated near the mouth of the river. They picked up a mechanical vibration under the flow of water. Combined with your observation, I believe I now have a complete hypothesis."

Odhiambo turned to gaze up at the great anomaly, continuing to speak as he regarded it with wonder.

"This structure is not built of any material known to man. Its construction techniques are a mystery. But its purpose is as clear as day," he said. "Our anomaly is a simple dam. And a dam exists for one reason. To generate hydroelectric power."

"Power for what?" asked Vedala.

"We will only find that out, my friends," said Odhiambo, pointing to the mouth of the tunnel, "when we go inside."

As the significance of that statement began to sink in, the satellite phone squawked. Holding her arm perfectly still, Vedala turned to the device with a surprised smile of relief. It was an expression that turned quickly to confusion and disappointment.

"Something is wrong," she said. "It's not connected to the

Iridium satellite constellation. It's connected to something else . . ."

Vedala was interrupted by a burst of static.

"Wildfire field team," hissed the satphone. "This is Kline. Do you read me?"

Peering upward into the only slice of blue sky visible from the jungle floor, Vedala's eyes widened in wonder. Several hundred miles above, the International Space Station was circling the globe. Vedala began to mentally calculate how long this transmission would last. It was probably a maximum of five minutes before the ISS would zip over the horizon and out of range.

"This is Wildfire. We read you. Repeat, we are alive."

"Roger that," replied Sophie Kline. "What's the situation down there?"

"Not good, but the mission is still viable. We've had no contact with Northcom and missed our rendezvous. Can you patch us through?"

"We only have a few minutes. I'll relay your message as soon as I'm over the horizon. Do you have any new data to share?"

"Stand by for a data transfer."

Stone was already hustling over to Vedala with his portable computer. Plugging the data port into the satphone, he initiated the data transfer.

On board the ISS, the monitors around Kline illuminated with data—the swollen trunk of a rubber tree, its latex sap bleeding into unnatural six-sided shapes. On another screen gruesome images of Machado casualties appeared, faces spattered with blood from gunshot wounds, skin flecked with metallic-looking chunks.

"I see you made contact. It looks like Brink took care of it," said Kline.

"Yes, he did," said Vedala.

"These men were infected. Do you know how?" asked Kline.

"We think they made contact with the anomaly."

Tapping Vedala on the shoulder, Stone whispered, "The rest of the data will have to wait until her next pass."

Kline saw an image of an indigenous boy—he was clearly alive, his face alert and cautious under a thin sheen of glistening red urucum. She expelled a sharp breath. The machinery of her mind had been processing, searching for clues that tied together the input she was seeing. Now she had seen a connection.

Gray ash. The boy had none of it on him.

"This boy lived, but the others didn't," she radioed. "Did he tell you anything? Did he say anything about an explosion?"

"He described a roaring in the jungle," said Vedala. "Two minutes."

"Of course," mused Kline, partially off-mike.

"Say again?"

"The AS-3 substance is harmless unless it's absorbed into the bloodstream. The men have ash around their nostrils. The boy doesn't."

Peng Wu was already calculating the meaning. "He wasn't allowed to get close to the anomaly. And he described the others as coughing. If an explosion aerosolized the Andromeda substance, it would have lingered as dust or smoke. The portal of entry would have been the respiratory tract, and the hosts were infected when the microparticle transmitted across the blood-air barrier in the upper lung."

"So if it's been blasted into smoke, you can breathe it. Otherwise, it only transmits through blood exposure, same as the first Andromeda Strain," warned Stone, remembering the ax wound in Brink's shoulder.

"What about the hexagonal scale patterns?" asked Vedala.

"Self-replication," answered Kline.

Vedala stared at the satphone with a look of confusion. She had one minute left of communication with the ISS.

"How do you know that?" asked Vedala. "Have you seen this before? Is there new data?"

"Retreat to the quarantine perimeter immediately," replied Kline in a clipped tone.

"Negative," replied Vedala, stubbornly. "On what basis?"

"I'm warning you," Kline continued, stumbling over the words in her haste. "Your safety gear is inadequate. Retreat to the perimeter."

"What are Northcom's missed rendezvous protocols?" asked Vedala. "Are we in some kind of danger?"

"I don't know. You've—"

"Why won't you put us through to Northcom?" demanded Vedala.

"I don't have the right equipment—"

"Bullshit. What's happening here? Why do you want us to leave this place?"

A solid five seconds of silence elapsed.

"Put Sergeant Brink on," said Kline with a tone of finality.

Vedala hesitated. She had grown darkly suspicious of Sophie Kline's behavior. Putting a finger to her lips, she quieted the group. Shaking her head, she mouthed: *Something is wrong.*

Speaking into the satphone with forced conviction, Vedala lied, "Brink is out hunting with the Matis. He should be back soon. We have fifteen seconds."

Static hissed over the line as the final seconds of the transmission ticked away, and then Kline spoke quickly: "Tell him . . . tell Brink to be extra careful with the Omega watch I lent him. Tell him it's very important. It's an *Omega.*"

Vedala glanced at her fellow scientists for clarification of Kline's bizarre statement. Her concerned gaze settled quickly on Peng Wu. The former soldier was biting her lower lip, cheeks flushed and trembling.

"Sophie? We fail to see how—" began Vedala.

Before she could say another word, Peng leaned forward and clicked off the satellite radio. The others stared at her in surprise.

Peng took a deep, shaky breath.

"Peng? What's wrong?" asked Vedala.

Without speaking, Peng reached into the kit bag hanging high on her slim hip. With shaking fingers, she produced a small black case. Carefully opening it, she slid out a vial full of viscous, amber-colored liquid. As she turned it slowly in the fading daylight, everyone was able to read the text imprinted on its side: **OMEGA**.

"I took this from Brink's personal effects," said Peng. "I'm sorry. I wasn't sure who I could trust."

Nidhi Vedala gently took the vial and case. She held the vial up to examine it, shaking her head at its contents. Carefully, she repacked the vial and slid the case into her pocket.

Having had no military experience, Stone was baffled. Tupa sat protectively at his side, eyeing the bulge in Vedala's pocket with suspicion.

"Are you saying . . . is that poison?" offered Stone.

Odhiambo cut him off.

"It is most likely a nerve agent," he said. "The kind that can only be produced by a state-sponsored program run by very smart and well-equipped chemists. Placed on any surface or in food or drink, this substance would kill us all quickly and without a struggle."

A wave of anger washed over Vedala. She threw the satphone to the dirt. Peng Wu placed a comforting hand on her shoulder.

"I don't know why," said Peng. "But I think it's clear . . . Sophie Kline just tried to have us all murdered."

DAY 4

BREACH

> Presidents and generals
> and all the important people
> in position to make the
> most important decisions
> are, by and large, the least
> equipped for making them.
>
> —Michael Crichton

Operation Scorched Earth

IN MORE WAYS THAN ONE, IT WAS THE DAWN OF A NEW day on board the International Space Station. As was her morning routine, Dr. Sophie Kline was floating in the ISS cupola module and looking down upon the world. *Her* world. Locked in a prograde orbit aligned with the rotation of Earth, the ISS was falling over the dark face of the equator. Stretching to the horizon, only a few lights twinkled here and there across the great black expanse of the planet.

The night before, Kline had finally spoken the dreaded code word.

It had been a last-ditch effort, a Hail Mary, and she knew it. Managing to place Brink on the ground mission had been thanks to both preparation and luck. Kline had ensured that a well-paid asset was stationed nearby to be selected if a call was put out, and it had been. Now there was nothing more to be done about the field team situation—the outcome of the gambit would be revealed with a message from Brink, or it wouldn't.

Kline found she didn't particularly care.

She turned her attention to the ground-monitoring equipment clustered in the cupola. Outside the windows, the last teal curves of the Pacific Ocean were disappearing in the west. Data from the ISS WideScat all-weather radar system painted a nearby monitor in shades of red and blue. It showed a map with a few blinking signatures: slow-moving commercial aircraft at an altitude of about forty thousand feet.

More importantly, there were four new signatures—moving fast.

Kline smiled.

Four state-of-the-art fighter jets were cruising low over the jungle, on a beeline for the anomaly—which was just over the horizon from Kline's location.

Stern's airstrike was under way, and Kline was glad.

The field team had made it too far, pushed too deeply into mysteries best left alone. Kline had warned them. Yet they had pressed on. It was largely due to the pigheaded stubbornness of Dr. Nidhi Vedala. And despite Brink's repeated assurances, a hired mercenary couldn't be fully trusted.

From the beginning, Sophie Kline had been amenable to a backup plan of aerial bombardment. Presumably the Wildfire field team would soon be incinerated in a hail of napalm and likely doused with some form of the inhibitor substance.

Kline activated another instrument. On the monitor, a shaky thermal satellite visual showed four contrails of exhaust raking across the night. At this rate, she estimated, the jets would unleash their deadly payloads at dawn—just after Kline's morning shift began.

It was truly ironic, thought Kline, as she looked down upon the slowly spinning world, that in a few hours Dr. Vedala would likely be crushed by multiple high-tonnage payloads of the same inhibitor substance she had invented to save life.

Dawn Strike

N THE HOT, HUMID AIR A THOUSAND FEET ABOVE THE Ucayali region of the western Amazon jungle, the gleaming skins of four F/A-18E Super Hornet fighter aircraft blazed pink with the first rays of dawn. Headed east, the jets roared at roughly the speed of sound directly toward a breathtaking orange-red eye rising over a vista of roiling green jungle. A thin expanse of mist rose over it all. The early-morning dew was evaporating, beading the silver jets with streaks of moisture.

The labyrinthine interior of the jungle below had remained impenetrable to wave upon wave of human civilization. It was a place where countless explorers had spent centuries searching in vain for mysterious artifacts.

Now, one had finally appeared.

No mist rose near the anomaly, only a foreboding pall of smoke trickling up from smoldering tree branches. After a series of mitotic growth events, the structure had stabilized on satellite footage as a long, slightly curved wall soaring nearly three hundred feet high at its center. On its northern side, a stagnant brown lake had formed where the river was blocked. A narrow shaft rose straight out of the water, a surreal sight at more than three-quarters of a mile tall. To the south, a stream ran out from under the obstacle, tracing a glittering trail along the wide banks of its former route.

Over six thousand miles away, General Stern stood in the wings of the launch control center in Peterson Air Force Base. The room had been built to accommodate the occasional public performance, with a viewing area for dignitaries or politicians to be photographed triumphantly overseeing a successful launch. At the rear, a pair of discreet doors allowed such celebrities to disappear without photo opportunities if things were to go explosively wrong, as they so often did.

It was after 3:00 a.m., yet the control center was crowded with experts of all kinds. Each of them had been called in to ensure the maximum probability of success for what was admittedly a desperate plan.

To that end, Stern had seized dedicated clearance from the CIA for the spectacularly expensive NIX-3 series reconnaissance satellite cluster. So far, the sensors had detected alarming levels of growth from the anomaly, and no trace of the Wildfire field team. The scientists had been lost somewhere between their last contact with the ISS and the anomaly perimeter.

Lost . . . and now, eighteen hours after a missed rendezvous, categorically presumed dead.

With a live view of the dark anomaly, the plan was to drop stripes of napalm along its outer edges. The infected area would be cauterized, isolated from the living jungle. Napalm would be followed by a payload of classified inhibitor substance—with the hope that it would shrink the structure, or at least ensure it didn't start growing again.

The plan was desperate for a variety of reasons.

First, it broke quarantine and potentially exposed the aircraft and pilots to a highly infectious strain of Andromeda. Second, executing an airstrike on foreign soil was the definition of an act of war—one that would likely precipitate a Brazilian counterstrike and total international discord.

The original Andromeda incident had itself nearly sparked a domestic nuclear disaster with worldwide repercussions. Yet General Stern could see that his current situation was clearly much, much worse. The analysts could sense his anxiety. Aside from crunching on an occasional tablet of Tums, Stern had only been listening, not speaking.

The room hummed with the subdued energy of hushed conversations. This whispered din would fade to full silence only when the room-wide speaker loop delivered occasional reports from the Super Hornet squadron commander, call sign "Felix," as it did now.

"Felix-1, painting target. Trail formation on me. We're gonna pop the approach, so be ready."

From the front of the room, an intern named Maxim Lonchev watched General Stern toss another brightly colored bit of calcium carbonate into his mouth. Sitting at a table that had been dragged in from the cafeteria, Lonchev was leaning over his tablet computer. Four minutes earlier, a subprogram had flagged an exception in the NIX-3 satellite data. The image in question was now laid out flat on the table at its maximum resolution.

"Master arm switch is on," reported the pilot.

The intern was frantically poring over the image, trying

to ignore a technical conversation between two other people sharing his table.

Lonchev had designed "Pillion," an artificial intelligence algorithm that analyzed visual data collected by the NIX-3 cluster. The rudimentary AI was unique in that it was a general-intelligence application with no particular modus operandi. Most algorithms were tailored to find very specific patterns, such as vehicle deployments or radar installations. Maxim Lonchev—acting against the advice of his academic advisor at the Stanford AI Lab—had designed an algorithm that simply looked for potential outliers—in other words, anything interesting.

As such, Pillion was an experimental effort, designed by a university student, and never expected to do much. The necessity of Lonchev's presence in launch control was, in fact, arguable—and he knew it.

Defining exactly what Pillion found "interesting" had become a principal research challenge. It was also the problem Lonchev now found lying on the table before him. He stared intently at the stitched-together black-and-white image.

"Tally the target," said the pilot. "We're headed downtown."

Pillion had registered an unlikely formation of tree branches. In a small strip of clearing along the anomaly, the configuration had simply been labeled "low probability." The problem was that this blurry image was a composite, generated by averaging multiple frames of video taken at different times of day from different positions. Lonchev was straining his eyes, trying to figure out why Pillion was showing him this stupid image of scattered branches.

"You want a coffee?" asked the analyst sitting next to him.

"No," snapped Lonchev. "Thank you. Sorry."

He winced as his voice echoed loudly. The cavernous room had grown quiet as the pilot spoke again over the radio.

"Let's get down on the deck. Holding cherubs two for final," he said in clipped pilot-speak.

In every image, the branches were hidden by the tree canopy or shadows from it, as well as the heat and electromagnetic interference washing off the surface of the anomaly. Reconstructed, the picture was blurry and choppy. Impossible to interpret.

"Alive?" asked the talkative analyst.

Lonchev looked up, hair mussed from running his fingers through it. "Yes, I'm alive. I'm also busy."

"No, *alive*," said the analyst, rotating the tablet until it was upside down. "Those tree branches are laid out in a message. See it there? 'Alive.'"

"Felix-1 is in hot."

Lonchev's mouth popped open into a surprised "Oh."

He scrambled to his feet, his knees loudly jarring the table, causing heads to turn. He stopped, breathing hard, his face flushed red with embarrassment. Legs shaking, he stared out at a room full of high-ranking officials who could make or break his career with a few words. Lonchev hesitated another second.

And then the graduate student began to shout.

Entry

COCOONED IN A HAMMOCK ILLUMINATED BY A HINT of gray morning light, Nidhi Vedala listened as the scream of jet engines died away. The flaring burst of napalm she expected had not cascaded through the canopy in fingers of bright flame. Nor had the scorching heat of a nuclear blast wave washed across the face of the alien structure. A relieved smile eased itself onto her face. Odhiambo's crude message of fallen tree branches must have been received.

It appeared the field team was going to survive another day.

The night had been utterly uneventful. Nothing living seemed to be left in this area of the jungle—a stark and disturbing contrast to the chaos of noise and life the team had experienced on the march to get here. Even the trees and plants seemed to shy away from the foreign material. Their high, skeletal branches reached like shriveled claws under the thin haze of smoke that rose from charred leaves. The near-total quiet combined with the unnatural heat and dryness made it feel as if the environment itself was being transformed around them, from verdant rain forest to . . . something else.

Stone's physiological monitoring logs showed that he had been thrashing with nightmares for most of the night—even worse than usual. The entire team had spent the hours of darkness drifting in and out of fitful bouts of unrest. Only the young Tupa seemed to sleep peacefully, comfortable in an extra hammock, his doubts and fears drowned in an inescapable flood of pure exhaustion.

Rolling out of her hammock, Vedala roused the rest of the field team and ordered them to assemble at the mouth of the anomaly immediately after breakfast. As Peng set about restarting the campfire, Vedala laced her boots tightly and reapplied inhibitor over her sleeved arms. Munching on a granola bar, she made her way alone through silent trees to the slick riverbank.

The structure had not undergone any more growth spurts in the preceding hours. Even so, Vedala felt she could sense a thrumming force inside the featureless structure. There seemed to be a kind of potential energy growing within, as if it was gathering itself up for another expansion.

Sitting on the dry tip of a hundred-foot log embedded in the sucking mud of the riverbed, Vedala let her feet dangle and studied the hexagonal mouth of the tunnel. The breach was human-size, positioned to the left of a cascade of yellow-brown water that flowed out from under the anomaly. Following the contours of the muddy riverbank, the scummy stream was heaped with mounds of froth.

Hazy morning sunlight fell in shafts over the hushed riverbank.

Vedala noted flakes of broken anomaly material scattered about the tunnel entrance. Most of the jagged stones lay among cratered streaks of mud. In some places, she could see empty holes—likely from pieces that had been harvested by the Machado. But the overall pattern of the streaks radiated away from the entrance. It gave the scene the kinetic texture of a debris field, as if the shards had erupted from the mouth of the tunnel.

Vedala's mind returned to Tupa's description of the angry god's roar, and Kline's admonition to run away.

A wave of air washed over the back of her neck, and Vedala heard the whir of a canary. She also smelled coffee. James Stone emerged from the trees, carrying a tin cup in each hand. He was already hypothesizing out loud.

"The breach there is caked in the same ash substance we found before," he said, pointing with a glinting cup. "Some pieces are missing from around the tunnel mouth. I've got the canaries on constant alert for airborne toxins, of course. But there don't seem to be any. Anyhow, we'd already know by now if there were."

Stone sat down on the log beside Vedala, handing her a cup.

"We'd be dead," he added.

"I've been mulling that," said Vedala. "The ash and flaked rocks are solid substrates. But a lot more material must have been vaporized by an explosion. The Machado breathed in the cloud of dust, only trace amounts, and it activated inside their bodies, slowly at first . . . but it drove them crazy. Very similar to Piedmont."

Vedala sipped her coffee.

"But why would it explode?" she asked. "Odhiambo says this area is volcanically dormant for five hundred miles in every direction. It's not likely to have been a natural process."

"I don't think it was," said Stone. "I'm not ready to reveal my pet theory without more evidence, but I think what happened was a mistake. A human mistake."

Vedala shot Stone a look of concern. She lowered her voice and faced forward as she spoke her next words.

"I look forward to hearing your theory. As you've seen, elements of this expedition have been compromised. Some people have been keeping secrets. And I need to be able to trust you, James."

"Look, I know it wasn't your idea to bring me, Nidhi, but I'm not some kind of a spy—"

"That's exactly what I mean. You're trustworthy because you were never supposed to be here. You're a wild card, Stone, and possibly a very lucky accident."

BY 11:03:24 UTC, the Wildfire field team was assembled at the mouth of the anomaly. They were watched from a distance by a wary Tupa. Respirators hung around their necks, and they wore headlamps on their foreheads. The team had reapplied the last of the inhibitor across their clothing and skin.

They were as prepared as they could be.

"All right," said Vedala. "I want everyone to march in single file. We're going to move slowly. If you see something, say something. Stone's canaries are going in first, so we'll have a map to work from. Slow and steady. No surprises."

The river murmured quietly in the background as Vedala added, "Remember, a certain someone doesn't want us here. Which is exactly why we've got to investigate."

"Deploying canaries," replied Stone, gesturing to the drones as they flitted one at a time into the tunnel. Turning to look into the forest, he added, "I just need a moment."

Stone tilted his head toward Tupa, who squatted on a nearby log with the blowgun across his knees. The boy hadn't left Stone's side since they'd made first contact, and his unhappiness now was not concealed. However, it had been decided that the safest scenario was for Tupa to wait outside for their return.

Vedala watched as Stone approached the boy with a smile and confident words. Asked to stay behind, Tupa was looking away from Stone with the distinct sheen of tears in his eyes.

Vedala couldn't suppress a sad smile.

Harold Odhiambo strode to the threshold of the tunnel, leaning inside with bright, curious eyes. For the xenogeologist, this was the realization of a literal childhood dream. The black tunnel had begun to blink with light as the canary drones illuminated their LEDs, flickering like fireflies into the dark throat.

Beside Odhiambo, Peng Wu was struggling not to hyperventilate. Sensing the onset of a panic attack, she was in the process of employing a deep-breathing routine taught in the taikonaut basic training regimen.

Odhiambo spoke to her in a calm tone, without any trace of judgment.

"Whatever is in there, Major Wu . . . we have no reason to believe it is hostile. Theoretically, this entire structure could be no more than an expression of a microparticle that doesn't know we exist. It is a natural wonder. Something ancient, possibly even from another star system . . . but here now entirely by accident."

"We don't know that," said Peng. "Not for sure."

"No, I suppose we don't. But Andromeda has never been found outside our own upper atmosphere. It is unique to our planet, some strange accident of evolution . . . unless you know something I don't?"

Their eyes met, and Peng almost began to speak before stopping.

"A prerequisite of information sharing is *trust*, Dr. Odhiambo. And I'm afraid there isn't enough of it going around."

Odhiambo noticed that Peng was staring coldly over his shoulder. Nidhi Vedala stood nearby, listening to the conversation. She seemed tense, her eyes sharp and calculating. When she spoke, there was a harsh edge to her voice.

"If you're aware of any danger to my team," said Vedala in a low voice, "now is the time to divulge it."

"I . . . " began Peng, before her mouth snapped shut. "I am not."

Odhiambo frowned. It seemed as if an opportunity for cooperation had just passed them by. Unfortunately, it was a chance that wouldn't come again.

Peng continued, "Regardless, I do see good reason to listen to Dr. Kline. She has the most intimate understanding of the microparticle. And she warned us not to proceed for a reason."

"Her warnings weren't backed up by evidence," countered Vedala. "And her judgment can't be trusted, for obvious reasons. Why are you so afraid?"

In response, Peng Wu said something very odd.

"I have . . . an intuition."*

The very mention of the word *intuition* caused Vedala to blanch. She was behaving as most scientists were trained to—immediately discounting the results of an emotion, a *feeling*, not backed up by solid evidence.

---

* Recent studies of intuition at Oregon Health & Science University have shown the strong influence of nonconscious knowledge on decision-making, as described in a study headed by Dr. Anna Long, and published as "Assessing Intuition: Exposing the Impact of Gut Feelings," *Journal of Social Psychology* 13, no. 7 (2016): 117–21.

She chose her next words carefully. Everyone knew that the loitering canaries would be recording this exchange.

"Our field team has a job to do, Major Wu. We are to enter and investigate the anomalous structure. Those are still our orders. If you wish to defy them, you may, but you do so with full knowledge of the repercussions."

Peng's machete was still in her hand, fingers flexed tightly over the grip. Each beat of her heart sent her arm quaking. She appeared to be experiencing hyperarousal, better known as the fight-or-flight response.

"I'll elucidate," Vedala added, stepping closer. "Since you are military personnel, you will likely be discharged. As a civilian, you will be prosecuted. Your career will be over. Possibly you'll lose your freedom, although I'm not overly familiar with the workings of the People's Republic military judicial system. I will assume they don't celebrate cowardice."

Peng nodded, shoulders slumping. She looked at the machete in her hand and forced herself to drop it to the jungle floor. Satisfied, Vedala turned sharply and moved to collect Stone from his goodbyes with Tupa.

Harold Odhiambo put a comforting hand on Peng's shoulder. He leaned in with excitement dancing in his eyes.

"Try and remember," he said, stepping over the threshold and into the tunnel mouth. "This is a scientific *adventure*."

Peng nodded without much enthusiasm, following Odhiambo into the structure.

Vedala followed a few seconds later.

Stone was the last to enter. At the opening, he turned to wave goodbye to Tupa. The boy was now sitting on his heels, perched on a hard-case full of extra food and supplies. He waved back listlessly. It had taken the last five minutes of arguing via the translating canary to fully convince the boy to stay behind.

The featureless black tunnel swallowed Stone quickly. The lights of the teams' headlamps danced on smooth walls. Deeper inside, the fluttering canary drones twinkled like distant stars.

Tupa, left alone in the hot, silent clearing, watched until the last flicker of light disappeared.

He paused for about thirty seconds and then hastily hopped off the hard-case and popped it open. Inside, he dug out an inhibitor-soaked shirt Stone had left behind. Shrugging on this "armor," he pulled a spare respirator over his head and wrapped the band of a headlamp around his fingers, dimming the bright light with his clenched fist.

At the entrance, he paused to pick up Peng's abandoned machete. Taking a last deep breath, he stepped across the threshold in pursuit of his friends.

The steel blade flashed once as the boy loped away into darkness.

Primary Descent

ONE AT A TIME, THE FIELD TEAM STEPPED INTO THE suffocating blackness. Coated in layers of inhibitor spray, each member wore long pants and sleeves, bright purple exam gloves, and a wing-shaped respirator tucked over nose and mouth. Four headlamps bobbed in the clear, hot air. Four sets of boots thumped off the hard flat ground, sending echoes racing up and down the seemingly endless corridor.

Ahead, the shifting swarm of canary drones flickered and hummed, their ultra-bright LEDs shining like dewdrops suspended in subterranean spiderwebs. The intense light reflected in unpredictable ways against the oily greenish walls—sometimes shimmering brightly, and other times absorbed into a flat blackness. When the milling drones passed near the scientists, their rotors sent down columns of hot, metallic-smelling air.

The team walked in silence, tense and wary, stretching their senses to the limit of perception.

"No airborne toxins, environment is still clean," murmured Stone every few minutes.

"I'm seeing a lot of residue," said Vedala, looking at Peng's bootprints as they appeared in a thin layer of damp ash.

"Yes, but no particulates in the air," said Stone.

"Even so, respirators stay on," said Vedala.

Every fifty yards, Odhiambo produced a small greenish-yellow tube from his hip satchel. As he cracked each one in his gnarled fingers, the tubes erupted into an ethereal emerald light. Dropping them on the ground, he left a trail of visual markers behind them—an indication of both elevation and the way out.

The tunnel cut straight into the structure, descending at a slow, nearly imperceptible grade. The walls remained feature-less, made of the same uniform substance, its surface seeming to waver like the dark-green glass of an old Coke bottle. The faint hexagon of daylight at the entrance was soon lost to view as the team steadily descended.

Stone provided rearguard, his stubbled face lit from below by the glow of his neck monitor. The hanging screen projected a rapidly expanding map constructed in real time by the canary swarm. So far it had depicted a very simple straight line, cutting into the anomaly for at least a quarter mile.

After approximately twenty minutes of slow progress, Vedala called a huddle.

"Status report?" she asked Stone.

"The corridor slopes down at a constant angle. It hasn't varied yet," Stone replied in an unintentional whisper. "Surface mate-rial seems totally consistent. The ash residue has solidified, and it's coating every surface, like the inside of a chimney. I'm not seeing any other passages, and the temperature is rising as we go deeper."

"The temperature change is consistent with the geothermal

gradient," said Odhiambo. "This is essentially a hole in the ground. Like a cave, but made of exotic material and with totally unnatural, nongeological features."

A sense of wonder had settled into Odhiambo's voice.

"I never thought I would see it," he mused. "A xenogeologist studies pictures, data collected across billions of kilometers of space. And here I am. Standing inside a piece of extraterrestrial architecture."

"Frightening, isn't it?" asked Peng.

"It is the most beautiful thing I have ever seen," said Odhiambo.

"And what exactly makes you so certain this is alien?" asked Stone.

"My assumption is based on the unique geological attributes of this environment. This substrate appears perfectly uniform. The interior void exhibits a six-sided configuration that perfectly mirrors the underlying structure of the microparticle. And I didn't say 'alien,' Dr. Stone. I said 'extraterrestrial.' You will recall that the first evolution of this incredible material was found lingering in the upper limits of Earth's atmosphere by the Scoop VII satellite."

"And it killed forty-six innocent people on first contact, followed by two soldiers, one pilot, one patrol officer, and five more in a nearby town," added Stone, his voice grave. "Men, women, and children."

"Before evolving into a benign expression," said Odhiambo.

"I wouldn't call the AS-2 plastiphage benign. Not if I were friends with the pilot who lost his life over Piedmont when every polymer in his jet was dechained and dissolved in under two minutes."

"Fair enough, Dr. Stone. You are right," said Odhiambo. "It

is easy for me to forget that your father was there, on the original Wildfire mission. This must all feel very personal to you."

Vedala was watching Stone closely.

"I believe it is alien," said Peng. "For my part."

"And why is that?" asked Vedala. "Intuition?"

"It is a microparticle found on the edge of space. No amino acids, no waste products, and a unique cellular structure. More machine than biological. Designed to survive in a low-oxygen, ultraviolet-rich environment. Every indication is that it was designed for a purpose."

"That, or it's an exotic terrestrial particle ejected into the atmosphere by a volcanic eruption or asteroid impact," replied Vedala. "Far from having come from outer space, it could have evolved deep under the earth's crust."

Peng said nothing more, staring at Vedala without expression. A clear wedge had appeared between the two, based on a simple miscommunication.

Specifically, the closest Chinese parallel to the word *intuition*—on the mainland, *zhijue*—does not directly translate into the Western understanding of the term. The notion of *zhijue* does not exist within the Confucian classics or in the traditional development of Chinese history, either, having been spawned after its introduction by Western philosophers in the 1800s.

The main difference between an Eastern and Western understanding of intuition, as laid out by Liang An in his work *Etymology: A Clash of East and West*, lies in its placement somewhere between instinct and intellect. In the West, the idea of intuition is ontologically identical to that of instinct. In the East, and from Peng Wu's understanding, the notion of intuition is based on *lixing*, i.e., the intellect. To her mind, intuition was a leap of faith made from a bedrock of fact.

The two scientists stared at each other without speaking. Their stalemate was broken only by an exclamation by Dr. Stone.

"Oh my god," he whispered hoarsely.

Stone's horrified face was outlined in light from his monitor. It disappeared as he flipped the glowing screen around to show the others. A flickering video feed was playing, gathered by a canary drone approximately two hundred yards ahead. The drone was hovering over an object sprawled on the ground.

It was a body, that much was clear.

The corpse was on its stomach, facedown. The limbs were curiously elongated. It didn't seem to be wearing clothes, though some parts of the skin were mottled darker than others. The remaining flesh was pale in the strafing light of the drone. Most disturbing, the body appeared to have sunk partially into the floor.

"It was crawling. Whatever it was, it looks like it was trying to crawl—" muttered Stone, before Vedala shushed him with a wave of her hand.

"Make no assumptions," she said. "Move the drone closer."

As the canary drew nearer to the corpse, the horrific image became clearer.

"What is it?" asked Stone, afraid to state the obvious.

"I don't know," said Odhiambo, "but it doesn't look human to me."

Evolutions

I N THE CUPOLA WINDOWS OF THE ISS, A RED LIGHT BEGAN
to blink. Kline watched it, hesitating. A call was incoming
from NORTHCOM at Peterson AFB.

Kline's interactions with General Stern had grown more aloof
as the hours mounted postrendezvous. She was not sure that
communicating with him would further her aims. Ultimately,
however, she decided to take the call.

[initiating satellite uplink—link established—connect]

ISS-KLINE

Kline here.

PAFB-STERN

Has there been any word from the team?

ISS-KLINE

Negative, Northcom.

PAFB-STERN

We have an indication they are alive. Were you aware?

ISS-KLINE

Negative.

PAFB-STERN

Are you monitoring the tower that's grown out of the lake? It's nearly a mile high. I'm desperate, Sophie. And pardon me, but so far your utility has been low. I expected more. Any ideas?

ISS-KLINE

Negative. Sir.

PAFB-STERN

[ten-second pause] Very well. Your involvement has come to an end, Dr. Kline. Thank you for your contribution. But our mission has failed.

ISS-KLINE

I disagree, General.

PAFB-STERN

Excuse me?

ISS-KLINE

My mission has only just begun. I wanted to let you know myself, in my own words.

PAFB-STERN

What are you—

[end transmission]

Cutting off the connection, Kline kept her eyes trained on the internal ISS camera feed. Her two fellow crew members continued their daily work, oblivious. As she watched them, Kline's physiological monitoring registered changes in respiration and heart rate that signaled her growing excitement.

This was unusual, as Kline rarely departed from a resting baseline. Through the use of deep breathing and mindfulness techniques, she normally kept her emotional state opaque to the physiological sensors and the prying eyes of the ground-based crew in Houston.

Today was different.

Kline employed no calming routines. Instead, she simply reached to her wrist and snatched off the watch-size Bluetooth wireless monitor. Deactivating it, she let the device float away— its signal gone dead.*

Dr. Sophie Kline was finished with pretense. She was done acting, lying, and hiding her emotions from constant ground-based observation. She had been concealing her true intentions for two years.

And now, those intentions were about to be revealed.

Heart thumping, Kline pulled out her custom robotic work-station interface. Slipping on the telepresence gloves and pulling her head-mounted display over her eyes, she flexed her fingers. A hundred yards away, the Robonaut R3A4 did the same.

The robot began to move its arms.

It typed on a keyboard, activating a suite of dedicated on-board computers located in the isolated laboratory module. The commands it was able to execute from this location had been

---

* The brain-computer interface embedded in Kline's motor cortex continued to record and send data to Mission Control. It was not as simple to remove.

given permanent emergency priority. In the event of a catastrophe, NASA had deemed it crucial that other ISS subsystems be accessible from the relative safety of the Wildfire lab.

A hostile action from within had never even been considered.

As she worked, Kline was blind to an ominous sight outside the cupola window just beyond her shoulder. A smudge had appeared on the nadir face of the Wildfire Mark IV laboratory module, still disguised as a Cygnus unmanned cargo vehicle after five years in operation. It was glowing violet in the vacuum of space, unnoticed. It flashed, a brighter purple, and then it was bigger.

Wearing her visor, Kline was seeing the world through a machine's eyes. Only the lower half of her face was visible, lips moving as she spoke quietly to herself. After years of grinding work, she had now embarked on a unilateral course of action. It was a plan known only to her, but one that would soon change her own life and that of every human being on the planet.

Sophie Kline's intention was to set the human race free.

Forensics

DEEP BENEATH THE AMAZON JUNGLE, AN UNRECOGnizable body lay slumped under the drifting LED lights of half a dozen canary drones. The inhuman figure seemed to be emerging out of the solid floor like a swimmer surfacing. In death it had been trapped, half consumed, facedown and perfectly still.

No camera feed could explain exactly what it was.

A hundred yards farther up the tunnel, the team paused, uncertain. This only lasted an instant. In her typical fashion, Nidhi Vedala was already waving them onward with impatience.

"On we go," she ordered, setting off down the tunnel. "Respirators tight. Eyes open. Prep your sample kit, Peng."

Taking small, steady steps, Vedala advanced until she had reached the maelstrom of flickering lights and humming drones. She aimed her headlamp down, tracking the bright beam along ridges of ruined flesh. Looking beyond the body, she noticed that the wall didn't reflect back—it was missing.

"There's an opening," she reported. "Rubble on the floor. Pitting on the walls. Probably caused by a kinetic energy release."

Odhiambo spoke up from just over her shoulder, cracking a fresh chemical light stick that bathed the walls and his face in electric-green shadows.

"Oh yes," he said, "certainly an explosion. And look at the surface features. See the striations? These fine grooves? Unique to this area of the anomaly. Almost crystalline, like quartz. Or perhaps like ice that has melted and been refrozen."

"What caused it?" asked Vedala.

"Probably a shock wave passing through the structure."

Vedala produced a slim digital camera from her hip-mounted kit bag. Stepping carefully around the body, she snapped a series of pictures. Once finished, she nudged the mass of flesh with the toe of her boot. The body swayed, shivering like gelatin, but didn't roll over.

"Careful, Nidhi," said Stone, unable to help himself. "We don't know what the hell that is."

Vedala pocketed the camera and kneeled. She curled her gloved fingertips under the corpse's cheek. Pulling firmly but gently, she twisted the head to the side to reveal the hidden face.

Only then did Stone realize he was holding his breath. He let it out.

"It's a man," said Vedala. "Seriously infected. Look at the nostrils."

Gray-green ash caked the nose and mouth. The cheeks were blemished with a patch of metallic hexagons. The chest and neck were fused with the floor, pulling grotesquely at the skin of his face.

"Get a sample, Peng," Vedala ordered, releasing the head and letting it sink back to the floor. "Let's compare it to what we've seen already."

"He is not indigenous," said Odhiambo, helping Vedala stand. "This person is a Caucasian male, or was. And you can see now he is wearing something . . . perhaps a lab coat or a uniform. The fabric is melted into his skin."

"There's part of a badge," added Stone, pointing with his light. "No name, just a number."

. . . k B . . . kstein #23402582

Vedala produced her camera and snapped a photo of the badge. She aimed her headlamp into the dark space beyond the corpse.

"He must have crawled out of this room," she said, stepping over the sprawled body.

"Slow down, Nidhi," called Stone. "I'm sending in the drones. We don't have any idea what's waiting for us in there."

Stone scrambled after Vedala, with Odhiambo close behind him. They were preceded by a whirring swarm of drones. Peng stayed behind, scraping a sample vial over the pale flesh of the corpse. After a long final gaze at the motionless body, Peng Wu rose and joined the rest of the team.

None of them noticed the boy, crouched and watching from the shadows.

"WHOA," SAID VEDALA. "This is big."

Her voice echoed back across an open expanse.

The canary swarm spread out into the emptiness to explore. The team remained by the doorway, crowded around Stone and his monitor. Nobody spoke as a series of hideous images flickered over the screen. Occasionally, Stone would flip over to the laser rangefinders to see the room topography. And to provide a bit of relief.

This was the site of a massacre.

The narrow passageway had opened into a vast space with an impressively high ceiling. The floor was littered with debris: shards of metal, broken rock, and more human bodies. Barely visible, three knobby cylindrical machines rose in a line. Red glowing emergency lights shone at their bases, and a faint humming was audible. A fourth cylinder was scorched black and leaning at a precarious angle, its casing shattered.

"What are those?" asked Stone. "They look like fermenting vats from a brewery."

"Not beer. Turbines," said Odhiambo. "As I expected, those are hydroelectric generators. The water flows under the dam and turns them, making electricity. The nearest one seems to be the source of our explosion."

Soaring around the turbine heads, a few canaries approached two tall beige cabinets located against the wall. Their metal surfaces were studded with dials and controls.

"The control panel," said Odhiambo. "Simple controls for simple turbines. These are small, the same kind of micro hydroelectric plants I have seen employed all across what is called the third world. From Afghanistan to Ethiopia. With twenty thousand dollars, a village of a hundred homes can have lights, refrigeration, water purification. And television, of course."

Odhiambo added the last example with a rueful smile.

"Let's get over there," said Vedala. "Carefully."

Moving together, the team approached a broad metal desk parked beside the panels. A body was slumped over it. A piece of debris had torn through the corpse, leaving the desk and cabinets beyond coated in a rusty spray of dried blood.

"Interesting," said Vedala. "This body isn't compromised. Looks like a simple puncture wound followed by bleeding out."

"Check the feet," said Peng.

The worker's boots had clearly fused together and then sunk ankle-deep into the anomaly surface.

"It's as if the room turned to quicksand," said Peng, twisting to look around. Vedala put a hand on her arm.

"We need to count the bodies," said Vedala. "See if we can identify who was here and where they came from."

For the next few minutes, the team cataloged half a dozen bodies scattered around the room. Most had melded into the surfaces where they stood or fell, with their clothing and equipment absorbed into the skin. All of it was flinted with hexagonal scabs—like frost growing over a windowpane.

The worst were the everyday items that formed part of this deformed human landscape: pens growing from a woman's forehead; two bodies partially absorbed into each other; swaths of fabric and human hair melted into mundane office furniture.

The room had become a graveyard of wreckage and twisted bodies, much of it unidentifiable.

All of this carnage emanated from the fourth turbine. A mound of crusted black ash surrounded a scarred metal casing that had been blown off. The detonation had vaporized a deep crater in the floor, and the path of superheated debris could be seen in a starburst pattern of streaks and gouges.

Over the hum of the remaining turbines, the team could hear the far-off roar of water under their feet.

Odhiambo began to hypothesize out loud, as was his habit. He spoke while holding a chemlight in one hand, walking and inspecting. As he gesticulated, the greenish light seemed to dance around him like swamp fire.

"Something went wrong with the dam turbine. It exploded. The detonation itself was surely lethal. But the shock wave also provided a burst of energy to the AS-3 substance this anomaly is constructed of. Triggered, it began to self-replicate using the available fuel on hand. Both inorganic material . . . and organic."

Peng stood frozen in the middle of the room, staring blankly at the drones. The only indication she was disturbed was in the way her front teeth were digging into her lower lip. Spread out, the other scientists were not paying close attention to Peng or to each other.

Vedala added to Odhiambo's hypothesis, her voice echoing through the empty space.

"So AS-3 is capable of pure energy conversion. Not surprising. Both known strains can self-replicate, given energy. If that nuclear fail-safe had gone off in the original Wildfire facility, it would have spawned enough Andromeda to end the world. We're seeing a smaller version of that here."

"On the bright side, at least it was temporary," added Odhiambo. "If the reaction had continued, these bodies would have been swallowed up. Instead, they are only halfway . . . eaten. It appears our unfortunate crawling man had at least a minute or two to try and escape."

Odhiambo looked back toward the room entrance.

"The tunnel leading outside," added Odhiambo, "acted as a natural chimney, concentrating and spewing this smoke into the jungle. It infected the Machado, as well as any animals in the vicinity. For them, it was a slower death."

"I think we're missing the bigger picture," said Stone. "If there are people in here, it means this isn't some extraterrestrial fluke. It's a *building*. And it was built by a human being, for a purpose."

The room fell silent.

"Stone is right. Do we all understand what this means?" asked Vedala.

As a lifelong professor, she was accustomed to employing rhetorical questions. "Someone has figured out how to use the Andromeda Strain," she continued, not waiting for an answer. "They've reverse engineered the microparticle to create this structure. And whatever this place is designed for, it needed at least a few highly skilled workers to operate it."

"Yes," said Odhiambo. "Most of this structure must have grown through the mitosis event we saw. But some pieces were too complicated for that. For example"—he waved his chemlight at the damaged curl of metal casing—"A turbine."

"It's amazing," Vedala mused. "This entire structure probably began as a single mote of reverse-engineered Andromeda material, encoded with growth instructions and the ability to make fuel for self-replication from anything nearby. The turbines and equipment are small enough to airdrop straight into the jungle. And all of it was installed by a skeleton crew who could have been lowered in on a single helicopter."

Leaning closer, Stone examined the burned husk. He kept his respirator tight over his nose and mouth. The explosion had vaporized a hip-deep chunk out of the floor. Inside it lay the blasted remains of the turbine—a scorched cylindrical frame the size of a refrigerator, still partially intact. From under it, he heard the rush of water.

Stone stood up and scanned the walls for cables and wires.

"One problem," he said. "The electricity generated by these turbines is useless if it can't be transported. And this electrical transmission equipment is small-scale. That makes sense, if all the equipment had to be airdropped in. But without larger transformers, the hydropower will attenuate before it can get anywhere."

"Unless it doesn't have to go very far," added Odhiambo, waving his chemlight at the spot in the crater where a bundle of frayed and burned cables emerged from the exposed innards of the destroyed turbine. The thick braid disappeared straight into the black rock of the floor.

Across the room, Peng was holding a long sheet of paper in one hand. A banner, torn and burned. Her face was blank.

"What have you got, Peng?" asked Vedala.

Peng held up the piece of limp paper.

GLÜCKWUNSCH ZU EINER GUT—

"It's in German," she said, her voice dull with fear. "'Congratulations on a job well done.' . . . They were only construction workers. And they were celebrating."*

Odhiambo turned to Stone, a worried look on his face.

"That means this station is complete. So where is the power going?"

"I don't know," said Stone. "The canary map ends here in this room. This structure is as simple as anything I've ever seen. Just a big mass, a tunnel cut straight through to this turbine room, and that's it. There aren't even doors."

"Building doors in a growing structure would be futile," said Odhiambo. "There is very little here that is not an organic part of the whole. But it isn't here for no reason. The power goes somewhere. Here, my friend, lend me your compass."

Stone complied.

---

* Forensic identification of the workers' remains traced them to an independent hydroelectric firm run by Germans, operating out of Mexico City, and known for working abroad on off-the-grid sites. No workers had yet been reported missing.

The rangy older man stepped over to one of the turbines. Holding the instrument near the floor, he began sweeping it back and forth. His eyes stayed on the compass needle.

As it fluttered, he stopped.

Taking careful steps around the room, Odhiambo used the relationship between current and magnetism to find a hidden line of electrical current. By watching the direction of the swinging compass needle, he determined the flow of current and followed a live wire across the room.

"The electricity goes this way," he said. "That canary survey puts us at nearly a kilometer deep. Well below the waterline. You said the transformer can push power only a short distance. Well, if we continue in this direction we will find ourselves . . ."

"Directly under the lake," said Stone. "It makes no sense."

Unfazed, Odhiambo methodically followed the line. It ended at a blank wall. He paused, frowning.

"I do not understand," said Odhiambo, standing under brightly lit canary drones. "The electricity flows this way. There should be some kind of duct or maintenance hallway, at least."

Stone rechecked his neck monitor. With a swipe of his thumb, he turned off the canary cameras and reactivated the laser rangefinders. The room filled with an invisible sweep of precisely measured beams of near-infrared light, projected from spinning mirrors in the hearts of the drones.

The monitor began to display the wall and floor surfaces in exquisite detail. Among the patterns and shapes, Stone saw the man-shaped outline of Harold Odhiambo. And under the feet of Odhiambo's silhouette, he saw the familiar lines of a hexagon.

"Harold, look down at your feet."

The silhouette on the screen looked down.

"I see nothing . . . wait, an imprint. But those are everywhere."

Stone lowered the monitor to his chest, where it dimmed itself. He was already walking toward Odhiambo. He had identified two barely noticeable grooves, visible only at submillimeter-level precision. Luckily, he recognized them for what they were.

Hinges.

Fight or Flight

TOLD YOU," SAID ODHIAMBO, SMILING. "THE ELECTRICAL conduits must lead somewhere. Otherwise the dam serves no purpose."

Leaning on his digging trowel, Odhiambo was able to unlatch the hatchway. He levered it open, and the hexagonal lid rose to reveal a dark hole. Inside, Odhiambo saw the glinting bones of a metal utility ladder leading down. The six-sided shaft cut straight into the substrate and disappeared into black depths.

"I thought you'd be more upset," said Stone, leaning over the shaft with a canary resting on his palm. "Now that we know this isn't an alien structure, after all."

"Oh," said Odhiambo. "We most certainly do not know that. In fact, I am more convinced than ever that this structure is alien in origin. Human involvement or not."

Stone looked at Odhiambo to see if he was joking. It appeared he was not. Shrugging, Stone removed his hand from under the glowing drone. It hovered in place for an instant, then began to slowly lower into the pit. The rest of the canaries continued to survey the control room.

"I guess we'll find out," said Stone.

The squawking of a loudspeaker startled everyone, but most of all Peng Wu. She let out a surprised shriek and clapped a hand over her respirator in embarrassment. Over the course of the exploration she had grown increasingly tense, to the point that now a facial tic had appeared under her left eye. Years of emotional mastery seemed to be fracturing under the strain of this mission and its secrets.

Embedded in the beige face of a bloodstained control panel, a small square speaker was sounding a transmission alert at full volume.

"Attention," announced a tinny voice. "I don't know if you can hear me but by my estimates, you should have reached the control room by now. If so, good work, Nidhi."

The team looked at each other in disbelief.

"That's Sophie Kline, isn't it?" asked Stone.

Vedala could only nod.

"What happened here was an accident. Nobody was supposed to get hurt."

Riddled with waves of static, the astronaut's words echoed through the room. Stone and Odhiambo left their rucksacks and equipment at the open mouth of the hatch. They joined Vedala, who was standing near the desk.

Peng Wu began to pace back and forth.

"No," Peng said. "No, no, no. This is not good. She's working with *them*."

Her attention split, Vedala cocked her head at Peng. *Them?*

Kline continued her monologue over the speaker. "I can't

explain to you what I have accomplished. And you could never understand my reasons. But I want you to know . . . this is for the good of all humankind."

Peng looked around in dismay.

"We have to leave here," she said. "She's not on our side. She's dangerous."

Turning to go, Peng collided with a small figure who had been hiding behind a dark, thrumming turbine. Tupa was knocked to the ground. The adult-sized T-shirt he wore billowed around him, ghostlike. Instantly on the attack, Peng began to raise her boot for a vicious stomp but the boy scrambled away, his borrowed machete clattering to the ground. Back on his feet, he stood exposed in the light of several canaries, chest heaving.

"Tupa!" shouted Stone, recognizing the boy's lanky silhouette.

As Peng stood staring, Stone rushed over and swept the boy up in his arms.

"Are you okay? What are you doing here?"

"Hi Jahmays," said the boy, grinning.

"I said we have to go," said Peng, her voice rising. "Now. All of us."

The former soldier seemed to already understand the dire implications of Kline's speech. Her resolve only grew as Kline's slightly slurred words continued to wash over them like rain, the echoes of each syllable chasing each other.

"I warned you to stay away. I warned you all. Remember that."

Turning in circles, Peng looked at the field team, eyes wide over the blunt nose of her respirator. "She's tried to kill us once already. She's going to try again. I'm calling for an evacuation. Now."

Vedala put her palms up, trying to calm Peng. "That's not possible. She's in orbit. You need to remain—"

At that moment, the shattered turbine began to try to restart itself.

The burned wreck had shut down automatically after the first, accidental explosion. Now, its safeguards appeared to have been remotely overridden. A disturbing shudder ran through the floor.

"Goodbye, team," said the soft voice, already lost in a static crack of lightning as electricity surged into the broken turbine engine mount, instantly vaporizing the remains of the rotor assembly.

A plume of billowing black smoke shot up from the husk.

"Respirators tight!" shouted Vedala, backing up toward the pile of rucksacks ringing the open hatchway. Odhiambo, Stone, and Tupa joined her. Knocked to her knees by the tremor, Peng swiveled her head desperately.

"Come on, Peng!" urged Vedala.

Standing up on shaky legs, Peng focused on the room's most obvious exit with a soldier's instinct. The only sure way out was across the cavernous room, beyond the dense smoke spewing up from the screaming remains of the turbine. It would be tight, but Peng was confident she could make it in time. If someone was going to escape to stage a rescue—or a body recovery—it would have to be her.

Escape was the only winning move.

"No!" ordered Vedala, kicking her backpack into the open hatchway. "Everyone after me!"

Voice muffled by his respirator, Odhiambo shouted, "Into the hatch!"

The plume of smoke had risen up into a foreboding column, smothering several loitering canary drones. Peng began to skirt around the obsidian cloud. After the initial shock wave had passed, the floor had turned spongy and soft.

Stone and Tupa launched themselves down the metal ladder and into the unknown. Older and slower, Odhiambo followed suit with surprising dexterity. Vedala was close behind, stopping only to scan for Peng.

She had stepped farther away.

The pillar of toxic dust was collapsing. It began to sweep across the room toward them. Peng's gaze was still fixed on the exit.

"Don't!" shouted Vedala.

Hands flat, Peng Wu launched herself into a sprint, legs slicing through knee-deep smoke. After a few lurching steps, her respirator slipped off her face and bounced around her neck. She continued accelerating in a beeline toward the tunnel exit, lips pursing as she tried to hold her breath.

"Damnit," muttered Vedala. She stepped lower into the shaft, only her eyes above the floor now. Her fingers were clamped tightly around the cold metal ladder. A rolling tide of smoke was churning toward her. Odhiambo's discarded light sticks glowed a bruised neon green within the black clouds, like ethereal lightning engulfed in a storm.

Peng tripped and fell.

Stumbling back up, she blindly groped her way forward. Then she collapsed into the blackness again, and disappeared.

Vedala took hold of the hatch over her head and paused another instant. She couldn't take her eyes from the spot where Peng had fallen. Under the spinning LEDs of disoriented canaries, Vedala thought she had seen movement.

Then a terrible sight lurched into view.

Peng's body reappeared, standing and falling again, then crawling. The infection had moved quickly, clearly penetrating her mucous membranes and propagating in her lungs. Incredibly, she took a choking breath, and managed to release a wailing scream of agony.

The tumbling wave of dust grew in Vedala's vision, and she slammed the hatchway shut as the toxic cloud rolled over its top.

THOUGH STILL FUNCTIONING, the power plant had been turned into a shrieking storm of poisonous ash. Every inch of the room was choked with gritty black smoke. The subterranean power station was now an abyssal hell, echoing with the screaming of torn metal as the damaged turbine quaked and rocked. The faint lights of disoriented canary drones streaked through the air, their cameras still transmitting.

Below them, Peng Wu was alive.

She would have felt the Andromeda infection closing her airways, like sandpaper on the back of her throat, but she was still crawling. Her knees and forearms were leaving faint indentations in the softening floor, and her clothing had dissolved into her skin, seemingly painlessly. Peng looked very tired, and she seemed to want nothing more than to lay her face on the floor and drift away to sleep.

But a glimmer of light from above caught her attention. And just before she collapsed for the last time, Peng managed to turn over onto her back. She gazed upward, her hair already fusing into the anomaly in tendrils of black on black.

Overhead, a white light was shining in the storm of ash.

It grew closer and brighter. She could detect a faint thrumming sound, and a gentle hot wind blew over her face as the angelic beacon descended. At last she saw that it was a canary drone, encrusted with metallic growths and spinning off-balance.

Twisting in the air, it plummeted down and landed right beside her face.

And in her final moments, Peng remembered her mission.

In a ragged voice, she turned her head and began to shout to the canary. She kept speaking as the infection closed up her throat and blocked her veins. She spoke as her body sank into the pillowy folds of the anomaly. Peng licked her metal-flecked lips, and she shared a last confession.

"The Andromeda Strain," she rasped, ". . . it's everywhere. Every planetary body. Mars. Moon rocks. Asteroids."

Huddled safely in the sealed hatchway tunnel, the remaining field team listened to Stone's monitor as it relayed this final message. In the darkness, nobody could see the tears leaking from Vedala's eyes and tracing cool paths around her respirator. Stone kept an arm tight around Tupa's bony shoulders. Odhiambo's eyes were closed, head bowed as if he were praying.

"We covered it up, NASA, JAXA, CING," said Peng, through clenched teeth. "Kline was right. Andromeda isn't here by accident. It was *sent*. Waiting for life. And it's been searching for *such a long time* . . ."

State of Emergency

SINCE ITS INCEPTION IN 1998, THE INTERNATIONAL Space Station has existed as a symbol of peace and scientific cooperation between the world's most powerful nations. Though these so-called superpowers often have conflicting interests, a sense of fellowship has prevailed among the many inhabitants of the ISS over the years. Astronauts form a common family, citizens of humanity working together above a shared world, men and women chosen from among the top scientists and pilots in the United States, Russia, Canada, Japan, Korea, the European Union, and a dozen other countries.

That unspoken integrity—an ideal maintained for over two decades with unbroken ceremony and courtesy on board the ever-expanding space station—was about to be shattered.

Dr. Sophie Kline was declaring war.

The decision-making process that led to Kline's next action has been much discussed. Most scholars have come to believe that the ISS was assembled in an era of relative naïveté, based on handshake agreements with no true safeguards. It is theorized that such an age of cooperation between superpowers will never again be possible, given the social, political, and intellectual climate that exists today.

Research and interviews, however, have led to a more optimistic conclusion.

What happened was most likely the work of a rogue scientist with unique traits. Kline's rise to success was unlikely, to say the least, given her severe disability. It was those years of suffering that forged her into something almost superhuman—a person who simply could not be broken, or stopped.

At the heart of Kline's indomitable spirit was a deep anger.

Kline despised the constant obstacles in her life—from the boundaries of her own body to the limits of scientific progress, and even the intellectual restraints erected by the scientific community to safeguard the human race.

Though laudable, her lifetime of achievements had not been spurred by a positive desire to open up new frontiers of knowledge. Rather, they were a sort of revenge. Kline had mastered the sciences quickly, violently, and with the express intent of putting them to use—the way one might break a horse in order to ride it.

Best estimates indicate that three years prior, Kline had become convinced that the Andromeda Strain was an attack on humanity. The tragedy is that Kline's secret actions from that point on had gone unnoticed or unchallenged due to her prestige status as an American astronaut.

Compartmentalized knowledge is a mainstay of spycraft and necessary for any governmental information dissemination process. As a result of a lack of information transparency, however, Sophie Kline and Peng Wu were the only active members of the Project Wildfire field team who knew the truth about the Andromeda Strain.

The original AS-1 variety had been collected by the Scoop satellite missions from Earth's upper atmosphere. Subsequently, the strain had been detected on every rocky body planet in the inner solar system. Traces of it had been recovered in 10 percent of regolith samples brought back by the Apollo trips to the moon.* And despite an unexplained landing failure of the return mechanism, the Stardust mission to Comet Wild 2 tested positive for the microparticle.

These instances had been humankind's only sample-return missions, though other spacecraft had carried specialized instruments for remote detection.

Most recently, the Hayabusa Japanese probe had made landfall on the tumbling, cigar-shaped asteroid BR-3. While it was there, an obscure sensor called Andro returned a seemingly innocuous reading, tagged onto the end of a larger report. The result was meaningful only to a small handful of researchers and military personnel.

Andromeda had proliferated across our solar system.

The scientists on the original Project Wildfire had been correct to invoke the Messenger Theory, first proposed by John R. Samuels in the spring of 1962. Simply put, the best way to find life in a mostly empty galaxy would be to send out a probe that could make copies of itself on arrival, and then spread those copies to other stars in an act of exponential exploration.

Kline had studied every aspect of the microparticle. She knew it thrived in hard vacuum, lasting for countless millennia

---

* Top-secret institutional knowledge of Andromeda necessitated the design and construction of Apollo-era mobile quarantine facilities, to ensure that astronauts returning from lunar missions did not trigger new infections.

and self-replicating without producing waste. It lacked amino acids, meaning no proteins, no enzymes or any of the "building blocks of life," and it was housed in a nonbiological crystalline cell structure.

Finally, she had come to a conclusion.

The Andromeda Strain wasn't a microorganism. It wasn't alive, exactly. The extraterrestrial microparticle was in fact a highly complex *machine*.

Kline reasoned that AS-1 had been a probe, designed to travel to other star systems and then make copies of itself and wait. For the last several hundred thousand years it had done just that. What it had been waiting for was triggered on February 8, 1967, in a small home on the outskirts of Piedmont, Arizona. On that day, a town doctor named Alan Benedict made the foolhardy decision to open the hatch of a salvaged Scoop VII satellite.

The Andromeda Strain had been waiting for life.

AS-1 infected living organisms, triggering an evolution into the AS-2 plastiphage configuration, which escaped from the depths of Project Wildfire and propagated in the atmosphere, dissolving the advanced plastics needed to reach low Earth orbit.

It had detected life, and then evolved into an insidious barrier.

And it is this conclusion that helps explain Kline's motivation. She saw the Andromeda Strain as yet another unfair obstacle among a lifetime of them. She believed the microparticle was designed with hostile intent—to detect life and then keep it from reaching planetary orbit. It was a *wall*, preventing our species from achieving its rightful destiny among the stars.

She would have considered it a personal affront.

Kline wondered how many other alien species had been

trapped. Privately, she speculated that this was the solution to the Fermi paradox, which asks, given the billions of Earth-like planets in the universe, *Where is everyone?*

Imprisoned on their home worlds by Andromeda, Kline assumed.

Humankind's first contact with an alien intelligence had not been a friendly affair. It had been a preemptive act of war.

And Sophie Kline was now preparing a counterattack. She had studied her adversary and painstakingly determined how to manipulate the microparticle into new configurations during her work in the Wildfire Mark IV laboratory. Her plan was to use Andromeda against itself, to destroy the obstacle it posed to human expansion into space, once and for all.

Kline had repositioned her remote manipulation station inside the Leonardo Permanent Multipurpose Module and closed the hatchway. Her hands were wrapped in teleoperation gloves and her head-mounted display was tight over her eyes as she took mental control of the R3A4 humanoid robot. The brain-computer interface to the station allowed her to send commands at the speed of thought.

The safeguards necessary to run a BSL-5 laboratory module on an inhabited space station called for emergency root access over the low- and high-level control infrastructure of the entire sprawling structure—an unprecedented level of backchannel command.

At UTC 17:24:11 a containment breach emergency was declared from inside the lab module. Like dominoes falling, every ISS subsystem, including communication, propulsion, and life support, relinquished its control. And as simply as that, Sophie Kline had seized total authority over the International Space Station.

Following standard emergency procedure, Kline's two crewmates made their way into the Zvezda service module. A cornerstone of the early station construction, the Zvezda was self-sustaining and outfitted with both Russian and American computer systems. A Soyuz crew return vehicle was docked on the module's aft port.

Kline had already moved to block all outgoing radio transmissions, sever connection to ground control,* and disable the onboard Wi-Fi. She then sealed the common berthing mechanisms (CBMs) in the Unity node connecting to the Zarya and Zvezda modules, effectively trapping the two other astronauts. And finally, she set all life support to backup power and cut the interior lights to conserve energy.

The SEP thrusters activated, converting electrical power collected by the solar panel array into continuous upward force. A shiver went through the entire structure, and a high-pitched whine could be heard. Objects in free fall, including the astronauts themselves, began to lower toward the deckside surface as the ISS rapidly gained altitude.

Yanking her head-mounted display up onto her forehead, Kline delivered a pronouncement over the station-wide closed-circuit camera to her two fellow astronauts in the Zvezda module.

"This is Dr. Sophie Kline. I am declaring an emergency and seizing station resources. From this moment until the emergency is over, you are to remain confined to your current module. Do not attempt to make outside contact. Do not attempt to leave your module. You will receive more information as

---

* This was a dangerous decision, as ground-based experts are responsible for monitoring and running nearly every aspect of the day-to-day ISS operations. Indeed, the ISS is perfectly fine running with zero crew, and it has been noted that with fewer astronauts, it actually stays much cleaner.

needed. But for the time being, the International Space Station is on lockdown."

The surprised faces of Yury Komarov and Jin Hamanaka oriented to the camera. Kline cut the feed, leaving only a black screen and stunned silence.

Of course, Kline's crewmates immediately set about defying her orders. They found the CBM passageway jammed from the outside, all communications equipment disabled, and electricity distribution cut to essential levels. Because life support connections are run along the outside skin of the station, regardless of whether the interior hatchways are open or closed, the astronauts remained safe inside their module, with plenty of air, food, water, and facilities for elimination.

What they were not in possession of was the ability to leave, or to easily communicate with the outside world. Thinking quickly, Jin Hamanaka retrieved a high-power laser diode from an optics experiment that had been stowed for return in the Soyuz. The class 3B diode was emerald green and powerful, though not classified as hazardous. Hamanaka was able to shine the battery-powered laser light through one of the small round windows of the Zvezda module toward the surface of the planet below.

At any given moment, an estimated several hundred amateur astronomers are watching the International Space Station as it passes overhead, visible from between two to six minutes. Now orbiting on a new axis, the ISS had attracted a flurry of attention from this small international community of "station gazers."

As it swept across the globe at 17,500 miles per hour, the ISS generated a rippling wave of surprise. A handful of attentive astronomers in Central America, Southern Europe, and the Middle East were bewildered to see the ISS cruising along without its exterior lights.

They all saw a bright green dot flashing in the belly window of the Zvezda module. Of those handful, more than half were familiar with the nautical language of Morse code. Of those, all were able to recognize the most famous message of all.

S O S
... — — — ...

The Tunnel

MAJOR PENG WU EXPIRED AT UTC 18:58:06, APPROXImately a half mile into the anomaly, infected by an aerosolized variety of the AS-3 microparticle. Nidhi Vedala was shedding silent tears at the bottom of the hatchway ladder. But a spark of anger was also growing in her chest.

Vedala could still see Peng Wu's final moments in her mind's eye—the woman's smooth, unperturbed face etched by a latticework of infinitely fine metallic hexagons. Peng's agonized shriek had sent a shudder of revulsion and grief through Vedala. Now, she focused on the cold steel of the ladder biting into her hip and tried to slow her breathing.

The glare of her headlamp was bright in the claustrophobic shaft. She was dismayed to see the beam swallowed almost totally by the relentlessly uniform material of the anomaly. Around her, she saw the faces of Stone, Odhiambo, and the boy Tupa, all staring in concern.

Their unmasked fear reminded Vedala abruptly that she was still the leader of this expedition—and that their mission was far from over. In many ways, she thought, the true mission had only just begun. A confident, if weary, authority returned to her voice.

"Okay," she said. "Let's regroup."

"Peng?" asked Stone. "Is there any chance she—"

He stopped when he saw Vedala's face. Instead of saying more, he reached over and gave her shoulder a squeeze.

"I'm sorry," he said.

The group stood close together in the mouth of another unlit tunnel. Like the previous tunnel, this one also appeared to slice a straight line into the darkness. The only difference was that this corridor was half as large, only six feet tall and as wide as a typical hallway. The glassy walls seemed to press in on them. The tunnel was altogether featureless, save for a round metallic conduit pipe running along one side, transmitting electricity to something deeper inside.

The one remaining canary had not detected airborne toxins, and the field team had their respirators around their necks, speaking in whispers by the drone's guttering light. Odhiambo passed out MREs, which they each chewed mechanically as they conversed. Tupa ate a granola bar and listened intently to the translations provided by the drone. Vedala had noted that the boy was absentmindedly holding Stone's hand. It looked as though the contact was comforting to both the man and the child.

"Peng said the Andromeda Strain has been found throughout the solar system, but the results were covered up," said Vedala. "First of all, could that even be true?"

Odhiambo's hand went to his chin.

"I believe so. There have been only a handful of successful sample-return missions: the moon, a comet called Wild 2, and the Itokawa asteroid. Every other nonterrestrial sample came from naturally occurring meteorites."

"Don't forget the upper-atmosphere missions that started all this fifty years ago," added Stone.

"And the Scoop missions, of course," said Odhiambo. "But access to so few samples is tightly controlled. It would be possible to suppress knowledge of the discovery of Andromeda in moon regolith, for instance. And if nonreturn probes were instrumented to look for it, the presence of Andromeda could easily be hidden during the data transfer process."

"In other words, you believe her," said Vedala.

"Of course I do," said Odhiambo. "These were her final words, and they were costly. She was in a great deal of pain."

"Then the Andromeda Strain satisfies the Messenger Theory," concluded Stone. "It has spread everywhere, waiting for life to emerge. Meaning there must be an intelligence behind it."

"Based on the Piedmont incident, likely a hostile intelligence," said Vedala.

"No wonder Peng was panicked," said Odhiambo. "With that knowledge, it was clear we were walking into extreme danger. A hostile alien structure."

"She kept her secret until it was too late," said Stone.

"She tried to warn us. I should have listened," said Vedala. "We could have been more careful."

"There are more immediate issues," said Stone. "Kline is trying to kill us, and we're buried a kilometer deep inside the Andromeda Strain."

"She's up there and we're down here," added Vedala, her jaw clenched. "Kline wants us dead, and we're going to figure out why. For now, we only have one direction to go."

Odhiambo was quiet for a long time before his eyes went back to the metal conduit running along the floor.

"I do not believe the location of this structure is an accident. It is perfectly equatorial, like the debris path of the Tiangong-1. But it is also located precisely at the mouth of a river that can provide hydroelectric power."

"So you think the crash of the Tiangong-1 . . ."

"It was a deliberate obfuscation, a red herring, so to speak, provided by Sophie Kline to mask her true goals. For some reason, I believe she needed the ISS to be moved into an orbit over this area, and the Heavenly Palace hypothesis provided a way to make that happen."

"Could that be true? Could Kline have really planned and built the entire anomaly from the ground up?" asked Vedala.

"As you said, the structure likely started as a speck of self-replicating material. Once she programmed its growth pattern, it would have been as simple as planting a seed in the dirt," responded Odhiambo. "The rest could have been orchestrated using personal wealth and connections with private industry. She is one person I would never underestimate."

"And yet we have no idea how much of this is on purpose, and how much is just a terrible mistake," said Vedala.

"We know that she doesn't want us here," said Stone. "She surely knew the *sertanistas* would notice the anomaly, but they wouldn't have the resources or knowledge to investigate properly. Wildfire protocol was only triggered when Eternal Vigilance detected outgassed particles matching the Piedmont incident. And that only happened due to an accidental turbine explosion. I think Kline's true goal was to work here for a while in isolation, letting the anomaly grow in the deep jungle."

"So these infections were not part of her plan," said Vedala.

"But whatever she's doing or trying to do . . . it's spinning out of her control. If this structure keeps spreading—or if some nation decides to drop a bomb on it—the AS-3 particle could end up consuming the entire world."

"The infamous Scenario F," mused Stone. "Total planetary extinction."

The Kenyan xenogeologist placed a hand flat against the wall, then pulled it away. His palm was glistening with condensation. "This tunnel has taken us under the lake. Whatever is using this electricity . . . it's hidden beneath the water."

With that knowledge, a palpable burden seemed to close in on the team. Stone could imagine the weight of hundreds of tons of water pressing down, squeezing itself into the tiny droplets emerging from the gray-green walls.

Standing on his tippy toes, Tupa whispered to the hovering canary. The device rotated to watch him, and the boy made a quick gesture. In response, the drone rose to head height and oriented to James Stone.

In its robotic voice, the canary translated, "We go now."

Glancing up the chute to the hatchway in alarm, Vedala was relieved to see that the seals were holding. None of the infected smoke had come in. She smelled only damp air and the metallic odor of the anomaly.

"We go now," said Tupa in halting English. The boy gestured and whispered at the drone once more, with urgency.

"There is a roaring," translated the canary.

"A roaring?" questioned Vedala, but Odhiambo hushed her. He closed his eyes, face aimed at the ceiling.

Listening.

"Water," said Odhiambo. "Water is coming."

Best-Laid Plans

D R. SOPHIE KLINE WAS NOT OVERLY TROUBLED BY what was occurring below. Though she knew full well the implications of her recent actions, her neural oscillations (measured constantly via the brain-computer interface) were once again concentrated between 8 and 12 Hz—an alpha state indicating a calm alertness.

The lives of her team members were no longer her concern.

Kline was minutes away from reaching a goal she had dreamed about for years. She had sacrificed family and personal relationships, devoting nearly every waking moment to reach this precise moment in time and (more importantly) space. And she had spent the day running a final experiment.

The ISS had continued accelerating, hour after hour, with nothing to slow it down. To the consternation of Mission Control, it had traveled over ten thousand miles beyond its normal orbit. It was much too late to stop now.

Even armed with hard data collected via brain-computer interface, the true mindset of an individual is impossible to fully reconstruct. Yet we are uniquely fortunate to have detailed records of Kline's neural state during these final moments, before all contact was lost. These data were worth considering, at least, given what Kline was about to perpetrate.

In her studies at the University of Washington, the renowned forensic psychologist Dr. Rachel Pittman discovered a type of anticipatory focus associated with committed scientists—a pattern consistent with Kline's neural data. Pittman found that scientists tend to score very high on delay of gratification (DOG) indices, an expected outcome, since researchers must often wait for years before receiving a reward for their effort. Kline's thought process at this juncture had shifted toward "anticipatory reward"—a mode in which the moral abhorrence of recent events seems insignificant compared to the scientific outcome.

The ability to delay reward—exhibiting supreme confidence in a hypothesis that has taken years to pay off—is what allowed Kline to achieve success, and it is what blinded her to the horror of her actions in these moments.

This is not meant to be an excuse, simply an explanation.

After seizing control of the International Space Station, Kline had spent an extra forty-five minutes retrieving and donning the Cardioflow, a pair of pressurized leggings designed to distribute blood from the lower body into the head. In microgravity, astronauts often report a "cloudy" feeling, as if they've been standing on their heads. These leggings were designed to squeeze blood up from the lower body to improve circulation, thinking, and comfort. If employed for too long, however, they could cause blackouts and, eventually, death.

The result, for the moment, was that as she completed her

final experiments, Kline felt completely fresh and clearheaded, for the first time since she had arrived on board the ISS. In video footage, her cheeks were flushed and her eyes bright and alert. She was seen smiling as she flexed her hands in the sweaty telepresence gloves, orchestrating control of the R3A4.

Inside the windowless pod of the Wildfire laboratory module, the fabric-covered arms of the R3A4 were in constant motion. Details of what followed are strictly classified, but a partial recording of the experiment was recovered.

The robot's work was being executed in a custom-built biological safety cabinet—an enclosure designed to limit exposure to biohazards while interacting with infectious agents. The sterilized robot had no need for gloves, much less the bulky blue positive-pressure suits and helmets employed by human researchers. The air within the laboratory module had been replaced with a nonreactive argon-nitrogen mix.

The cabinet was embedded in the wall, a well-lit cradle with a hood of glass allowing space beneath for the robot's arms to operate. Inside, negative air pressure pulled air up through a HEPA filter to prevent particles from escaping the cradle and polluting other microgravity experiments.

Cameras mounted under the cabinet hood were meant to meticulously record every experimental trial. Working backward from this point in time, forensic videographers discovered missing tape going back several years—evidence that Kline had carried out (and covered up) a long series of illicit experiments. All told, over one hundred hours of experimentation were unaccounted for, most of them occurring in fifteen-minute segments.

Under the magnification built into its vision system, the R3A4 turned its gaze to a sample of AS-3, trapped under a flat glass slide. It had been created in secret by Kline herself, by modifying the existing samples discovered five decades before. The tiny six-sided microparticles had been arranged in a line. Scaling her hand movements to 1:50,000—approximately one micrometer per five centimeters—Kline used her unique mental interface to puppeteer the steady hands of the R3A4 through an experimental ballet that was breathtaking to behold.

In the form of a machine, all of Kline's human vulnerability had been stripped away—she was now operating in a realm of perfect scientific experimentation. No human hands could ever manipulate an object at this scale and with this amount of grace. With confident swoops and dips of her robotic end effectors, she painted the line of Andromeda microparticles with a catalyst agent. Seconds later, she painted the same area with a growth substrate of liquid carbon dioxide.

The reaction was swift and mesmerizing.

Each microparticle of AS-3 began a version of the "mitosis" witnessed in larger scale on the anomaly. The sum total began to dance and skitter under the glass plate. Kline watched as the faint line began to grow in two dimensions, soon taking on the shape of a stamp.

Moving quickly—indeed, well beyond the limits of human ability—Kline applied a growth-inhibiting agent to the top and both sides of the expanding particles, curtailing their voracious spread. Even so, some of the particles along these faces began consuming a small portion of the experimental tray. In places, the ceramic surface crumbled into a gray, ashlike substance.

The R3A4 moved quickly, avoiding contact with the rapidly multiplying microparticles. Its ortho fabric-coated hands gleamed with a thick coating of Vedala's inhibitor substance, applied during its construction to prevent reactions with either Andromeda strain.

A structure began to emerge on the macro scale—a ribbon shape, about as wide as a sheet of paper and thinner than a human hair. It continued to grow along its bottom edge only, like a scarf weaving itself longer and longer.

The ribbon soon expanded beyond the confines of its experimental tray. In a swift motion, the robot drew back an arm and rapped its knuckles across the face of the biological safety cabinet. On the second rap, the cover shattered into floating glass shards (all use of polymers had been curtailed, for obvious reasons).

At some point in the past, Kline had reset the force allowances on the robot's actuators. Electric motors by their design can exert instant and crushing torque—making them more than capable of tearing themselves apart. As a result, these motors were limited by an acceleration profile coded into the software and monitored by three independent and redundant sensing systems. But disabling this acceleration profile would have been possible for an expert.

By removing the safety constraints, Kline had greatly multiplied the Robonaut's ability to move in ways that could be both constructive and destructive.

Reaching through thick slivers of broken glass, the R3A4 pulled out the tray containing the metallic ribbon. It was now over a foot long and continuing to grow. The robot carried the ribbon to the crown of the Wildfire module—the overhead point at which the module was docked to the Harmony node, and from there attached to the entire International Space Station. It was a location chosen to complete the ruse that the laboratory was simply a cargo module.

The robot pressed the dormant end of the ribbon against the bare metal wall and painted it with another dab of accelerant.

In seconds, the AS-3 material seemed to sink into the module hull structure. The smooth wall near this mating point began to shimmer a familiar gray-green color. The materials were combining as the accelerant was consumed, the aluminum of the hull interlacing with the AS-3 microparticle. In a subsequent temporary chain reaction, metallic tendrils spread through the hull. The other end of the ribbon hovered weightlessly, growing longer, rippling like a swimming snake.

A shrill alarm began to whine.

Kline's monitor flashed the following warning message:

> ARGON LEVELS 10%, NITROGEN 22%,
>
> COMBINATORIAL GASES OVERCOMPENSATING—
>
> PLEASE REFILL CANISTER—CANISTER EMPTY—ALERT

The carefully balanced atmospheric levels inside the module—designed to be inert and nonreactive—were changing rapidly. The leading edge of the expanding ribbon was consuming the air itself. Sustained by a steady appetite of atmosphere, the ribbon kept growing as the infinitely adaptable microparticle searched for any available fuel to continue its self-replication.

Kline ignored the blaring alarm, and the sound soon faded to nothing as the atmosphere was further consumed.

The ribbon began to spit and twist, like a downed electrical wire. The leading edge brushed over the carapace of the R3A4. On contact, it sent up a roil of smoke that was itself consumed by the swiftly growing material. The inhibitor seemed to have prevented the ribbon from fusing with the robot's fabric skin.

In any case, the machine did not react. There were no pain sensors built in for Sophie Kline to feel.

Instead, the machine's black lenses were focused on a small point in the deckside hull. Pausing as if to take a deep breath—an action that was actually occurring in the module occupied by Sophie Kline—the R3A4 flexed its multijointed legs and launched itself across the cylindrical module.

As it soared, the machine pulled back its fist. On contact with the far wall, it unleashed a punch with all the force it could muster. The servo motors in the punching wrist shattered on impact as its gold-anodized aluminum knuckles dented into solid hull. The blow wrenched several fingers into awkward angles, snapping beige-white Vectran tendons like moist cartilage, creating a grisly semblance to human injury.

Drawing back the mangled endoskeleton of its hand, the Robonaut punched the same spot again.

And again.

On the fourth blow, the hull of the Wildfire module breached. What little atmosphere still remained was explosively evacuated through the fist-size hole in the side of the module.

Designed to withstand depressurization events up to 15 PSI per second, the Robonaut was not harmed, although its bearings emitted tiny particles of lubricating grease as the air evacuated from them.

Ignoring its damaged hand, the machine eagerly leaned forward. Through the new hole, the R3A4 gazed upon the blue face of planet Earth, shining thousands of miles below.

Inundation

BASED ON INTERVIEWS AND DATA RECOVERED FROM the last canary drone, the flood began with a groaning that could be heard somewhere deep in the guts of the anomaly, growing into a rumbling bass that resonated everywhere. A wet-pavement aroma of moisture filled the air. By this time, a thin carpet of cold water had already swept past. Tupa was a dim shape in the distance, sprinting after the light of the lone surviving canary, his bare feet smacking the tunnel floor.

The field team looked at each other in dismay for a split second, headlamps illuminating a haze of water vapor rising into the air. Then, without speaking, they broke into a measured trot. Vedala led, with Stone and Odhiambo following in single file. With a swipe of his finger, Stone set the canary's LED to full illumination. The tunnel ahead erupted in stark white light.

"Odhiambo?" called Vedala, panting. "That sounds seismic. Is the anomaly growing again?"

"Doubtful. This is definitely a hydrological feature," said Odhiambo. "Feel the pressure in your ears? That is from a lot of water filling an empty void."

Moving with a slight limp, Odhiambo fished a fresh chem-light from his kit pocket and cracked it. The eerie light swung back and forth in his fist as he clambered forward. The exhausted scientists were moving with growing panic, boots thumping into a skim of water darkening the metallic floor.

The disturbing roar was building all around them.

"This tunnel is a tiny volume compared to the lake," said Odhiambo. "And I'm afraid it will flood very, very quickly."

Tupa sprinted in easy strides. Navigating by the light of the drone, the boy had pulled out far ahead of the others. As he ran, his feet dipped deeper into the water. Farther back, Stone and Vedala now ran side by side, panting but keeping the same pace. The surging water was seeping into their boots now, igniting a panic that drove them forward faster.

Odhiambo, older by nearly two decades, kept up for a few minutes. Then he began to slow, grimacing and holding his side. Though the roar of water was deafening and the chilly liquid clearly rising, his body simply would not allow him to keep pace with the others, adrenaline or not.

As the water rose to his calves, however, the lifelong spelunker understood innately that his life depended on reaching an exit on the other end of the tunnel.

If, indeed, one existed.

When Stone turned to check on him, Odhiambo raised a hand to shoo him forward.

"Go!" he panted. "I'll catch up."

Stone ignored Odhiambo's advice and stopped. Reaching an arm around the older man's shoulders, he ushered him ahead. Vedala had not slowed, trying to catch up with Tupa. Stone could glimpse her eyes occasionally as she glanced back over her shoulder to check on his progress.

Nearly two feet of frigid brown water had already risen around the team's legs, nearly up to their thighs. They stampeded forward in a chaos of panting and splashing and metallic echoes. Every scattered droplet was shadowed and lit by the flickering, dancing light of their headlamps.

A scream came from up ahead.

"Tupa!" shouted Stone, torn between helping the old man beside him and the young boy up ahead.

"Jahmays!" came an echoing reply from somewhere in the distance.

Struggling through the splashing turmoil with one arm around the sagging shoulders of Odhiambo, Stone thought to check the monitor hanging around his neck. From the canary camera feed, he saw why Tupa was shouting. The boy had reached the end of the tunnel.

On the far wall, a metal ladder rose into darkness.

Odhiambo had been right about the speed of the flood. The lower rungs were already submerged in sloshing river water. Tupa had climbed the ladder to get above it. And at the top, he'd found another hatchway.

Tupa punched and clawed at the closed portal, to no avail.

Still pulling Odhiambo along, Stone shouted to Vedala ahead in the darkness: "Nidhi! There's a locked hatchway ahead! Tupa can't get through!"

The nimble woman increased her speed, calling over her shoulder, "Got it!"

As the ice-cold water rose to his waist, Stone slogged forward, helping Odhiambo along as fast as he could. The old man was shaking violently now, wheezing with each breath. He had pushed his body well beyond its limits. And yet he held on to Stone with a grim strength, forging stiffly ahead.

It was quieter now. The roaring had hushed, along with the splashing.

Both men tossed away their backpacks. Now they were moving through what felt like cold lead, pushing forward on numb feet, their clothing soaked and heavy. The only warmth was their arms around each other, and even that heat was fading.

"Stone," said Odhiambo, between labored breaths. "It is true that men must capture fire. Otherwise we do not survive. But this fire . . . it does not belong to us."

Odhiambo gripped Stone by the forearm, looking into his eyes.

"This fire belongs to the *gods*."

"Come on, Harold," replied Stone, pulling his arm away. "We'll philosophize later. The end is just ahead."

"Too far, I'm afraid," panted Odhiambo, nodding at the dark water. It had risen above his waist. "For me, but not for you."

Stone kept moving.

At the other end of the tunnel, Vedala had reached the ladder. Tupa was clinging to the rungs. A pressurized hatch waited at the top. Vedala noticed a number pad on the wall—a lock that required a key code. Climbing up two rungs past the boy, Vedala reached overhead and punched in random numbers.

The door beeped a negation after four digits.

"Good," muttered Vedala.

At least the hatchway had power. And now she knew it was a four-digit code comprised of numbers only, leaving only ten thousand possible combinations.

Below her, Tupa had hooked an elbow through the ladder. His lips were bluish in the light of the canary, and he was trembling.

His wet hair was plastered across his forehead and the last of the fearsome red paint had washed off.

His face was that of a little boy, scared and cold.

Twisting her body to access her hip pack, Vedala began to desperately paw through its contents. The remaining canary drone was beeping a low battery alert, strafing the nearby walls with fading light, throwing lunatic shadows as it avoided the rising black surface of the water.

Vedala finally found her digital camera and turned it on.

Swiping through a grid of images, she paused when she saw the first corpse they had found inside the anomaly, then continued scrolling hastily through a series of pictures. Finally, she zoomed in to see what she had been looking for—barely visible on a twisted body that was half dissolved in the floor.

It was a work badge, along with an ID number.

. . . k B . . . kstein #23402582

Vedala tried to pull the camera closer to her face with shaking fingers. Fumbling, she dropped it. The camera fell into the water and sank. The light of it flickered to the bottom and disappeared.

"Damn it," she cried.

Meanwhile, Tupa was pulling himself up the rungs to avoid the rising water. The boy was pressing his rail-thin body against her hip. They were either going to die here together or be born again through the hatchway above.

Vedala closed her eyes to concentrate. She reached up and punched in the last four digits of the badge code she had seen, hoping that her memory wouldn't fail her in this panic. Saying a silent prayer to Krishna, she dug a finger into the enter key.

The hatchway beeped a chirpy positive, and an electromagnetic bolt thunked open as the hatchway unlocked.

"Yes!" shouted Vedala.

Her triumphant voice was swallowed in the shrinking space. Glancing down, she saw the water was nearly up to the tunnel ceiling. Stone and Odhiambo were still nowhere to be seen. Tupa was looking upward, regarding her with silent fear in the fading light of the canary. The boy's teeth were clenched together to keep them from chattering.

Vedala threw open the hatchway over her head and ushered Tupa past herself and into the unknown above.

Dropping back down into the water, Vedala peered into the narrow crevice of blackness between the tunnel ceiling and the water's surface. She could no longer touch the bottom without going under, but Stone and Odhiambo were taller. They could still make it, she hoped.

In the stark glare of her headlamp, the corridor had shrunk to just a foot-high trapezoid of space that stretched away into darkness. None of Odhiambo's greenish chemlights were visible. The last remaining canary had already followed Tupa up the shaft and out of the hatch.

"Stone! Odhiambo!" Vedala shouted.

The only response was the whoosh of a damp breeze as the rising water pushed the remaining air out of the tunnel. Staring into the dark with a lump growing in her throat, Vedala blinked with surprise—she thought she had seen a faint glimmer of light, perhaps a headlamp.

But she couldn't be sure.

Farther up the tunnel, Stone and Odhiambo were bobbing forward on their toes, the water up to their necks. They had heard Vedala's call but couldn't take a breath deep enough to shout a response. The two of them were trapped in a claustro-phobic sliver of air just below the ceiling.

They weren't going to reach the end in time.

"We have to swim for it," said Stone. "Okay?"

"See you on the other side, James," said Odhiambo. "It has been an honor."

Head tilted back, Stone took a last glance at Odhiambo. The old man offered him a sad smile. Stone understood this was goodbye. He gave Odhiambo's shoulder a squeeze under the water and took a final gasp of air, his lips pressed to the ceiling. With that, Stone dropped under the surface and began kicking his legs. For the first few seconds, he felt the presence of Odhiambo beside him.

Then that awareness was lost in the panicked throbbing of his lungs, the crushing cold and utter blackness of the water around him, and the occasional slippery metal wall of the tun-nel against his shoulder or hand. Stone groped ahead blindly until his eyesight erupted in pinpricks of light.

Finally, his fingers closed around a metal bar—a ladder.

With that, he felt a hand close around the collar of his shirt and haul him up. He saw Vedala through a blur of water as he emerged, gasping and coughing, into blessed air. Then he fell to the ground, wheezing and blind.

The Wildfire field team leader continued to watch the swirl-ing water rise, her lips pressed together in a white line. She re-fused to give up hope.

"Come on, Harold," she muttered. "Swim, old man."

Fifteen seconds passed. Thirty.

The water rose to the lip of the hatch. Vedala waited un-til the final seconds as it began to overflow. As Stone coughed violently, lying on his back nearby, she reluctantly pressed the hatch closed and locked it. Swallowing a shudder in her lungs,

Vedala felt the heat of tears mingling with river water on her cheeks.

Dr. Harold Odhiambo passed away at approximately UTC 23:10:07 on day four of the expedition. The cause of death was anoxic cerebral injury due to drowning. He was the third member of the Wildfire team to perish under violent circumstances.

Unfortunately, he would not be the last.

Activation

DETAILS OF THE REMAINING PORTION OF KLINE'S FINAL experiment could not be recovered. The cameras on board the Wildfire Mark IV laboratory module had been ruptured by the intentional breach, and the R3A4 ceased to transmit its video. Logs of Sophie Kline's brain-computer interface were available, but too complex to re-create the activity of the Robonaut.

Instead, the next few moments were captured in a shaky handheld video recorded by the two other astronauts on board the ISS. Held captive for hours, Yury Komarov and Jin Hamanaka had been forced to bear witness from their temporary exile within the Zvezda service module.

Jin Hamanaka was hovering before the largest Earth-facing window of the module, a sixteen-inch porthole in the main working compartment. She was a trim astronaut who wore her dark hair in a tight ponytail, known among her JAXA colleagues for having a famously loud laugh. She wasn't laughing now, as she continued to flash a scavenged laser pointer in an SOS signal. At this point, the beam was noticeably dimmer. And more disturbingly, Earth itself was also noticeably farther away. The ISS had continued to accelerate and gain altitude.

The cosmonaut Yury Komarov, stocky and bearded, was positioned across the module near a partially disassembled wall panel. He had spent the last few hours trying to piece together a functioning radio from parts scavenged from ancillary systems, without much success.

As a precautionary measure, both astronauts had changed into their pre-EVA uniforms. It had been decided between the two of them that nothing was off the table in terms of safety. A hasty retreat into the Soyuz spacecraft and an emergency descent were likely, though the risk of sabotage was high.

Surviving this situation was far from guaranteed.

This was the reason that Komarov had turned on his personal GoPro camera. He had set it to record and let it float ignored through the module. The hope was that, in the worst-case scenario, a record of what happened would at least exist.

Click-click-click. Click, click, click. Click-click-click.

"Call it a day with that, why don't you?" asked Komarov over his shoulder. He winced at each click of the laser pointer button. "They know we are in distress. Look how far from home we are."

Hamanaka seemed not to have heard him.

Thirty seconds passed, punctuated by the repetitive clicking of the laser. Komarov looked up in annoyance. He had just opened his mouth to speak again when an impact violently jarred the module. The entire ISS infrastructure shook along its main trusswork, the solar panels flapping like great wings.

Komarov's mouth snapped shut in alarm.

Grabbing the tiny camera, he pushed himself toward Hamanaka. "What was that? What is happening?"

Hamanaka turned to him from the window, her face pale and lips trembling. She placed a hand over her mouth.

"Jin?" asked Komarov.

Her eyes turned to the window. Moving her gently out of the way, Komarov pressed his face to the glass.

"What is that cloud?" he is heard asking. "Why is it . . . it's growing darker. It is—ah, *gospodi!*"

Komarov turned to Hamanaka, his jaw working. The Japanese astronaut had quickly composed herself. Her brow was furrowed as she began to work through the implications of what they'd seen.

"It is a debris plume," said Hamanaka in a quiet voice. "Forward deckside. The Wildfire module is breached."

Komarov found a different vantage point through a nearby nine-inch portal. He watched the rupture in disbelief.

"There is something else," added Hamanaka. "On the side of the module. Some kind of new growth is spreading. Dark purple."

The Russian astronaut shook his head. His toes were lightly curled under a bar on the forward wall of the module, not straining, placed perfectly to maintain position without expending too much energy. Komarov was on his third visit to the station, a veteran, and until Kline's coup he had been commander of this mission.

"This is too much!" he exclaimed, breath misting the inch-thick, quadruple-paned circle of glass. Komarov had forgotten to aim his camera outside, and it was now trained on the side of his concerned face. The following data was reconstructed through footage collected by an external camera mounted to the truss segment.

A glittering debris cloud still lingered near the Wildfire module. Komarov could be heard repeating the word *no*, again and again, as he watched the hole opening wider. The breach was ejecting a steady plume of wreckage. Reduced to shocked silence, Komarov watched as the dull golden face of the Robonaut R3A4 emerged from the jagged hole.

It looked around slowly, as if in wonder.

The Robonaut R3A4 was leaving the confines of the BSL-5 protected Wildfire module in which it had been built. The humanoid robot carefully squeezed its bulky body through the ragged breach and into the vacuum.

Turning, it reached back into the hole.

The robot teased out the ribbon filament. In the harshly lit images, the ribbon was tattooed with an alien sheen of hexagons, like dull dragon scales. The length of it spilled from the breach like a lolling tongue.

Even from a distance, and even at this early juncture, it was clear that the ribbon was still growing rapidly. The white-hot front edge glowed like smoldering coals. Anchored within the module, the ribbon now trailed after the ISS like a fishing line cast into a current.

Its surface was sparkling, presumably as it absorbed stray molecules of debris and atmosphere.

This frightening sight was visible to the ISS crew but too distant to be observed by the hundreds of astronomers watching from around Earth's equator, both professional and amateur. NASA itself had "requested a look" from several orbital security assets of the US military. They saw a metallic ribbon, razor-thin and glinting in the sunlight, stretching away from the space station toward Earth. After a day of constant acceleration, it was plain to see that the ISS had progressed to a distance of nearly twenty thousand miles—toward geosynchronous orbit.

What remained unseen was even more concerning.

Imagery recovered after the fact revealed a luminous patch of violet on the Wildfire module. The encrustation had been expanding steadily, not in hexagons but in pulsing, serpentine tendrils. Now the size of a dinner plate, it flashed green and then purple as it spread across the hull in a starburst pattern.

Distinct from AS-3, it was the birth of a new evolution.

DAY 5

ASCENT

> Of all the ways you can limit yourself, your own self-definition is the most powerful.
>
> —MICHAEL CRICHTON

A New Paradigm

ENVELOPED IN A SHROUD OF DARKNESS DEEP BENEATH the anomaly, the remaining survivors of the Wildfire field team would have found themselves exhausted and without hope. They had just witnessed the deaths of two team members. Their supplies had been lost, including Stone's backpack. The final canary lay still, out of batteries. Shivering and wet, Stone and Vedala sat back-to-back, leaning against each other with Tupa curled on Stone's lap. Their body heat had slowly begun to dry them.

In the dark unknown, the touch of other people must have been reassuring.

Based on postincident interviews, the team could discern only that the floor beneath them was flat and hard—made of the same material as the rest of the structure. Their fingers could make out the faint traces of hexagons etched in its surface. And though they couldn't see the space around them, it was full of echoes. An eerie whistling sound came and went, almost like melancholy singing, emanating from someplace high.

The team was too fatigued to explore further.

This expedition had gone utterly wrong. Death was now the most likely outcome. The only question was how quickly the end would come. Leaning his back against Vedala's, Stone kept one arm wrapped around the boy's bony shoulders. Despite their worries, they all three succumbed to a deep and dreamless sleep.

It was daylight that woke them.

"James," whispered Vedala. "Look."

Blinking his eyes open, Stone realized he could now see the room around him. A shaft of blazing morning light was falling from a hexagonal opening high in the ceiling. The light was faint by any normal standards, but having been in the dark for so long, Stone found it nearly unbearable to look at. Tupa had crawled off his lap and was yawning and staring at the room in surprise.

"A hole in the ceiling? How?" asked Stone. "We're under a lake!"

"I have no idea," said Vedala. "Look at this place, it's so strange."

Shading his eyes, Stone lowered his gaze. Like the rest of the anomaly, every surface he saw was made of the dark gray-green AS-3 substance. The room was six-sided, with a hexagonal pillar rising from the dead center, right through the open shaft in the ceiling. Some kind of platform, made of human materials like steel and glass, had been built around the central pillar.

"It's like a cathedral," mused Stone, standing and stretching. His low voice echoed into the heights, and indeed he felt a reverence that was almost religious. The feeling, however, was laced through with a sickening fear. "What could it be for?"

"This is what the dam is meant to power," said Vedala. "It's also the only man-made equipment I've seen besides the turbines."

Stone approached the steel platform. He felt a warm hand take his and looked down to see Tupa. The boy had been through a lot in the last two days, but right now his expression was one of curiosity. It was an impulse that James Stone shared. Together, they walked slowly toward the center of the room.

The man-made platform was floored with metal grating, and it wrapped completely around the central hexagonal pillar. Footings had been placed around the edges, perhaps to support an enclosure that hadn't been fully installed yet. The rest of the room was littered with wooden crates. Some containers had been opened and emptied, but others were still wrapped in heavy canvas, stained with mud and water. It looked as though they had been parachuted into the jungle, along with the rest of the equipment used in the power station.

"Whatever it is," said Stone, "it isn't completely finished."

Vedala was already standing on the platform. Her head tilted back in awe, she was looking up through the hole in the ceiling. For an instant, Stone found himself thinking she was beautiful there, captured in the dim light falling from above, her smiling face bright beneath a tangle of reddish-black hair.

"What do you see?" he asked, approaching.

"Something that's never existed on this planet before," she replied.

Joining her on the platform, Stone gazed upward.

The shaft and the central pillar housed within it proceeded upward for what looked like a mile. At the top, a pale blue dot of sky shone.

"How . . ." asked Stone, trailing off.

"It must have been growing, along with the rest of the anomaly," said Vedala.

A speck of cloud passed far overhead, and they felt the room cool slightly. Their hands found each other. Standing together, the two scientists silently contemplated the wonder of this structure.

"Jahmays," said Tupa.

The boy was sitting on a rolling office chair in front of an instrument panel. It had been fitted against the far wall like a long desk, with exterior conduit running to the central platform. Self-consciously letting their hands go, the scientists joined the boy.

"It's a control panel," said Vedala, running her fingers along the metal surface. She studied the simple scattering of buttons and levers for a long moment, frowning. Finally, she turned a key and flipped a switch.

The panel lit up and began to hum. Tupa shot back in his rolling chair, cackling with surprised laughter as it rolled smoothly over the floor.

"It's got power," said Vedala. "Maybe that platform spins like a centrifuge? Or the spire could be some kind of communications antenna?"

"No, that doesn't seem right," responded Stone. "Why would it need *so much* electricity? Why build a million-ton structure and leave it under a lake? None of this makes any damn sense. Maybe Odhiambo would know . . ."

Stone stopped, remembering the last squeeze of his arm, the feel of losing his friend in the cold black water.

"It's okay," said Vedala, putting a hand on his shoulder. "We're going to figure this out. Who better than us?"

Stone smiled ruefully. "A couple of overeducated scientists? You're right. Who better?"

"Jahmays," called Tupa.

The boy was using a metal bar to paddle himself across the

room in the desk chair. Rowing toward them, he looked utterly ridiculous. Nonetheless, he had a very serious look on his young face as he slid out of the chair and put down the improvised oar.

Tupa pointed at the spire, then looked back at them.

Using his hands, Tupa drew a vertical line in the air, then moved his hands up and down the imaginary length of it, clenching and unclenching his hands as if he were climbing a rope.

Stone stared, uncomprehending. He glanced over at the last canary drone where it lay like a dead bird, beyond repair. He shook his head.

"Rope?" ventured Vedala.

Tupa smiled, pointing again at the central pillar that rose through the shaft and then continuing his gesture.

"I don't understand. Why rope? What's it for?" asked Stone.

Tupa shook his head and spoke slowly in his own language, still moving his hands in a climbing motion.

"A rope," said Vedala, making a similar motion, "is to climb."

"Climb," said Stone, miming the gesture and then putting his hands up in a shrug. "To where, Tupa?"

Beaming, Tupa pointed straight up. He stood on his tiptoes, stretching his entire body taut and pointing as high as possible. Then he began to wiggle his fingers over his head, lowering them, watching the scientists with wide eyes.

The boy stopped, seeming very proud of himself.

"The stars," said Vedala, an astonished smile growing on her face. Vedala turned to Stone. "A rope to climb to the stars.

"The kid is right," she said. "That spire is a tether. It's meant to connect to a rope hanging down from the heavens.

"Kline has built a space elevator."

Finger of God

AMATEUR REPORTS OF A FIRE IN THE SKY WERE INI-
tially dismissed out of hand by major news agencies. Sporadic messages on social media were ignored. It was the
now-infamous "finger of God" video that finally caught the
world's attention.

The shaky seven minutes of footage was taken from a smart-
phone held in the sweaty palm of Sra. Rosa Maria Veloso. She
was on a flight from Buenos Aires to Tapatinga to visit her sister
and nephews. That morning, TAM Flight 401 happened to be
crossing over the Amazon jungle at an altitude of approximately
thirty-five thousand feet. The sunrise—Sra. Veloso's intended
subject—was spectacular, painting the endless canopy below in
daubs of fire and shadow.

But it was not the reason this video went viral.

"Dios mío" could be heard, repeated by different voices around
the plane.

Just above the starboard wing, a miles-long curve of red light was slowly rippling across the upper atmosphere. Shining like a rind of flame, the arc resembled a crack in the dome of the heavens. It flowed downward like a molten waterfall, tracing its way across the sky as it continued to grow.

The miraculous material had accumulated many tons of mass at this point. Only a few atoms thick and as wide as a sheet of paper, it had grown to an incredible length of over twenty thousand miles. Visible only as a streak of light, it hung like a mirage, seeming to waver without moving.

It was a sight that many on board Flight TAM 401 would go on to describe as "biblical."

And yet the ribbon had been built by a mortal woman.

Composed of AS-3, the tether was shimmering as it reproduced itself at an astonishing pace. On reviewing the "finger of God" footage, experts at the Oak Ridge National Laboratory theorized that the Andromeda Strain was fueling itself by consuming molecules of nitrogen and oxygen in the atmosphere.

Seismic data collected from Brazilian radar installations placed along the border of Peru were also able to confirm that the ribbon was producing a continuous sonic boom along an entire fifteen-mile segment—a crackling thunder that was faintly audible across much of the southern hemisphere.

The top of the ribbon descended from a gleaming dot, visible from the ground only through telescopes. It was the International Space Station, located just beyond geostationary orbit over this exact point on the equator, and supporting the mass of the ribbon with the centrifugal force of its five-hundred-ton bulk. Kline had long since activated the Progress cargo module thrusters, as well as those of the solar electric propulsion device, pushing the ISS through a classic Hohmann transfer orbit and into this special position.

At an altitude of exactly 22,236 miles, an object's orbital velocity and period reach a sweet spot that almost perfectly matches Earth's rotation. The tether's center of mass was located at this point, and it was growing both down and up at the same time. This resulted in a stable orbit that kept the ISS hovering directly above a single familiar point on the planet's surface—the anomaly.

Kline's plan was culminating in a literal blaze of glory.

The ribbon trailed over the Amazon, the sheer weight of it overcoming the effects of variable winds. In an incredible feat of coordination, its leading edge had reached a specific spot above the jungle: a black spire, rising a mile into the sky from a circular brown lake.

The "finger of God" video did not directly capture the moment of contact. But just above the jungle canopy, the gossamer ribbon was sweeping over the treetops toward the black spire. Made of the same material, they seemed to exhibit a magnetic attraction to one another. The ribbon was out of sight as it touched the spire, sending a burst of light and energy that flared in all spectrums.

The two fused on contact.

In the video, reflections of the energy burst could be seen racing across the sky like heat lightning. The long arc of the ribbon faded to a silver line of light that seemed to bisect the heavens. And then the glowing line simply winked out, leaving only pale pink morning sky.

Slowing down, the material had cooled and faded to a near-invisible black. It was now an incredible umbilical cord reaching from the International Space Station to its anchor point on the ground.

The AS-3 material held its structure, even under the titanic force of its own weight and the pull of a five-hundred-ton counterweight.

In the final frames of the video, Sra. Veloso had lost sight of the ribbon, but the camera remained trained on the wing where it was last seen. In the background, a hushed conversation could be heard, in a mix of Portuguese and Spanish.

Translated to English, the last words spoken in the video were not far from the truth. "My god," said Sra. Veloso. "The heavens are broken. It is the end of the world."

Realignment

FTER FIVE DAYS OF CONTINUOUS EMERGENCY OPERA-
tion, the team at Peterson AFB was growing haggard. The
normally pristine control room was littered with empty
paper coffee cups, mounds of research material, and hundreds
of scribbled notes. The console operators on the "orbit one"
shift, from 11:00 p.m. to 7:00 a.m., wore lines of exhaustion under their eyes that the promise of overtime pay could not erase.

At the command console, General Stern was coming to
terms with the nightmarish knowledge that one of his Wildfire team members had gone rogue on board the International
Space Station. Compounding that disturbing fact was his missing field team on the ground. Stern's assumption at this time
was that his career was over.

He had failed, utterly.

A preauthorized backup field team had been dispatched when
the primary team had missed rendezvous. But the beta group
was currently anchored at the quarantine line and moving at a

snail's pace. Meanwhile, foreign governments had been paying attention, and rumors of something in the Amazon had finally begun to leak. Countries around the globe were scrambling teams of commandos, scientists, and flocks of every variety of journalist—all of them pouring into Central American airports. The mayor of the British territory of Bermuda had even sent a group of alien linguists.

Stern sighed, feeling the sidelong glances coming from his room of worn-out analysts.

Thankfully, news of the ISS going dark had been explained as a training exercise. The constantly patrolling American fighter squads over the Amazon had dissuaded any unwelcome visitors from penetrating the jungle quarantine, including a limited Brazilian Air Force. And the unlucky passengers of TAM 401 were currently sequestered on the tarmac at a military airstrip in western Bolivia. Stern estimated the civilian eyewitnesses could be held for the rest of the day, but not longer.

Unfortunately, the "finger of God" video had already been shared online.

The only recourse had been to hand the video situation to military information support operations. Formerly known as psyops, these air force veterans had moved beyond dropping leaflets from transport aircraft years ago. Now, multiple task force groups were busy generating misleading articles in multiple languages, using AI to generate "deep-faked" versions of the original video and spreading a series of conspiracy theories about the true intentions and background of poor Mrs. Veloso on all types of social media.

Stern resisted the urge to sigh again.

The general understood keenly that it would only be a matter of time before an international incident was triggered. The likelihood of a military conflict had increased to over 90 percent, according to an event chain simulation report sitting on his desk. The highest likelihood was a territorial dispute between Brazil and the United States, fomented by the action of disguised Russian or Chinese actors infiltrating the area.

All attempts to contact the International Space Station had failed, and it was impossible to send more astronauts without cooperation from the station. The field team was also impossible to reach, and had been since their last desperate message was discovered. In short, Stern was out of ideas.

That was about to change, for better or worse.

Stern later described the moment the call came in from Sophie Kline as one of immense relief. "Everything up to then was standing on the gallows with a rope around my neck. I was glad when she called. It meant the lever had been pulled, and I could finally get it over with."

An encrypted message from the ISS came through at UTC 11:04:11. General Stern promptly took it offline and into his backroom office, away from the looming monitors and room-wide main speaker loop. Watching him through the window glass of his small office, analysts noted among themselves that Stern exhibited no reaction during the call besides weariness.

Stern began the call by waiting fifteen seconds as Kline determined how she was going to compose her message.

"Go ahead," he urged. "Out with it, Kline."

"General Stern. You can't be very happy with me right now."

The general snorted. It was quite an understatement.

"But I don't need you to be happy. I only need you to understand," she continued. "You and everyone else are afraid the Andromeda Strain will be weaponized. What I have to tell you is that its true purpose is not as a weapon. In actuality, the Andromeda Strain is an immensely powerful *tool*."

"Kline, listen to me," responded Stern. "You're brilliant, but

stand down. Give this up, whatever it is. You can't make unilateral decisions for an entire species—"

"Then who does? You? Another man in a uniform? Today, I
am making the decision. And I choose freedom."

"You've chosen treason," he pointed out, wearily.

The conversation had gone quickly off the rails. Stern's
hopes for a rational resolution were fading. He was beginning to
suspect mental illness was playing a large part in this situation,
based on Kline's grandiose language.

Which is why what happened next was so stunning.

It is well known among security specialists that the majority
of hacks are not carried off by reprogramming computers, but
by manipulating the human beings who control the computers.
In other words, hacks are usually carried off through convinc-
ing conversation, which is in itself a complex skill. Advanced
social engineering requires meticulous preparation and a deep
knowledge of your subject.

In this case, Kline demonstrated both.

In particular, the astronaut seemed to understand that Stern,
as the father of four children, had a practical and rather plodding
defensive mindset. The brunt of his focus had always been on
protecting his nation from the machinations of *other people*, above
all else.

"We must protect our country, General," she said. "At some
point in the past, our atmosphere was seeded with a hostile extraterrestrial microparticle. For over fifty years we've known
about it . . . and been able to do nothing. The struggle of trying to understand the Andromeda Strain became its own fight.
Questions that were once complicated and profound eventually
became very simple: *Which nation will figure out Andromeda first?*

"Well, I have your answer. We did. The United States of
America."

The general was listening now. He was listening very intently. "Get to the point," he urged.

"I made a key and I unlocked the door, General. The knowledge of how to reverse-engineer the Andromeda Strain is inside my head; the data is inside the Wildfire Mark IV laboratory module on board this station; and the experiment itself is unfolding on a grand scale over one of the most uninhabited areas on earth. The Amazon basin is a sacred ecological hub where any nation will think twice about deploying nuclear weapons, and it's the place where we can most efficiently reap the benefits of our discovery."

"This is manipulative, even for you, Doctor," said Stern, putting a hand to his forehead and wiping away cold sweat. "You've taken 'act first and ask forgiveness later' to an entirely new level."

"*We've got it.* Do you understand, General? This genie is out of its bottle, and it can't be put back. But the genie is *ours*."

"Okay, I'll bite. What have you made?"

"The Andromeda Strain tried to trap us on this planet. Instead, I hijacked its incredible physical properties to build a ladder to the heavens. General, we own a fully functional space elevator, with this space station acting as counterweight. The United States now has the capacity to put thousands of tons of material into orbit for next to nothing in cost. It's a new manifest destiny, and it will be our people who spread to every corner of this solar system."

"A space elevator," said Stern, sitting down.

"The instructions were just under the surface. Andromeda is a machine, and not a particularly complex one. Reverse engineering the strain is my gift to the human race, and in particular to the United States of America. General . . . I defy anyone to stop me—to stop us, I mean. We, as a species, we will *ascend*."

Stern was quiet for a long moment, one hand again pressed to his forehead. He had not missed the mania lurking under Kline's passionate voice. Her proclamations were pompous to the point of absurdity. He later reported his striking realization: "Having overcome the personal barrier of physical disability, Sophie Kline had focused all her genius on destroying what she saw as the civilizational barrier presented by the Andromeda Strain."

And the implications were staggering.

It was dawning on the general that if it really worked, Kline had created a machine more valuable than anything that had existed in the history of humanity. An asset of such incredible utility would instantly upset the balance of world power. To protect and exploit such an asset would require staggering economic incentives to the other superpowers; it would hinge on the naked threat of sheer military muscle; and it would call for a thousand ludicrous promises to everyone else.

These were all things the United States had in surplus.

Stern seriously considered the proposal for a moment.

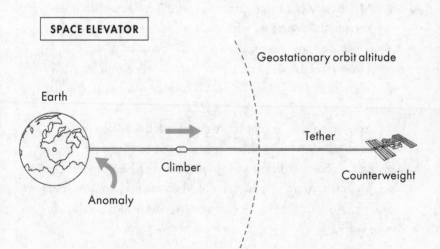

SPACE ELEVATOR

Kline had been correct in predicting that, as a father, Stern would be a devoted protector. However, she had not considered the fact that, like most parents of teenagers, the general had also become an expert at constantly and soberly considering insane demands—and then denying them.

"Kline, you've put our species at risk. Your elevator is built from something we don't fully understand. It could easily wipe out every living thing on this planet. Right now, I want you to focus on getting yourself and your crewmates safely back to Earth. I'd very much like for you to avoid the death penalty."

"I've been living under a death penalty since I was a child," replied Kline. "That threat doesn't scare me, so here's a threat of my own. I've already informed the Russian and Chinese governments of exactly what I just told you. They are mobilizing substantial military resources to determine who this machine truly belongs to. Make no mistake, they will claim it if they can. So you can either take my offer, or rest assured *they will*."

"So the patriotic talk was all posturing," said Stern. "You've got no real loyalty to anyone."

"My loyalty is to humanity, General," responded Kline. "I suggest you make history with me. Or get out of my way."

Ten seconds of tense silence passed.

"I understand," said Stern, finally. "But a decision like this is above even my pay grade, Kline. I'll contact you again in a little while."

"You have thirty minutes," responded Kline, disconnecting.

Stern put down the phone. He stepped to the glass door of his back office, letting it swing open into the command center. An entire room of analysts looked up at once, conversations ceasing. Nodding at the closest analyst, Stern spoke in a calm, even voice.

"I'll need another cup of coffee, please," he said, moving into the room slowly and rubbing his eyes. As he reached the command console, Stern added one more thing, as if he had just remembered.

"Oh, and I suppose I'll need to speak to the president. As soon as possible."

Z-Axis

THE THREE SURVIVORS SAT TOGETHER IN THE CENTRAL chamber, listening to the wind whistling high above. The sight of the bright shaft in the ceiling and the spire rising through it had grown no less bizarre and exhilarating.

And if nothing changed soon, Stone knew the view would be his last.

The chamber was beginning to feel more and more like a tomb. An exhaustive search had revealed only a single half-finished opening: another hexagonal tunnel opened at an angle through the wall, likely used to bring in the supplies. Only the size of a wooden crate, the passage was too narrow to imagine squeezing through. He supposed eventually they would have to try.

The prospect of survival was growing dim.

Stone and Vedala had at least worked out how the structure functioned. The concept of a space elevator wasn't novel, hav-

ing first been proposed in 1895 by the Russian scientist Konstantin Tsiolkovsky. Generations of physicists since then had
repeatedly determined that the idea was scientifically possible,
but not plausible—not without radically advanced construction
materials.

Most important, the tether needed to be incredibly strong
and flexible—each individual thread able to sustain at least
150 GPa (gigapascals) of force. Meanwhile, the counterweight
needed to have hundreds of tons of mass and be parked beyond
geostationary orbit. And finally, a mile-high compression tower
had to be built on Earth's equator.

These were all impossible requirements, or had been.

Armed with the reverse-engineered Andromeda Strain,
Kline had *grown* a ground-based compression tower and tethered it to the only large enough counterweight available to
humankind—the International Space Station. Currently, she
was accelerating just beyond geostationary orbit. The distance
of over twenty thousand miles had been formidable, but newly
launched communications satellites routinely reached it in a
matter of hours.

Kline had constructed a tower, a tether, and a counterweight—leaving one final component.

The platform in the center of the room was a robotic
climber—a cargo platform that could scale the miles-long tether.
It ascended using a simple device that looked like two rolling
pins. As the pins rotated they would compress the ribbon and
pull the platform up. The electric motors were powered through
the conductive material of the tether itself.

It was a simple and elegant design.

The dam had been constructed both to provide hydroelectric power for the climber and to create a lake on which the

ground station could eventually float—affording the entire base station some degree of movement. In this way, the tether could be maneuvered around potential debris or obstacles in orbit.

But understanding the function of the anomaly had done nothing to save them.

Tupa had remained occupied for a little while, leaping between wooden pallets loaded with crates and untying the ropes. Bright and curious, the boy had proven extremely capable. He had soon wrenched the lids off each crate. Inside, they found no food or water. It was all construction material and tools to be used to complete the elevator.

One particular crate had triggered a shout of surprise from the boy.

Rushing over, Stone looked inside, only to see his own incredulous face staring back from a gold-mirrored visor. It was a neatly packed space suit. Throwing the lid of the crate to the ground, Stone found there was a set of two—one large and one small. The pristine white and gold outfits were lying on a bed of packing peanuts, looking like overweight kids sinking into a ball pit.

"Those aren't regular issue," said Vedala. "Kline must have used her connections in NASA to get hold of prototypes. The Z series."

Vedala pointed to an insignia on the shoulder of one suit. In plain lettering, it read "Z-3." On examination, the suit was smaller and sleeker than the traditional bulky white "extra-vehicular mobility unit" suit known as an EMU. The upper torso was a hard shell, and the back opened up neatly for a person to slide quickly inside. Made of advanced composite materials and Kevlar-laced ortho fabric, the entire outfit was light enough for Stone to lift with one hand.

A variety of other NASA-issued accessories accompanied the

suits, including a collection of "tether hooks"—modified carabiners used to secure astronauts to the exterior of the International Space Station during EVAs.

The astronaut gear was almost comically out of place in the middle of the Amazon jungle, yet it made the purpose of this room feel all the more real.

Stone and Vedala sat together on the hard floor, out of ideas. Before them, they had laid out every item they had available. Their final manifest included a few MRE meals, a bladder of water from Vedala's kit, some battery packs, and the dead canary drone. Most frustrating, they still had the Iridium satellite phone. But the shaft had proven too narrow to allow a signal. Without a clear line of sight to the sky, the phone was a useless hunk of black plastic.

"If we drink river water from the hatch, I think we could survive in here for over a week. But it won't be pretty," said Vedala, with resignation. "It's likely that Stern or someone else will try to destroy this structure before then."

"How could he even begin to do that?" asked Stone.

"Probably not with a nuke. They learned their lesson on that. I'm guessing conventional explosives. Or napalm."

Stone took a deep breath, letting his eyes travel upward again. He imagined a waterfall of liquid fire coursing down the throat of the shaft. Then Stone's eyes stopped moving.

He blinked several times, putting a hand to his forehead.

"Wait," he said. "Wait. The tether conducts electricity to the climber, right?"

"Right."

"Then it will also conduct a radio signal. We're sitting here staring at the world's biggest—"

"Antenna!" exclaimed Vedala, climbing to her feet. "How could we have been so blind?"

• • •

THE SATELLITE RADIO had been weighing down Vedala from the beginning of the journey. Cradling it in her hands, she connected the external antenna mount to the filament wire. Stone had already wrapped the other end of the exposed wire around a contact point on the climber. Now, in theory, the phone should have finally become operational. Even so, she held her breath as she activated it.

The cool blue screen flickered, numbers swirling.

It was attempting to reach the Iridium satellite constellation located in polar orbit above the continent of South America.

The satphone numbers blinked and disappeared.

"Well, it was worth a try—"

Stone was interrupted as the satellite phone chirped a connection. A digital warble came from the handset, punctuated by a connection beep and a series of inscrutable clicks.

"This is Northcom, come in," said a familiar voice over the satphone speaker phone. "Wildfire? Is that you?"

Vedala lifted the satphone.

"General Stern, this is your field team. It's nice to hear your voice," she said.

"Copy that," said Stern. "The feeling is mutual. What's your status?"

"We entered the anomaly yesterday. The main structure is a hydroelectric dam. The secondary structure is a space elevator, but I'm sure you already know that. During the exploration we were joined by a boy from a local tribe, and . . ."

Here Vedala paused, swallowing.

"And myself, Dr. James Stone, and the boy are the only expedition members still alive. We are now located at the base of the elevator."

The line was silent for fifteen seconds as Stern absorbed the news.

"You're at the bottom of the spire?" asked Stern.

"That's right."

"I'm sorry to hear about the losses," Stern said, finally. "There've been major operational changes. Have you heard from Kline?"

"We believe Kline is responsible for our casualties. She reverse engineered the Andromeda Strain and built this anomaly. She's on a crusade."

"I agree with you, but this is out of my hands. Your orders are to stand down and wait for evacuation. That device is now the property of the United States government. It's valuable beyond belief."

Vedala held out the satphone, thunderstruck. Stone gently took it from her hand. A theory had been coalescing in his mind, and now it had finally taken shape.

He just needed the evidence to back it up.

"Sir?" said Stone. "I need to ask you an important question. Have you seen any indication of another mutation on board the ISS? Anything strange?"

There was no response for thirty seconds.

"What do you know, Stone?" came the reply.

"It's only an educated guess, sir. But if I'm correct . . . you should be seeing another type of mass conversion. This one is probably spreading through the Wildfire laboratory module. And it's outside Kline's control."

"How could you know—"

"Yes or no, General?" urged Stone.

"Yes," Stern said finally, in a weary voice. "It hasn't been easy with the ISS twenty-five thousand miles up. But our orbital imaging assets have revealed some kind of . . . infection, spreading across the outer surface of the Wildfire module. An hour ago, it began to consume a portion of the adjoining Leonardo module. It's made of a different material. Dark purplish strands, almost organic looking."

Stone handed the satphone back to Vedala.

"We've got to go up," he said.

"What the hell are you talking about?" she asked. "Even if it were possible, why?"

"My pet theory. The first Andromeda evolution was triggered on contact with life. The AS-2 variety adapted to eat polymer and escape the confines of Wildfire. Since then it's been floating in the upper atmosphere, waiting to evolve again. And now I believe Kline has triggered the next evolution."

"How?"

"The new infection . . . it's another response to stimulus."

"You mean Andromeda responded to being reverse engineered?"

"Exactly."

"And what makes you so damned certain?"

"Because it was *too easy*," said Stone. "Andromeda is the most advanced technology we've ever seen. It's ancient, sent here from the stars. Kline may be brilliant, but I don't believe the microparticle could have been reverse engineered unless it allowed itself to be."

"I see. And what do you think it's evolving into now?" asked Vedala.

"It doesn't matter, Nidhi. It's self-replicating, and we have no way to stop it. I don't know what it is, and I don't want to ever find out."

The light of the satellite phone pulsed as Stern spoke again, urgency in his voice. "Can you identify it? How we can stop it from spreading?"

"Whatever it's becoming," Stone said to Vedala, "it's already consuming the International Space Station. If we don't go up there and find a way to stop it, it will eventually climb down the tether and infect our planet."

Vedala considered before replying, "There's another solution. The military can sever the tether. Hit it with a missile."

Stone shook his head. "Even if we could convince them to try, it wouldn't work. The ISS is moving at well below escape velocity, and there are thousands of miles of tether above us. If we sever the line down here, the sheer weight of it will slowly drag the space station into destructive reentry."

"Which would spread burning Andromeda material across the planet," finished Vedala.

"Cut the tether and the infection falls. Wait, and the infection will come down the tether. Like I said, we have to go up. If Kline made this substance, maybe we can force her to unmake it," said Stone.

"Or I can do it for her, using her own tools," added Vedala.

Stone nodded. "There is no other choice."

Vedala considered this for a moment, chewing her lip. She took a deep breath and gazed up the spire. Then she spoke into the satphone.

"General," she said, "I need you to listen to me very carefully."

Mission Preparation

S TONE FELT ENERGIZED, BUT ALSO ODDLY DISSOCIATED. The shining steel climbing platform rested silently on its roost like science fiction come alive. The technical challenge was how to activate and operate this unprecedented machine.

The personal challenge was finding the guts to go up.

"This control panel works," called Vedala. "And I did my best to cut off Kline's remote access. But the ISS is barely beyond geostationary orbit, which only cancels out the weight of the tether. Think of it as a teeter-totter with the fulcrum at geostationary orbit. The weight of the tether is on one side, and the ISS on the other. The ISS is much heavier, so it can sit close to the fulcrum. But until it moves farther away, there just isn't much lift capacity. For now, this space elevator isn't fully operational."

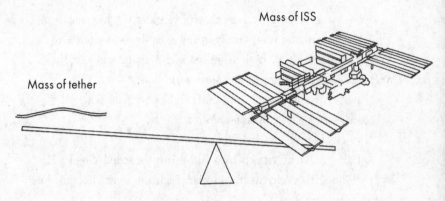

Mass of ISS

Mass of tether

Geostationary orbit

"Emphasis on fully, Doctor," said Stone. "The lift capacity is proportional to the distance of the counterweight beyond geostationary orbit. Stern said the ISS was at about twenty-five thousand miles up, so it can carry some weight."

"The question is, how much?"

"I don't know. But it will be a ratio of the lift weight versus the counterweight. If the ISS is five hundred tons, and essentially at geostationary . . . I'd give us one percent, or maybe half that. About two and a half tons."

Surveying the platform, Vedala shook her head.

"Then we're grounded," she said. "The motors alone weigh a ton. And with the metal platform, the rollers, and the infrastructure . . . it's not even close."

"You're right, it isn't," said Stone, leaning over and rummaging in a crate. "Not unless we make a few deletions."

"We'd have to strip it down to a metal catwalk and the motors," said Vedala, inspecting the climber. "That leaves no room for life support. The vacuum will kill us, if the cold doesn't get us first."

Stone was staring at her carefully, gauging her reaction. Under one arm, he was now cradling a bulbous white helmet. With his other hand, he had pulled a Z-3 space suit out by its neck, spilling packing peanuts across the floor.

"Luckily, we have two spacecraft right here," he said.

"No," said Vedala, eyeing the suit.

"I'm afraid yes," replied Stone.

A half grin had settled into his thinly bearded cheek. His eyes shone with excitement and fear. Leaning over the suit, he began brushing it off.

"We won't have much shielding," he added, "but we'll be warm and we'll be able to breathe. The faster we go, the better, since we'll have to travel right through the Van Allen radiation belt."

Vedala paused, watching him to see if he was serious. He was.

Slowly, she also began to smile. Stone's excitement was contagious. She stared at the helmet with an almost sickening thrill building in her stomach.

"This is doable, isn't it?" she asked.

"Technically, it's doable," he replied, looking up at her. "It's insane. But it's doable."

"Then that'll have to be enough," said Vedala, putting a hand on Stone's shoulder. "We're all that's left of Project Wildfire, Dr. Stone. Let's go finish our mission."

AS VEDALA ACTIVATED the control panel, Stone began to shove cargo boxes off the climbing platform, delighting Tupa, who nimbly avoided the wreckage as each wooden crate crashed to the ground. Once the platform was empty, Stone sparked a portable acetylene torch he had discovered in a tool crate, pulling a pair of welder's goggles over his eyes.

It was time to make those deletions.

With a few precise cuts, Stone began stripping off chunks of nonessential infrastructure. A haze of smoke from the torch soon rose, and a pile of twisted metal began to build around the robotic climber. Stone was careful to stay away from the motors and the central infrastructure, but everywhere else he was ruthlessly efficient.

As he worked, Stone was wondering what they would find at the other end of the tether. Hopefully, a makeshift docking bay. If that hadn't been constructed yet, they could end up climbing straight to their deaths—in a collision with the ISS that would likely kill them, Kline, and the rest of the astronauts on board. Or perhaps they'd suffocate in their suits while searching for a way in.

It was a risk they'd have to take.

The ribbon at the top of the spire continued to make its curious singing sound as they worked.

"What do you think that noise is?" asked Stone.

"Probably the sound of the tether growing," replied Vedala. "From a nanotech perspective, the closest analog is bird bones. It's amazing, really. Their bones naturally deposit calcium where the stress is greatest. Keeps them light and strong. My guess is the Andromeda material is doing the same thing. Self-replicating in places where the stress is tearing it. That would be the middle of the tether. As the particles self-replicate under extreme stress, the entire ribbon vibrates. Basically, we're hearing the longest guitar string ever made."

Ultimately, it was decided to remove even the heavy metal casings from the motors. The platform was reduced to the rolling-pin climbing mechanism, an exposed electrical motor, and a narrow skirt of metal grating.

By this time, Vedala had worked through the operation of

the control panel. It was exceedingly simple. A lever to activate power to the climber and then a launch button to send it up to the ISS. Vedala theorized that Kline had designed it to be basic enough for an amateur to operate.

And she planned to test that theory.

As Stone and Vedala prepped the pair of space suits, Tupa was growing more sullen. Sharing a look with Vedala, Stone paused and approached the boy. Kneeling before him, Stone shook his head sadly.

"I'm sorry, Tupa," he said, explaining the best he could. "No kid-size suits. No . . . armor."

Tupa turned away angrily.

Stone put a hand on the boy's shoulder, gesturing with his other hand. "I will come back, Tupa. I will find you. I promise."

Without the translating drone, Stone had to hope Tupa would understand the gist of his words. The boy refused to look at Stone, hair hanging in his eyes. He was scared and sad and trying not to show it.

Stone stood up.

"I promise," he repeated.

"But we do need your help," interjected Vedala, motioning to the control panel. She spoke slowly, using her hands. "Do you want to push buttons?"

Looking over at the glowing red buttons, Tupa couldn't help letting out a small smile of anticipation.

"Bottons?" he asked.

"Yes," said Vedala. "But very, very carefully."

Destination ISS

WITHIN HALF AN HOUR, THE TWO SCIENTISTS WERE
fully enclosed in the Z-3 space suits and perched on the
narrow platform that ringed the climber, their legs dangling over the edge, like two children on a swing set. Each was
secured to the metal grating with an improvised safety belt made
of rope and tether hooks, looped through the Z-3's hip anchor
points.

Stone could feel the electrical power coursing through the
bones of the platform, thrumming through his entire body. The
interior of the helmet was spacious, and the visor perfectly clear.
A radio was embedded in the metal collar ring where the helmet
connected to the suit, and he could speak easily with Vedala on
a local channel selected with a chest-mounted control knob.

At the moment he chose not to speak, as he was concentrating on not throwing up the MRE he had just eaten.

It occurred to Stone that this is what astronauts must experience as they waited for liftoff on the landing pad—ready to

risk life and limb to climb to the stars. He felt a squeeze on his hand and looked over to see Vedala smiling at him through her own fear. She had lifted the reflective visor layer on her helmet so that her face was visible, and to Stone she looked very small and very brave.

"You ready?" she asked, her voice transmitted over the local radio and into Stone's helmet.

"Not even close," said Stone, squeezing her hand back.

Vedala nodded, then turned to Tupa. She gave the boy a thumbs-up.

As they had practiced, the boy punched the correct button. The lever had already been set to the proper velocities—a slower speed for atmospheric travel, then accelerating to top speed once in the frictionless vacuum of space.

"We're doing this," said Vedala, as the platform shivered. "We're really doing this—"

The climber leaped upward.

The two rolling pins at the top rotated, accelerating rapidly, clamped tightly against opposite sides of the spire. Before he could catch his breath, Stone watched Tupa's small upturned face recede below.

And then the boy was gone.

With gut-wrenching speed, the platform launched straight up along the spine of the spire. They were accelerating at a breathtaking five Gs for approximately five seconds, the smooth interior walls of the shaft flying past like highway pavement only an arm's length away. When they reached the top of the spire, a startling jolt rocked the platform as the climbing mechanism clamped down on the thin ribbon tether.

The platform abruptly transitioned into bright daylight.

Vedala and Stone blinked in stunned disbelief as they emerged from the darkness of the shaft into a vivid blaze of green and blue light. For an eyeblink, the lake was stretching away around them, flat and mysterious. Then it was replaced by the emerald-green roof of the jungle beneath a dazzling, clear blue sky.

The wind hit them both like an invisible sledgehammer.

The Z-3 suits were not incredibly aerodynamic, and the platform had already accelerated to a brutal speed. The violent turbulence was shocking in both intensity and volume—pinning both scientists to their seats, mute and paralyzed.

Gloved fingers clinging to the metal grating, Stone held his breath and felt the quivering of the platform against his back and thighs. Fat drops of condensation streaked over the exterior of his helmet visor as the humid jungle air washed over him. He could feel hot sunlight raking over his chest, and also the veins of cool water flowing over his skin through the webbing of the suit's coolant system.

He looked upward through his visor.

The ribbon filament tether curved away to dizzying infinity. It was bent at a slight five-degree angle westward, Stone realized—a result of the Coriolis effect of the spinning planet. When he glanced back down, Stone could glimpse the channel of rushing river water as it poured through the front of the dam. The trail of water quickly faded into a brown scribble. In seconds, the massive bulk of the anomaly had been reduced to a black dot far below.

Moving at top atmospheric speed, the platform had reached five hundred miles per hour—a relative crawl compared to the eighteen thousand miles per hour required by rocket-based launches into space. The ascent was steady and smooth, ripping through the dense lower atmosphere and set to reach low Earth orbit in minutes.

Vedala and Stone were undertaking a challenge completely outside the human experience. The scientists were piloting a novel mode of transportation on its inaugural voyage, an achievement on par with the first powered flight. They were living proof that science fiction can mature into science—that simply dreaming a thing, no matter how incredible, is the first step to bringing it into reality.

"Good?" asked Vedala. Her voice echoed in Stone's helmet, barely audible over the rush of wind and the thrum of the electric motors. Stone managed a shaky thumbs-up.

The space suits' portable life support systems activated in response to the environment around them. Thermal regulation clicked on, warming the water-filled tubes laced around their bodies. Oxygen was already circulating in the suits, and excess carbon dioxide was being scrubbed, both providing air to breathe and pressurizing each suit against an already dwindling atmosphere. On the exterior of each helmet, low-energy LEDs illuminated.

Looking to Vedala as they tore through a cloud bank, all Stone could see were her helmet lights flickering through a rush of pale mist.

Emerging above the cloud, Stone saw that in just a few seconds they had transitioned from a skyscraper view of the anomaly to a view of the Amazon from the world's highest mountains, and finally to seeing Brazil from the height of an aircraft—albeit one dangling from a string.

The intimidating Amazon jungle sprawled beneath them, cloaked in low-hanging clouds bathed in golden daylight. From here, the jungle terrain that had felt endlessly claustrophobic an hour ago was no more. The once fearsome rain forest had revealed itself to be delicate and finite, already fading away.

One minute and twelve seconds into the journey, the climber had reached an altitude of nearly forty-two thousand feet above Earth. Through streaks of water and the tissue-paper shreds of clouds screaming past, the scientists could see only their own legs hanging over an unthinkable drop. They lingered in this gray purgatory for seconds that felt like hours.

And then the reverie exploded into chaos.

A dark shape loomed in the cloudy distance, moving fast. Stone shouted "What—" over the radio, before he was drowned out. A Russian-built Sukhoi Su-57 fighter jet had shrieked past the tether at a distance of only a hundred feet. It was followed almost instantly by an American F/A-18E Super Hornet in hot pursuit. The two supersonic jets, each moving at over a thousand miles an hour, produced a double shock wave that sent a vicious shudder through the ribbon.

For a split second, Stone caught the wink of sunlight off the helmet visor of a pilot who was looking up, watching them in awe.

Vedala and Stone clung to the ledge, straining the tether hooks they'd used to keep themselves attached to the platform. Engulfed in a blinding white haze, with fighter jets screaming past, the scientists could only huddle together.

Ten seconds later the platform emerged above the pillowy cloud.

In an iconic long-distance photo taken by a Brazilian reconnaissance plane at the extreme top of its operational ceiling, the two survivors were seen one last time during the ascent—two tiny specks of white-gold humanity, seated side by side as the glinting metallic platform rose, clinging to a line of silver light over a surreal landscape of billowing white clouds.

Below them, swarms of fighter jets still jockeyed with each other for position over the Amazon jungle—each pilot waiting on orders. A frenzy of diplomatic overtures and dire threats was unfolding between nations. By all indications, the world was on the brink of war. And rising above this churning scrum of billions of dollars of advanced military hardware was a delicate line of ribbon filament. This tether to the stars had emerged in five days to become the most valuable structure ever built— worth more than every grand pyramid, ornate medieval castle, or towering superskyscraper combined.

With no guidelines established and no forewarning, the international bureaucratic apparatus had been caught off guard. This leap into the future had happened too fast. Ultimately, no nation was prepared to pull the trigger.

Despite all the noise and confusion, nothing happened.

Lethally armed jets thundered to and fro in the cloudy depths below, the roar of their engines receding, their diminishing shock waves reverberating through the tether long after they were lost from view. The shadowed predators snapped at one another, bared their metal fangs, but they did not strike.

Now the danger lay above, not below.

An eerie silence had set in as the atmosphere diminished. There was no longer enough air to transmit sound. The roar of the wind faded. Now, Stone and Vedala could feel more than hear the muted singing of the ribbon and the whine of the electric motors pulling them inexorably higher.

The sight of the ground far below had transformed into an abstract painting, too far away and beautiful to inspire a true fear of falling.

Vedala finally lifted her gaze and gasped when she saw the horizon. It had been only about six minutes, hardly enough time to catch her breath from the stomach-wrenching initial acceleration. Earth's curvature was already visible in nebulous shades of blue and white. The climber had passed through the ozone layer and into the mesosphere, miles higher than any spy aircraft or weather balloon had ever traveled.

In this silence and stillness, it had just become clear that Stone and Vedala were leaving the planet and all its inhabitants behind.

Stone spoke. "It's amazing," he said. "Beyond beautiful."

The two remaining field team members stared in awe at the world as they had never seen it—an expanse of twinkling ocean, wrinkled mountains, and a horizon of brilliant light where all color and beauty faded into the cold emptiness of outer space.

"It is beautiful," responded Vedala. "Seven billion people living under that thin layer of atmosphere. It looks so delicate and fragile. Because it is."

A few more minutes passed in mutual appreciation before they turned back to the job at hand.

"Do you think Kline can be reasoned with?" asked Stone. "Can she undo what she's started?"

"No. What's done is done."

"How are we going to fix this?"

"We're not, James," replied Vedala. "The Andromeda Strain is like an oil spill. Once it's happened, we can't stop it. All we can do is try to contain it. We've got to try to keep it from spreading."

A sudden acceleration cut off the conversation.

Earth's atmosphere had been left behind, along with its gravitational pull. Blood was rushing to Stone's head, bloating his face and clogging his sinuses. Eyes fixed on the ribbon above, his mental orientation shifted. Now it seemed as if he were falling away from Earth.

In microgravity, he had lost all sense of up and down.

Without any atmosphere to provide drag, the climber soon reached a velocity of over 7,500 miles per hour. The only indication of the great speed was a trembling vibration.

No stars were visible at first; the reflection of the sun on the Pacific Ocean washed out the sight of them. But soon countless pinpricks of light emerged: the combined output of a trillion other solar systems, stained reddish near the horizon and then melting into the faint bluish patina of the Milky Way.

For just over three hours, the scientists bore silent witness to the raw beauty of the universe.

A lurching deceleration was the only indication the platform was approaching its destination. The trip had carried them to an elevation of over twenty-five thousand miles. The dark bulk of the International Space Station loomed above, and the planet had receded to a blue marble far below.

"Do you see it?" asked Stone.

Fear was audible in his voice, even over the static-filled radio feed.

The ISS was made up of a pieced-together collection of cylindrical modules, zigzag trusses, and acres of gracefully draped solar panels. It was the length of a football field, hovering dark and silent. Plumes of gas jetted from the Progress module as the ungainly structure continued to accelerate away from the planet.

"Roger that," replied Vedala. "We're not a moment too soon."

The underbelly of the Mark IV Wildfire laboratory module had been clawed completely open. The ribbon disappeared into the broken module, forming a kind of dock. In the sharp light of the vacuum, Vedala and Stone could see where a patch of the module had turned a slick, wet-looking purple. The material was roiling and moving, as if parasitic worms were exploring under its skin.

"The new evolution is here, and it's spreading."

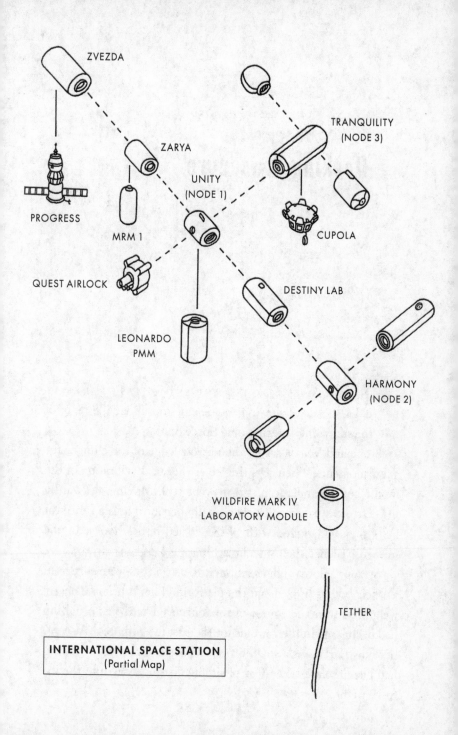

ZVEZDA

ZARYA

PROGRESS

MRM 1

UNITY
(NODE 1)

TRANQUILITY
(NODE 3)

CUPOLA

QUEST AIRLOCK

DESTINY LAB

LEONARDO
PMM

HARMONY
(NODE 2)

WILDFIRE MARK IV
LABORATORY MODULE

TETHER

INTERNATIONAL SPACE STATION
(Partial Map)

Docking Procedure

THE PLATFORM REACHED THE END OF ITS TETHER AT UTC 17:02:42, slowing to a silent stop under the belly of the sprawling International Space Station.

Stone and Vedala sat on the narrow ledge of the climber for a few moments. Their legs tingled as the steady vibration of the motor cut off and the platform went still. Moving awkwardly in their pressurized suits, they finally began to unsnap the seat belts they had rigged with NASA-issued tether hooks. In the immense silence their own breathing was loud in their ears.

Strapped down tight for hours, the scientists were surprised as their bodies lifted from the platform. They'd become nearly weightless over the course of the journey. The threat of falling had been large in their minds for the first few minutes of ascent, but now Earth was a small orb far below, and the fear of falling had been replaced by a fear of simply floating away into the infinite night.

"We need a way in," Vedala said over the radio. "Our oxygen and heat aren't going to last forever."

Feeling his boots pressing lightly into the platform's grating, Stone realized he wasn't completely weightless. The ISS was still ascending, generating a faint acceleration that simulated gravity. Falling off the platform was truly a risk. One slip, and they'd plummet into infinity—a slow death by asphyxiation.

Stone looked over to see Vedala inspecting their makeshift dock. The exterior illumination around her visor glimmered, wreathing her face in a ghostly light. Her eyes had settled on the remains of the Wildfire Mark IV laboratory module directly above them.

"The Robonaut is missing," noted Stone.

"The lab module is completely infected," said Vedala, over the radio. "It's probably been absorbed into the mass. We certainly can't go in that way."

"Then how do we get inside?" asked Stone.

"I don't know," said Vedala. "But I think I know someone who does."

Vedala reached out and tapped Stone on his chest with her gloved fingers. Confused, he peered down at her hand. A brilliant dot of green laser light was dancing over her padded glove.

Thirty yards away, the face of Jin Hamanaka was barely visible through a small hatch window of the Russian MRM1 module, attached to the Zarya. Despite everything, she was smiling with a mixture of joy and relief. Seeing the state of the climber, she had realized immediately the newcomers couldn't be Kline's allies. Aiming carefully, she pointed the green dot upward, to a gleaming silver cylinder.

The Quest airlock module.

Mated with the starboard port of the Unity node, the airlock was above them, oriented parallel to the planet's surface. The stubby cylinder was flared at the end, where an airlock hatch was placed for American astronauts to enter and exit during routine EVAs.

"Bingo," said Vedala, giving a thumbs-up to Hamanaka.

"Right behind you," said Stone, as Vedala began to pull herself up the climbing platform. Grip by grip, the two made their laborious way along the side of the climber, taking care not to touch the ribbon itself. At the top of it, they stopped to rest beside the rollers. The rest of the way up was blocked by the infected Wildfire module.

But the Leonardo module was a small leap away, attached vertically to the Unity node near the middle of the station. It was a jump they'd have to make to avoid touching the infected remains of the Wildfire Mark IV laboratory module above.

"Slow," warned Stone. "The ISS is accelerating. If we fall, it's a hell of a long way down."

Vedala nodded. "Be sure to tether as soon as you make the jump. Think of this as mountain climbing. No mistakes."

Neither scientist had experience moving in low gravity, but neither had any choice. Fortunately, the extreme safety-mindedness of NASA meant that the exterior of the station was littered with convenient grab bars. And the tether hooks were expressly designed to clip on to these safe harbors during routine EVAs.

"Here we go," Vedala said, tensing to leap.

With a sharp hop, she launched herself across the flat blackness of space. The surface of the Wildfire module passed by just above her head. Turning without much control, she flailed an arm, her glove swinging dangerously close to the infected surface.

"Watch out!" cried Stone into his helmet radio.

Falling in a short arc, Vedala collided awkwardly with the

silver Leonardo module. Scrabbling with both hands, she slid helplessly down the featureless metal exterior. Finally, she managed to break her fall against an external antenna array. She took a few ragged breaths before turning and waving Stone onward.

"Piece of cake," she said.

Stone crept to the edge of the climber, keeping his arms away from the Wildfire module overhead. He tried not to look at the purple-tinged stripes of material. As he leaped, he imagined he could almost feel the infection radiating off its contaminated surface.

Landing hard just above Vedala, Stone clung to the module with his fingertips. Reaching up, he took hold of a golden EVA handrail mounted securely to the white fabric-covered main truss. The aluminum alloy infrastructure was designed as a highway, and it was studded with plenty of dog-bone handholds, named for their distinct shape. Hanging on tightly, Stone and Vedala stopped to breathe for a moment.

The moment wouldn't last long.

Vedala was the first to spot the white flash of the Canadarm2 robotic arm, just over Stone's shoulder, as it accelerated toward them like a felled tree. Curled against the trusswork of the ISS, the fifty-foot-long, seven-jointed arm had silently begun to move. Without a word, Vedala yanked Stone down with all her might. As she did, the metal arm smashed into the strutwork where he had been resting. A wrenching scream echoed throughout the ISS as the powerful arm dragged across the trusswork, leaving crumpled metal in its wake.

"It's Kline," gasped Vedala. "She's controlling it."

The long clumsy arm dragged itself back up, spraying bits of metal and flakes of paint. It was in a default configuration, with only a flat plate of metal attached to the end. Recovered from the strike, the arm reoriented toward Vedala.

But Stone was falling toward Earth.

Flailing, he dragged his gloved fingertips down the side of the Leonardo module. The antenna array that had caught Vedala crumpled under his feet. Rolling down the side of the module, Stone lashed out with one hand and caught hold of the remains of the antenna. It came away in his grasp, broken. Then he jerked to a stop. A single thin wire still tethered the dislodged antenna to the module, like a tenuously clinging root. Panting, his feet dangling over the glowing planet below, Stone looked up toward Vedala.

"Nidhi," he managed to grunt. "Move!"

Vedala threw herself to the side as the multijointed robotic arm came streaking toward her. Having already taken care of Stone, it was now trying to sweep Vedala off the strutwork.

As she backpedaled, the robotic arm caught Vedala across the chest.

The collision bruised Vedala's rib cage, but she managed to grab hold, clinging to the robotic arm as it dragged her off the structure.

Through a spray of spinning bits of wreckage, Stone could see as Vedala was shaken like a rag doll. He pulled himself up inch by inch, careful not to snap the narrow wire. Finally, he clasped fingers around the bottom lip of the Leonardo module. With a decent grip, he could begin climbing. The entire space station shook as the long white arm bucked back and forth, trying to fling away Vedala's small form.

"Hold tight, Nidhi. I'm coming to get you."

Reaching the top of the module, Stone shoved one arm through dented trusswork. He paused, racking his mind for an idea. Blue-white light from his helmet LED strafed the metal around him, revealing nothing useful. As a roboticist, he had realized that Sophie Kline had total mastery over the largely automated ISS. She would be capable of assuming control over almost any subsystem.

But Stone hadn't counted on the robot arm—the possibility had simply never entered his head. The hulking boom was designed to help dock multiton cargo modules as they arrived. Kline would have stripped the motor limit safeguards from it, of course. Controlling such a huge device was normally a slow process, requiring delicate control and a great vantage point—

The robot arm had no touch sensors of its own, Stone realized.

The machine could only be controlled by sight, which required cameras. But he saw no cameras mounted to the scarred length of the robotic arm.

"James!" shouted Vedala, desperation in her voice.

The arm had stopped shaking. It was now accelerating with purpose toward the infected mass of the Wildfire module. If she couldn't shake Vedala off, Kline was planning to crush her, pressing her body into the pulsing infection that streaked across the module's surface.

With a quick glance around, Stone found what he was looking for.

Launching himself wildly along the strutwork, Stone soared toward the golden squares of a solar panel. He grabbed awkwardly with heavily gloved hands. The flexible black and golden material bent and then crumpled, bits of black glass spraying away in slow motion. Ignoring the mess, Stone held on until his momentum was absorbed.

Then Stone climbed the trusswork, not stopping until he could see his own reflection in the black eye of a large pan-tilt camera.

Below him, Vedala was desperately trying to escape from the arm. The boom continued to swing across empty space, leaving a choice between suffocating in free fall or being eaten alive by the microparticle.

Reaching with his whole body, Stone managed to grasp the head of the camera and rip it off its mooring.

The last sight Kline registered through her camera feed was Stone's mirrored visor. Then the video failed as he bashed the camera against the side of the ISS.

Stone couldn't find any more cameras mounted within view. Below him, he saw the robot arm slowing down, confused, with Vedala still hanging on.

"I think she's blind," Stone reported over the radio. "You have to let go."

"Roger that."

Silhouetted against the face of the planet, Vedala's small figure released the robot arm. Stone held his breath as her body spun slowly in space. She had executed the dismount perfectly, albeit slowly, soaring on a lazy trajectory toward the dark cylinder of the Progress cargo module. The narrow Russian module was mounted vertically at the rear of the station, sprouting two solar panels like dragonfly wings. Underneath, its engine was still spewing gas as it pushed the ISS upward.

Vedala collided with the Progress, scrabbling her fingers against the matte black fabric surface. Blind, the arm had continued on its collision course with the Wildfire module. It silently plowed into the infected surface, sending a disturbing tremor through the entire ISS. Vedala cried out, grabbing at the solar panel mounts. Dangling from the Progress module with one arm looped over a panel, she kicked her legs as bursts of jet propulsion erupted from the module's engines, inches from her boots.

"Climb, Nidhi. Meet me at the airlock," urged Stone. "You can do it."

Lunging, Vedala got a hand around a window porthole and was able to pull her entire body up in the low gravity. Moving slowly and warily, she managed to ascend the module.

The robotic arm continued to sweep back and forth in a blind rage. Kline was now groping for them in the dark.

But Vedala's size worked to her advantage. Staying low, she crawled along the strutwork until she reached Stone at the airlock—out of reach of the sightless, groping appendage below.

As she arrived, Stone reached out a gloved hand and pulled Vedala up. He leaned forward until their visors were touching. From this distance, they could see each other's faces clearly. Both were flustered, breathing hard, their cheeks flushed with extreme overexertion.

"Great work, Dr. Vedala," said Stone.

"Thank you, Dr. Stone," she replied. "It's a shame we haven't even gotten started yet."

Vedala turned to the airlock, examining the controls before activating the depress pump. Stone continued to scan the area for any new danger. He had learned the hard way that Kline was both devious and intelligent. Working together, the two were finally able to push the hatch open to reveal the cramped crew airlock inside.

In their elation, neither scientist noticed that the airlock was empty of the myriad items usually stored inside while it was not needed. If they had, they would have realized that it had been used by someone, and recently.

Stone's Theory

Y ANKING OPEN THE EQUIPMENT AIRLOCK DOOR AF-
ter repressurizing, the scientists emerged into the Unity
node—an American module serving as a kind of central
hallway. The open space was dim and hazy, a few emergency
lights blinking silently.

The layout of the ISS had been greatly simplified by Kline's
takeover.

An aft hatchway leading back to the Zvezda and the rest
of the Russian portion of the station was locked shut with an
improvised metal bar. Through a blur of smoke, they could
see scarred metal and melted plastic. Below them, the deckside
hatchway to the Leonardo module was also closed tightly—but
not damaged.

"There's been a fire," said Stone.

"And it's been put out," said Vedala. "Or there'd be nothing
left."

Their helmet-mounted lights strafed the darkness as the two floated to the center of the Unity node. Across from them to the port side, the Tranquility node was deserted, its cupola windows shuttered. Only one other passage remained, leading toward the front of the station—to the American-built Destiny laboratory and the modules beyond it.

Stone tapped his helmet.

"Let's stay suited up," he said. "Just to be safe."

Vedala nodded, wrapping her fingers around a blue handrail above the hatchway. For a moment, she simply rested there.

The Destiny lab, primarily occupied by American and Canadian astronauts, was cluttered with dozens of inscrutable experiments. They had all been abandoned, the detritus floating eerily in the darkness. Exploring the gloomy space, they peeked beyond into the Harmony node but found nothing in it or the adjoining Japanese and European science labs.

None of the computers or radio systems were functioning.

Returning silently to the Unity node, Stone and Vedala shared a glance. Kline had to be located below them, in the Leonardo module. The module was located directly adjacent to the Wildfire Mark IV laboratory. Having seen the Leonardo module from the outside, they knew it was most at risk of infection.

It was not clear whether Kline was aware of this fact or not.

Stone and Vedala floated together before the round hatchway leading "down" into the Leonardo module. The dark glass of the hatch's observation portal revealed nothing about the module beyond.

It was time to face Sophie Kline.

Using the chest-mounted display and control unit, Vedala and Stone each set their suit radios from local to stationwide. They listened for a moment, hearing nothing.

"Dr. Kline?" radioed Vedala. "Are you there?"

Stone noticed the soap-bubble lens of a camera placed above the hatchway. He studied it for a long moment, considering. Finally, he nodded to Vedala and took hold of the lever to open the hatch. It would open quickly, as it was impossible for Kline to lock the door from the inside without damaging it and trapping herself.

As he laid his gloved hands on the lock bar, Stone heard a burst of static from the speaker inside his helmet. He paused, glancing at Vedala.

From the look on her face he knew she had heard it, too.

"Dr. Kline?" asked Vedala over the radio. "Can you hear me? This is Nidhi Vedala, head of the Wildfire field team and your direct superior. I am ordering you to stand down."

The helmet radio pulsed with a gentle ripple of laughter.

In the background of the transmission, Stone caught a strange rustling sound. It evoked a mental image of desert sand, caught in the wind, rustling over endless dunes. He shuddered reflexively.

A voice began to speak—the mildly slurred words of Dr. Sophie Kline, oddly intimate coming from inside the suit helmets.

"Dr. Vedala and Dr. Stone," said Kline. "Congratulations. You've just made history. The first human beings to ride a space elevator. The first of many."

"Enough, Sophie. Can you stop this?" asked Vedala. "Or is the chain reaction spreading out of your hands now?"

"The question is not *can* I stop this, but do I want to? And the answer is no."

"Dr. Kline," said Stone. "I understand your theory about the Andromeda Strain. You're very smart, but you're dead wrong."

For a moment, there was no response.

"Let me tell you a story, Jamie," replied Kline. "Once upon a time, there was a town called Piedmont. It was a small town, and the people there were good. They cared for each other. They raised families. But one day, a *thing* fell from the stars. On that day the good people of Piedmont died, their blood solidified in their veins. Or they killed themselves and each other. Drowned themselves. Shot themselves. Slit their own wrists. Did you know, Jamie, that some of those poor people even abandoned their own babies in their cribs to die?"

Stone's face had gone white behind his visor, eyes fixed on the hatchway. A muscle in his jaw was twitching as he gritted his teeth.

"Nobody has called me Jamie since I was a little kid," he said.

"I've done my research on you," replied Kline. "And I know . . . this *thing* that fell to Earth was a sophisticated tool, designed to evolve into many forms—all with a singular purpose: to find life and to keep it on the planetary surface, forever. The Andromeda Strain has lingered in our atmosphere for eons. It's been found everywhere in our solar system, where it waits for life to develop. When we brought it down to Earth, it killed every living thing it touched. The blood of those people triggered the Andromeda Strain to evolve. It knows we're here, and it's trying to trap us.

"It took fifty years, but one person learned to master the alien tools. Me."

Stone's eyes were welling with tears. With effort, he swallowed and regained his composure. Then he began to speak quickly and with purpose.

"Sophie, I am sorry, but you're mistaken. The plastic-eating strain of Andromeda wasn't a barrier to trap us. It was a test for intelligence. The goal of the Andromeda Strain isn't just to detect life, but to detect *intelligent life*. You thought you were reverse engineering it, but you were taking a test. You passed, and now you've triggered something else . . . a new evolution."

A sound like a sob came through the speaker, cut off quickly. Stone continued.

"Vedala's inhibitor made me think of it. The Andromeda strains ignore each other because they're all stepping stones on a path that's leading somewhere. I don't know why Andromeda is searching for intelligent life, or what it's becoming now. But if we don't stop this chain reaction, we are *going to find out*."

Stone made his final plea: "I think you know . . . this thing has hurt us both. We don't have to forgive, but we have to look at it objectively. Help us, Sophie," he said. "We can't stop what's happened. But maybe we can isolate it."

The speaker hissed in silence for thirty seconds. To her credit, it appeared that Kline was truly considering Stone's words. Finally, her soft voice emerged from the sea of random static.

"This is your final warning," she said. "Do not open that door. It would be very dangerous for you . . . and for the other astronauts on board this station."

Stone lowered his head in defeat. Turning to Vedala, he nodded. Lips pressed tight with determination, Vedala decided to put the mission back on course.

"Dr. Kline, I'm afraid we cannot trust your judgment anymore," said Vedala. "Consider yourself under arrest. We're coming in now."

Reunited

WITH A SHARP YANK, STONE CRACKED OPEN THE hatchway along its lock bar. Planting his feet on the wall, he slid the hatch up and out of the way. Swirling tendrils of smoke began to pour out of the darkness.

Clad in ponderous space suits, Stone and Vedala pulled their bodies through the short cylindrical passageway. Their external LEDs sent fingers of light ahead, illuminating very little.

The Leonardo module contained eleven hundred cubic feet of volume in a cylindrical frame that was the exact size of the *Discovery* shuttle payload bay in which it had been delivered. The interior walls were flat, made of express racks with rounded backs that fit into the cylindrical module like four pieces of pie. Pale white, the racks were mostly hard metal, bristling with white packing cubes and lined with blue grip bars. On the far wall, a hanging computer monitor glowed. There were no windows.

It had been a utilitarian, almost boring storage module—repurposed as a remote workstation by Kline.

But today, something had gone very wrong. The interior space was engulfed in ominous, swirling sheets of thin smoke. The surfaces of the express racks were stained with soot.

Stone noticed that the far end of the module was darker than the rest—the wall seemed to be made of violet glass. The contamination had clearly spread from the Wildfire Mark IV laboratory module to the Leonardo module, directly through the vacuum. It had come through the hull and into the interior express racks.

Luckily, the infection had begun from the far end of the module. It hadn't reached up to the hatchway and the rest of the ISS. Not yet.

But where was Sophie Kline?

Stone felt fingers clamp tightly over his bicep. Vedala was beside him, fixed in a kind of primal fear. Following her gaze, Stone caught a glimpse of the end of the world.

"Oh, Sophie," he said. "Oh no."

Something that looked like Sophie Kline was stretched out against the far wall of the module. She lay on her back wearing a microphone headset, eyes closed, blond hair splayed behind her. Her arms were floating in the posture of crucifixion. Her legs were not visible—they had been partially consumed, disappearing into throbbing folds of infected metal.

She wasn't moving.

Stone stared at the infected body, limbs frozen, fixated.

"Dr. Stone, I need you to listen to me," said Vedala, her voice hoarse with barely contained panic. "Dr. Kline is infected with the evolved Andromeda Strain. She needs immediate medical attention. I'm going to need your help."

When Stone did not react to her words, Vedala grabbed him by the shoulders and turned him around forcibly. Clinking her helmet into his, forehead to forehead, she made eye contact.

"Dr. Stone. I need your help. Now," she repeated.

"Yeah, yes," replied Stone, emerging from his reverie. "Of course. But what can we do?"

Vedala turned to look closer at Kline's body, thinking practically.

"Our only choice is to amputate her legs. If we can move her away from the infection site, maybe we can buy some time for an interrogation."

Kline's eyes opened.

Stone bit down on a shout of alarm. Somehow, Kline was smiling at them through what must have been excruciating pain, her cheeks smudged with soot, marine-blue eyes clear and piercing and alert.

"Very practical thinking," said Kline. "But it's no use. I don't have any revelations for you."

"Sophie," said Stone. "You're dying."

In the shifting smoke, Stone saw tears shining on Kline's cheeks. He could make out bits of black soot speckled across her lips and tongue.

"We're all dying, Jamie. Some of us faster than others."

"Whatever it is you've triggered, it's spreading with no way to stop it," replied Stone. "If it descends down the ribbon and reaches the planet's surface, everyone and everything will die."

Now Kline was staring intently at Stone.

"Maybe that will happen. Maybe not. We've both known death, haven't we, Jamie? You and I see the truth of the situation. And the truth is that sending humanity to the stars is *worth the risk*."

"Sophie, please," said Stone.

"Not only am I free now," she said, face flushed with excite-ment, "but we as a species have been set free."

Only now did Stone fully understand that it was far too late to save Kline. Most likely it would never have been possible. All the momentum of her life had been carrying her forward on this path, to these final moments.

"This," continued Kline. "This—"

Kline winced as she turned her head. Moist-looking tendrils of Andromeda were spreading radially from her trapped body, like veins under the surface of the module's skin. "This is a last triumph over this so-called body of mine. This body that never cooperated, that always tried to fail on me. Now it's going to become part of what *I* created."

Sophie was shivering, her voice ragged.

"I risked everything—*gave* everything—to destroy the bar-riers that face our species. I never let this broken body beat me, and I won't let you either."

Holding to a wall grip with one hand, Vedala spoke steadily and calmly. "Last time. Can you stop it?" she asked, softly.

Kline blinked. Tears separated from her eyes and floated into the darkness like small, delicate planets. She reached up with a gloved hand and pulled the head-mounted display over her eyes.

As the visor came down, her eyes rolled backward and her lips and fingertips began to twitch.

"She's passed out," said Vedala, turning. "We need more in-formation. We're going to have to wake her up."

"No," replied Stone, a hand latched over Vedala's shoulder. "No, I don't think so."

Stone was frantically scanning the walls of the module. He could find no danger. Even so, he began trying to pull Vedala up toward the open hatchway and back to the Unity node. Not understanding, Vedala pushed him away.

"I think she may be seizing," said Vedala. "Look how the status light on her neural implant is blinking—"

"Something's wrong," Stone said, turning away. "We've got to get—"

Loud as a gunshot, a mangled metal fist punched into the express rack beside Stone's head. The blow shattered a set of gauges and sprayed cubes of safety glass across the module. By reflex, Stone shoved off the wall and floated haphazardly toward the other side of the module.

The smooth metal face of the Robonaut R3A4 met his gaze.

Kline had activated the machine and piloted it through the hatchway with predatory stealth. It must have been on board all along, hiding. Stone watched as it leaped gracefully between blue handrails, gripping them with insectile, multijointed legs. Unlike the astronauts, this machine was designed expressly for locomotion in a microgravity environment—it was perfectly at home here.

The R3A4 advanced mutely and without hesitation.

"Stone!" shouted Vedala.

The robot launched itself at the off-balance man, one mutilated hand snarled with bits of jagged metal and the other with fingers outstretched. Each digit of the robot's hand was designed to apply five pounds of force—altogether it could apply over a hundred Newtons, twice the strongest grip of an adult male, and more than enough to crush human bone.

Flailing in microgravity, Stone almost managed to dodge the attack.

The robot caught hold of Stone's boot with its good hand. Stone shouted in pain as the machine crushed his heel in its grip. Kicking hard, he managed to escape with his boot intact and undamaged, crashing against the opposite wall. Farther down into the module, the walls were pulsing with dark wrinkles of infection. Above him, the face of the robot was silhouetted against dull red emergency lights. Stone was cornered.

Until Dr. Vedala grabbed the Robonaut from behind.

Although the R3A4 roughly occupied a human form factor, its center of gravity was wildly different. With vision equipment located in its relatively light head, processors in its stomach, and a slim backpack full of heavy batteries, the robot occupied an unevenly distributed mass of 330 pounds.

This unexpected difference surprised Vedala as she tried to take hold of the robot's shoulders. Designed to efficiently maneuver heavy cargo, and under the control of an experienced pilot, the R3A4 had no trouble flipping the scientist and launching her violently across the module.

Vedala's helmet smacked into the open metal hatchway. Her body instantly went limp, floating halfway into the Unity node.

Moving with a freakish, arachnid-like dexterity, the R3A4 began climbing the wall toward Vedala's body. Stone noticed how the machine continuously kept an eye on the motionless form of its controller. Kline still lay partially embedded in the depths of the module, her fingertips twitching in their instrumented gloves.

Stone pushed himself up toward Vedala. As he floated closer, he scanned the smoky room for a weapon.

His gaze settled on a long metal tube with bright orange fabric wrapped around its base: a fire extinguisher. Grasping it in both hands, he planted a foot against the wall and swung it as hard as he could into the side of the Robonaut's head.

It hit with a satisfying crunch.

There was no pause, no need to shake off the blow: the machine was made of rigid carbon fiber, stainless steel, and aluminum alloy. The impact had slightly damaged the neck struts, permanently cocking the head to one side. But it had caused no serious damage.

The robot turned to face Stone.

Sophie Kline had felt the attack as a jarring of the cameras and a newly limited range of motion in her neck. She easily directed the R3A4 to snatch the extinguisher from Stone. He threw himself backward, turning away just as Kline's robotic puppet pitched the extinguisher back at him like a fastball.

The metal cylinder glanced against the bubble visor of his helmet, shattering the faceplate. A shard sliced open his forehead. The dented fire extinguisher pinwheeled away.

Blinking away tears, Stone choked and gagged on the smoke now flooding into his open helmet.

Blood was sprouting in pendulous beads across the gash in his forehead. As he swiveled his head to get his bearings, the droplets detached and hovered before him like a handful of dark rubies.

On the far end of the module, more tendrils of the Andromeda infection were surrounding Kline. The jelly-like surface seemed molten now, quivering, giving Stone the gruesome feeling of being inside some kind of alien organ.

A few yards away, Vedala had just come to.

"Stone?" she said, her voice still projected from his collar microphone. "Where . . . what's happening?"

Turning at the sound of Vedala's voice, the robot continued to skitter along the wall of the module back toward the scientist. Kline seemed to know the location of every grip, moving the robot faster than Stone thought possible. The machine was too far away, too strong, and too fast to stop. And it was headed straight for Vedala.

Stone turned to Kline's trembling body.

"Sophie!" he shouted. "Stop this! I'm warning you!"

Sophie Kline had no intention of stopping, of course. Alone and dying and fueled by an iron will, she had engineered an unprecedented scientific achievement. Stone knew even as he spoke that she would never, ever stop.

Stone ripped open a Velcro pouch on the chest of his suit and retrieved a small case. Coughing, ears ringing, he could barely see through the blood and smoke.

At the hatchway, the R3A4 had closed in on Vedala.

Still disoriented, the scientist was trying in vain to pull herself into the dark mouth of the Unity node. But she was too slow. The machine caught her neatly by the ankle, gears purring as it twisted her leg in a sharp motion. The ligaments inside Vedala's right knee snapped.

Vedala screamed in pain and surprise. The sheer brute strength of the machine was impossible to fight against.

On hearing Vedala's cry, Stone's face went blank.

In his gloved hands, he was holding a small black case. Inside was a glass vial etched with the word **OMEGA**. After Peng had found it on the body of Eduardo Brink, she had given it to Vedala for safekeeping. The poison was among the items Vedala had wanted to leave behind. Stone had taken it partially to make sure no harm came to Tupa, but also in case of a darker outcome he hadn't wanted to acknowledge to himself.

Stone ripped open the case to reveal the vial. He did not issue another warning. Like the machine, he did not hesitate.

Prying off the cap with a smooth flick of his wrist, Stone launched it toward the grotesque remains of Dr. Sophie Kline. The tiny vial sailed across empty space, rotating slightly, venomous liquid escaping the lip of the glass cylinder in a spatter of tiny yellow droplets. For an instant, they formed a miniature meteor shower, all speeding together across the expanse of the module.

Stone heard another shrill scream as the R3A4 began dragging Vedala back into the module by her wounded leg. He could only watch helplessly as it raised its disfigured fist to silence her cries.

Sophie Kline never saw the droplet of neurotoxin that glanced off her lower cheek. Absorbed through the skin, it attacked her nervous system, immediately scuttling the delicate neural connection to the Robonaut R3A4 humanoid robot. Across the module, the machine froze in place with one fist poised to strike.

"Omega," said Stone, sadly. "The end of all things."

Kline reflexively yanked off her goggles, eyes locking onto Stone's. Her jaw began to work silently, trying to get out words, tendons standing out in her neck. A sliver of drool escaped her lips as she expelled a final breath.

"You," she said.

It was over in seconds.

At UTC 17:58:11 Dr. Sophie Kline, remote scientist for Project Wildfire, expired on board the Leonardo module of the International Space Station. Official cause of death was asphyxiation due to a cutaneously absorbed nerve agent that disrupted control over autonomic functions.

Kline's body had gone still, and the light had left her open eyes.

Scanning the smoky room, Stone saw Vedala. She was still floating near the exit to the Unity node. Behind her visor, Stone could see she was breathing hard and in extreme pain.

The Robonaut had drifted away. Frozen in its last position, it rotated in place like an abandoned sculpture, bumping gently into an infected wall gone dark and smooth as obsidian. Purplish specks had already appeared on the machine's Kevlar-reinforced outer fabric.

Stone pushed himself up to Vedala, where she waited at the open hatch leading into the Unity node.

As he approached with his arms extended, the two scientists embraced. Up close, Vedala's face registered shock at his shattered helmet. In the reflection of her intact visor, Stone could see his own sweaty, bloody face—and the twin trails of metallic soot streaking below his nostrils.

It was the telltale sign of infection.

"Oh, James," said Vedala, backing away through the portal. "Oh, I am so, so sorry."

Goodbyes

STONE LOOKED PAST HIS OWN REFLECTION AND INTO the visor of Nidhi Vedala. She was watching him, oblivious to the emergency lights and smoke. Her eyes were hard and afraid and sad.

He understood.

If the soot was on his nostrils, then he had aspirated the microparticles into his lungs. And whether this was the reverse-engineered strain or its mysterious new evolution, there could be no doubt—he had been infected.

"It's okay," he said, keeping his distance. "I know you're injured, but you can still fix this. Close the hatchway. Free the other astronauts. Decouple the station from the infected modules."

"No, James," she sputtered. "No, it can't . . ."

Stone took hold of the hatchway door with both hands, moving quickly, his mind still numb to what was happening.

"I'm sorry, Doctor. You know the protocol. The infection has to be quarantined."

As he unlocked the hatch, he heard her trembling words. "Does it hurt?" asked Vedala. "Are you in pain?"

"No. I don't feel anything yet."

Considering this, Vedala's brow knitted. "That's not right. Normal onset is within a few minutes," she said. "You should feel it by now."

"It doesn't matter," said Stone.

Turning, he glanced back at what remained of Sophie Kline. Her corpse seemed to be staring at him, gray-blue eyes wide open, her body fusing with the writhing mass of the far wall. Tendrils of inky-violet matter had roped over her chest, as if a kraken were pulling her under the surface of dark waters.

Kline had finally become one with her creation.

But the infection had not yet reached the hatchway. There was probably still time, but not much.

"You have to go now," Stone said. "Take care of Tupa, will you? Be sure and find him. He's going to need you."

Vedala nodded, swallowing tears.

Stone cleared his throat. He forced himself to speak without emotion.

"I am proceeding to close the hatch, Dr. Vedala."

"James, no . . . there has to be another way—"

"I wish there was," he said, tightening his grip on the hatch.

Vedala's genius intellect was racing now, sprinting desperately through scenarios in which James Stone lived. She felt something in the back of her mind, the tickle of a thought struggling to reveal itself. But time was up.

There was no happy solution.

"Thank you, Nidhi," said Stone, as he lowered the hatch the

first few inches. His voice was clear and haunting in her helmet radio. "Thank you for everything. I would have liked it . . . if we could have had more time together."

Over Stone's shoulder, Vedala could see the Andromeda infection spreading molecularly through the infrastructure of the module—traveling relentlessly closer to the rest of the ISS. The remains of the Robonaut floated in a slow circle, half its golden face revealed.

"Goodbye, James," said Vedala. "Godspeed."

Reluctantly letting go, she began to float backward. Stone tugged on the hatchway and began to slide it down. Through its circular porthole, Vedala watched his determined face and tried to ignore the pain pulsing in her damaged knee. Braced against the wall, he dragged the hatchway closed inch by inch.

As he worked, Vedala made a final confession over the radio link. "When you joined this mission, I thought you'd been chosen because of who your father was. That's why I hated you, even though we'd never met. But I was wrong, James. I want you to know that. It doesn't matter who your father was—you were the right choice."

Stone paused briefly, before making a confession of his own.

"Don't feel too bad. I had my own reasons for coming. And Jeremy Stone was actually my adoptive father," he said. "All of it was classified, but Stern must have known. My birth name was Jamie Ritter. Fifty years ago, I was one of two survivors of the first Andromeda incident. I was the baby."

Stone could feel the vibration of the infection through the soles of his boots. The time for goodbyes was over. Wincing, he hauled on the lever to close and lock the hatchway.

It jammed.

Vedala had shoved the dented fire extinguisher into the gap.

She planted her feet against the wall and hauled the hatch-way open with both hands. Before Stone could react, she had grabbed him by the chest and yanked him into the Unity node.

"Nidhi!" he shouted, but it was too late.

A rippling swell of infected material was closing in on the hatchway, expanding in serpentine paths. Stone had no choice but to help Nidhi close and seal the hatch. Then he turned and shouted, "What the hell do you think you're doing—"

He didn't finish the sentence. Nidhi had pulled him to her, pressing the cool surface of her half-mirrored visor against his broken helmet. Inches away, she was grinning, her eyes bright and wet.

Vedala spoke with the calm confidence of a person who has been the smartest person in the room for her entire life, with no exceptions made for this room, thousands of miles above planet Earth.

"James, the only scenario in which you can be infected this long without symptoms is that you're not infected. Understand?"

"I breathed it in. And I can't have formed an immunity. It's impossible."

"True. But when you were a baby, your lungs were infected with AS-1. It couldn't kill you then because your blood pH was too alkalotic-basic, from crying. But when it evolved into the AS-2 variety, your lungs remained coated with benign micro-particles."

"And . . . the Strains ignore each other," added Stone.

"It's the basis of how my inhibitor spray works."

"Oh," he said.

"Exactly. Your past exposure renders you effectively immune to infection via the lungs. This is why you're here. This is why Stern picked you at the last minute. On a damned hunch."

Intercepted Transmission

IT WAS A LITTLE AFTER NOON AT NORTHCOM CONTROL center at Peterson AFB. General Rand Stern was thinking to himself that it was lucky his four daughters had grown accustomed to his occasional unexplained absences. They were good kids and had always been very understanding.

The general stood at the head of the room with his hands clasped tightly behind his back. A scrap of paper with an authorization code number was clenched in his fingers. He was pondering whether he would survive to make this particular absence up to his wife and children.

Stern had never felt more helpless in his life.

On the front screens, footage from various orbital telescopes—some military or government, and others seized from private institutions—showed multiple angles of the International Space Station. It was growing increasingly distant, still running dark. The bizarre ribbonlike tether stretched away from it, barely visible, like the thread of a spiderweb floating on the wind.

Whatever had been happening inside for the last hour was invisible from the ground. After the fiasco with the robotic arm, there had been no sign of the field team. In near total silence, a cloud of tension had settled over the control room.

Stern knew a life-or-death fight had occurred. He just didn't know who had won.

"Sir," said Stern's lead analyst. "There's no sign of them. Perhaps it's time?"

"Not yet," replied Stern, his voice quiet and commanding. "When it's time for that . . . if it's time, I will advise."

"Yes, sir."

"For now," ordered Stern, "keep Felix and King squadrons on rotating assignment. All fighters are weapons hot and authorized to protect the tether at all costs."

Stern looked dumbly at the paper in his hands. Spoken out loud, the authorization code would activate Operation Zulu.

Two hours and sixteen minutes earlier, the general had asked for and received presidential authorization for the operation—a secret action plan that, in a single word, would trigger a waterfall of thousands of alerts disseminating down to local municipalities across the United States and its territories and possessions. The unprecedented call would first evacuate members of the upper government to predetermined safe areas. Second, it would declare martial law nationwide.

In addition, Zulu would summon the entire half-million-person force of the US National Guard to their local stations; activate all police and fire department personnel to their command stations; and alert a grassroots network of church leaders and city shelters to begin making preparation for mass casualties. All doctors and nurses would be dispatched to emergency shifts at major metropolitan hospitals.

In military scenario planning, Operation Zulu had been designed for a single unlikely purpose—as a last-ditch response to a full-scale surprise ground invasion from a combined coalition of enemy nations.

Incredibly, an even worse scenario was unfolding.

Stern was considering the activation of Operation Zulu as a response to the high probability of ground and water contamination by a self-replicating extraterrestrial microparticle, which would likely progress northward from infection sites around the equator. First, a wave of refugees would arrive from Mexico and Central America—tens of millions, fleeing reports of a boiling sea of infection. Next, the nation would face an unstoppable chain reaction that would consume soil, air, and water.

The end of the world, in not so many words.

Most of the analysts flinched when the room erupted in a snakelike hiss of radio static.

"Houston says ISS comms are back online, sir," called an analyst, two fingers pressed to his earpiece radio. The room erupted in murmuring and a sudden burst of applause that Stern silenced with a glance.

"Put the loop room-wide," responded the general. Seeing the surprise on his analyst's face, he added, "Mission Control in Houston can hear this, and so can Moscow. We're all in it together now, good news or bad."

The analysts shot each other grave looks as speakers around the room crackled with static. Stern's fingers were locked together behind his back in a painfully tight grip around the damp authorization code. His face was calm.

Standing at the head of the room, Stern looked like a captain about to go down with his ship.

"We're getting activity on the line, sir," reported the analyst, as static began to resolve into words. "These comms are between ISS modules. Not directed to us. Audio is patchy. Putting up a real-time transcription."

< . . . >

ISS-HAMANAKA

. . . tell us what to do.

ISS-STONE

My colleague has a lower leg injury. She's barely mobile. Do you have medical facilities?

ISS-HAMANAKA

I can treat her. I'm coming out now.

ISS-STONE

Thank you. The hatchway is cleared. Komarov, can you stabilize life support systems and contact Mission Control? Tell them . . . the infection has almost spread to the tether. Once it does, Vedala estimates it'll reach the planet's surface in an hour, maybe a lot less.

ISS-KOMAROV

They can hear us now, Stone, if I'm not mistaken.

HOU-CAPCOM

This is Houston. Proceed.

ISS-STONE

Right, okay. Hi. I need every brilliant brain down there in Mission Control. First, confirm what happens if we sever the ribbon Earthside.

HOU-CAPCOM

One minute . . . Stone, we calculate that if we sever that ribbon Earthside, the weight of it will slowly pull the ISS into destructive reentry. That outcome won't change until the ISS is well beyond geosynch . . . at least thirty-five thousand miles.

ISS-STONE
_____
Then it's not an option.

HOU-CAPCOM
_____
Right. And we've got more bad news. If the ISS decouples from
the infected modules up there, the weight of the ribbon will
drag them back to Earth. So I'm afraid we're not seeing a solution
from down here.

ISS-STONE
_____
What if . . . what if the ribbon could be severed at a midpoint?

HOU-CAPCOM
_____
That's interesting. [urgent off-mike whispering] Based on mass
calcs, it could work. Earthside tether is subject to the most
gravitational pull, so it's by far the heaviest. We need to separate
the ribbon at . . . around thirty miles up. That removes enough
weight to send the ISS and upper tether into escape velocity.
The lower portion will be short enough to fall to Earth without
reentry burn. The ISS will need to decouple from the infected
modules immediately afterward, then hit a full deceleration
profile to avoid being ejected into deep space.

ISS-STONE
_____
So you're saying it *is* possible—

PAFB-STERN
_____
Stone, this is General Stern. It won't work. Thirty miles is too damn
high. An ICBM would aerosolize the ribbon material and defeat
our purpose. Likewise, our surface-to-air missiles have a max vertical
range of twenty miles. The maximum service ceiling for our aircraft
in the area is thirteen miles, not even half of what we need.

ISS-STONE
_____
There is one way.

PAFB-STERN

. . . you're not seriously—

ISS-STONE

I'll go back down the climber. If I can sever the ribbon at thirty miles, I could parachute down. . . . Houston, what do you think?

HOU-CAPCOM

Jesus. Uh, yeah, yes. Hold one second. . . . Master inventory shows an old pumpkin suit from the Shuttle days. Stored in Zarya.
It's . . . an advanced crew escape suit, ACES, with a parachute.
There's a drogue and a main stage. Hopefully still functional.

PAFB-STERN

It's too high.

HOU-CAPCOM

Record is twenty-five miles. Technically, it's feasible . . .

ISS-STONE

How about cutting the tether? Can we mix something together? Make some kind of a bomb?

HOU-CAPCOM

Uh, no . . . no way. [nervous laughter] The tether is much too strong . . . and it will regenerate. To blow that thing, he'll need a focused [off-mike whispering] . . . well, he will! [scuffling sounds]

ISS-STONE

Hello? Are you there?

HOU-CAPCOM

Dr. Stone, you'll need a modular shaped-charge explosive, designed specifically to cut metal.

ISS-STONE

Well, that's impossible.

. . .

ISS-STONE
_____

Houston?

. . .

HOU-CAPCOM
_____

Tell him, sir. You've got to tell him.

. . .

PAFB-STERN
_____

I can neither confirm nor deny details of certain, uh, orbital
experiments, but I can say . . . that item is available.

ISS-STONE
_____

You've got to be kidding me.

HOU-CAPCOM
_____

Komarov, can you collect the ASAT package—

ISS-KOMAROV
_____

Already on it, Houston.

HOU-CAPCOM
_____

Then it's a plan.

ISS-STONE
_____

It's a plan.

ISS-KOMAROV
_____

Dr. Stone, I wish we could toast your voyage home properly. But it
must suffice to say *udachi.* Good luck. You are a brave man.

[communication terminated]

Stern looked down from the front screens to find a room full of ashen-faced analysts staring at him. He stared back, blinking slowly. Finally, the comms operator cleared his throat and spoke.

"Sir, if this fails . . . should we prep Zulu?"

Stern let his gaze settle on the analyst's face. He noted the circles under the man's eyes and the stubble on his chin. There was a coffee stain on his shirt pocket, two days old at least.

"No," said General Stern. "No, I'm afraid it's already too late for Zulu. This is either going to work, or it's not. In fact, all nonessential personnel . . . go home to your families."

Stern turned and walked toward his back office, adding, "That's an order."

Super-Terminal Velocity

HURRY," URGED NIDHI VEDALA, HER FACE PRESSED TO a dark porthole window of the Zvezda module. "The new infection is contained, but not for long."

Outside, organic strands of infected material had webbed between the Wildfire and Leonardo modules like gristle between lobes of meat.

"Hush," said Jin Hamanaka, inspecting a carbon-fiber splint strapped to Vedala's right leg. The splint had been preceded by an intramuscular injection of twenty milligrams of morphine. "You're going to feel tired and nauseous now. It's okay to rest."

"Uh, no," said Vedala, turning to the backup remote workstation. "I've got a lot of work to do."

Blinking to focus, Vedala accessed the computer. She pecked at the keyboard, scanning through Kline's programs. Finally, she reached a simple screen with the words: "**DESCENT PROFILE**."

```
● ● ●              DESCENT PROFILE

      Atmospheric Velocity:   [ 500 mph     ]

      Vacuum Velocity:        [ 7,500 mph   ]


                         Initiate downline mass transfer?

                                          [ Y ]  [ N ]
```

"Here we go."

Vedala's urgent voice echoed in stereo inside the headsets of Komarov and Stone. Back to back, the two were deep inside the Destiny laboratory module. The white walls of the module, one of the largest pieces of the ISS, sprouted metallic blue handrails and neatly packed express racks full of equipment, experiments, and no small amount of redundant junk. Stone's suit was connected to the module's service and cooling panel via a universal umbilical line. As they spoke, it recharged batteries and replenished oxygen and water supplies. The battered suit had already been inspected head to toe for damage and hastily approved by the crew.

Komarov had retrieved the bright orange ACES survival suit, stripped out the parachute, and roughly affixed it to Stone's back. The Russian had assured Stone that the old chute was designed for high-velocity emergencies just like this—except that the person wearing it usually didn't know the danger was coming ahead of time.

"So it is even better for you, right?" Komarov had asked.

Now the Russian had his arms buried in an experimental tray, rummaging with bright eyes and humming a tuneless song.

"Do you see it?" Stone asked. "Houston says it's in there. Payload rack number two, portside."

"Yes, yes," said Komarov. "It is a delicate situation. Have patience."

The Russian hauled out a long golden canister. Then he lifted a bright steel ax that had been floating by his side. The muscles in Komarov's forearms bulged as he began using the ax head to pry the end off the canister.

"I would go myself, you know," said Komarov, voice straining as he worked at the canister. "But I have been up here for six months already. My legs are like rubber, and besides, Houston wouldn't trust me."

"Where did you get an ax?" asked Stone.

Komarov shook his head dismissively. "All Russian modules have a little ax by the door. Waste of money to run utility lines outside the module, like the Americans do. Instead, if we have an emergency and the door needs to close all the way—you have the ax."

"The ax? For what?"

"For the utility line. Chop, chop. *Then* close the door."

Stone was left speechless, and glad the fight with Kline had occurred on an American module.

Komarov finished prying open the canister. From inside, he gently extracted a smaller canister the size of a flower vase. A hollow copper cone was mounted to the front, giving it the look of a missile or a huge bullet. A thick golden pin was attached to a dangling O-ring jutting from the back of the device.

"There," said Komarov. "Simple as that."

The weapon had clearly come out of a hunter-seeker satellite. And it was obviously something nobody wanted to talk about. Stone frowned.

Seeing Stone's expression, the Russian shrugged.

"Chinese do it all the time. At least we are more discreet."

"How does it work?" asked Stone.

"Secure the device with this end pointed at the tether," said Komarov, holding up the metal cone. "Detach the pin, and two seconds later, kaboom. Got it?"

Stone nodded.

"I'm ready. Open the airlock."

"Ah, one more thing, my friend."

"Yeah?"

"I don't know. Maybe you want to put on a functioning helmet?"

Stone touched his face with a gloved hand, feeling blood rushing to his cheeks. Komarov laughed loudly, clinging to a handrail to keep himself from floating away in his mirth. The Russian astronaut was soon securing Nidhi's old helmet over Stone's head and face, locking it securely with a few expert movements.

"Americans, *bozhe moi*," he muttered, shaking his head. "And you think *we* are the reckless ones."

Moments later, Stone had maneuvered himself and the shaped-charge canister into the Quest airlock.

With a last thumbs-up, Komarov closed the hatchway and activated the depress pump. Stone felt the odd shivering sensation of evacuating atmosphere. A coolness crept over him, and the recharged interior heaters began warming his thighs and chest. Over the last few hours, Stone had gotten used to wearing the Z-3 space suit. After his taxing ordeal with Kline, however, it had begun to feel like iron armor hanging over his already fatigued muscles.

As Stone waited, he spoke into his collar mike.

"Nidhi? How are the controls looking?"

"No . . ." came a soft reply.

"No? Nidhi? What's wrong?"

"Puh-roblem," finished Vedala, words slurring despite a clear attempt to concentrate. "No problem. I have got it covered."

"How much morphine did they give you?"

"A medically necessary amount. But James, here's what I want to say. I wanted to say . . . you don't have to do this."

"If I don't, a lot of people will die. Including people I care about."

"That's what I mean," said Vedala. "Not for me. You don't have to do this for me. I knew the risks. I don't need saving."

"I am doing this for you, Nidhi. But I'm also doing it for *him*, you understand?"

"Tupa," said Vedala.

"He's alone down there. Andromeda took his family. It took away the only world he ever really belonged in . . ."

Stone stopped speaking. Composing himself, he continued slowly. "I'm going back for him. Somebody did the same thing for me, once."

Stone felt a tremor pass through his suit as the exterior airlock unsealed. A red square of light on the wall flashed green. It was time to go.

"Wish me luck," said Stone.

Vedala couldn't bring herself to answer.

IN THESE LAST moments, Stone's physiological signs, monitored by the pressure suit, registered near total exhaustion. His respiration was soon labored to the point that he was unable to communicate effectively via radio, and he appeared to be fading in and out of consciousness. Moving slowly, as if underwater, he navigated across the devastated exterior of the International Space Station.

Earth seemed so very small and far away.

Stone carried a bulky load on his back, comprised of the flight parachute and the shaped-charge canister. Maneuvering was nearly impossible. He was forced to stop and gather his strength multiple times. At each instance, it was unclear whether he was resting or had passed out completely.

After twenty minutes, Stone stopped moving.

"James?" radioed Vedala. "James, you have to keep going. The infection could jump to the ribbon any second. You have to get down there before *it* does."

Twenty seconds of static played over the line.

Finally, Stone responded between deep breaths. "Prep the climber, Nidhi. I'm securing myself. Be ready to decouple the ISS and decelerate directly after detonation. We'll send the rest of this mess into deep space."

As a result of the proximity of the infected modules, the internal temperature of the ISS had risen by ten degrees. The ventilation and cooling systems were taxed well beyond their limits. Cut off from Mission Control for over twenty-four hours, myriad problems had been left unattended and unmonitored.

Finally liberated, Hamanaka and Komarov had quickly reestablished radio connections to Moscow and Houston. With the help of hundreds of Earthside scientists in both nations, they were efficiently working their way through a triage list of life support and environmental problems. Groundside, mathematicians were feverishly working out thrust and decoupling calculations for remote execution at the proper time.

Only Vedala had been left to visually monitor the infection outside. And from what she could see, the situation didn't look promising.

The twitching filaments were absorbing the Wildfire and Leonardo modules, slowly combining them into a single malleable globule of black-purple metal, its surface flickering with a skein of greenish light. Vedala couldn't be certain it wasn't the morphine, but she thought she had glimpsed disturbing shapes emerging from the seething mass. Sinuous limblike twists of metal. Other, more complex surfaces that reminded her of circuit boards.

The Andromeda Evolution was progressing.

It took another twenty minutes for Stone to secure himself and the explosive charge to the climbing platform. He first used tether hooks to attach himself once again to the narrow ledge of metal gridwork that encircled the climber. Next, he strapped the explosive canister to the base with a handful of Russian cable ties—extremely strong solid copper wires, looped on both ends.

Last, Stone used a tether hook to snap a short primary leash to the grated floor of the climber. Then he placed a much longer, secondary leash around the golden pin at the rear of the shaped-charge explosive. Both tethers were connected securely to anchor points on his waist.

Sweating and nearly delirious in his pressurized suit, Stone sat down on the lip of metal. In the distance below, he could see the round curve of the entire Earth—frighteningly far away. The ribbon itself was barely visible, just a glimmer. Even so, he could feel it singing through the bones of the climbing platform.

Dr. James Stone gave a final thumbs-up.

"Ready," he reported, "as I'll ever be."

"James," said Vedala, letting the moment stretch out. "I want you to live through this. Okay?"

"It's just an overgrown roller coaster, Nidhi. Let's start the ride."

Vedala reluctantly punched the release button.

The climber lurched, sending a shudder through the entire ISS. Then the rolling pins at the top of the climber began revolving in reverse. The stripped-down, barely functional climbing platform began accelerating downward. Within seconds it had reached a cruising speed of 7,500 miles per hour.

The bottom dropped out of Stone's world.

On board the ISS, the solar panels began to tremble as the mass transferred down the tether. Otherwise all was still, save for an eerie humming as vibrations traveled through the ribbon.

STONE CLUNG TO the base of the shaking metal platform, aching fingers pushed through the gridwork. Staring out the mirrored visor of his helmet, he watched breathlessly as Earth slowly began to grow larger.

He was moving at over 7,500 miles per hour. On Earth's surface this speed would have been astounding, but it was less than half the normal orbital speed of the International Space Station. In microgravity and without air friction, it was hard to notice any movement at all.

Every few minutes, Stone checked the canister at its attachment point, making sure it was still secure. If he was unable to detonate the charge, or if it failed to sever the tether, then whatever alien mind was behind the creation of the Andromeda Strain would very likely wipe out the planet.

But all Stone could really think of was Tupa, alone and abandoned in a quarantine zone, and the promise he had made to the boy. To distract himself, he focused on walking through the mental steps necessary to complete his task. And in that way, over two hours elapsed.

"How's it going down there?" asked Vedala, her voice nearly drowned out over the thrumming in Stone's helmet.

"Hell of a view. Status?" he radioed back.

"Less than two thousand miles to go. Once you hit atmosphere at around a hundred miles, we'll slow you down."

"Good, that's—"

At UTC 21:11:20, the climber was hit by a severe tremor. The origin was from somewhere above, and it sent the platform wobbling side to side with multiple g-forces. The unexpected jolt threw Stone from his perch. The short primary leash held, and he was left dangling from the edge of the falling platform. The soaring length of ribbon sliced past, only inches from his wildly kicking boots.

Dust particles shaken off the platform impacted the ribbon above and below, igniting into a blazing shower of sparks. Stone prayed his suit integrity would hold as the fan of light coursed over his dangling feet.

For nearly three minutes, the climber swung and rocked. Legs pedaling over nothingness, Stone swung by his tether like a rag doll. Then, with a final shout of utter exhaustion, he managed to lunge onto the metal gridwork and pull himself back up. For several minutes, Stone simply recovered his strength.

"What—what was that?" he finally radioed, panting.

"The infection has spread to the ribbon," said Vedala. "It's traveling down toward you, and it's moving fast."

"How fast? Is it moving faster than I am?"

"I can't tell. Just hold on, and I'll advise. You only need ten more minutes."

Stone waited, but he could feel the lie in Vedala's shaking

voice. The smooth descent had been replaced by a gritty constant tremor, like a car passing from paved highway to cobblestone. Stone imagined that the tensile strength of the ribbon had shifted slightly. The nanoscale conversion process was turning the atoms of the tether into the new evolution of Andromeda material.

Similar, but not the same.

Stone's stomach lurched as the platform decelerated upon reaching the extreme upper atmosphere. To avoid being torn apart by air friction, he was slowing to a still punishing speed of five hundred miles per hour. The planet had once again grown to encompass nearly his whole field of vision. Looking upward, he saw that the upper portion of the silvery tether had turned deathly black.

"Will I have enough time, Nidhi?" he radioed. "Tell me the truth."

"You only have fifty miles left—"

"The truth!"

"The ribbon is thin, James. It's going dark so fast. Ballpark . . . it'll overtake you in minutes. Two, maybe three."

Stone quickly did the calculation in his head. Moving at five hundred miles per hour, he would need six minutes to cover the final fifty miles. It was a simple math problem with a terrible answer—he needed to travel fifty miles in two minutes.

"I have to accelerate," said Stone. "It's simple, Nidhi. Fifty miles in two minutes. Three times faster."

"That's Mach 2. You'll experience reentry burn," said Vedala. "It'll kill you."

"We have to try," said Stone. "Nidhi. We have to try."

Vedala registered the desperation in Stone's voice.

Any other person might have paused; might have waited until it was too late. Despite feeling the rapidly fading effects of her morphine dose, Dr. Nidhi Vedala clearly understood every variable in this equation, including her own emotions.

She punched the button.

"Hold on tight," she said.

Stone couldn't respond—his breath was caught in his chest as the climber instantly accelerated downward with the full force of its electric motors.

"I'll radio when it's time to detonate and jump," said Vedala. "Get ready. This is going to hurt."

On the last point, it wasn't clear whether Vedala was talking to James or to herself. Everyone involved understood that Stone's probability of survival was now essentially nil.

Stone could hear and feel the piercing vibration of metal on metal; it seemed to scream through his bones. His vision shook along with the quaking platform.

"Maximum acceleration—"

Vedala's voice was drowned out by a chaos of shaking. Stone felt blood rushing into his head as the downward acceleration pulled him up off his seat. It was just as well, as the metal undercarriage was already heating up as it collided with particles of the upper mesosphere. Staggering, he pushed up to a standing position.

He looked like a man on a ledge to infinity.

"Fifty seconds," said Vedala, though Stone could no longer recognize the voice he was hearing. Around him, a corona of flame flared like a waterfall of light falling upward.

For several seconds, Stone considered it beautiful.

"Friend, be careful," urged Komarov over the radio. "You are going to burn yourself to a cinder. From here you already look like a fireball."

Stone felt a new vibration. Looking up, he saw that microscopic pieces of the rolling mechanism were disintegrating. The speed and friction were too much. As the invisible particles collided with the ribbon above, they burst into a soaring rooster tail of flame.

"I'm okay, I'm okay," radioed Stone. His voice was barely discernible in the roaring static. He was now moving well over a thousand miles per hour.

This would be his last discernible radio communication.

Images of the catastrophic final descent were collected from low-angle telephoto shots on board a trio of B-150 long-range bombers operating at their maximum service height. The spy aircraft captured a surreal sight—a cone of bluish flame cascading up the curving thread of white light. Barely visible inside the inferno was the solitary figure of a man, standing silhouetted in wavering lines of flame. Beyond the cone of fire, the cold empty blackness of space draped itself over a blue-white horizon.

The sound was not transmitted over radio, but Stone screamed into his suit as his forehead accidentally touched the glass of his visor. He was scalded instantly. The fabric exterior of his suit was charring, and the bottoms of his boots had begun to melt.

"Thirty seconds," said the voice in his helmet.

The gridwork around Stone's feet had begun to glow red, and flecks of molten metal were dribbling up and streaking past like meteors. Moaning, gritting his teeth, Stone reached down and found the leash around his waist. Following it with both hands, he focused on the golden pin mounted at the rear of the shaped-charge canister.

Amazingly, it was still secure.

On the backs of his eyelids, Stone could see a white-hot desert. A woman was there, lying on her back. She had been hurt badly. Blood had spilled from her wrists in a tide over the grains of sand. The image was from a classified black-and-white photograph that had become a memory that had become a nightmare.

"Fifteen seconds," said a voice. "Hold on, James."

With a gloved hand blackened by flame, Stone disconnected his primary tether hook. That left only the secondary tether, attached to the golden pin. In nuclear strategy circles, this detonation method was known as a "fail-deadly." As opposed to a fail-safe, the explosive was sure to trigger if there was no human operator present to stop it.

"Stay with me."

Eyes closed, teeth bared in agony, Stone clung to his tether and cried evaporating tears as the inferno rose up around him. Against the glare of pure blazing light, he forced his eyes open and glimpsed the green bulk of the South American continent. The sight made no logical sense to him. It was simply a swirl of colors—an impossibly beautiful rendering of green, teal, and brown.

It had nothing to do with his current life of pain.

He'd found the image in the Andromeda materials. His birth mother, lying dead in the Arizona sand. Her blood had turned to dust, and it was rising in a swirl on the hot wind. It was his only photograph of her, his only memory of her face.

Millisecond by millisecond, Stone felt his consciousness stripped away into the roaring chaos. He could feel the desert heat, swallowing him up, carrying his blood away on its oven-hot breath—just as it had done for a mother and father he would never know, for a world he had never had the chance to grow up in, an entire life that had been stolen.

James heard a far-off voice whispering in his ear. It was a gentle voice. He struggled to hear what it was telling him.

"Mama?" he asked.

"Now," the voice said. "Now, now, now."

James Stone felt his knees buckle. He turned and fell backward from the burning platform. He felt the secondary tether snap and trigger the shaped-charge explosive. With a concussive thump, the canister detonated in a pale puff of smoke.

There was no visible effect for fifteen seconds.

The subsequent wink of flame occurred at a height of thirty-seven miles above the surface of the earth, well beyond the troposphere. It was a peculiar sight for those who observed it firsthand. And of those few witnesses, none observed the speck falling below the blast.

It was a speck in the shape of a man.

RESOLUTION

> . . . we understand what's
> happening now . . .
>
> That's the important thing.
> That we understand.
>
> —MICHAEL CRICHTON

Out of Eden

THE EXPLOSION WAS VISIBLE FROM OVER TWO HUNDRED miles away in every direction. It occurred at the epicenter of a constantly evolving patchwork of international quarantines, ordered by various government agencies with differing levels of enforcement capability, including the United States, Russia, China, Brazil, Peru, and nearly every other equatorial nation. The airspace above the canopy was under patrol by multiple squads of American, Russian, and Chinese fighter jets.

Yet there was only a single ground-based observer—the boy called Tupa.

After the climber had ascended, the boy had managed to squeeze out of the half-finished tunnel in the spire wall. Dropping thirty feet into the lake, he swam to shore. He found nobody there, so he waited.

And he watched.

According to the boy's eyewitness account, the silver tether in the sky began to swing. A dark dot fell down along it, followed by a blackness. From the top down, the silver tether was darkening. Then an orange spot flashed in the sky, leaving pale smoke on the wind. The black upper ribbon rose into the heavens. The bottom portion fell slowly, draping itself harmlessly over miles and miles of tropical wilderness.

Tupa watched this in awe.

And then, by his own account, he put his face in his hands and he cried.

The boy was ten years old. He was utterly alone. And he had just witnessed what was surely the death of the only person he had grown to trust.

Four minutes later, through eyes blurred with tears, Tupa was also the first to observe what looked like a small red-and-white cloud. The strange thing was falling slowly toward the earth, rotating lazily in the air.

And hanging beneath it, Tupa saw the silhouette of a person.

THE VOICE SEEMED to be coming from very far away.

"Jahmays," it said, the sound muted, barely audible.

James Stone cracked open his eyes and saw his own face reflected faintly from the interior of his helmet. He winced at the sight of a nasty blister growing on his forehead. And then, incredibly, he smiled. Looking past his own reflection, he could now see the upside-down, grinning face of Tupa.

Groaning in pain, Stone reached up and detached the charred helmet. The boy helped him wrench the equipment off his head, and he felt the familiar warm wash of humid jungle air on his skin. The red-and-white parachute lay twisted about him like a burial shroud, along with torn branches and shredded vines.

Stone sucked in a breath of fresh air and held it in his aching lungs. He wiggled his fingers and toes. Finally, he exhaled and closed his eyes for a long moment.

He felt a small hand take his.

"Jahmays," said Tupa, his voice clear and bright.

"Tupa," croaked Stone.

On his knees, the boy leaned over and pressed his forehead to Stone's briefly. Then the boy sat up and began pointing at the sky and speaking rapidly in his own language. His initial description of what had happened was punctuated with gestures, enthusiastic gymnastics, and an array of sound effects that would be familiar to just about any ten-year-old in the world.

"Tupa," repeated Stone. "Good to see you, buddy."

JAMES STONE HAD lived his entire life in the shadow of his famous father. He had never married and never had children. Instead, he had devoted himself single-mindedly to upholding the high expectations of his family legacy.

Stone had believed that joining the Wildfire field team would be the definitive adventure of his lifetime. He couldn't have been more wrong.

The following partial document, shared with the permission of Dr. James Stone and Dr. Nidhi Vedala, says more than any historian could explain.

IN THE CIRCUIT COURT OF THE STATE OF CALIFORNIA
FOR THE COUNTY OF LOS ANGELES
FAMILY LAW DEPARTMENT

In the Matter of the Adoption of:

TUPA,
A Minor Child.

Case No. [Redacted]

PETITION FOR ADOPTION
Authority: P.L. 21.135(1),(2)(d),
P.L. Ch. 109; P.L. 109.410(4)

Petitioners, James Stone and Nidhi Vedala, married, respectfully petition to adopt this child as follows . . .

Epilogue

ON THE OFFICIAL RECORD, THE HIGHLY IRREGULAR orbital path of the International Space Station was attributed to an emergency avoidance maneuver necessitated by a debris field, coupled with a training exercise exploring emergency preparedness in the event of an extreme shift in the Van Allen radiation belts.

Soon after the incident, the National Indian Foundation of Brazil received a large grant from an unknown benefactor. As a result, a vast swath of the Amazon was marked for conservation and its perimeter effectively quarantined. An international coalition of researchers was approved to study the area.

The North American Aerospace Defense Command, housed at Peterson Air Force Base, trained its ground- and satellite-based radar networks on the pair of cargo modules that had been decoupled from the International Space Station. Initial readings showed a nonreturn, nonthrusting escape trajectory out of the ecliptic plane. Telescopic measurements taken from the ISS (itself now on a return trajectory) indicated that the object was rapidly spinning on every axis—completely out of control.

As expected, the modules had been flung away from the planet and were headed toward deep space, forever.

Within minutes, however, total rotational deceleration was observed on all three axes—a maneuver normally possible only through a complex and fuel-hungry "de-spin" procedure. The trajectory of the debris began shifting back toward the ecliptic plane—as if it were being guided. Without onboard fuel, the only explanation was that a mass shift maneuver was taking place. By redistributing interior mass, it is possible to make course corrections without fuel.

This behavior was officially attributed to an outgassing of atmosphere still contained in the module, via punctures caused by impact with a micrometeoroid swarm. Unofficially, it was clear that the infected debris was steering itself.

In the last few images snapped before distance rendered visible light useless, only an amorphous shape was seen, markedly different in each snapshot. Etched hexagonal patterns were visible on the object surface. When it was last detected, the mass was predicted to be on an intercept trajectory with the gas giant Saturn.

What exactly happened after the debris impacted Saturn is unknown.

However, a cluster of news articles released soon after this event are worth noting. Both scientific journals and the popular press reported on a bizarre curiosity, without drawing conclusions. One such article is excerpted below:

SWIRLING HEXAGONAL STRUCTURE
SPOTTED ON SATURN

SOURCE: EUROPEAN SPACE AGENCY

The twenty-year Cassini space mission has culminated in the detection of a massive hexagonal storm front swirling around the north pole of the planet Saturn, scientists confirmed today.

In a study based on imagery captured by the $4 billion USD Cassini space probe, which was intentionally crashed into the planetary surface soon after reporting its data, researchers hypothesize that the 32,000-kilometer-wide weather structure is generated by a jet stream of air moving through the dense clouds of Saturn's upper atmosphere, and fueled by the rotation of the planet.

"The hexagon is simply a byproduct of weather patterns," Dennis Verulam, of the Cassini imaging team, said of the bizarre finding.

Although researchers are certain of their findings, there is still one aspect of the hexagonal vortex that remains a mystery—it seems to be growing larger.

IN A SPARSELY attended classified closed session of Congress, key participants in the second Andromeda incident were called before the Committee on Science, Space, and Technology. General Rand Stern was questioned by Congresswoman Laura Perez on the outcome of the event. With a major disaster averted, the main focus was now on "getting back to normal." This seemed a possibility, for the most part.

A partial transcript of the conference follows:

. . .

Q: Stern, what's the concrete outcome here? The threat is over. Are we back to a benign particle?

A: It appears so, Congresswoman. But we don't understand the last evolution of the Andromeda Strain. We recovered some research from our deceased scientist—

Q: Terrorist, you mean. Let's stay focused. You and your team rebuffed an attempted biological terrorist attack. We commend you for it. The Wildfire field team members who were killed will be posthumously medaled, classified of course. And now, having confirmed the airborne particle is harmless . . . all's well that ends well.

A: Thank you, but this incident may not be over.

Q: How so?

A: We still have the issue of the radio signals.

Q: General Stern, are you going on record, telling this committee that we are now receiving signals from Saturn? From little green men?

[laughter from the room]

A: No, ma'am. That is not what I'm saying at all.

[Stern stands to address the committee]

A: What I am telling you is that there is a new structure on Saturn. It is hexagonal, like our microparticle. It is large, and growing bigger. And yes, ladies and gentlemen, it does appear to be transmitting radio signals. But not to us.

References

Listed below is a selected bibliography of unclassified documents, reports, and references that formed the background to the book.

DAY ZERO

1. Crichton, Michael. *The Andromeda Strain*. New York: A. A. Knopf, 1969. Print.
2. Cuvington, P. "Civilizational Self-Destruction: A Self-Fulfilling Prophecy." *Journal of Anthropological Philosophy* 11, no. 4 (2007): 81–89.
3. Diaz, K., et al. "Unmanned Aerial Mass Spectrometry for Sampling of Volcanic Plumes." *Journal of the American Society for Mass Spectrometry* 24, no. 2 (2015): 210–26.
4. Herbert, N., R. Dejong, and J. Qin. "Marvin: A Vision-Based Rapid Aerial Terrain Mapping Algorithm." *GIScience & Remote Sensing* 38, no. 1 (2013): 26–51.
5. Holland, R. J., and B. Moore. "A Practical Experience of the Law of Large Numbers." *Proceedings of the National Academy of Sciences of the United States of America* 31, no. 2 (1947): 25.

6. Jax, Renaldo, and Martin C. Williams. *Automated Logistics and Decision Analysis (ALDA)*. No. TR-87. MIT Operations Research Center, 1973.

7. LeBlanc, Jerry. "The Strain of Michael Crichton." *Southwest Scene*, May 1971, 18–23.

8. Lee, R. S., B. Waldinger, W. Dorn, and U. Mitchell. "Ultra-Wideband Synthetic-Aperture Radar Interferometry." *Computer Graphics and Image Processing* 14, no. 1 (1998): 22–30.

9. McCallum, B. "Geo-Printing: Using Ultra High-Resolution Optical Imaging to 3-D-Print Highly Accurate Terrain Models." *Journal of Geoscience Education* 42, no. 1 (2014): 156–78.

10. Pavard, F. "Intergenerational Discounting and Inherited Inequity." In *Proceedings of the Eleventh International Conference on Social Economics*, 226–32. San Francisco: Morgan Kaufmann, 1982.

11. Singh, A. L., R. Bishop, and A. Nilsson. "Tactile Spatial Acuity: Discrimination Thresholds of the Human Lip, Tongue, and Fingers." *Journal of Neuroscience*. 11, no. 8 (2016): 7014–37.

DAY ONE

1. Wise, Robert, dir. *The Andromeda Strain*, featuring the documentaries "The Andromeda Strain: Making the Film" and "Portrait of Michael Crichton." Universal City, CA: Universal Pictures Home Entertainment, 2000. DVD.

2. Chaloner, J. B. "Forensic Analysis of Skylab Initial Ascent: What Went Wrong." In *Proceedings of the Tenth Lunar and Planetary Science Conference*, 143–57. Houston: Holt, Rinehart & Winston, 1979.

3. Heitjan, U., et al. "Classifying Emotions using FCM and FKM." *International Journal of Computers and Communications* 1, no. 2 (2007): 21–25.

4. Koza, D. E., M. Teller, and T. Wright. "Hall Thrusters for High-Power Solar Electric Propulsion." *Physics of Plasmas* 8, no. 5 (2001): 2347–54.

5. Kroupa, B. and V. Williams. *ISS Cupola Window TCS Analysis and Design*. SAE Technical Paper No. 1999–01–2003, 1999.

6. Liu, Bo, and P. Etzioni. "Adaptive Super-Resolution Imaging via Stochastic Optical Reconstruction." *Science* 222, no. 4853 (2010): 610–13.

7. Puri, M., A. Goldenberg, and N. Serban. "Advances in Treatment of Juvenile Amyotrophic Lateral Sclerosis: A Review." *Acta neuropathologica* 104, no. 3 (2012): 359–72.

8. Smith, S. "Emergency Debris Avoidance Strategies." *AIP Conference Proceedings* 595, no. 1 (2001): 480–92.

9. Stender, K., and T. Reddy. "The Mental Prosthesis: Assessing Juvenile Adoption Success of the Kinetics-V Brain-Computer Interface." *IEEE Transactions on Rehabilitation Engineering* 8, no. 2 (2000): 144–49.

10. Vedala, Nidhi, et al. "Demonstration of a Metamaterial with Zero Optical Backscatter." *Nano Letters* 11, no. 4 (2017): 1606–9.

DAY TWO

1. Bramose, R. O., et al. "Robonaut: NASA's Humanoid Telepresence Platform." *IEEE Intelligent Systems and Their Applications* 14, no. 5 (2000): 47–53.

2. Odhiambo, H. *An Introduction to Modern Xenogeology.* Cambridge, England: Cambridge University Press, 2014.

3. Rezek, John, and David Sheff. "Playboy Interview: Michael Crichton." *Playboy Magazine,* January 1999, 73–75.

4. Stone, J. "CANARY: Towards Autonomous, Self-Charging MAV Swarms for Environment Mapping over Extended Loiter Times." *Journal of Intelligent & Robotic Systems* 51, no. 1 (2016): 329–43.

5. Taplin, John. *Robber Barons of the Jungle: A History of the Amazon Rubber Boom.* New York: New York University Press, 2010.

DAY THREE

1. Besag, Ixna. "Traditional Mythology of Amazonia: Tupi-Guarani Family Lore." *Ethnohistory* 37, no. 2 (1998): 299–322.

2. Dawid, Stephan. "Gesture-Enhanced Universal Language Translator System." US Patent Application No. 11/342,482.

3. Heitjan, W., et al. "A Bioactive Paper Sensor for Discriminative Detection of Neurotoxins." *Analytical Chemistry* 71, no. 13 (2009): 5272–83.
4. Novick, S., and R. Lindley. "An Oral History of Traditional Medicines in the Javari Valley River Basin." *Fitoterapia* 60, no. 2 (1999): 124–29.
5. Odhiambo, H. "Adaptive Cancellation of Rhythmic Vibration across Distributed Seismic Data." *Geophysics* 46, no. 10 (2013): 1577–90.
6. Pole, Christopher. "Flight Testing of the F/A-18 E/F Multirole Fighter Aircraft Variants." *Proceedings of the IEEE* 7, no. 19 (2001): 198–204.

DAY FOUR

1. Harville, D. "Parallel Microhydroelectric Power Generation in Off-Grid Environments." *Power Technology and Engineering* (formerly *Hydrotechnical Construction*) 17, no. 10 (2013): 495–99.
2. Lonchev, M. "Pillion: An Image-Based Architecture for General Intelligence." *Artificial Intelligence* 44, no. 1 (2017): 1–64.
3. Long, A. C. "Assessing Intuition: Exposing the Impact of Gut Feelings." *Human Relations* 54, no. 1 (2011): 67–96.
4. Pittman, Rachel. "Delay of Gratification and Anticipatory Focus: Behavioral and Neural Correlates." *Proceedings of the National Academy of Sciences* 112, no. 16 (2011): 13288–300.

DAY FIVE

1. Diehl, Digby. "Man on the Move/Michael Crichton." *Signature Magazine*, February 1978, 36–37.
2. Drayson, V. L. "Does Man Have a Future?" *Tech. Rev.* 119:1–13.
3. Tsiolkovsky, Konstantin. *Dreams of Earth and Sky.* Moscow, 1895.

IT IS EXCITING TO BE SHINING A SPOTLIGHT ON the world that Michael so brilliantly created over fifty years ago with his groundbreaking novel *The Andromeda Strain*, and to collaborate with Daniel H. Wilson on the sequel. *The Andromeda Evolution* is—first and foremost for Crichton fans—a celebration of Michael's universe and a way to introduce him to those discovering his worlds for the first time.

There are so many people to thank for this remarkable journey, starting with Laurent Bouzereau, Ernest Cline, and our incredible team at Harper: Jonathan Burnham, Jennifer Barth, Sarah Ried, Lucy Albanese, John Jusino, Leah Wasielewski, Katie O'Callaghan, Tina Andreadis, Leslie Cohen, and their entire publicity and marketing groups. I would also like to thank my agents at WME: Jennifer Rudolph Walsh, Jay Mandel, and Kimberly Bialek; as well as Will Staehle, Jennifer Fisher, Filmograph, the teams at HarperCollins Australia and UK, Michael S. Sherman, Megan Bailey, Laurie Reis, Laurie Fox, and Michael's faithful fans. And the remarkable Daniel H. Wilson for his masterful storytelling and collaborative spirit.

Last but not least, I am indebted to Michael's daughter, Taylor, and to our son, John Michael, for their love, support, and encouragement in our shared mission to keep the Crichton legacy alive for many years to come.

—SHERRI CRICHTON

MICHAEL CRICHTON (1942–2008) was the author of the bestselling novels *The Terminal Man, The Great Train Robbery, Jurassic Park, Sphere, Disclosure, Prey, State of Fear, Next,* and *Dragon Teeth,* among many others. His books have sold more than 200 million copies worldwide, have been translated into forty languages, and have provided the basis for fifteen feature films. He wrote and directed *Westworld, The Great Train Robbery, Runaway, Looker,* and *Coma,* and created the hit television series *ER.* Michael Crichton remains the only person to simultaneously have the number one book, film, and television series in a given year.

DANIEL H. WILSON is a Cherokee citizen and author of the *New York Times* bestselling *Robopocalypse* and its sequel, *Robogenesis,* as well as ten other books. He recently wrote the Earth 2: Society comic book series for DC Comics. Wilson earned a PhD in Robotics from Carnegie Mellon University, as well as master's degrees in Artificial Intelligence and Robotics. He lives in Portland, Oregon.